Ignite

Clov ~~ies~~

D0889035

Melanie Harlow

For fans of the Cloverleigh Farms Series,
thank you for loving this world like I do.

Welcome back.

You deserve someone who makes you feel like you've been struck by fucking lightning. Don't you dare settle for fine.
Roy Kent, "Ted Lasso"

One

Dex

"**D**ADDY," A SMALL VOICE WHISPERED.

I lay completely still and kept my eyes closed. My alarm was set for six and hadn't gone off yet, but my daughters had been up for at least twenty minutes. I'd heard them talking through the thin wall separating my bedroom from the one they shared in my crappy apartment. Now they were playing their favorite game, which was to stand next to me while I slept and talk shit about me.

"Daddy." The voice was a little louder now, and I recognized it—my five-year-old, Luna. "We heard you snoring."

I continued playing possum.

(And for the record, I don't fucking snore.)

"Daddy always looks so funny when he sleeps." Luna got the game started. "Don't you think?"

"Yes." That was Hallie, my eight-year-old. "He makes grumpy faces."

"And weird breathing noises."

"Yeah. And he's so hairy."

"Daddy's not *that* hairy," Luna whispered defensively. "Just some right there."

Since the blankets were at my waist, I imagined her little

finger pointing at my chest, although they often made fun of my hairy legs and scruffy jaw.

"Yeah, but have you ever seen his armpits?" Hallie asked. "They're *super* hairy."

Just to mess with them, I flopped one arm over my head, putting one armpit on display.

"Ew." Luna giggled. "You're right. Gross."

"I'm never getting tattoos," Hallie announced. The girls were both fascinated and horrified by the ink on my biceps.

"Me neither."

"Why would anybody let someone draw on them with a *needle?*"

"I don't know."

"You could just use a permanent marker and it wouldn't hurt."

"That's a good idea," Luna said enthusiastically. "Let's do it on each other later."

I was about to sit up and inform them there would be *no* fucking tattoos given with permanent markers on my watch—I could already hear their mother yelling at me for it—when Hallie said, "Let's poke him."

One of them poked my ribs with a bony finger.

"Grrr." I growled long and low and opened one eye. "Who poked the bear?"

"She did." Standing beside my bed, they pointed at each other.

The hall light lit them from behind, illuminating their messy hair and summer nightgowns—Hallie's had owls all over it and Luna's had a unicorn on the front. I couldn't see their feet, but I knew Luna's were bare and Hallie had socks on because she hated being barefoot, even in summer.

"What do you want?" I grabbed the covers and pulled them over my head. "I'm hibernating."

2

"Hibernation is for the winter, Daddy," said Hallie. "It's August right now. You're just sleeping."

"Am I?" I said from beneath the blanket.

"Well, you *were*."

"You know why?" Coming out from beneath the covers, I reached over to the nightstand and tapped my phone screen. "Because it's not even fucking five a.m., and that is what normal human beings do at this hour."

"Mom says you're not supposed to say that word around us," Hallie reminded me.

"Mom's not fucking here." Remembering not to curse was a tough job after twelve years in the Navy, something my ex didn't seem to appreciate.

"Can we get up now, Daddy?" Luna tugged the blankets impatiently.

"No. I didn't even get up this early in boot camp."

"But we can't sleep." Luna hopped onto my bed, climbed over me, and got under the covers.

"Why not?"

"We're too excited about the new house."

"Oh." I was excited about today's move too—I'd never liked this apartment. And despite being called the Luxury Harbor Complex, the place was neither luxurious nor anywhere close to the harbor.

But I hadn't had much time or choice when I was looking for somewhere to live after Naomi asked me to move out two years ago. All I wanted was somewhere close to the elementary school, somewhere I could afford, and somewhere not too far from the fire station where I worked. As soon as I moved in, I'd started saving for a down payment.

The new place wasn't big by any measure—it was a two-story, attached townhouse. But it was an end unit, much roomier and newer than the apartment, and the surroundings were way better. There was a grassy area for the girls to play out back, a park within walking distance, and a pool. We'd have two full bathrooms, a garage, and I wouldn't be able to hear anyone else's arguments, toilets, or televisions through the walls.

Was it enough to make up for the fact that they'd have to go back and forth between two places for the rest of their childhood? Or wonder why their mom and dad didn't love each other anymore? Or erase from their memory all the fights they'd heard?

Probably not.

But it was somewhere we'd get a fresh start, a permanent place to call home, and a chance for me to prove I could be the kind of father I wanted to be.

That was enough for me.

"Listen, girls." I yawned loudly. "Moving into the new house is exciting, but I promise it's still going to be that way once the sun comes up, so let's try to get a little more shut-eye."

Hallie scrambled into the bed too, forcing me to move to the middle to accommodate them both. "Can we sleep in here?"

"Do I have a choice?"

"No."

"Then I guess you can. But go turn off the hall light first."

Hallie dutifully got out of bed, switched off the light, and hurried back under the covers.

"And you have to actually sleep, okay? No talking," I ordered.

"Okay."

Stretching out on my back, I closed my eyes, knowing the silence wouldn't last. Sure enough, not ten seconds went by before Luna spoke up.

"Daddy, can we please ride in the truck today?"

"No."

"Why not?"

"Because there's no time. You guys can stay with Aunt Bree and your cousins while Uncle Justin and I get the big stuff moved in."

"What about after the big stuff is moved in?" Luna asked hopefully.

"We'll see. Go to sleep."

It would have been easier to make the move when I didn't have the girls, but the timing shook out this way, and I refused to give up any of my days with them. My work schedule—twenty-four hours on and three days off—and the custody arrangement meant that I only got them two days a week, and those two days were always shifting around.

Naomi was willing to be flexible, but since she had to arrange her client appointments at the salon based on my work schedule, I'd promised her I wouldn't ask for changes once the calendar was set for the month—although that never stopped her from trying to see them during my days or nagging me about things she didn't think I could handle, like Luna's nut allergies or Hallie's compulsive tendencies or any kind of scheduled appointments.

"We'll bring our stuff and stay the night in our new beds tonight, right?" Hallie pressed.

"Yes." Frowning, I remembered there was something else I was supposed to do tonight—make an appearance at an engagement party for Chip Carswell, my best friend from high school.

If it was anyone else, I'd have blown it off, but I hadn't seen Chip in several years, and he was only in town for one night. He pitched for the White Sox, and time off during the season was severely limited. I'd have to bring the girls to the party with me, but maybe that would be good because it would give me an excuse to get in and get out fast. Parties weren't really my thing.

But I'd told Chip I'd be there, and I didn't take my word lightly.

"Daddy?" Now it was Hallie.

"Hm."

"I was wondering."

The girl was always wondering. She asked more fucking questions than anyone I'd ever known and never accepted an answer she didn't like.

"It's too early for wondering," I told her. "No wondering before six a.m. That's the rule."

"You can't just turn off wondering, Daddy. It's not like a TV."

"Can I at least mute it?"

"What I was wondering about," she went on, pretending she hadn't heard me—a particular skill of hers, possibly learned from her mother—"was did you have to wear boots at boot camp?"

"Yes."

"Is that why it's called that?"

I yawned again. "Sure."

"Was it like summer camp?"

"No. Except that it was hot."

"What did you do there?"

"A lot of push-ups."

"Is that how you got your muscles?"

"Some of them."

"And you held your breath under water a long time, right?"

"That was SEAL training."

She was quiet a moment. "When Mommy first told me you were a Navy SEAL, I pictured you in a dark blue seal costume."

Eyes closed, I cracked a smile. "Yeah?"

"Yes. And your whiskers were light blue. And I imagined

you worked somewhere like Sea World. Swimming in a tank and doing tricks for people, and they'd clap for you."

"That would have been more fun than what I did."

"What *did* you do?"

"Lots of things." Mostly I'd just tried to keep my team alive and our gear intact. Which wasn't that different from being a single dad, really.

"Mom says she never knew where you were or what you were doing."

"That's because I couldn't always tell her."

She lay back and settled under the covers again, turning onto her side to face me. "You were gone a long time."

"I know." As always, I felt torn when faced with the truth. I was proud of my career, but it had come at a price—my marriage, seeing my kids born, watching them take their first steps, hearing them say their first words. Three years ago, when I'd come home for good, Hallie hadn't wanted to hug me—she knew I was her daddy, but I was unfamiliar to her in person. And little Luna screamed her head off when I held her. She had no idea who I was.

I knew guys in the military who could shrug that stuff off, but I wasn't one of them. I didn't want to be one of them.

"But you're not going away anymore, right?" Hallie reached over and took my arm, hugging it close like a stuffed animal.

"No. I'm not going away anymore." Thanks to gunshot wounds in my right leg that had rendered me unfit to be a SEAL, my Navy career was over. No fucking way was I going to take some boring desk job. I'd been offered a teaching position at sniper school, and I'd considered it, but Naomi had made it clear that if I took the position, she wasn't coming with me to Indiana—that she and our daughters would remain in Michigan where we'd grown up. She wanted a familiar home, she wanted family nearby, she wanted stability, for herself and for the girls . . . and I couldn't blame her.

I'd told the Navy I was out and moved back here, taking a job as a firefighter and trying to ease back into civilian and family life. But the marriage hadn't survived, and I was now a single dad.

Truth be told, I liked it better this way.

And most days I thought I was doing a decent fucking job of it, although I swore too much, burned a lot of dinners, and couldn't get Hallie's pigtails even to save my life.

But I was here, I was trying my best, and I always put my children first—which was more than my father had done.

And despite the charred hamburgers and constant F-bombs, the girls liked being with me, and they always gave me extra long hugs when it was time for them to go back to their mom.

They often told me they loved me, and I was still getting used to hearing it—and saying it back.

On one side of me, Hallie snuggled closer and brought up her knees, which jabbed me painfully in the hip. On the other side, a sleeping Luna rolled over, slapped a hand on my chest, and kicked me. But they were still breathing, which meant I'd successfully kept two humans alive for one more day.

I called that a victory.

I woke up before my alarm went off and carefully snaked my way out of bed without waking the girls, which required tactics in stealth and breath control that rivaled what I'd learned in sniper training. But today was going to be hectic, and I wanted just one cup of coffee in the calm before the storm. With one final glance at them, I silently threw on a TCFD T-shirt and traded my sweatpants for a pair of jeans.

In the kitchen, I stuck a pod in the machine, and finished packing up a kitchen box while it brewed. My lease wasn't up here until the end of the week, so I didn't have to completely empty the place out, but I wanted to get as much done today as possible. My sister's husband, Justin, who was also a firefighter on the same shift as me, was helping to move the big stuff this morning—not that there was much of it. The plan was to drop the girls off at their house and then go get the truck. Bree, my younger sister, would bring them over later.

While the girls were still asleep in my room, I stripped their twin beds and stuffed the bedding into big garbage bags. Then I lugged the mattresses aside and grabbed a screwdriver, removing the headboards from the frames. The dresser they'd used at my apartment was already empty, and each of them had a suitcase packed and ready to go. Their clothing for today was laid out on the dresser top.

I was double checking that the closet was empty when they came shuffling into the room.

"Is it time to get up now?" Luna asked hopefully, scratching her belly.

"Yes," I said. "Get dressed and we can go for donuts on the way to Aunt Bree's."

"Mom doesn't let us have donuts," she said.

"Mom's not fucking here," replied Hallie.

"Hey!" I gave my older daughter a sharp stare. "No cursing."

"But you do it all the time."

"That's because I'm a grouchy old man, and I earned the right."

Hallie stuck her hands on her skinny little hips. "How come Mom says she's still young and you say you're old, but you're both thirty-four?"

"Mom says she's young?" Luna sounded surprised as she tugged off her nightgown.

"Yes," Hallie answered, spying the mattresses I had propped against the wall. She began running at them full speed and bouncing off again. "Last week when she told us she and Bryce were getting married, I said I didn't know brides could be as old as her, and she said brides could be any age as long as they believe in happily ever after."

At the mention of Naomi's boyfriend, a wealthy guy we'd gone to high school with I'd never much liked, I snorted. The thought of that asshole succeeding where I'd failed made me want to punch things.

And as for happily ever after, good fucking luck.

"What about you, Daddy?" Hallie asked, flinging herself at the mattress again.

"What about me?"

"Do you believe in happily ever after?"

"No." I handed Luna her socks. That's when I noticed she had gum in her hair. Frowning, I examined the remnants of the watermelon Hubba Bubba the girls had begged me for at the store yesterday.

"Why not?"

Annoyed, I turned to face her. "Because most adults outgrow fairy tales once they stop thinking like children. I'm one of them."

Hallie made a face. "That's stupid. No one is too old to be happy."

"Never mind." I tossed Hallie's shorts and shirt at her. "Get dressed while I find the scissors. If I can't get that gum out of Luna's hair, I have to cut it out."

Luna gasped and covered her matted blond curls with her hands. "No! Last time, you made it uneven and Mom yelled at me because I'm not supposed to have gum. And you were supposed to know that."

"Sorry." I held up my hands. "I'll do better this time."

"You promise?" She eyed me warily, reluctant to let go of her head.

"Yes."

"Make him pinkie swear," said Hallie as she yanked up her shorts.

I held out my pinkie, and Luna hooked her tiny finger over mine. "I swear to do a better job this time," I told her. "Now you swear to stop trying to chew gum and eat your hair at the same time."

She laughed. "I promise."

Just after eight, I hustled the girls out the door, slightly behind schedule. As anxious as they were to move into the new place, they could dawdle like it was an Olympic sport.

But it had taken me a solid twenty minutes of working on the gum in Luna's hair before I gave up and cut it out, and then Hallie hadn't been able to find her lucky penny. After turning the apartment upside down and mopping her tears—"but you gave me that lucky penny on my first day of school last year and I need it for this year too or else I won't be okay!"—I promised her I'd come back and look for it later, but we had to get going in order to pick up the truck on time. She was still sobbing as I hurried them out to the parking lot, where Luna tripped on a loose chunk of asphalt and skinned her knee.

Now both girls were crying.

I carried Luna back into the apartment as she howled in pain, Hallie following close behind, the lost penny momentarily forgotten in light of the bloody knee.

Setting Luna on the counter, I cleaned her off and dug through the box labeled BATHROOM until I found a bandage.

"Those are plain." Luna sniffed tearfully at my beige Band-Aid. "Mom has pink ones with Hello Kitty on them."

I clenched my teeth. "Do you want to go by Mom's house to get one?"

"Would we still have time for donuts?"

"Probably not."

The girls exchanged a look. "Then I'll have the plain," Luna said. "But kiss it first."

I kissed the bandage and she giggled. "Not the Band-Aid, Daddy. My strawberry."

Leaning over, I kissed the red abrasion on her knee, then gently covered it with a boring beige Band-Aid. "I'll get some better ones at the store, okay?"

"Okay. Ask Mom where she gets the Hello Kitty ones," she said as I lifted her down.

"I'll think about it."

Twenty minutes later, we were heading for my sister's house, eating glazed donuts and banging our heads along to some hard rock, which the girls called "Dad music." In the rearview mirror, I looked at my daughters, and as always, I was half-stunned to see them sitting back there—was I really a *father?*—and fully knocked out by how much I adored them. Sometimes I thought I might be having a heart attack when I looked at them. The feeling was that powerful.

Hallie had my dark hair and brown eyes as well as my stubborn streak and smart-ass mouth. She had Naomi's lightly freckled nose and relentless need to ask questions. Physically, Luna was her mother through and through, from the blond curls to the dimpled smile, but she was much more easygoing, and she always laughed at my jokes.

I turned down the music. "So how did I do this morning?" This was another game they loved—giving me a score based on how well I'd handled the morning. I'd invented it to distract them from missing their mom in the early days of the split. "Ten, right?"

"I don't know about ten," Hallie said. "I think there should be a point off for cutting Luna's hair."

"But that was *her* gum," I argued.

"Still. And then my lucky penny got lost."

"*You* lost the penny!"

"And you didn't have Hello Kitty Band-Aids," Luna added, wiping her hands on the front of her shirt.

"That's three things," Hallie said. "And ten minus three is seven."

"Seven out of ten?" I shook my head. "No fucking way. I need at least an eight."

"You did let us sleep in your bed," Hallie allowed. "I guess we could give you a point for that."

"And we'll give you another one for a ride in the truck!" Luna added.

"Hmmm." I pretended to consider their offer. "So I'd get a nine out of ten?"

"Yes," they answered.

"Fine. But I'm playing Dad music the whole time." I cranked up the volume on Aerosmith and rolled down the windows.

Nine out of ten wasn't perfect, but I'd fucking take it.

Two

Winnie

I LIKE A WELL-MADE MAN AS MUCH AS THE NEXT GIRL, BUT I NEVER *truly* considered myself a creeper until the day my next-door neighbor moved in.

Around one o'clock that day—a Saturday—I was sitting on my bedroom floor painting my toes when I heard the sound of a truck with noisy brakes in the parking lot. My windows were open, and after the truck's engine shut off, I heard two male voices.

Intrigued, I stood up and walked on my heels over to the front window. Nudging the curtain aside, I peeked out and saw two muscular guys in jeans and T-shirts rolling up the truck door and pulling out the loading ramp.

I recognized one of them—the tall one with the baseball cap, dark scruffy jaw, and gray T-shirt. Yesterday afternoon, I'd seen him coming out of the condo next to mine just as I was pulling into my driveway after work. The end unit had been empty for a couple months but had recently been sold—maybe he was the new owner? I'd have introduced myself right then, except that he'd seemed in a hurry, only giving me a quick nod before jumping into a dusty black, older-model SUV the next driveway over and taking off.

But this was definitely the guy. It was hard to tell how old he was from up here—maybe late twenties or early thirties?—but he was tall, with big shoulders and biceps that bulged inside the sleeves of his shirt. He yelled something to his friend, and I noted the deep, gruff voice.

Curious, I watched him and his buddy unload furniture off the truck. My cat, a brown and white tabby, nudged my ankle with her nose, like she wanted to see him too.

"I don't blame you, Piglet," I said, bending down to scratch behind her ears. "He's hot, even if he doesn't look too friendly."

The guy never smiled. He moved quickly and purposefully, like he didn't want to waste any time, and he didn't interact much with his buddy. But something about his clenched jaw, broad chest, and surly demeanor intrigued me—along with the shirt he wore, which said TCFD.

Traverse City Fire Department?

Immediately I imagined him carrying me from the inferno formerly known as the Woodland North Townhomes, soot darkening his face, my arms looped around his sturdy neck. After gently setting me down a safe distance from the blaze, he'd rush back inside to rescue Piglet, barley making it out before our end of the building collapsed.

I was half in love with him inside five minutes.

"I bet he's one of those guys with a hard shell and a soft center," I rhapsodized to my cat. "Someone who acts tough but has a big heart beneath his armor. A beast just waiting for his beauty!"

Piglet meowed like she agreed—or maybe it was a warning.

Because this is the problem with me.

I think I'm good at reading people when actually what I'm good at is wishful thinking. Letting fantastical notions about guys run away with my brain rather than seeing who they really are. It's not because I enjoy getting my heart broken—although that's often the result—but because I'm hopelessly romantic and I don't know how to pace myself.

There's even a name for it—emophilia.

Sounds like a disease, right? Like something in your blood? But it's actually a personality trait, my therapist told me, and it means you fall for people fast, easily, and often. You dish out your deepest, most vulnerable feelings for people like popcorn at the movies.

Here's my heart, sir. Would you like butter and salt with that?

I've been this way as long as I can remember. In elementary school, my best friend Ellie might *like* a new boy, but I would announce I'd met the boy I was going to marry. In middle school, she'd write down the name of her crush in our secret notebook while I named all the children I was going to have with the cute kid who sat next to me in Life Skills. When we went to the bridal store to find prom dresses, I tried on at least six wedding gowns, because I was positive my boyfriend and I were going to be together forever—even though we'd only been dating a month.

Of course, he broke up with me right before we left for college, and I spent my first month at Michigan State pining for him.

Until I fell head over heels for Andrew from Wisconsin, who was majoring in agribusiness and planned to go home and take over his family's dairy farm. The rest of freshman year was spent rhapsodizing about our life on the farm, where I'd milk our cows every morning and then come in to whip up waffles from scratch for all the guests staying at our B & B. The fantasy was complete with a Pinterest vision board, and my farm outfits were adorable, as were each of our six farm children and two farm dogs.

Alas, Andrew turned out to be a two-timing jerk, and my golden dreams of gingham dresses and towheaded toddlers on the prairie were crushed alongside my romantic hopes.

But my hopes were resilient, and I'd fallen wildly in love at least three more times during college. In fact, I even got engaged during my senior year—to a graduate student in finance who was heading for a job on Wall Street.

I glanced down at my left hand, where I'd worn a diamond ring for precisely six weeks, which was how long it took for Merrick to change his mind about taking me with him. Ellie and both my older sisters assured me I'd dodged a bullet, since they thought Merrick was possessive, demanding, and full of himself, and while I could see their side of it, I'd always found his confidence attractive.

His cheating, however, was not, and he flat out told me he realized he wasn't ready to have sex with only one person for the rest of his life, especially not when he was heading for New York City, and there were bound to be a lot of hot models there.

Asshole.

So instead of moving to the Big Apple, I'd moved back home to northern Michigan, adopted a cat, and taken a job working at Cloverleigh Farms.

Which was great—I'd always loved Cloverleigh Farms, which was owned by the Sawyer family. I'd practically grown up there because my father was the CFO, and when I was just four, he'd married the youngest of the five Sawyer sisters—Frannie, my amazing stepmom, who'd raised me.

The inn was beautiful, an elegant, old-fashioned estate with twenty guest rooms, a bar and restaurant, and gorgeous lobby with cathedral ceilings, a wide central staircase, and a giant fireplace that was always ablaze in the winter months, making the place feel warm and cozy.

There was also a winery on the premises, as well as a wedding barn, all nestled among hundreds of acres of vineyards and orchards. The old red horse barn was still there too, and

I recalled many a childhood summer afternoon spent playing in there with my sisters while our dad worked.

My official title was Hospitality Specialist, which meant I did a little bit of everything. Over the summer, I'd run week-long summer camps for kids, organized live music nights on the winery patio, assisted at wine tastings both on and offsite, and helped with weddings whenever my sister Millie needed an extra pair of hands—she was the event coordinator there. I also filled in at the front desk reception quite a bit, and a few times I even tended bar.

My parents had helped me buy this condo, which was only about ten minutes away from the house where I'd grown up. They still lived there with my two youngest sisters—the twins, Audrey and Emmeline, who'd been born a few years after my dad had married Frannie and were now sixteen. I saw them all every Sunday for family dinner.

I was happy here, even if I hadn't found my true purpose yet.

My phone buzzed on the floor where I'd been sitting, and I tore myself away from the window to answer it. Ellie calling, the screen said. I took the call and wandered back toward the window.

"Hello?"

"Hey. What are you up to?"

"Painting my nails and spying on my hot neighbor."

She laughed. "I didn't know you had a hot neighbor."

"I didn't until today. He's moving in right now." I watched him carry a large cardboard box down the ramp. "At least, I think he's hot. It's hard to tell for sure since I'm stalking from the second-floor window."

"What's he look like?"

"Tall, dark, and broody."

"Ooh. Tell me more."

"He's wearing a shirt that says TCFD. It's very tight."

"A firefighter! How old, roughly?"

"Not sure. Maybe thirties?" I watched him walk back toward the truck, pause, and lift off his cap before wiping the sweat from his forehead with his inner arm. My breath caught. "He just took his hat off."

"And?"

"Hotness confirmed."

"Is there a wife or girlfriend?"

"Not that I've seen."

"Well, what are you waiting for? Go introduce yourself."

Suddenly he glanced up in my direction, and I backed away from the screen. "Shit. He just saw me being all Gladys Kravitz at the window."

"Gladys who?"

"Gladys Kravitz! The neighbor lady from *Bewitched* that was always standing at her window spying on everyone."

"What the hell is *Bewitched*?"

"It's a classic sitcom! Comfort TV! You've never seen *Bewitched*?" To remove temptation, I went downstairs into the kitchen.

"No, I rewatch *Friends* for comfort like everyone else who isn't ninety. Listen, it's not weird to be friendly to a new neighbor. Go say hi and welcome. Bring him a pie or something." She laughed. "But no falling in love with him. Give it at least a week."

"Haha." I opened the fridge and stared at the contents, possibly hoping to find a stray pie. But the only sweet thing in there was my half-eaten chocolate Frosty from yesterday with a plastic spoon sticking out of it, which I didn't think would make a very nice welcome gift. "You're just trying to sabotage me so you can win the bet."

"I'm going to win the bet anyway," she said with confidence. "I can't believe you made it in the first place."

Honestly, I couldn't either. It must have been the vodka.

Three months ago—right after my engagement imploded—Ellie and I went out for drinks, and I announced I was swearing off men.

Ellie had laughed. "Ha! You won't last six months."

"Wanna bet?" I'd challenged, tossing back the rest of my second martini and licking vodka off the last olive on the bamboo pick.

She'd raised one eyebrow. "It's May, Winifred. You think you can make it to *November* without falling in love? *You?*"

"Definitely," I'd replied, and then hiccupped.

"I admit," Ellie said to me now on the phone, "I didn't think you'd even make it to the Fourth of July."

"See?" I gloated, although generally, I did enjoy having a significant other on national holidays. And bank holidays. And especially Hallmark holidays.

"But fall is coming," she said suggestively. "Cuddle weather."

"Doesn't matter." I took a quick bite of the Frosty before closing the fridge. *"I* am the boss of my feelings."

"Glad to hear it. But if you fall in love before Thanksgiving, you still owe me the thing."

I shuddered. I did not want to owe her the thing. "I can absolutely make it to Thanksgiving. In fact, let's make it Christmas."

"Christmas!" She burst out laughing. "Now you're just talking crazy. You didn't even like being single at Christmas in seventh grade."

"Well, this is an all-new Winifred talking. And I am perfectly capable of *not* falling in love—not even with my hot new firefighter neighbor." But apparently, I wasn't capable of minding my own business, so I decided to go check and see if the mail had come yet.

I opened the front door, peeked into my mailbox for half

a second, then looked toward the parking lot. He was standing next to the truck, looking at his phone.

And that's when I saw two little girls jump out of a minivan and run toward him. "Daddy!"

I smiled triumphantly. "Guess what?" I whispered. "He's not single, so it doesn't matter. His wife just arrived with their two kids—actually, make it four kids." I watched a dark-haired woman get out of the car, and retrieve a toddler and a baby in a carseat.

"*Four* kids?"

"Yep. Two girls, a boy, and a baby." Relieved, I grabbed the mail and went back inside. "Crisis averted."

Ellie sighed. "Damn. I really want you to owe me the thing."

"Never gonna happen." But at least now I could introduce myself and make friends with the new neighbors. As easily as I fell in love, I did *not* go for married men. To console myself, I took another spoonful of Frosty, then put it back in the fridge. "Are you still coming with me tonight?"

"Yes. In fact, that's why I called. What's the dress code?" Ellie was my date for my cousin Chip's engagement party.

"I'd say cocktail casual," I said, heading back upstairs. "I'm sure there will be people in jeans there, but also some dressed up."

"What are you wearing?"

I reached my bedroom and opened my closet door. "I'm thinking dark flared jeans, halter top, heels."

"Which top? The stripes?" Ellie and I knew all each other's favorite outfits.

"Yes."

"Okay, I'll go that direction too. What time should I pick you up?"

"The party starts at seven," I said. "So maybe like quarter to?"

"Okay. What are you doing the rest of today?"

"Not much. I have some errands to run, but other than that, just painting my nails and stalking the nice people next door." Unable to resist another peek, I went over to my bedroom window and looked out again—the two little girls I'd seen were running up and down the truck ramp. "Maybe I'll pick something up at Plum & Honey while I'm downtown and take it over there. I bet those kids would like my mom's cupcakes."

"Good idea."

"What about you?"

"We started the harvest this morning, but I had to come in and clean up because Mia asked if I could handle a meeting with a prospective wedding couple this afternoon—which I really don't want to do because that is not my job."

I smiled. Ellie always referred to her mother by her first name, and it drove her crazy. "But that's so fun, getting to make someone's wishes come true. Making their dream a reality."

"It's not *my* idea of fun. Brides are insane. Even perfectly normal women lose their minds once that ring is on their finger. I'm never getting married."

"You just like butting heads with your mother."

"I can't help it. She keeps asking me what my life *plan* is."

I sighed. "Your mom always did love a plan."

"And I keep telling her, my plan is for them to fire the perfectly great head winemaker they've had at Abelard for fifteen years and promote me, because I'm twenty-two and I know everything."

"Solid strategy."

"Actually, I think she's just wondering when I'll stop taking up one of their guest rooms and move out. I keep telling them if they want me to be able to afford rent somewhere they should pay me more."

Ellie had recently moved back home after spending practically our entire senior year in the south of France, doing an internship at a vineyard her dad's family owned. She spoke fluent French, because her dad had been born there and he spoke nothing but French to her and her brothers growing up. Now she lived and worked at Abelard Vineyards, her parents' winery, which was on Old Mission Peninsula, only about twenty minutes away.

"Ell, you can totally afford a place around here," I told her. "It just won't be as fancy as those guest rooms at Abelard."

"Listen, as I've explained to Mia and Lucas, I need to be able to live in the lifestyle to which I've become accustomed. It's their fault for accustoming me to it, right?"

I laughed. "I'm not sure that's how it works." Downstairs, I heard someone knocking on my front door. "Hey, I have to go. Someone's at my door."

"Okay. See you tonight."

Three

Winnie

ENDING THE CALL, I HURRIED DOWN THE STEPS, WONDERING if it was one of my new neighbors. A mirror hung on the wall near the front door, and I glanced at it.

My dirty blond hair, which I had not brushed yet today, was pulled back in a haphazard ponytail. I wore no makeup, and while I'd changed out of my pajamas earlier, the outfit I wore—ripped denim shorts and a cropped white top—wasn't what I'd have chosen to make a good first impression. The bottoms of the shorts were all shredded and the shirt had a coffee stain on the front. I was barefoot too.

Whoever it was knocked again.

Oh, well—I tightened my ponytail and opened the door. Then I smiled, because through the screen, I saw the two little girls from earlier standing side by side on my porch.

"Well, hi there," I said, opening the screen door.

"Hi," said the taller one. She had dark hair pulled back into two pigtails—one was considerably higher than the other one—and beautiful brown eyes. It was sweet the way she held her little sister's hand. "We live next door now, and we wondered if you had any Hello Kitty Band-Aids."

"I have a strawberry." The younger one—whose frizzy

blond curls framed a round Kewpie doll face—popped up one knee. "See?"

Leaning over, I examined the red mark. "Oh, no! How did you get that?"

"I was running in the parking lot," she said, like she was ashamed. "And then my dad gave me a Band-Aid, but I lost it."

"It wasn't a Hello Kitty one," the dark-haired sister clarified. "It was plain brown."

"Well, I'm not sure I have any Hello Kitty bandages, but I'm sure I can find something." I glanced behind them, but I didn't see any adults, and the truck had been moved to the far side of the lot. "Is it okay for you to come in?"

The girls looked at each other. "I think so," ventured the older one cautiously.

"Where are your parents?"

"They're not here," said the little blonde.

"Oh." Thinking it odd that their parents had just left them to their own devices in a new place—no way was the older one even ten yet—I motioned them inside. "Okay, well, why don't you come in while you wait for them? My name is Winnie."

"Like Winnie the Pooh?" the smaller one asked, and even though I'd hated the remark as a kid, I'd learned to embrace it as an adult. It usually brought a smile, and that was something good.

"Exactly." I grinned as they stepped in. "And I even have a cat named Piglet."

Their smiles widened. "I'm Hallie, and this is Luna," said the big sister.

"Can we pet your cat?" asked Luna.

"Sure," I said, leading the way down the hall. "She gets shy around new people, but I know where she likes to hide."

The girls eagerly followed me into the kitchen, which opened up onto the living room. A sliding glass door led to a patio out the back. "This is just like ours," said Hallie, looking around. "But flipped around."

"I think all the units in this building are the same," I told her, coaxing a trepidatious Piglet out from her hiding spot in the pantry. Immediately Hallie and Luna dropped to their knees and cooed over her, and eventually Piglet braved moving close enough for them to pet her.

"Wow, she must really like you," I said, rifling through my shoulder bag. Somewhere in there I had a makeshift first-aid kit, and I thought I might have stuck some princess Band-Aids in there during the weeks I'd run summer camps.

"Do you have parents?" asked Luna, looking around.

I smiled as I pulled the kit from the bag and poked through it. "I do, but they don't live here."

"Are you married?"

"Nope. I live here alone."

"Do you *want* to get married?" asked Hallie.

"Someday."

"Does that mean you believe in happily ever after?"

I laughed. "Doesn't everybody?"

"Not Daddy," replied Hallie, "but I do."

"Me too," added Luna.

"Hey, look what I found!" I held up a pink bandage. "It's not Hello Kitty, but it's better than plain, right?"

Luna looked up from Piglet and smiled. "Much better. Can I have it?"

Hallie elbowed her sister.

"Please?" Luna added, scooting toward me on her bottom.

"Of course." I dropped to my knees and carefully put the Band-Aid over the mark on her knee. "So how old are you girls?"

"Five." Luna flexed her knee and smiled.

"Eight," said Hallie. "I'll be in third grade this year."

"And I'm going to be in kindergarten!"

"That's so exciting!" I stood up and threw away the wrapper. "You have a little brother too, right? And a new baby?"

Hallie and Luna both looked confused. "No," Luna said. "But we'd *like* a baby. Or a hamster."

"I thought I saw your mom with a little boy out front," I said. "And an infant carseat."

"Our mom was here?" Hallie questioned, her face scrunching up. Then something clicked. "Oh! That's not our mom. That's our Aunt Bree. And the boy is our cousin Peter. Same with the baby. His name is Prescott. He's only two months old."

"It's Daddy's two days right now," said Luna.

"He gets us two days a week," Hallie explained. "Because of the divorce."

"Oh." I nodded in understanding, feeling sympathy for them. My mom had taken off when I was younger than Luna. I knew what it was like to be a child of divorced parents. "So just your dad is moving in here?"

"Yes." Hallie sighed. "And we love our dad, but he's really grumpy right now because one of the legs on the couch broke and he can't afford a new one, so he had to find his tools and try to fix it himself. That's why we didn't want to ask him for another Band-Aid."

"He gets grumpy a lot," Luna added. "And he snores."

I laughed. "A lot of dads do."

"He's also really hairy, and he swears too much," announced Hallie.

Her little sister confirmed this with a nod. "He says it was because he was a SEAL."

"Not the kind at Sea World," Hallie clarified quickly. "The kind that wears a uniform. But he is a very good swimmer."

"Guess what?" I smiled at them. "My dad was a single dad too, and he also used to swear a lot."

"Was he a SEAL?" Luna asked.

"No, but he was a Marine," I said. "And he always told us

that once you're a Marine, you're always a Marine, so we had to put up with his cursing."

"Did it make your mom mad?" Hallie wondered. "Our mom gets really mad about it."

"I don't think she knew," I said carefully, "but I had sisters too, and you know what we did?"

"What?" they asked.

"We had a swear jar, and every time he said a bad word, he had to put money in the jar."

"How much money?" Hallie asked, her dark eyes wide.

I shrugged. "Depends on the swear. Most words were fifty cents."

"Our dad says the F-word a lot," whispered Luna, glancing at the cat like she was afraid Piglet's ears might be offended.

"The F-word was a whole dollar," I told them.

The sisters exchanged a delighted look.

"And then every month, my sisters and I would take turns choosing where to donate the money. When it was my turn, I always chose an animal charity."

"Our dad says there's a pool here," Hallie said excitedly, off to a new subject with the speed of an eight-year-old. "Do you know where it is?"

"Yes."

"Can you show us?"

I paused. "Yes, but I think we should wait to ask your dad for permission."

A vigorous rapping on the aluminum frame of my screen door made us all jump and sent Piglet scurrying back into the pantry.

"I bet that's Daddy," Hallie said. "We didn't tell him we were coming here. He might be mad."

Flustered, I hurried from the kitchen toward the door, where I could see the imposing masculine silhouette of him through the screen—wide shoulders, thick arms, trim torso.

Pushing open the door, I could see he was just as handsome as I'd thought.

And clearly upset.

His dark eyes were clouded with worry, his brow was furrowed, and his jaw was clenched. "Sorry to bother you, but have you seen—"

"Daddy!" Luna came running up the hall with Hallie close behind.

At the sight of his girls, the guy relaxed his shoulders and expression somewhat. "You guys cannot just run off like that. I didn't know where you were."

"Sorry," Luna said contritely. "I needed a new Band-Aid."

"And we didn't want to ask you because you were already being a grouch about the couch," Hallie added.

"Hey, that rhymes. Grouch and couch." Luna smiled up at her big sister with admiration. "Daddy was a *grouch* about the *couch*."

I smiled, but judging by his expression, their father was not amused.

"Please come in," I said, stepping back to give him space. I held out my hand. "I'm Winnie."

"Just like the Pooh!" Luna said.

Although I was used to the joke, I felt my cheeks grow warm.

"I'm Dex." He didn't exactly smile, but at least he unclenched his jaw and gave me a nod. He appeared a bit older than I'd originally guessed—he had some gray at his temples, and a few faint lines on his forehead. But when he wasn't frowning, his dark scruff framed a beautiful mouth, with a slightly fuller lower lip.

"Nice to meet you," I said, my pulse quickening as he shook my hand.

He gestured to the girls. "These two strays are my daughters, Hallie and Luna."

"She knows us already, Dad," said Hallie impatiently.

"She gave me the Band-Aid." Luna showed off her knee. "It's much better than yours."

Dex rolled his eyes and looked at me again. "Sorry for the intrusion."

"Not at all. I'm sorry about the couch, and I hope the rest of the move goes well. If you need anything, just let me know."

"Thanks." He looked at his kids. "Let's go, girls."

"Can we go swimming now, Daddy?" Hallie asked, tugging on his shirt.

"No. There's too much to do. You can unpack while I put your beds together." He pushed the screen door open.

"What about a ride in the truck?" Luna asked, taking his hand. "You promised."

"We'll see," Dex answered, shepherding them off the porch. He glanced back at me without smiling. "Thanks again."

"Anytime." I shut the front door, leaned back against it, and squeezed my eyes shut.

Damn, he was handsome. My heart was still fluttering.

"It's fine," I told myself. "It's fine that my new next door neighbor is a hot firefighter and single dad with muscles for days and dark, broody eyes. It's fine, because *I* am the boss of my feelings."

Slowly, I started walking up the stairs, skimming my palm along the banister and wondering if his abs were as hard and sculpted as his jaw. Then I snatched my fingers off the wood as if it was hot.

"I am also the boss of my *hands*." I started up the steps again, imagining what it would be like to feel his scruff against my cheek, maybe bite his lower lip.

"And my teeth," I said defiantly. "I'm definitely the boss of my teeth. I will not bite my nice new neighbor."

But I paused when I reached the top. "Unless he asks me to."

Four

Dex

"**Y**OU TWO CANNOT JUST WANDER OFF THAT WAY," I scolded as we walked back to our place. I'd only been gone for twenty minutes, tops—after parking the truck out of the way, I'd run out to the hardware store to get a metal bracket for the broken couch leg. When I got back, the girls were nowhere to be found. "You know you have to ask permission to leave the house."

"We couldn't find you," Hallie said defensively as we crossed our driveway. "And Uncle Justin said it was okay to go outside as long as we didn't go in the parking lot, which we didn't."

"Where's Aunt Bree?"

"She had to take the boys home for a nap."

"You were supposed to go with her."

"We didn't want to."

"Next time, wait for me." I opened the front door for them, and they slipped into the house. "Got it?"

"Yes, Daddy," they said together, but I could have sworn I saw Hallie roll her eyes. For good measure, I gave one of her pigtails a tug. "You know these are crooked, right?"

"Hey! *You* did them!" Giggling, she scooted away from me and darted up the steps.

"I like 'em that way," I teased, following her and tugging the second one. "Makes it easy to recognize you from behind."

Up in the girls' room, Justin and I put together the girls' twin beds while they put their clothes in the dresser.

"Dad, do we have a jar?" Hallie asked, carrying her clothes in neat piles over to the drawers she'd designated as hers.

"A jar?" I tightened a bolt holding the headboard to the frame on Luna's bed. "What for?"

"To collect money every time you say a bad word."

Justin laughed. "A swear jar?"

"Yes," Hallie answered. "That's what she called it."

"That's what *who* called it?" I asked, irritated.

"Winnie."

"Who's Winnie?" Justin asked.

"She's our new friend that lives next door." Hallie refolded a few things before placing them in a drawer.

"She gave me a Band-Aid," said Luna, who clearly didn't give a shit about keeping anything folded and was shoving things in drawers willy-nilly. "See?"

Justin dutifully examined the knee she displayed. "Very nice."

"She said her dad was always saying bad words too, so she and her sisters made a swear jar."

"Fuck that," I said.

"The F-word is a dollar, Daddy. You might not want to say it anymore." Hallie's tone was solemn as she lined up her shoes in the closet *exactly* the way she liked them.

My brother-in-law laughed again. "That's nice there are kids next door for you guys to play with. How old is Winnie?"

Luna giggled. "She's not a kid."

"She looks like one," I muttered.

"I don't know how old she is," Hallie said thoughtfully. "Maybe a teenager?"

"That could be good," Justin said, testing the stability

of the frame and headboard. "You'd have a babysitter right next door."

"I think she's older than that, but not by much." My knees cracked as I rose to my feet. "Okay, let's put the mattresses on."

"I think she's pretty," Luna said.

"Oh yeah?" Justin gave me a teasing glance as we hauled one twin mattress over to Hallie's bed and tossed it on. "Is this true?"

I shrugged and turned around to grab the second one. "I only saw her for a minute." During which I'd tried not to notice how short her shorts were or glance at the bare skin showing beneath her crop top.

"It's true," said Hallie with confidence. "She's very pretty."

"And she likes animals," Luna said, watching us place the mattress on her bed. "Can we get a pet here, Daddy?"

"No." I looked around for the garbage bags full of their sheets and blankets. Were they still downstairs?

"But why not?" Hallie followed me out of the bedroom and down the steps. "You said the old apartment didn't allow pets but this one does."

"How do you know?"

"Because Winnie has a cat. Her name is Piglet. And cats are very clean, I've read about it."

"I told you, Halsy pal, we can't have a pet because I work twenty-four-hour shifts. There would be nobody here to feed it." I spied the two bags at the foot of the staircase and handed one to her. "Take this up to your bedroom."

"Maybe Winnie could feed it when you're not here," she said, lugging the bag up the steps.

"No."

"Why not?"

"Because I don't want a stranger in our house."

"She's not a stranger. She's a friend."

"We don't even know her, Hallie." Frowning, I followed her into the bedroom and dumped out the contents of the bag onto the carpet. "She could be a lunatic. Or a serial killer."

"But she has princess Band-Aids. And she believes in happily ever after!" shouted Luna.

"Then she's definitely a lunatic."

"After you know her better, can you ask her?" Hallie pleaded.

"I'm not getting a cat. There's nothing to ask."

"Daddy, can we paint the walls in here pink?" Luna asked, hopping onto her mattress and starting to jump.

"Not pink, purple!" Hallie began bouncing up and down on her bed too.

I held up Luna's fitted sheet and studied it. "Should I wash this stuff first?"

"Maybe. Smell it," Justin shrugged.

I sniffed the sheet—it smelled like maple syrup. "Guess I should. Come on, girls. I'll teach you how to do laundry. Whoever finds the box with the detergent gets a ride in the truck."

Squealing with excitement, they leapt off their beds and took off running, elbowing each other to get ahead as they raced down the stairs.

A few hours later, the laundry was done, clean sheets were on the beds, and the truck had been returned. I'd let the girls ride in it while Justin followed in my SUV, and they'd chirped like magpies the whole time. My head was fucking *pounding*.

After dropping my brother-in-law off, we returned to our new home to see the girl from next door on our front porch.

"Winnie's knocking on our door!" Luna said excitedly from the back seat. "Hurry, Daddy!"

No sooner had I pulled into the garage than the girls un-buckled their seatbelts and bolted for the porch. It was like they'd spotted a celebrity.

I got out of the car slowly, eyeing the door that went right into the kitchen and wishing I could just slip inside without talking to anyone. But I walked around to the front door.

The girl still had those tiny shorts on, and my eyes were immediately drawn to her legs again. And since she faced away from me as she spoke to the girls, I accidentally got a good eyeful of the way the denim hugged her ass before I forced myself to look down at my feet.

Knock it off, old man. Just because you haven't had sex in over a year doesn't give you permission to gawk. She's way too young for you.

"Winnie brought us cupcakes," Luna called out as I ap-proached, gesturing at a white bakery box in Winnie's hands. "And she says they don't have nuts in them!"

"They're from my mom's pastry shop, Plum & Honey." Winnie smiled brightly at me as I climbed the steps, causing the tiniest catch in my chest. "One of my little sisters has nut allergies too, so she's very careful."

"She said there's two in the box for each of us." Hallie clapped her hands with excitement.

"I wasn't sure which flavors you'd like, so I just chose some of my favorites—sugar cookie, chocolate chip pancake, maple bacon cinnamon—"

"Bacon!" Hallie and Luna looked at each other and made their *that's disgusting* face, generally reserved for meals I'd botched and asked them to eat anyway.

"Bacon on a cupcake?" Hallie was incredulous. "That doesn't sound good at all."

Winnie laughed. "I know it probably doesn't to a kid, but I like it."

"You can have that one, Daddy," Luna said benevolently.

It actually sounded fucking great to me—I'd eat bacon on anything. But I said nothing as I moved around the trio to unlock the front door.

"Will you feed our cat?" I heard Luna ask Winnie behind me.

"Oh, do you have a cat?"

"No," I said, giving Luna a menacing glare over my shoulder. "We don't."

"But we might get one in the future," Hallie said.

Luna tried again. "Will you feed our future cat?"

That made Hallie laugh. "Future Cat sounds kind of like a cartoon or a superhero. Hey, maybe our cat will have superpowers!"

"And we can get it a little cape," Luna said.

"There will be no cats, with or without superpowers," I announced.

"He's still grouchy about the couch," Hallie said to Winnie, who tried not to laugh. "And because he has to go to a party tonight and he doesn't like them."

"Go on inside now, girls," I ordered, propping the screen door open with my back. "We have to start getting cleaned up soon. I want to leave before seven."

Luna beamed up at Winnie. "We get to go to the party too."

"How exciting! Well, I won't keep you—I just wanted to drop these off." She met my eyes and handed over the box with a smile. "Welcome to the neighborhood."

There was that hitch in my breath again, like a loose thread snagging. The girls were right—she *was* pretty. Her eyes were deep blue and fringed with thick black lashes, and she had dark blond hair streaked with gold. It was pulled back from her face, which was shaped like a heart. When I took the box from her, my fingers brushed the back of her hands, and I didn't like the way it sent heat rushing up my arms. "Thanks."

"My pleasure." One more smile, and then she moved past us and bounced energetically across my driveway, which separated our front doors. Jesus, she even *moved* like a kid.

But I found it hard to take my eyes off her, and when she turned back to glance at me, she caught me staring.

Embarrassed, I quickly turned and went inside the house.

"Daddy, can we have a cupcake now?" Hallie asked, washing her hands at the kitchen sink.

"I guess."

I set the box on the kitchen counter and found a knife to slice through the sticker sealing it shut. The girls opened the top, squealing like it was Christmas morning. Each of them grabbed a gigantic cupcake and started inhaling it.

"Mmmm," said Hallie as she took a big bite of pink frosting that almost looked like it sparkled. "This tastes like cotton candy."

Luna had dark brown frosting on the tip of her nose. "Mine is chocolate."

"Are you going to have one, Daddy?"

I washed my hands and came over to look inside the box. There were four cupcakes left, all different, and one of them had bacon crumbled on top of caramel-colored frosting. "Maybe I will."

The girls laughed as I took the wrapper off and opened my mouth wide enough to bite the thing in half. "Mmmm," I moaned, and I wasn't pretending—the thing was fucking delicious. I ate the entire cupcake standing right there at the counter. The girls couldn't quite finish theirs and left me to clean up the mess while they went upstairs to choose party outfits.

"I'll be up in a minute to turn the shower on," I yelled, hunting around for a roll of paper towels. I really wished Chip's party wasn't tonight—I hadn't unpacked half my shit yet. I'd be lucky to find a comb and some deodorant.

But I wanted to see my old friend, and he'd already texted me that bringing the kids was no problem at all. He said he was looking forward to meeting them, and so was Mariah, his fiancée. I'd never met her, but judging by how fast Chip had proposed, I figured she must be pretty cool. Chip wasn't the kind of guy to make a rash decision.

As I stuck the cupcake box in the fridge, my phone vibrated in my back pocket. I pulled it out.

"Speaking of rash decisions," I muttered.

Naomi and I had been high school sweethearts who'd broken up after graduation, but we'd hooked up again a few years later when I'd been home between tours. Getting married had been an impulsive move fueled mostly by nostalgia and beer.

I debated letting her go to voicemail, but since I had the girls, I took the call. When she had them, she was pretty good about letting me call and say goodnight.

"Hello."

"Hey. How was the move?" she asked breezily.

"Fine."

"You're all settled in?"

"Yep."

"Because if there's nowhere for them to sleep tonight, you can always bring them back here. I'm sure you have a lot to do."

"Their beds are all put together, Naomi. They even have clean sheets on them."

"Look at you." She laughed. "What are you doing for dinner? Do you have a kitchen together yet?"

"Actually, we have Chip's engagement party tonight."

"You're taking them to a party?" The pitch of her voice rose dramatically, as if I'd said I was taking them to a strip club. "You don't want to do that. Why not bring them here?"

"Because it's my time with them, Naomi. And they want to go."

"Will they have dinner there?"

My headache returned with a vengeance, and I started hunting around a kitchen box for the ibuprofen. "I'm sure there will be food. It's a party."

"Make sure Luna doesn't eat anything with nuts."

"She won't. They won't be hungry for a while anyway, they just ate cupcakes."

"*Before* dinner?"

"Is there something you want, Naomi?" I asked through clenched teeth. "Otherwise, I need to go up and get them in the shower. I don't want to be late."

"Are you okay? You sound stressed."

"I have a fucking headache, and I can't find the ibuprofen. Now what do you want?"

"I was going to ask to talk to them, but never mind," she said. "I can tell you're overwhelmed, and I know how you get when you can't handle things."

"I'm not overwhelmed, I have a headache!" I barked. "And I can fucking handle anything right now except you trying to barge in on my time with the girls! I'll bring them back to you tomorrow, and don't fucking call me before then!" I ended the call and shoved my phone into my back pocket as I stormed toward the stairs.

"Um, excuse me?"

Startled, I glanced to my left, and through the screen door, I saw Winnie on the porch.

Fuck. She'd probably just heard me yelling at Naomi. Exhaling, I moved toward the door and opened it.

"Can I help you?" I asked, more tersely than intended.

She looked a little nervous, not that I blamed her, as she held out a small pink box of Band-Aids. "I had these lying around and thought Luna might want them for her knee. Band-Aids sometimes come off in the shower, so . . ."

I reached out and took them from her, noticing she was careful not to let our fingers touch this time. "Thanks."

"That's it—I just wanted to—um, okay, have a good night." She turned to leave, and I probably should have let her.

"Wait a second."

She faced me again, her expression still wary.

"I'm sorry about that." I gestured over my shoulder with the pink box. "My ex-wife—the girls' mom—knows how to get a rise out of me."

"Oh, that's okay. It's none of my business, and I didn't really hear anything." It was obvious she'd heard everything.

I nodded slowly. "Well, thanks for the Band-Aids. Luna will appreciate it."

Her smile was back, along with that stutter in my chest. "Good. Enjoy your night."

"You too."

She turned around and went down the steps, cutting across the lawn to her place with that same youthful bounce in her step. Glancing down at the box, I shook my head—of *course* she had a whole thing of pink princess Band-Aids. I shut the door and trudged up the stairs to get the kids cleaned up.

Hallie went first, after a brief attempt to get me to let her wear socks in the shower. As usual, I refused, explaining again that the entire house had been thoroughly cleaned before we moved in, and I'd been here yesterday to make sure of it.

While she was getting dressed, I made sure Luna washed her hair and used soap, then helped her get dried off. After hanging up their towels, I double-checked that they'd chosen appropriate clothing and was just about to get in my own shower when I heard a series of high-pitched beeps.

"What's that?" Hallie said, scrunching up her face.

Instantly on high alert, I put my hand up. "Shh."

I heard it again, and recognized it as a smoke detector

going off, but not in our house—we were hearing it through the walls. "Stay here."

I raced out of their room and took the stairs down three at a time, jumping to the bottom with five to go. Barreling out my front door, I ran over to Winnie's and knocked. The alarm was clearly coming from inside her unit, and when she didn't answer the door, I made a split-second decision to bust in.

Fortunately, the door wasn't locked.

I shouldered it open, relieved when I didn't see or smell smoke right away. Winnie's townhouse was laid out exactly like mine, and I immediately realized the detector going off was upstairs. Racing up the steps three at a time, I reached the master bedroom doorway just in time to see Winnie climbing onto a suitcase, one hand reaching toward the ceiling to disconnect the unit.

My jaw dropped.

She was totally naked and dripping wet.

One hand was clutching a small towel to her chest that didn't fucking hide *anything*. Behind her, steam from her shower billowed from her bathroom, which must have been what set off the alarm—some detectors are that sensitive. Behind me, I heard clamoring on the stairs, and a second later both Hallie and Luna rushed into the bedroom.

Startled, Winnie looked over and saw us. Her eyes went wide as she screamed, lost her footing, and toppled backward off the suitcase. She landed hard on her ass, arms and legs flailing like a rag doll.

Averting my eyes, I strode over and disconnected the unit while she scrambled toward the bathroom on her hands and knees, presumably in search of a bigger towel.

But then she slammed the door . . . and didn't come out.

The eighty-five decibel alarm had ceased, but the sirens in my head continued.

I looked at the girls. Luna had her hands over her mouth.

Hallie's eyes were wide, and she pointed to the bathroom door. "Winnie was naked," she whispered. "We saw her bum."

"Quiet," I scolded angrily. "You two were supposed to stay at our house. You didn't follow my orders."

"But Daddy, we were scared," Luna said. Her hair was still wet and tangled. "We came to find you."

"We'll talk about it later, but when I tell you to stay put, you stay put—especially in an emergency. Understand?"

They nodded.

"Now go back to our house, both of you."

"But what about Winnie? Is she okay?"

I went over to the bathroom door and knocked, trying not to picture her naked. The shower wasn't running anymore. "Winnie? Are you okay?"

"I'm fine!"

"Are you hurt?"

"I'm fine!" she repeated in the same false, bright tone.

A tiny smile inched onto my lips. "Are you sure?"

"Uh huh!"

"It must have been the steam that set off your smoke detector."

"Yes, it happens sometimes when I forget to open the windows in here."

"It's good that it's sensitive, but open them now, okay? I should hook this back up."

"I will."

I hesitated, then spoke again. "Sorry to barge in on you like that. I'm a firefighter and a dad, so I take smoke detectors seriously. They're kind of my thing."

"Haha, it's okay!" She was still trying to sound brave and cheerful, but her voice cracked, making me smile again.

Clearly, she was not going to risk looking me in the eye after I'd seen her naked, and I couldn't really blame her. After making sure both windows in her bedroom were open, I reconnected the battery in the detector. Then I went over to the door and spoke through it once more. "I reconnected it. I'll lock the door on my way out."

"Thank you!"

"Okay, girls. Let's go." I glanced around quickly before herding the girls from her room—walls painted a soft gray, neatly made bed with a white comforter, ten thousand pillows in every shade of pink, fuzzy white rug on the wooden floor. Would have been nice if she'd landed on that rug when she hit the ground, but she'd gone down just beyond it.

As we went down the stairs, I couldn't help chuckling as I recalled her mad dash for the bathroom on her hands and knees. I'd never seen anyone crawl that fast—not even the kindergartners during the home escape and exit drills when they came to the station for a fire-rescue visit. But I felt bad for her—she was going to have a hell of a bruise on that hip.

Shoving the memory of her bare ass from my mind, I hurried out the door, making sure it locked behind me.

"Was the noise from her smoke alarm?" Luna asked as we walked back to our place.

"Yes."

"How come the alarm went off if there was no fire?" Hallie asked. "Was it like a drill?"

"No, it was the steam from her shower. But it's good that the alarm went off, because that means it's working. That reminds me—first thing tomorrow, we make our emergency plan and set a meeting spot, okay?"

"Okay."

I opened the screen door to our place—they hadn't even bothered to shut the big door—and shooed them inside. "We will also talk about what the consequences will be for not doing what I say."

They nodded solemnly as we went up the stairs.

"I still can't believe we saw her bum," Hallie whispered to Luna.

"That's enough." I swatted her backside lightly before ushering them into their bedroom. "I have to get cleaned up, so comb your hair, find your shoes, and be ready to go in ten minutes."

"But I need help, Daddy," said Luna. "I can't get the tangles out by myself."

"Baby," snickered Hallie, grabbing her brush and easily pulling it through her smooth, damp hair.

"Shut up! Yours is just easier because it's straight!"

"Stop," I ordered, dropping onto the foot of Hallie's bed. "Bring me the comb, Loony Toon. I'll do it. I'm awesome at getting tangles out of hair."

"But not gum," Hallie said.

I picked up a stuffed animal—a penguin she called Rupert—and threw it at her. When it hit the floor, I heard a coin go rolling beneath the dresser.

"My lucky penny!" Hallie dove for it, reaching under the dresser where it had rolled. "I forgot I put it in the hole in Rupert's belly last night!"

"I get a point back for finding it." I took the comb from Luna's hand and started working through the tangles from the bottom.

"I don't know if that counts as *finding* it," said Hallie, "but okay."

"So ten out of ten for today?"

"I *guess*," she said, like she was doing me a favor.

I pumped my fist. "Fuck yeah."

"That's another dollar, Daddy," Luna said. "Remember the swear jar."

"There's no way I'm having a swear jar in this house, girls. I'll go broke."

"Or maybe you'll stop swearing," Hallie said.

I leveled her with a look. "Not. Fucking. Likely."

But later on, when I went into the kitchen to grab my keys, I noticed one of the girls—or maybe both of them—had taken the cupcake box out of the fridge while I was in the shower and written on top of it DADDYS SWAIR BOX (MONEY FOR FUCHUR CAT).

I peeked inside and saw that at least they'd left the cupcakes in the fridge. Shaking my head, I closed it up again.

I could say one thing for them—when they got an idea in their head, they did *not* let it go.

Five

Winnie

I TEXTED ELLIE AND TOLD HER I WAS RUNNING LATE AND NOT TO pick me up until fifteen minutes *after* seven.

It was a lie, but I knew Dex and the girls would be gone by then, and I couldn't risk running into them outside.

I was *mortified* by what had happened earlier.

Mortified and sore—I had a bruise on my ass the size of Texas.

When I saw her pull up, I said one last prayer I could make it to her car unseen, pulled my straw beach hat lower on my head, put on my darkest sunglasses, and opened the front door. When I was sure the coast was clear, I yanked it shut behind me and dashed for her white Honda without lifting my chin from my chest.

Throwing myself into the passenger seat, I pulled the door shut and hunched down. "Twenty-four Maple Lane! And step on it!"

"Calm down, we're not even that late. And why are you wearing that hat?"

"I'll explain in a minute." I winced as I shifted on the seat to buckle my seatbelt. "Ouch."

"What's wrong with you?"

"I'm injured."

"From what?"

I slunk down farther in the seat. "Just drive, okay? I'll tell you about it once we're out of the parking lot."

She did as I asked. "Okay, we're out of the lot. Now what the hell happened?"

I lifted my head up just enough to peer out the passenger window. Satisfied I'd made my escape, I sat up straight. "I fell off a suitcase."

"Why were you on a suitcase?"

"I was trying to disconnect the ridiculously sensitive smoke detector in my bedroom, which goes off sometimes when I take a shower because of the steam."

"Don't you have a stepladder?"

"It was downstairs, and I was naked and soaking wet."

She laughed. "Oh, you'd already gotten *in* the shower?"

"Yes." I took off the hat, tossed it in the back seat, and fluffed my hair. "But I haven't even gotten to the worst part yet."

"Worse than falling off the suitcase?"

"Much worse." I shuddered. "Dex saw it happen."

"Who's Dex?"

"My new neighbor."

"The hot firefighter?" Her voice rose in surprise.

"Yes." I pictured him standing there in my bedroom doorway, his dark eyes on my naked body, his jaw practically on his chest.

"And *why* was he in your bedroom?"

"Apparently he heard the smoke alarm through the wall and came to see if I was okay."

"Oh, sweet Jesus. Why didn't you grab a towel?"

"I did! But it was more like a hand towel."

Ellie laughed. "So he could see—"

"Everything," I confirmed, slinking down in my seat again. "He saw everything. They all did."

"Who's they?"

"His little girls were there too."

"Well, so what?" Ellie shrugged. "He's a first responder. That's practically like a doctor, Win. Those guys are used to that stuff. And his daughters are just kids."

"There's more."

We pulled up at a red light and she looked over at me. "More?"

"After I went down on my ass, hand towel flying, all my bits on display, I was so desperate to get to safety that I *crawled* to the bathroom."

Ellie burst out laughing, banging the heel of one hand on the steering wheel. "Just like stop, drop, and roll! I bet he was impressed!"

"Stop making fun of me, this is serious! I've never been so traumatized in my entire life. I have to *move* now."

"Oh, for heaven's sake—you do not have to move, Winnie." The light turned green and we moved forward again. "The guy was probably just as embarrassed as you were."

"Maybe. But he's gotta think I'm a total idiot. After I barricaded myself in the bathroom, he stayed for a minute to reconnect the alarm and ask if I was okay." I cringed and shook my head. "I just kept saying, 'I'm fine!' like a crazy parrot and wishing the ground would open up and swallow me."

"Stop being so dramatic. So the guy saw you naked—who cares?"

"Naked and crawling on the floor," I reminded her.

"Fine. Naked and crawling on the floor. It's traumatizing right now, but it's a great story and someday you guys will be able to laugh about it."

"Like you're able to laugh about finding the box of sex toys under your parents' bed when you were sixteen?"

"NO. That was a whole other level of trauma." Ellie shuddered. "I can't even believe you just brought that up."

"Oh, come on. It was funny."

"Winnie, there was a whip in that box! And a blindfold!"

"I know." Distracted for a moment, I shook my head. "I still can't imagine your parents—"

"Please stop talking."

I laughed. "Sorry."

"I wonder if he went home and told his wife he just saw the new neighbor lady naked."

"Oh! Turns out, there is no wife."

She glanced at me. "I thought you saw her."

"That was his sister. He's a single dad—only two of those kids were his. Hallie and Luna." I cringed again. "The ones who saw me naked."

"A hot single dad, huh?" Ellie was clearly intrigued. "And he's right next door. Imagine that."

"Actually, I don't know that he's single. Just that he's not married. He might have a girlfriend."

"And he might not."

"Don't get any ideas," I told her, even though I'd already had *plenty* of ideas about the hot single dad next door, who'd only moved in like six hours ago.

"But I like ideas," Ellie said, pulling up in front of my Aunt April and Uncle Tyler's house.

"You just want to win the bet," I said. "But I told you—I am the boss of my feelings, and I'm off romance until Thanksgiving."

"Christmas," she said with a grin. "You changed it to Christmas, remember?"

"Right. Christmas."

"Remind me whose house this is," she said as we turned up the driveway. "I get all your aunts and uncles confused."

"April and Tyler Shaw—they're Chip's biological parents. They had him when they were super young and gave him up for adoption, but they reconnected when he was like eighteen. I grew up calling him my cousin."

"April is one of your mom's sisters, right?" We went up the porch steps and knocked on the door.

"Right." While we waited for someone to answer, I thought about my new neighbor again. "I forgot to mention that before the whole wet and naked debacle, I went over to his house to drop something off and heard him yelling at his ex-wife."

"She was there?" Ellie's eyes widened in surprise.

"No—on the phone. Something about being able to handle anything except her trying to butt into his time with the girls. Gave me flashbacks of hearing my dad on the phone with Carla when I was a kid." Carla was my biological mom, but she'd moved to Georgia before I was even out of diapers, and growing up, I'd only seen her about once a year.

"Huh. I wonder how recent their divorce was."

"I wonder when I'll be able to face him again without wanting to die. How long do you think it'll be before he forgets he saw me naked?"

She laughed. "*Cherie*, you're twenty-two and you've got a kick-ass bod. He will never forget he saw you naked."

Unfortunately, my cousin Frankie, who's fourteen, pulled the door open right then and caught the end of Ellie's sentence. Her brown eyes widened. "Who saw you naked?"

"No one," I said, giving Frankie a hug and Ellie a look to keep her silent.

"Come on, who?" My cousin looked back and forth between Ellie and me eagerly. Ellie zipped her lips and threw away the key.

I sighed. "This hot guy who moved in next door to me," I said as we went inside. "I accidentally set off the smoke detector in my house, and—"

But then I lost track of my thoughts, because right there

in the living room was Dex, looking less sweaty but just as gorgeous as he had this afternoon. Hallie and Luna hung off him like monkeys, like they were begging for something he'd already said no to.

Dex and I locked eyes, and I couldn't speak. My entire body was flushed with heat, and I knew my face had to be crimson.

"Winnie!" The girls spotted me and came racing over. "What are you doing here?"

"Um—I was invited." Tearing my eyes from Dex, I looked down at them and tried to smile, but my heart continued to race. "This is my aunt and uncle's house, and the party is for my cousin Chip. What are *you* two doing here?"

"Chip is Daddy's friend from high school," Hallie said. "They played baseball together."

"Really?" Over their heads, I met Dex's eyes again and smiled weakly. "Small world."

He nodded, looking like he had no idea what to say.

Chip entered the room and handed Dex a beer. "Here you go. Should take the edge off moving day."

Dex grabbed it and tipped it back immediately, taking a few long swallows, while Chip noticed me standing there.

"Winnie, hey!" Coming forward, he gave me a hug. "Long time, no see."

Rising on tiptoe to hug my tall, handsome cousin, I struggled to get my wits back. "Great to see you, Chip. And congratulations on your engagement."

"Thanks. I need to introduce you to Mariah—April kidnapped her for a minute, but I'm about to steal her back."

Letting go of Chip, I tried to act like an adult. "Remember my friend Ellie?"

"I think so." Chip smiled warmly and shook Ellie's hand. "Glad you could make it."

"My pleasure," she said. "Congratulations."

"This is my friend Dexter Matthews." Chip put a hand on Dex's broad shoulder before gesturing to the two girls. "And these are his daughters, Hallie and Luna. Guys, this is my cousin Winnie and her friend Ellie."

"Oh, we already know Winnie," Hallie informed him.

"You do?" Chip grinned down at her in surprise.

"Yes, she lives next door," said Luna excitedly, bouncing up and down. "We saw her bum today!"

Record scratch.

Horrible silence.

Chip looked confused. "Her what?"

"Her bum." Luna patted her own backside while I held my breath and tried to make myself disappear. "We saw it when we were in her bedroom today."

"Luna!" Hallie elbowed her sister. "Daddy told us in the car not to tell that story tonight. You're gonna get us in trouble and then we can't go swimming tomorrow."

"I for*got*." Luna rubbed her shoulder and looked up at Dex. "Sorry, Daddy."

Dex struggled for words and came up with, "Fucking hell, Luna."

"Boy, I could really use a glass of wine," Ellie said brightly, putting her hand through my arm. "How about you, Win?"

"Yes, please," I squeaked.

Chip looked relieved to exit the room and the conversation. "Come with me. There's a bar set up in the kitchen, and that's where April and Mariah are too. I'll introduce you."

Although part of me was tempted to make a run for the door, I let Ellie commandeer me, and we followed Chip out of the room. Before I could stop myself, I glanced over my shoulder to see if Dex was still standing there.

He was, and he was looking at my butt.

But as soon as he realized he'd been caught doing it, he turned around and walked in the other direction.

***

The large rectangular kitchen table was laden with dishes and platters and multi-tiered serving stands of hot and cold hors d'oeuvres, but my eyes went straight to the bottles of wine lined up on the island.

It was self-serve, so while Chip went to drag Mariah away from April, Ellie chose a rosé for us and poured two glasses. She handed me one. "Here. This will help."

Grateful, I took a few sips. "Thanks. But I think I have to leave after this drink. Will you go get my disguise from the back seat of your car?"

She laughed. "Will you stop? It's fine. It's hilarious, actually. I don't know who was more embarrassed, you or Dex."

"Me." I took another swallow.

"You were right about him, by the way. The guy is gorgeous. And built." She sipped her wine. "Doesn't smile or talk much, but with that jaw and those shoulders, does it really matter?"

"Stop."

"Maybe you should ask to see his bum, just to even the score."

"No!"

"Why not? I bet it's a nice bum."

"You're not helping, Ellie."

Thankfully, Chip appeared with a beautiful young woman at his side I knew immediately was his fiancée, since not only was he holding her hand, but he was staring at her with the biggest puppy-dog eyes I'd ever seen. "Mariah, this is my cousin Winifred and her friend Ellie," he told her.

"Hello," I said, holding out my hand. "It's so nice to meet you. Welcome to the family."

"Thank you." She smiled and shook my hand, then she bit her lip. "You're . . . Frannie's daughter? One of Mack's girls?"

I smiled, impressed. "Very good."

She blushed a little as she laughed. "I'm trying. Chip went through all the family names on the drive here from the airport—"

"She took notes," Chip said, giving her shoulder a squeeze. "And studied them like there was going to be a quiz later."

"I did," Mariah admitted. "But it's really nice to put faces to the names. There are so many of you!"

Ellie held out her hand. "Don't worry—I'm not a family member, so you don't have to memorize me. But congratulations on your engagement."

"Thank you so much." Mariah smiled at Ellie. "Do you live in the area?"

"Ellie's family owns Abelard Vineyards on Old Mission Peninsula," I said. "It's really beautiful—you should visit if you have the time."

"Too bad our new restaurant isn't open quite yet," Ellie said. "You could come for dinner."

Mariah, who didn't appear to be much older than Ellie and me, looked up at Chip. "I really wish we had more time here. We just have the one night."

"We'll come back, babe." He kissed her forehead. "Promise." To us, he said, "Mariah's family is from Michigan too, a little south of here."

"I grew up in Bellamy Creek," Mariah said.

"Oh, I know that area!" Ellie nodded enthusiastically. "It's such a cute town. About two hours from here, right?"

Mariah nodded and smiled. "Yes."

"Is your family here tonight?" I asked.

"No, we visited my family a few weeks ago, and we do want everyone to get together soon, but since Chip's extended family is pretty big, I sort of wanted the chance to meet everyone first without having to make tons of introductions." Mariah smiled at me. "I just met your mom and dad. They're so nice—everyone is," she said, laughing. "I just want to keep all the names straight."

"You're doing fine. Can I get you another glass of wine?" Chip asked his fiancée.

"Yes. I set my glass down somewhere outside—I think at Mack and Frannie's table," Mariah said.

"I'll find it. Be right back."

Mariah watched him walk away so adoringly, Ellie and I exchanged a private look of mock disgust.

"When will you get married?" I asked her. "Have you guys decided yet or is it too soon to ask?"

She laughed. "If it was up to Chip, we'd be married already—he does *not* care about having a big fancy wedding."

"Most guys probably don't," Ellie said with a smile. "We do a lot of weddings at Abelard, and I had to meet with a couple today about theirs, and the dude could not have cared less about any of it. Meanwhile, the bride was like, 'That's not *quite* the right shade of ivory I want for the linens. Do you have anything closer to ecru? Perhaps more of a creme brulée?'"

Mariah laughed. "That will not be me. I don't have the whole thing visualized in my mind or anything—and it doesn't have to be huge. I'd like something intimate, just family and close friends. We're sort of limited by the baseball calendar as to when we can do it, so we're thinking maybe February."

"This February?" I asked in surprise.

She nodded. "I know it's only six months away, and most brides plan ahead at least a year, but I'm hoping we can pull something off."

"I'm sure you can," Ellie said confidently. "And I bet you'll have an easier time finding a venue in the winter."

"April said I should talk to Millie about Cloverleigh Farms." Mariah tucked a strand of hair behind her ear.

"You should," I agreed. "I saw her car on the street, so she's here somewhere. And if Cloverleigh is all booked up during that time, check out Abelard. It's not far from here, and it's gorgeous. Cloverleigh is more American rustic chic, but Abelard is vintage south of France." I kissed my fingertips. *"Très belle."*

"That sounds beautiful. So you're a wedding planner?" Mariah asked Ellie.

"No, I work for the winery. My mother is who you want—her name is Mia Fournier. She's the manager at Abelard and coordinates all the weddings."

"Thanks," Mariah said. "Next time we're here, I'll definitely check it out."

Chip returned with a full glass of white wine, handing it to Mariah. "How's it going?"

"Great," she said. "We're talking about the wedding."

He looked at us. "I voted for Vegas with an Elvis impersonator officiating, but I don't think I'm going to get my way."

I gave his chest a playful shove. "You're not."

He grinned. "I'm gonna grab another beer and check on Dex since he doesn't really know anyone else here."

"He knows Winnie," said Ellie. "He's seen a lot of her lately."

I gave her a murderous look.

"That's so crazy that he moved in next door to you." Chip hesitated. "And I wasn't going to ask, but what was that about them . . . being in your bedroom today?"

Sighing, I took another long sip of wine and told them the story. By the time I got to the part where Luna announced to the living room that they saw my bum today, Mariah was wiping tears. "I'm sorry, I shouldn't laugh. That fall must have hurt."

"My pride took the bigger bruise," I said, "but I'll be okay. The wine is helping."

"I'll get you another glass." Chip took my empty glass and

headed for the island. A moment later, he came back with it and took off in search of Dex.

Ellie and I chatted with Mariah for a few more minutes, asking her about her job with the White Sox. "I'm in media relations," she said, "which basically means I'm a liaison between the team and the press."

"Do you like it?" Ellie asked.

"Yeah, I do. I've always loved sports, and at one point, I thought about broadcast journalism, but turns out I like being behind the scenes." She shrugged. "I could always try broadcasting in the future, but I guess it depends where Chip and I end up."

"Is he planning on staying in the game for a while?" I wondered.

"I'm not sure," Mariah said. "Pitching is really hard on the body. Most pitchers retire before age thirty. Chip is thirty-four, so he's like a grandpa." She laughed.

"You'll keep him young," I told her with a smile.

"That's what I always say!"

"How old are you?" Ellie asked.

"I'm twenty-four." Mariah glanced over at Chip and grinned. "People are always teasing him about robbing the cradle."

"A ten-year gap isn't too crazy," Ellie said. "That's like your dad and stepmom, right, Win?"

I nodded. "Yep. And they've been together for eighteen years."

Mariah smiled. "Good to know."

"Maybe he'll retire and you guys could move up here," Ellie said.

"We've actually talked about that." She lowered her voice. "Although he doesn't want me to say anything to anyone, because he hasn't made a decision. But we want kids pretty soon after we're married, and I'd like to be closer to home once that happens. Family is really important to me."

Even though I was happy for Mariah and Chip, I felt a momentary twinge of envy—how exciting to be planning a future together, and thinking about a family of their own. I knew most people my age put those things off until they were closer to thirty or even older, but I'd always imagined myself as a young wife and mom. I had a lot of love and energy to give, and it made me happy to give it, so why keep it to myself? I just needed to find the right person to share it with.

After Christmas, of course.

Chip approached with a beer in his hand but no Dex by his side.

"Did you lose your friend?" Mariah asked.

"I did. He just texted me." Chip frowned. "Apparently one of the girls is allergic to tree nuts and ate something that gave her a reaction."

I gasped. "Oh no—it's Luna! Was she okay?"

"He said she's fine, but he needed to get her home and give her some medication."

"Poor thing," Ellie said.

"Are they coming back?" I asked.

"He said they might," Chip replied. "He just needs to see how she's doing in half an hour or so. I hope they do."

I nodded, concerned for the little girl. "Me too."

We moved out to the patio, where I said hello to my dad and Frannie, my sister Millie, and lots of other relatives and family friends. I felt sorry for Mariah as she made the rounds with Chip because I knew she was frantically trying to remember everyone's names.

Every now and again, I scanned the crowd, looking for Dex and the girls, but they never returned. I couldn't stop thinking about Luna and wondering if she was okay.

When Ellie dropped me off around ten-thirty that night,

I wondered if it was too late to knock on their door and check in on her. I didn't have Dex's number or anything, or else I'd have sent a quick text.

In the end, I decided against knocking, since I didn't see any lights on in their front windows. Instead, I waved good-bye to Ellie and let myself in, ditching my high, block-heeled sandals by the front door.

In the kitchen, Piglet came wandering out from her hiding spot seeking attention, and I bent down to give her some. "What do you think, time for bed?" I asked her, scratching behind her ears.

But I wasn't tired yet, so I grabbed a spoon and the remains of my Frosty, and went out to the patio. I had a small table, two chairs, and a few potted plants out there, which I realized I'd forgotten to water the past few days.

Setting the cup on the table, I lit my citronella candle to keep the mosquitoes away and went back inside to fill the plastic pitcher under my sink. Back on the patio again, I began pouring water into one of the pots. "I'm sorry, kids," I said to my plants. "I forgot to feed you, didn't I?"

"Happens to me all the time," said a deep voice to my left.

Six

Dex

"**O**H!" STARTLED, WINNIE SPILLED WATER OVER THE side of the flowerpot and touched a hand to her chest. "I didn't see you there."

"Sorry," I said, rising from the cement. I'd been sitting there for the last half an hour, leaning back against the brick, nursing a beer and enjoying the silence. "Didn't mean to scare you. I don't have any furniture out here yet. Or candles."

"Then you're probably being eaten alive," she said. "The mosquitoes are awful out here at night."

I shrugged. "I have all the lights off, so they haven't bothered me much."

"How's Luna?"

"She's fine. It was a very mild reaction—she just needed an antihistamine."

"Oh, good," she said, sounding relieved. "I was worried when you didn't come back."

"The antihistamine makes her sleepy, so we ended up just ordering pizza and watching a movie. They both fell asleep on the couch without brushing their teeth—don't tell their mother—and I had to carry them both to bed."

She mimed zipping her lips.

"But they were sad about missing the party. I had

to promise them we'd go swimming right after church tomorrow."

"Sounds like fun. Would you like to sit over here?" she asked, gesturing toward the chairs on her patio.

My first instinct was to say no—as much as I wanted to deny it, I was attracted to her, and spending time together out here in the dark seemed like a bad idea.

But then I reconsidered—maybe by getting to know her better, I could defuse the tension, stomp out the spark. Every word out of her mouth would remind me of how young she was, right? For fuck's sake, she was out here drinking a chocolate milkshake. And I didn't want her to think I was an asshole, especially after she'd heard me yelling at Naomi on the phone. We'd have to live next door to each other for a while. Better to be friendly.

I glanced behind me—I'd be able to hear the girls through the screen if they called out. Their bedroom window was also open above us. "Sure. I'm going to grab another beer. Can I bring you one?"

She hesitated, and for a second I panicked.

"Wait—you're old enough to drink, right?"

She laughed. "Yes."

"I saw the milkshake and I wasn't sure."

"Nope—that's just my chocolate Frosty from yesterday. Those things are my favorite, but this one is definitely past its prime. I'll take you up on the beer, thanks. And no worries, I'm twenty-two."

Fuck. Twenty-two.

"Be right back." Feeling like I was contributing to the delinquency of a minor anyway, I went through the sliding door into my house, set my empty bottle on the counter, and swiped two cold ones from the fridge. My sister had brought a six-pack over for Justin and me earlier, but we hadn't touched it.

Before going back outside, I set the bottles down and crept up the stairs to peek into the girls' bedroom—both of them were sound asleep. After a quick check to make sure they were both still breathing, I snuck back down the stairs as silently as I could.

But before I went back to the patio, I ducked into the downstairs bathroom, switched on the light, and checked my reflection. Immediately I sort of wished I hadn't, because my hair looked grayer and my forehead more wrinkled than I remembered. I tried to relax my facial muscles. I fussed with my hair. I tucked in my plain white T-shirt.

Then I frowned at the glass. What the fuck was I doing?

I reminded myself again that *she was way too young for me*, even if I was the kind of guy who'd mess around with a woman he'd have to see coming and going all the time— which I wasn't. And the last thing I needed was an awkward situation when I'd moved here for a fresh start. That meant keeping my hands to myself.

Even if she was the prettiest woman I'd seen in a long, long time.

Even if the memory of her bare skin would taunt me every time I closed my eyes.

Even if I'd frantically jerked off while thinking about her in the shower earlier—which would *not* happen again.

I untucked my shirt again, turned off the light, grabbed the two beers, and went back outside. Over on her patio, the milkshake was gone and she was setting a plate on the little table with a maple bacon cupcake on it.

"I only had one of these, but it's yours if you want it," she said, dropping into one of the chairs.

"I had one earlier." I sat in the other chair and popped the caps off both bottles.

"Verdict, please. Do you agree with your girls that bacon does not belong on a cupcake?"

"No. It was fucking delicious." I handed her a beer. "Here you go. It's no chocolate Frosty, but it's cold and wet."

She laughed. "Thanks." Clinking her bottle against mine, she said, "To new neighbors."

I drank when she did, trying not to stare at her lips on the bottle.

Setting her beer on the table, she stretched out her legs, pointing and flexing her bare feet. "High heels," she said with a sigh. "They look good, but they hurt like a bitch."

I wasn't sure how to respond to that, but she *had* looked good in those heels and those jeans and that tiny little top. From the moment I'd seen her walk into the party, I'd been unable to think straight, and not just because I was scared she could read my mind about the whole getting off to her in the shower thing.

I cleared my throat. "I'm, uh, sorry again about earlier."

She flipped a wrist. "It's okay. Someday I will forget how hideously embarrassing that was."

"You have nothing to be embarrassed about," I said quickly.

"Just the fact that my new neighbors saw my bum," she joked, reaching for her beer.

I frowned. "The girls have no fucking filter."

She smiled at me sideways. "That's what they said about you."

"Oh yeah?"

"Yes. They told me all sorts of interesting things about you when they came over today."

Groaning, I tipped up my beer. "Like what?"

"Ohhh, how grumpy you are, how much you snore . . ."

"Assholes," I muttered.

"They also mentioned how hairy you are and that you swear too much."

"*That* is a fucking lie."

She laughed—an adorably girlish little giggle—and said, "I told them about the swear jar my sisters and I used to make my dad put money into whenever he cursed."

"I heard about it," I grumbled. "Thanks a lot."

"You might have met my dad tonight—his name is Declan MacAllister, but everyone calls him Mack."

"I don't think so," I said, sort of glad I hadn't had to look her father in the eye tonight. "So how are you related to Chip again?"

"We're actually not blood-related, but I consider him my cousin. His biological mom is April Sawyer, and my stepmom—who's been married to my dad since I was four—is Frannie Sawyer. They're sisters."

"Oh." I stared out into the dark for a moment, remembering events from the year I'd met Chip. He'd moved up to Traverse City just before our senior year of high school and we'd hit it off right away. We were both on the baseball team, which had been really exciting that year, not only because our record was so good but because Tyler Shaw—the recently retired MLB pitcher and most famous graduate of our high school—had come back to town and was helping out the coaching staff.

"That was pretty fucking wild, discovering that our coach was actually Chip's biological dad," I said, "not to mention that it was *Tyler Shaw*."

Winnie nodded. "Yeah. I was too young to know what was going on at the time, but I've heard the story."

I braced myself. "Were you even in school when we graduated?"

"Barely," she said, giggling again. "I was in kindergarten."

Jesus.

I took another swallow. "Luna's age. She starts kindergarten this year."

"Is she excited?"

"I think so. It helps that Hallie is already there, although she can get anxious about things."

"How so?"

"She's a little bit of a germaphobe, doesn't love eating in the cafeteria, also likes to have things *just so* in her desk, and if a kid borrows a colored pencil and doesn't put it back exactly the right way, she loses her shit."

Winnie nodded. "That must be tough on her."

"It can be, because her behavior comes off as weird to the other kids. She hates being barefoot, so she's always wearing something on her feet. Even in the pool, she wears swim socks."

"What about in the shower at home?"

"Naomi, the girls' mom, sometimes allows it to avoid a fight, but I don't. That probably makes me the mean parent, but I believe in consistency, and the doctor said it's better for her if we *don't* allow the compulsive behavior."

"Does the doctor think she'll grow out of it?"

"Too hard to say right now, but it's possible." I hesitated, then went on. "Naomi thinks Hallie's anxiety stems from worrying about me when I was gone."

"I heard you were a SEAL. But not the kind at Sea World."

"Not the kind at Sea World. They would have liked that much better." I studied the label on my beer bottle, picking at the edge of it with my thumb. "I was gone a lot when they were tiny. Back-to-back tours."

"But it's not like you had a choice about that."

"No, but the fact remains—I wasn't there when either of them were born, and I missed a ton of milestones after that. I had to watch both of them take their first steps on video." I paused. "I don't regret my choices, but I feel bad about the things I missed."

"And your ex blames Hallie's anxiety on your absences?"

"She doesn't exactly put it like that, but it's pretty clear that's the case." I paused and added, "I think she blames a lot of things on my absences."

She was silent at that, and I was embarrassed.

Why the hell was I telling Winnie about this? I never talked about this stuff with anyone, let alone a near-stranger. I was trying to think of a way to change the subject when Winnie gracefully moved the conversation in a different direction.

"Well, they seem like sweet, polite, adorable girls—when they're not talking about my bum." She brought her heels to the edge of her chair and wrapped her arms around her legs, setting her chin on her knees the way a kid would. "I hope they don't give you too much grief about the swear jar."

I harrumphed. "Too late for that. They already made one, although it's more of a swear *box*."

She laughed. "Oh yeah?"

"Yeah, they used the cupcake box. And they wrote on it. It says 'Daddy's swear box—money for future cat.'"

She burst out laughing, her head falling back, and I thought about putting my mouth on her throat. Did she wear perfume? What would her skin smell like? Quickly, I looked away and tipped up my beer again.

"So they want to get a cat?"

"Yeah, they're always on me about getting a pet, and Hallie likes the idea of a cat because they're supposedly clean animals. But my shifts at the fire station are twenty-four hours, so having a pet doesn't really work."

"I could help out," she offered. "If you just let me know which days you work, I can come by and feed her or him. And I can tell you where to go to adopt one."

"You're not helping," I told her in my best grumpy dad voice. "I don't want a fucking cat."

"Listen," she said, dropping her feet to the ground and reaching for the cupcake. "I know what happens when little girls have their dad wrapped around their fingers. They get what they want."

"Oh, really." I watched her peel the wrapper from the cupcake, my eyes on her fingers. They were long and slender, and her nails were painted to match her toes in a bright, fiery red. The thought of that hand wrapped around my cock jumped into my head uninvited.

"Yes. My sisters and I always had our dad's number." She broke the cupcake in half, then sucked frosting off her thumb, which made my dick start to get hard.

"Maybe I'm not as nice as your dad." I tried to sound menacing, but I was so fucking turned on it was difficult. "Maybe I'm better at saying no."

She laughed like she knew better than I did. "Maybe. But even a Navy SEAL has some weaknesses."

Blowjobs, I thought, watching her lick her fingers and imagining her tongue brushing across the tip of my cock.

"Here." She pushed the plate with the cupcake on it toward me. "We can share."

I wasn't hungry, but I needed the distraction, so I picked up one of the halves and bit into it.

She picked up the other, and we ate in silence for a minute. I did my best to keep my eyes off her mouth, since I was struggling to keep my thoughts clean and felt like an asshole about it. When I was done, I wiped my hands on my pants.

"Oh, sorry," she said, popping her last bite between her lips. "I should have brought us napkins. I'll get some."

"It's okay. I should go." We stood at the same time, putting us practically chest to chest.

She looked up at me and swallowed. Parted her lips.

Don't do it, dickhead, I told myself.

But she was right—I did have weaknesses, and right now her mouth was at the top of the list.

Without another thought, I took her by the shoulders and

crushed my lips to hers. She made a soft sound of surprise, and I felt her body lean into mine. She rose up on her toes, opening her mouth so I could taste her—a tantalizing combination of salty and sweet. She twined her arms around my neck, and I moved my hands down her back. Her tongue grazed mine.

Stop this right the fuck now, said a voice in my head.

But not only did I ignore it, I hitched her up by the back of her thighs, and she gasped against my lips as she wrapped her legs around me. Grabbing her ass, I pulled her tight to my lower body and moved her up and down my cock.

On the table, the candle crackled and spit, making both of us jump. I set her down hard and backed into my chair, putting distance between us. "Fuck." I held up my hands, as if she'd asked me to put them where she could see them. "I'm sorry."

"No, don't be sorry." She shook her head. "It just—it just happened."

I stood there for one second longer, watching her chest rapidly rise and fall, feeling like I couldn't catch my breath either—and I knew if I didn't get out of there, I'd end up with my tongue in her mouth again.

Or maybe other places.

"Goodnight," I said, and quickly retreated into my house.

Once I'd shut the sliding door behind me, I went into the kitchen and braced myself against the counter with two fists. Closing my eyes, I hung my head.

What the fuck? What had possessed me to do that? Was I really so weak? The girl was only twenty-two! She was twenty-fucking-two, and I was thirty-four with two young daughters, and I had no business putting my hands on her. For fuck's sake, she was nearly closer to Hallie's age than mine.

Furious with myself, I went to the fridge and took another beer out, popping the cap off with an angry twist. It reminded me that I'd left the two empty bottles on her table—now she probably thought I was one of those assholes who never cleaned up after himself and expected a woman to do it, just like my dad.

Leaning back against the counter, I took a long drink and vowed not to touch her again. If that meant I had to keep some distance between us, so be it. I'd just keep my head down if I saw her. Wave and keep on walking.

It wouldn't be easy, but I was good at doing hard things. Wasn't that why I'd become a SEAL in the first place? I could still hear my father laugh when I told him that's what I wanted to do. A hard-drinking gambler and drifter, he'd served some time in the Navy long before I was born, and never held down one job for long. Tired of his cheating, my mother threw him out when I was ten, and he'd been in and out of our lives after that with no consistent pattern. He often disappeared for months at a time. Our mother, who was loving and kind, always worked two jobs to support us.

But she had a soft spot for him that refused to harden, and she always let him back into our house when he felt like coming around—and even into her bed sometimes. It used to make me sick to think about it, so I tried not to. I hated the days when I'd come home from school or practice and saw his truck in the driveway. I felt sorry for my mother because she said she couldn't help loving him, but I was also angry with her for being so weak, so easily manipulated. By the time Bree and I were teenagers, we could see she was only going to end up hurt again when he left—because he always left. No matter what that lying asshole said, he always left again.

But he happened to be around the day during my senior year that a Navy recruiter had come to school. I'd come home excited to tell my mom what I'd decided to do with my life, since I'd never been sure before, and she was always on me to make a plan.

When I'd walked into the house, there he was, sitting at the kitchen table, drinking a beer and watching my mom cooking dinner. "Son," he'd said as I came up short at the sight of him. He used the word like a weapon.

I refused to call him Dad. I refused to acknowledge him at all.

Instead, I turned to my mom and started telling her about my talk with the recruiter and how he thought I might be a good fit for the SEALs. Over at the table, my father had busted a gut. "You'll never be a SEAL," he said derisively. "You know how hard that is? I knew guys way tougher than you who couldn't hack it."

I glared at him, my hands curling into fists. "Watch me."

I didn't see him again for almost a decade—he had the nerve to show up at my mother's funeral and claim he was sorry, and I nearly lost my mind and threw the punch I'd been dying to throw for twenty years. My sister and Naomi had to calm me down.

Bree kept in touch with him for a while, but I told her not to tell me anything. I didn't care if I ever heard his name again.

But I supposed he had taught me some valuable lessons— how *not* to be a father. How important it was not to let anyone make you feel weak. How good it felt to prove someone wrong when they doubted you.

Turning around, I dumped the rest of the beer in the sink. The last thing I wanted was a hangover in the morning. My girls deserved better.

After turning out the lights, I went upstairs, checked on them one last time, and went into my bedroom.

Five minutes later, undressed and under the covers, I lay with my hands behind my head, wide awake and unable to stop thinking.

About the past. My mother and father. Naomi and me. Our marriage had failed for different reasons than my parents'—I hadn't been unfaithful, and to my knowledge, she hadn't either—but we just hadn't loved each other enough to make up for lost time, for our differences, for failed expectations, for hurtful things that couldn't be unsaid.

I thought about Chip and Mariah and hoped it would work out better for them. It certainly seemed like some people were able to figure it out. Maybe it was the luck of the draw. Or maybe it helped to grow up like Chip had, in a house with a mom and a dad in a good marriage. Seemed like Winnie had grown up that way too.

Not that she'd been a grownup very long.

Stifling a groan, I flopped onto my stomach and shoved my head under my pillow, trying not to think about her perfect round ass, her bare wet breasts, water dripping down her warm, smooth skin. I imagined licking droplets from the stiff peaks of her warm pink nipples. I remembered what it felt like to pull her toward me and press my hard cock against her. What would it be like to cover that body with mine, to move inside her, to make her moan beneath me?

She was probably in bed now, just a few feet from the other side of this wall.

It was too close.

Seven

Dex

"LOOK AT THE WAY HIS NOSTRILS FLARE WHEN HE SNORES."

Hallie's voice came through the fog of a restless sleep.

"Yeah." Luna giggled. "Is that hair in his nose?"

"Ew, I think it is. I never noticed that before."

"Maybe he cuts it," Luna said. "I saw him giving his bushy eyebrows a haircut once."

More giggling. "I'm glad my eyebrows don't look like that."

"They kind of do."

"Do not!" Hallie was indignant.

"I just mean they're dark like his. But don't worry, yours aren't as fuzzy. Daddy's are like black caterpillars crawling over his eyes."

Hallie snickered. "Totally."

Silence for ten blissful seconds. And then.

"Daddy has an outie. I have an innie."

"Me too."

"Outies are funny-looking."

"I know."

The next thing I knew, one of them stuck a finger in my belly button. I opened my eyes. "Seriously?"

Luna, whose finger was still on my belly button, grinned. "Did that wake you up?"

"Your shit-talking woke me up."

"We want to go swimming," Hallie said.

"We have church first. You have Sunday school."

"Can't we skip it?"

"No. Your mom would kill me. Bring me my phone please."

"Where is it?"

I tried to think where I'd left it plugged in. "Try the kitchen."

Hallie left the room and went downstairs while Luna hopped onto my bed, but instead of getting under the covers, she started jumping on it. "Are we going to get a cat today?"

"No." I moved my lower body out of the way so she wouldn't crush the family jewels. "We have church, and then we can swim, and then I need to go to the grocery store. There's still lots of unpacking to do too. Plus, I haven't yelled at you enough yet for disobeying me yesterday. And we need to make our emergency plan."

Hallie appeared with my phone. "It's seven-twelve," she said as she handed it to me, then proceeded to join Luna in jumping on my bed.

"I see that." I also saw that I had texts from Chip and from Naomi, who'd also called several times. "What should we do for breakfast?"

"Donuts again?" asked Hallie hopefully.

"How about bagels?" I frowned at the message from Naomi, which had been sent sixteen minutes ago.

I heard Luna had an allergic reaction last night at the party. I can't believe you didn't tell me. Did you take her to the ER? CALL ME.

After a deep breath, I looked at Chip's text, which had been sent around midnight.

Hey, I hope everything is okay.

Really sorry about the allergic reaction.

Our flight doesn't leave until two so if you're up early and have time for coffee let me know.

"Stop jumping, I have to type something," I told the girls. "Why don't you go get dressed? Nice clothes, please. Something that matches."

They performed a dismount and raced for their room, while I shot Chip a quick note.

All good here.

We're heading for church shortly, but maybe you could swing by here on your way to the airport? We should be back by ten-thirty.

I didn't want to deal with Naomi before getting some caffeine in my bloodstream, but I forced myself to call her back.

"Why didn't you call me?" she shrieked upon picking up.

"Morning," I said, mostly to piss her off.

"Dexter."

"What?"

"I asked you a question! Why didn't you call me after Luna had a reaction?"

"Because it wasn't that big a deal. All she needed was an antihistamine. I handled it."

"I still had a right to know it happened! You should have notified me right away. Instead, I had to hear about it from someone at the bakery this morning."

"Sorry," I said. "I didn't think it was necessary."

"Well, it was. I'm still their mother, even when they're with you. I need to know about medical emergencies."

"It wasn't a fucking emergency," I snapped.

"Watch your mouth—are the girls right there?"

"No. They're getting dressed for church."

"I want to talk to Luna."

"You'll see her at church."

"Now, please."

Deciding it wasn't worth the fight, I took the phone into the girls' room and handed it to Luna. "Your mom wants to talk to you."

Luna put the phone to her ear. "Hi, Mommy. I'm fine. Yes." She looked up at me. "Yes. Okay. I will. Bye." She gave the phone to Hallie. "She wants to talk to you."

Hallie got on while I crossed my arms over my chest. "Hello? Yes. It was fun, but we weren't there too long." She looked around the bedroom. "Yes. It's nice. Uh huh. And the neighbor lady is really nice too. Her name is Winnie, like the Pooh, and she has a cat named Piglet."

"Okay, give me the phone," I said, nervous the next words out of Hallie's mouth would be *we saw her bum*. "You can tell her about all this another time."

Putting the phone to my ear, I walked back to my room. "Satisfied?"

"I guess. But please call me next time, okay?" Her voice had softened. "That's all I ask. It's hard enough to be away from them for days at a time, and I . . . I just need to know they're okay. And it's so hard when you won't talk to me."

Great. Now she was crying. I didn't want the sound of her sobs to affect me, but the truth was, it did. I took the edge off my tone. "Fine. If there is another allergic reaction, I'll call you."

"Or any medical thing."

My jaw clenched. "Or any medical thing."

"Thank you, Dex. I appreciate it. I don't mean to intrude on your time with them."

"I have to go," I said. "They're waiting for me."

"Okay. I'll see you at church."

"Fine." Ending the call, I tossed my phone onto the bed and rubbed my face with both hands.

Marriage was a fuck ton of work, and I hadn't been good at it, but damn—divorce was a bitch too.

I didn't plan on doing either of them ever again.

Fifteen minutes later, we were ready to go. As I backed out of the garage, I didn't even glance in the direction of Winnie's house.

But Hallie spoke up. "Hey, maybe we should ask if Winnie wants to go to church with us."

"We're not doing that," I said.

"Do you think she's awake?" Luna asked.

"No idea."

"I wonder if her car is in the garage," Hallie said. "She's old enough to drive, right Daddy?"

"She's twenty-two," I told them. "Yes, that's old enough to drive." And vote and drink, I thought—but *barely*.

Shoving the thought of that kiss from my head, I concentrated on the road.

"I wonder what she does for a job," Luna said.

I realized I'd sat outside with her for at least twenty minutes but I had no idea what she did for a living. "I don't know."

"Her mom owns a bakery," Hallie recalled. "Maybe she works there?"

"She might." For a second, I wondered if it was possible Winnie had been the *someone at the bakery* who'd told Naomi about the allergic reaction last night. But how would she have known who Naomi was?

"That would be a fun job," Luna said. "Baking cupcakes all day."

"Hey, that's the place our cupcakes were from!" Hallie shouted, pointing out the window. "Plum & Honey. It matches the sticker that was on the box. And the sign says open."

"Can we go there, Daddy?" Luna pleaded. "Maybe Winnie is working."

"I thought you wanted bagels," I said, panicking slightly at the thought of facing Winnie this morning after I'd rubbed her crotch against mine last night.

"No, let's go to the bakery," Hallie said.

I looked around but didn't see any other breakfast options, and of course, there was an open parking spot right in front of Plum & Honey. Cursing the universe, I pulled into it and the girls cheered.

As they unbuckled their seatbelts, I flipped down the visor mirror and checked my hair, trying to fix where it stuck up a little on the side I'd slept on. Then I sniffed the collar of my dress shirt—it was the same one I'd worn to the party last night, but I'd taken it off and hung it up as soon as we'd gotten home. I hadn't felt like ironing a new one this morning, so I'd just thrown it on again. It smelled like cologne, which I figured was okay.

What about my breath? Had I brushed my teeth? I'd been so annoyed about the phone call with Naomi, I might have forgotten. I exhaled into my hand and sniffed. I couldn't smell anything, so maybe I was fine. At least I'd trimmed the nose hair.

That's when I locked eyes with a perplexed Hallie in the mirror. "What are you *doing*?" she asked, blinking at me.

"Nothing." I snapped the visor shut and opened the door. "Come on, let's go or we'll be late."

"But why were you smelling your hand like that?" she persisted as they scrambled out of the back seat.

"No reason."

I opened the bakery door and followed them inside, relieved when I didn't see Winnie behind the counter. The girls, however, were disappointed, and went rushing up to the woman standing near the register. She might have been

Winnie's stepmom—she seemed like the right age, and I thought she looked familiar. Maybe I'd seen her at the party last night.

"Hello," she greeted them, her smile warm and welcoming. "What can I get for you?"

"Is Winnie here?" Hallie asked.

The woman looked surprised, then she laughed. "Not today. Do you know Winnie?"

"Yes, she's our next door neighbor."

"We met her yesterday," Luna said excitedly. "Does she work here?"

"No, but she comes in here a lot. She's my daughter." She lowered her voice and spoke behind the back of her hand, like she was telling them a secret. "She says she comes here for me, but I think she just likes the free cupcakes."

The girls laughed as I approached the counter. It smelled delicious in here—like sweet, buttery cinnamon rolls were in the oven. And something about the scent reminded me of Winnie . . . maybe because of the cupcake we'd shared last night?

"So you must be Hallie," Winnie's mom said, pointing to Hallie. "And you must be Luna."

"Yes," Luna said. "But how did you know?"

"Winnie told me all about you last night at the party." She looked up at me with gray-green eyes that crinkled a little at the corner and smiled. "Hi. I'm Frannie MacAllister."

"Dexter Matthews. It's nice to meet you."

"You too. I was sorry to hear about little Luna's allergic reaction. I have sixteen-year-old twins, and one of them has terrible food allergies." She hesitated, her expression turning apologetic. "I'm a client of Naomi's at the salon, and we've chatted a little about the challenges of dealing with them. She was in here this morning, and I asked how Luna was—judging by her reaction, she hadn't heard about it. I'm sorry if I caused any friction."

Now it made sense. "No worries," I said easily. "We're divorced, but I spoke with her this morning."

She nodded and turned her attention back to the girls. "Well. What can I get for you? And don't worry—no nuts in anything!"

While the girls asked her about every single muffin, roll, and pastry under the glass, I checked my phone again to see if Chip had gotten back to me. He had—a couple minutes ago, he'd texted that they were just waking up and planning to have breakfast with his mom, sister, and stepdad at nine, but could swing by my place around eleven. All I had to do was give him the address.

I sent it to him and asked him to text me when he arrived, since we might already be at the pool. He immediately responded that was no problem and he'd see us soon.

"What about you, Dexter?" Frannie MacAllister asked once the girls had chosen their breakfast. "Can I get you something?"

I glanced at the display case and ordered a slice of quiche.

"Good choice," she said. "The ham and gouda is one of Winnie's favorites too. She might have even created this recipe—she's an excellent cook."

"Daddy is a terrible cook," Hallie announced. "He tries, but he burns everything."

Frannie laughed. "Winnie's dad isn't a very good cook either. But he's good at other things, like I'm sure your dad is."

"He's good at putting out fires," said Luna proudly. "He's a firefighter."

"*That* is a *very* important job." Frannie smiled as she took a slice of quiche from the tray. "Now, will this be for here or to go?"

"To go," I said, still a little wary of running into Winnie. "Thanks."

A few minutes later, we were sitting in the church parking lot, the girls eating their muffins in the back seat, me devouring a slice of quiche in the front, trying to avoid getting anything on my white shirt. "Girls, could you please stop telling everyone you meet embarrassing things about me?"

"What kinds of things should we tell them?" Luna asked.

"How about saying nothing at all if you don't have anything nice to say? Wasn't that what Bambi said?"

"It was Thumper who said that, Daddy," corrected Hallie.

"Whatever. Just no more telling people things like I snore or I swear or I have hair in my nose."

"But you do," Luna said with a laugh.

"Tell them about the hair on my chest. I like that hair." I finished off the last bite of crust and checked the bag for a napkin. "Or my muscles. Can't you guys tell people what big muscles I have?"

"We *could*," allowed Hallie, "but muscles aren't as funny as hair. And we decided we don't care if you swear anymore."

"You don't?" No more napkins in the bag. I opened the glove box.

"No, because we need money in the box for Future Cat. So swear all you want."

"Fuck," I muttered, unable to find another napkin anywhere.

"That's a dollar-fifty, Daddy."

"A dollar-fifty!" I turned around and looked at them in the back seat. "You said yesterday the F word was only a buck."

Hallie smiled sweetly. "Prices go up on Sunday."

"Because of Jesus," added Luna.

Turning around again, I grabbed the wheel and slumped down in my seat.

After church, I stood on the steps next to fucking Bryce for ten solid minutes while Naomi looked the girls over, as if she was expecting to find evidence of neglect. "You're sure you're all right?" she kept asking Luna.

"I'm fine, Mommy."

Bryce kept busy on his phone the entire time, probably checking the value of his stock portfolio. He came from a wealthy family and never tired of telling people about his Harvard degree, his investments, or his sailboat. It drove me insane that once he married Naomi, my daughters were going to live in his house. They didn't belong to him.

"Hals, do you want me to fix your pigtails? They're not even." Naomi reached for one of the elastics I'd put in.

Hallie pushed her hand away. "No, it's okay. We're just going swimming."

"We have to go," I said impatiently. "I'll have them back by five."

Naomi sighed and kissed them both. "Okay. Be careful in the pool please. And don't forget sunscreen!"

I took the girls by the hands and walked them back to the car. On the ride home, I let them choose the music, and I think they knew I was bothered by something, because after I pulled into the garage and turned off the engine, Hallie unbuckled her seatbelt and hugged me from behind. "You get a ten this morning, Daddy."

I patted her skinny forearm. "I do?"

"Yes."

I looked over my shoulder at Luna. "Well, do you agree?"

"Yes," she said, grinning at me. "It's anonymous."

"She means unanimous," Hallie explained.

"Thank you." I opened the car door, feeling a little better. "Who's ready to go swimming?"

The girls had just gotten into their bathing suits when Chip and Mariah arrived. Since the kids were impatient to get in the water, we went out to the pool and sat in chairs near the edge. I sprayed Hallie and Luna down with sunscreen and made them wait a minute for it to dry, which they counted off standing on the pool's top step, then jumped in.

While they played in the shallow end, Chip and Mariah talked a little about what I'd missed at the party and how they were anxious to come back and look at some wedding venues.

"I've heard Cloverleigh Farms is beautiful," Mariah said, "but Chip's cousin Winnie mentioned Abelard Vineyards too."

At the mention of Winnie's name, my blood warmed, but I was careful not to visibly react. "I've never been there, but I've heard it's nice."

"We thought about Chicago too, but we're worried not everyone would be able to make the trip down, especially if we do it in the winter," Chip said. "Mariah's family doesn't live too far from here, so this makes more sense."

"You're thinking this winter? Like before spring training?"

"Yeah." Chip hesitated. "Actually, I'm thinking of retiring after this season."

For the first time, I looked away from the kids. "Seriously?"

He shrugged. "My arm is shot, I'm tired, and I feel like I did what I wanted to do. I'm sort of ready for the next phase of my life. We'd like a family."

I focused on my girls again. "Will it be hard to walk away?"

"If you'd have asked me that last year, I'd have said yes. But today, I can honestly say no." He put an arm around Mariah and kissed her head. "There's more to life than baseball."

I laughed. "That's something I never thought I'd hear Chip Carswell say."

He chuckled too. "Times have changed, haven't they? But after a while, you start to realize what really matters, and it's not the money or the fame or the speed of your fastball."

"I don't know, those things sound pretty nice to me."

"They are," he said, "but I look at you and your girls and think it's so fucking cool what you have. I'd easily walk away for that."

"Can we watch our mouths around here, guys?" Mariah whispered, glancing around at all the families at the pool.

"I do love being their dad," I said. "But I worry that the divorce is gonna mess with them forever. Or that I won't able to give them everything they deserve. Or that I don't have enough time with them."

Mariah leaned over and touched my shoulder. "My dad raised me on his own until I was nine, and I know it's not easy. He was a cop and worked long hours, and he used to worry about the same things. But the time he *did* have with me—he made it count. You do too, I can tell."

"Can you find a job with more traditional hours?" asked Chip. "Would that help?"

"Maybe. But I can't fucking sit behind a desk. And I like what I do and who I work with. I have decent benefits. I like having three days in a row off." I shrugged. "I sometimes think about doing something on the side for a little extra, but I'm not sure what."

"You should talk to Tyler," Chip said. "He's got that sports complex and I'm sure he could use you as a trainer. You'd be good at that. You know how many guys would love to be trained by a fucking Navy SEAL?"

"The problem is my schedule. It's never the same week to week."

"He'd work with you." Chip was confident. "You should get in touch."

"You guys should do something together," suggested Mariah.

"You're moving back?" I asked in surprise.

"We're thinking about it." He looked at his fiancée. "With her family and mine up here, we don't really have a reason to stay in Chicago."

"That would be cool," I said. "We could round up Fitz and Jimmy, get the team back together."

Chip laughed. "That would be something."

"Oh my God, you guys should!" Mariah exclaimed. "My dad and his friends played in this senior men's league while I was growing up—in fact, they're still playing—and going to the games was so much fun."

"Uh, I think some people might complain if we had a retired MLB pitcher in a senior men's league," I said.

"I'll take a little something off my fastball," joked Chip. "I'll keep my eyes closed. We'll put a fake name on my jersey."

"You'd still strike out every jackass at the plate. We'd be disqualified before the inning was up."

He grinned, looking eighteen again. "Be a hell of an inning though. Then we'd go for beers."

"Fuck yeah," I said. "Count me in."

Eight

Winnie

SUNDAY MORNING, I WOKE UP AROUND NINE, WHICH WAS LATER than usual—probably because I'd lain awake half the night thinking about that kiss.

That *kiss*.

Rolling onto my side, I hugged a body pillow close to me, arms and legs wrapped around it. If I closed my eyes and held my breath, I could transport myself right back to that electric moment when we'd both stood up at the same time, as if it had been choreographed by divine intervention.

Neither of us had moved. Time stopped ticking. My heart hung suspended in my chest, poised to fall.

And then—*and then*—he'd taken me by the shoulders and crushed that mouth to mine, the one I'd been thinking about all day. Usually, his jaw was all clenched and tight, but suddenly his lips were open, his tongue was on mine, his scruff brushing against my skin.

I'd felt that kiss right down to my toes.

Then all of a sudden, it was over. And he was gone.

Moaning, I rolled onto my back and burrowed under the sheet again. Kissing me had obviously been an impulsive move on his part, and judging by the apology that immediately followed, one he felt bad about.

But there was no reason he should regret it. And I hoped he didn't think I was mad about it . . . I'd enjoyed every second of that kiss.

That *kiss*.

But still, it was probably best if it never happened again.

Not only because it could make for an awkward situation having to live next door to each other, but because I knew myself—I could easily start to crave the way he'd made my heart pound, the way he'd given me butterflies, the way he'd stolen that kiss from me like he knew he couldn't afford it but he had to have it anyway.

Bringing my fingers to my lips, the swoony feeling came over me again, and I let the hum reverberate throughout my body. I pictured him, and heat began to pool at my center. The eyes. The mouth. The shoulders. The chest. The arms. Those hands that gripped my ass and moved me like he owned me.

I let my imagination travel down his body to places I hadn't seen . . . rippling abs. A deep, sexy V line. A big, hard cock. His weight between my legs.

My hand moved down my chest, slipping into my underwear, my fingers easing between my thighs.

Then I sat up and swung my feet to the floor. "No, no, no. I'm not going there. It was one kiss, it happened, it's done. I'm not allowed to obsess over it. I am the boss of my feelings."

But I wasn't feeling particularly bossy there in bed, so I got up, used the bathroom, and threw some workout clothes on. Grabbing my yoga mat from my closet, I went downstairs and spread it out in the living room. Normally, I didn't do anything without having a cup of coffee in the morning, but this seemed like an emergency situation—I needed to distract my mind and body with something more physical, channel the pent-up energy into something more productive than getting myself off.

Twenty minutes later, I felt more centered, relaxed, and

in control. When I checked my phone, I saw a message from Ellie. **Coffee and power walk this morning?**

Sure, I replied. **Meet at P & H?** My mom's coffee at the pastry shop was the best.

Give me twenty, she texted back.

I sent her a thumbs up and went upstairs to make my hair more presentable and put on socks and shoes. At the top of the steps, I stopped and pressed my ear to the wall, on the other side of which was the smaller of the two bedrooms of Dex's unit.

Would it be the girls' room? Were they getting ready for church? Already there? Or what if he'd given them the master with its own bathroom and taken the smaller bedroom for himself? Was he in there getting dressed?

Frowning, I pushed myself away from the wall. It was going to take some effort today to keep him from infiltrating every thought.

I had to be vigilant, which meant no stalking or spying. I needed to ditch the Gladys Kravitz routine and put my energy into something else—maybe while we walked, Ellie and I could plan a road trip or something. Or brainstorm a new guest amenity at Cloverleigh Farms. Or partner up on some autumn wine tastings—Cloverleigh and Abelard.

I needed a distraction.

"Hi, Mom," I called, entering Plum & Honey and holding the door open for an elderly couple on their way out. Even though she was technically my stepmom, I'd been calling her Mom since she married my dad.

"Hi, sweetie." She smiled at me from behind the counter. "What are you up to today?"

"Meeting Ellie here for coffee and then we're going to take a power walk."

"Nice. Want coffee to go or for here?"

I glanced around. Plum & Honey only had a few tiny tables, but there was one open. "For here."

"You got it." She placed two cups and saucers on the marble counter and began to fill them from the pot. "Did you have fun last night?"

Immediately I thought about the kiss, although I knew she was referring to the party. "Yes."

"Mariah seems sweet." She replaced the coffee pot in the machine.

"She does."

"And young."

"She's only ten years younger than Chip, Mom. Same as you and Dad."

"I know." Shaking her head, she took a couple scones from the case and put them on two plates. "I guess I feel like twenty-four is very young to make a lifelong commitment. You hardly know who you are yet."

I rolled my eyes. "You were what, twenty-seven when you married Dad?"

"Twenty-eight."

"Okay, twenty-eight. That's only a few years' difference."

"I know, I know." She laughed at herself. "Maybe I'm just remembering the panic I felt when I thought you were getting married at twenty-two."

My smile faded. "That's different. Merrick was obviously not the right *choice* for a lifelong commitment, but it doesn't mean I wasn't ready to make one."

"I know." She held up her hands. "And I remember very well what it was like to be young and want to make my own decisions, whether they were mistakes or not. You have to be free to stumble along the path, which is why I didn't say anything negative to you about Merrick even though I knew all along he was not the one for you."

"Next time, you could at least drop a hint," I said wryly, picking up both saucers.

"Deal." She took the plates with scones on them and came around the counter, following me to the empty table. "By the way, your new friends were in this morning."

I sat down and looked up at her in surprise. "My new friends?"

"Dexter Matthews and his girls."

The butterflies returned. "Oh."

"They came in to grab breakfast before church." She laughed as she set down the plates. "The girls were looking for you. They thought you might work here."

I smiled. "They're so funny."

"They are. And Dexter seems nice."

"Yes."

"And very handsome. I'd never met him before."

I shrugged, trying to play it cool. "I guess."

"His ex-wife Naomi does my hair."

"Oh really? I didn't know that."

She sighed, twisting her fingers together. "I've heard her side of things—she definitely isn't shy about discussing her personal life at work. But her side isn't the only one."

"What does she say about him?"

"The usual stuff any ex-wife would say. She doesn't think he tried hard enough to make the marriage work. She said he was gone a lot when they were first married and that was tough." My mom shrugged. "She's called him some names."

"He's a good dad," I said, feeling the need to defend him. "A really good dad. Those girls adore him."

"I could tell when they were in here. And she never says he's a bad father, just a shitty husband." She shrugged. "But like I said, there are two sides to every relationship story."

I knew she was thinking about my real mom, and how shitty things were for my dad after Carla left. I also remembered very well the things Carla used to say to my sisters and me about our dad, and how upset it used to make me. I'd get terrible stomachaches over it. "I hope Naomi doesn't say those things in front of the girls."

"I don't think she does," my mom said. "She's said before that she doesn't believe in one parent badmouthing the other in front of the kids. I think it's more like the salon is her safe space to vent." She thought for a moment. "She'll often rant for a bit and then apologize and say something like, 'I've known him forever and he's a good person, but he just turned out to be wrong for me.' I guess they were high school sweethearts."

Out of nowhere, a sharp bolt of jealousy zapped me in the gut. "When did they split up?"

"I think maybe a year and a half ago? Two years? I know it's final though, because she's already engaged again."

"Good for her," I murmured, picking up my coffee for a sip.

"Anyway, it was nice to meet them today. And I'm so glad Luna's reaction was nothing scary."

A few customers entered the bakery, and Ellie was right behind them. "I better get back to work." My mom patted my shoulder. "Thanks for coming in, sweetie."

Ellie waved to my mom and joined me at the table. As soon as she sat down, she took an elastic from around her wrist and gathered her reddish-brown hair into a ponytail. "Hey. Sorry I'm late. Mia cornered me on the way out to make sure I know the tastings I have to cover for today. I don't know why she thinks I have no brain. We went over the schedule yesterday. She's so fucking type A, I don't know how my dad deals with it."

"No worries." I took another sip of coffee.

"What's wrong?" Her light brown eyes scrutinized my face.

"Nothing."

"Nice try." She tightened the ponytail and picked up her coffee. "If you don't spill the tea, I'll keep complaining about my mother. Is that what you want?"

I laughed a little. "I was just talking to my mom about Dex."

"Does she know he saw you naked?" Her eyes gleamed wickedly over the rim of her cup.

"*No*. Apparently he and the girls were in here this morning looking for me."

"Oh?" She tilted her head. "That's interesting."

"And she told me that Noami—his ex-wife—cuts her hair. So every six weeks she gets an earful about what a shitty husband he was."

"That's not cool."

"No, but I suppose it could be true. I don't really know him."

"I guess not."

"But . . . he seems nice." I played with the handle on my coffee cup. "He came over last night and sat on the back patio for a bit."

Ellie's mouth fell open. "And?"

"And we talked."

"*And*?"

"And I got to know him a little better," I said, reluctant to give her the entire truth right up front. "He's actually kind of funny and sweet beneath his grumpy exterior."

One of her eyebrows peaked.

"And he loves those girls so much. He talked a little bit about feeling bad for being away so much when they were babies. He missed a lot of milestones." I took another sip of coffee. "I think he wants to make up for that."

"Sounds like a good guy so far," she said. "How long did he stay?"

"Maybe half an hour? Just long enough to have a beer and share a cupcake."

"You two shared a cupcake?" Her eyes twinkled again. "How romantic."

"Not like that—I mean, we didn't, like, feed each other bites or anything. We just . . . each ate half. And then he said goodnight and went home."

"That's it?"

"Yes. Mostly." I picked up my coffee and looked out the window.

"Winifred." Ellie set her cup down and leaned onto the table with her elbows. "What happened between sharing the cupcake and saying goodnight?"

"It wasn't a big deal," I said quickly.

"What wasn't?"

"He apologized right away."

"Apologized for what?"

I held my breath for a second, then gave in. "For the kiss."

Ellie's jaw dropped. "There was a kiss?"

"There was *one* kiss."

"And?" she demanded impatiently. "How was it?"

"So hot," I said, fanning my face. "Like, *really* hot."

Leaning back in her chair, she grinned slowly.

"What's that smile?"

"It's a victory smile, because I'm going to win the bet," she said, her tone smug. "You made out with a hot dude, and you've got that look in your eye."

"What look?"

"The look that says *I can't stay long, I have to go pick out a china pattern.*"

"I do not have that look," I argued, trying to arrange my face in a more casual expression. "He didn't *propose*. He just kissed me. I'm perfectly capable of kissing a man without wanting to marry him."

"Since when?"

I glared at her. "Anyway, it won't happen again."

"How do you know?"

"Because he apologized right afterward and left. Obviously he didn't mean to do it."

She rolled her eyes. "You don't kiss someone by accident, Win. It's not like stepping on their foot."

"Whatever." I waved a hand in the air, like a magic wand—like poof, he was out of my head. "It would never work anyway. He's too old for me, he's newly divorced, and I'm not really interested in dating someone with a lot of baggage. We're just going to be friends."

"If you say so." Ellie picked up her cup again.

"I do," I said emphatically. "And that's that."

After we finished our coffee and scones, Ellie and I took off on our power walk, a three-mile loop we'd been doing pretty much every Sunday morning all summer. As we huffed and puffed under the hot sun, we brainstormed different ideas for projects we could work on together.

"I love the idea of a joint wine tasting," Ellie said. "Abelard and Cloverleigh make different enough wines that it could be really interesting."

"Do you think a series or a one-time event would be better?"

She thought for a moment. "If we can get it on the calendar, why don't we try a one-time event later this fall? If it goes well, we could make it a series next summer during the high season."

"Good idea." We looked both ways and crossed a side street. "Where should we do the first one? Abelard or Cloverleigh Farms?"

She shrugged. "Either place would work. It's too bad our

new restaurant won't be open for another couple months. That would be the perfect space—intimate and cozy, amazing view of the vineyard."

"What's the holdup?"

"You name it. Materials, labor, contractor delays. Even my dad has lost his temper a couple times about it, and you know how laid-back he usually is. Originally it was supposed to open in October. Now they're saying it might not be ready until after the holidays, and the chef my dad wanted couldn't wait. He took a job somewhere else."

"That stinks."

"They're interviewing chefs again, but they're not finding anyone who's right."

"I could ask my sister Felicity if she's interested," I said. Felicity, who lived in Chicago, had gone to culinary school and was now a food scientist.

"Do it. My parents keep mentioning Gianni Lupo and I would rather eat dirt than work with him."

I laughed. Growing up around here, the Lupo brothers were legendary. There were three of them, and they were all loud, reckless, and rowdy, constantly in trouble at school for breaking rules or getting in fights—often with each other—and one of them was usually in a cast or sling from some dare they couldn't resist or stupid thing they'd done to show off. They weren't mean, except to each other and other boys just like them, but when they weren't tearing each other apart or pulling pranks at school, they loved teasing girls.

Ellie had grown up with the Lupo brothers because their mothers were best friends, but she didn't have one nice thing to say about them, especially Gianni, who was our age. Not that I entirely blamed her—he'd always tormented her relentlessly. It hadn't helped that they'd grown from scrappy, skinny boys with gangly legs and scabby elbows into gorgeous, brawny teenagers with unfair bone structure, thick tousled hair, and irrepressible grins.

Then there was the infamous night of the Cherry Festival when we were seventeen, which involved a dunk tank, several pies in the face, and a highly controversial game of Seven Minutes in Heaven.

"I still haven't forgiven him for what he did to me," Ellie said. "It was so humiliating."

"Come on, that was five years ago. We were in high school. Maybe he's matured by now."

She gave me a look that would have singed hair at twenty feet. "Guys like Gianni Lupo don't mature, Winnie. They don't have to, because even though they get older, they can just keep dating younger girls who don't know better."

"I thought he was in California. Wasn't he doing some next generation version of the reality cooking show his dad was on?"

"Yeah. *Lick my Plate*," Ellie sneered, rolling her eyes. "I can't even believe my parents are considering hiring that clown."

"I will reach out to Felicity and see if she's interested."

"Thank you. That would save me from death by testosterone. Or going to prison for murder."

I laughed. "What are friends for?"

Later that afternoon, I was unloading the dishwasher when I heard a little voice coming in through the sliding screen door. "Hi, Winnie."

I glanced over and saw Luna and Hallie standing on my patio, wrapped in large towels, their hair wet and dripping. "Well, hi," I said, noticing Hallie wore swim socks. "You finally went swimming, huh? Did you like the pool?"

"Yes," Hallie said. "Will you come out and swim with us?"

"Me?"

"Daddy said we could ask you." Luna paused. "Well, at first he said no, we weren't allowed to bother you, but then we bugged him until he said yes."

I laughed. "Sometimes that works."

"So will you?"

Glancing at my phone, I saw it was just after three. I could hang out with the girls at the pool and still have plenty of time to clean up and make it to my parents' house for six o'clock dinner. "Okay," I said. "I just need a few minutes to get my suit on. Do you want to come in?"

"We can't," Hallie said, glancing over her shoulder toward the pool area. "Daddy said we have to stay where he can see us. And we're still sort of in trouble for wandering off yesterday."

"But we have our emergency plan now," added Luna seriously. "If there's a fire, we're going to meet at the pool gate."

I nodded. "That's a good plan. Okay, I'll be right down."

I hurried upstairs and opened a dresser drawer, debating between a skimpy two-piece and more family-friendly tank. Considering the situation, I decided on the blue and white striped tank. It had a low V in the front with a ruffled neckline, but wasn't too revealing. I didn't want to look like I was trying to be sexy or get Dex's attention.

Tossing a cover-up on over my suit, I put on flip-flops and grabbed a towel. Downstairs, the girls were patiently waiting for me on the patio. I slung my pool bag over my arm and put on my sunglasses, sliding the door shut behind me. "Okay," I said. "Let's go."

They scampered across the lawn like puppies, and I walked fast to keep up. Beyond the black fence, I saw where Dex was reclining in a lounge chair, the back propped all the way up so he could see all the way to my patio door. His feet were crossed at the ankle, his arms were folded over his chest, and he didn't look all that thrilled as we approached. I wondered if he'd been hoping I wasn't home.

"See? Told you he was hairy," Hallie said to me.

Luna raced ahead. "We found her!" she cried, trying unsuccessfully to open the gate. "She said yes!"

Dex got out of the chair and came over to open the gate. "I see that."

"Hi," I said, ignoring the way my heart was thumping at the sight of him in dark blue swim trunks. His chest was every bit as magnificent as I'd imagined, and not at all too hairy, despite what his daughters thought. His six-pack abs were taut beneath golden skin, and my eyes immediately wandered to the trail of hair beneath his belly button and the V lines that showed above his waistband.

As the gate swung shut behind me, he hitched up his suit, as if he'd caught me looking.

I quickly looked up and tried to smile. "How was church?"

"Fine." His dark hair was wet and messy, and I couldn't read his eyes behind his aviator sunglasses.

"The girls got you in the water already, huh?"

"Yeah." He ruffled his hair in a boyish gesture. "I keep trying to get them out of here, but it's impossible."

"Well, it's a gorgeous day," I said, walking over to where Hallie and Luna had dumped their towels on the cement, right at the foot of their dad's chair. "And school starts in what, just over a week? Gotta enjoy this while you can."

The pool was crowded and there were no other lounge chairs available, but Dex moved his towel and spread it out on the ground. "Here. You can sit."

"Thanks, but I don't think the girls asked me out here so I could work on my tan," I said with a laugh. Hallie and Luna had already jumped into the shallow end and were shouting for me to join them.

"You don't have to swim if you don't want to," he said. "I told them not to bother you."

"It's no bother," I said, removing my shoes and sunglasses. After tossing my cover-up on the chair, I noticed him looking at my body but trying to appear as though he wasn't. "I'm just going to put some sunscreen on real quick."

I leaned over and pulled a can of SPF 50 from my bag, giving my face and shoulders and chest a quick mist. "Want some?" I offered.

"No, thanks." He dropped to his towel on the cement and sat with his forearms draped over his knees.

After tucking the can back into my bag, I walked down the steps into the pool, conscious of his eyes on me.

"Are you coming in too, Daddy?" Hallie yelled. "We can have a tea party with four people now."

"Nah, you guys don't need me."

As I played with the girls in the water—tea party, judging their handstands, proving I could still do three backward somersaults in the water without taking a breath—I was aware of him watching us, and I told myself he was just a concerned dad keeping a cautious eye on his children in a pool without a lifeguard.

But when I got out and dried off, I could sense him wrestling with his focus again—his gaze kept straying to my chest.

"Daddy, can we have another popsicle?" Luna asked, putting her towel over her head like a nun's habit.

Dex checked his phone. "It's time to go in."

"No!" both girls said at once.

"Okay, you can go get another popsicle, but that's the last snack before dinner, and we have to clean up soon. I have to have you back at five or I'll get yelled at."

Grinning, they tossed off their towels and took off toward their back door.

I smiled at him. "Softie."

He made a noise, something between a growl and a grunt.

I glanced at the empty lounge chair. "Are you sure you don't mind if I sit here?"

"Go ahead."

I spread my towel on it and stretched out, disappointed when he kept his eyes straight ahead on the pool, although I did notice the way he had one hand clamped tightly around the opposite wrist, like maybe he was afraid of where that hand might wander if it were set free.

My knee? My thigh? My hip?

I liked that he might want me like that, even if it couldn't go anywhere, especially after being dumped for the *prospect* of banging a New York model.

The guy was hot, and catching his eye felt good.

Really good.

Nine

Dex

S HE WAS SO CLOSE TO ME I COULD SMELL HER—COPPERTONE
and chlorine had never been so sexy—and I considered
moving away from her chair a little.

I kept my eyes straight ahead, but it took effort. She had
an amazing body, and even though her swimsuit wasn't revealing, I'd already seen what was underneath it. And no matter
how badly I wanted to forget that kiss, I couldn't stop thinking about it.

She seemed comfortable with the silence between us, but
I was squirming with guilt.

And other things I didn't want to feel.

"I'm sorry again about last night," I said quietly.

"It's fine. No apology necessary."

Which should have been my cue to shut up and move
on, but it really fucking bothered me, how attracted I was to
her. How badly I wanted to get my hands on her body. How
I'd lain awake half the night thinking about all the things I
wanted to do to her.

I had to make sure she didn't want me the same way, or I
was doomed. "I just didn't want to give you the wrong idea."

She turned her head to look at me, shading her eyes. "The
wrong idea about what?"

I refused to look at her. "About me. I'm not, you know, interested in you like that."

"I never thought you were."

"Good. Because it was just a stupid mistake."

She stared at me for another ten seconds, then dropped her arm and turned her face to the sun again. It had to be seventy-five degrees out here, but I swear I could feel an icy cold wind coming from her direction.

A minute later, she stood up, grabbed her things, and left without saying a word.

Stop her, you asshole, I told myself as she let herself out of the gate.

But I didn't.

I watched her walk back to her place and disappear into her condo without a single backward glance.

And I breathed a sigh of relief.

"Mommy!" Hallie unbuckled her seatbelt and hopped out of the car.

"Hi, Halsy pal!" Naomi scooped Hallie into her arms and hugged her tight. "I missed you."

"But you just saw me this morning."

"Doesn't matter." Naomi rubbed noses with her. "I always miss you when you're not with me. And oh my goodness, look at that sunburn."

I helped Luna down from the back seat and opened up the back to get their things.

"You're all pink too!" Naomi looked at me reproachfully as I set their things down on the driveway. "Dex, did you not put sunscreen on them?"

"Of course I did. But they were in the pool, and it was hard to keep getting them out to reapply."

"And Winnie came swimming with us!" Luna said excitedly.

I flinched at her name.

"Who's Winnie?" Naomi asked.

"Our neighbor with the cat," replied Hallie. "Remember? I told you about her."

"Oh, right. That's nice." But Naomi was distracted as she examined the girls' faces. "We need to get some aloe on those cheeks and noses. I bet your shoulders are all burned too, huh?"

I bit my tongue.

"Say goodbye to your dad and go in the house. I'll be in in a minute."

One at a time, the girls came over and hugged me tight, their tiny arms wrapped around my neck. I held them close and pressed my lips to their damp, chlorine-scented hair.

"I love you, Daddy," they each said.

"I love you too," I told them. "I'll call you this week and I'll see you on Saturday, okay?"

"Okay." They went into the house, and Naomi faced me, hands on her hips.

"Sorry they're not showered," I said. "They wanted to stay in the pool so long, we ran out of time."

But she didn't seem interested in bitching about that for once. "So how was the party last night?"

"Fine."

"What's Chip's fiancée like?"

"She seems nice."

"They got engaged fast, didn't they?"

"I guess."

"I heard she's young."

I ran a hand through my hair, impatient to leave. Naomi had always loved to gossip, and I hated it.

"Like ten *years* younger than him," she prodded.

I shrugged. "Maybe."

"Didn't you meet her?"

"Yeah. But I didn't card her or anything."

She rolled her eyes. "Never mind. I don't know why I bothered to ask."

"And what difference does her age make anyway?" I pushed, suddenly in the mood to fight. "You and I are the same age. We knew each other forever before we got married, and our relationship still didn't work."

Her eyes narrowed. "Our relationship didn't work because I was the only one in it."

"I wasn't here."

"Even when you were here, you weren't in it, Dex." She backed away, holding her hands up. "You know what? I don't want to have this argument again. And that's the beauty of divorce—I don't have to."

She went into the house and shut the door, leaving me fuming in the driveway.

What the fuck was I doing? I didn't want to have that argument either. I jumped into my car, threw it into reverse, and took off so fast my tires squealed.

The truth was, I wasn't mad at Naomi, I was mad at myself. I'd hurt someone that didn't deserve it, all because I didn't trust myself to keep my goddamn pants zipped.

If it hadn't been a work night, I might have found a dive bar and gotten good and drunk, maybe gone home with a hot cocktail waitress and gotten rid of this fucking pent-up aggression, but since I had to be at the station at seven a.m., I hit the drive-thru and went home alone.

I arrived at work the next morning by six forty-five, swapping places with the guy who had my position on the previous shift. Since I hadn't slept all that well, I was tired and crankier than usual during all the chores we had to get done every morning—put out our turnout gear, check the radios and air packs, bring the apparatus outside, run the pump and emergency lighting, inventory each compartment for proper gear and equipment.

After that, it was on to station housekeeping—cleaning the bathroom, emptying the trash, vacuuming the carpets, mopping the floors, sweeping out the bay, landscaping. I never minded the work, especially since I'd much rather clean than cook. And since the rest of the guys agreed I was the worst at making the evening meal, I was often allowed to trade my kitchen duties for other tasks.

After lunch we had a meeting with the Lieutenant and then some medical training, but eventually I was able to hit the gym for a workout. It wasn't anything big or fancy, but it was clean and functional, and there was enough equipment to punish myself sufficiently, or at least take my mind off the gorgeous girl next door.

Justin joined me, which was fine, although I wasn't in the mood to talk. My brother-in-law had known me long enough to read the signs, but when I was done on the treadmill, he got off the machine he'd been on and came over.

"You okay?" he asked.

I shrugged, walking slowly on the belt to cool off. "Fine."

"You haven't said a word all day."

"I'm tired, I guess."

"How was your weekend with the girls?"

"Good." My mood lifted a little at the thought of them. "Thanks again for helping with the move. I appreciate it."

"No problem. You get all unpacked?"

I made a face. "Fuck no. I spent yesterday sweating my ass off at the pool and telling them five hundred times that no, we can't get a cat."

Justin laughed. "You know you're going to get them a cat. Give it up."

"And who's going to feed it while I'm here?" I stopped the belt completely and got off.

"Your neighbor. What's her name again?"

"Winnie."

"Right. Like the Pooh."

I thought about her bright, happy smile and girlish laugh and felt like shit again. "I don't think Winnie is all that anxious to do me any favors."

"Why not?"

Exhaling, I wiped my face with a towel. "I said something shitty to her yesterday."

"Why?"

"Because I'm an asshole." I tossed the towel in a laundry basket, then picked the whole thing up.

"True," Justin said, following me to the laundry room. "But what was it you said?"

I dumped the dirty towels into the washing machine and added soap. "I made a remark about not being interested in her."

"Why the hell would you say that?"

I turned the dial on the old machine and pulled the knob. "Because I *am* interested in her. Sort of."

"Sort of?"

I frowned. "I'm interested in doing things to her I shouldn't, because she's so fucking young it should be illegal."

"How old is she?"

"Twenty-two."

"Oh." He seemed relieved. "That's not *that* young."

I turned around and leaned back against the machine, folding my arms over my sweat-soaked chest. "Have you talked to any twenty-two-year-olds lately?"

Justin, who was thirty-seven, shook his head. "Can't say I have."

"They're *young,* dude. She was in fucking kindergarten when I graduated high school."

He laughed. "Hey, I'm five years older than Bree."

"That's not as bad. And Bree was like thirty when you guys met. This girl was drinking a fucking Frosty when I went over there Saturday night."

"You went over there Saturday night?"

"Just to her patio. I was sitting on mine having a beer when she came out to hers, and I wanted to apologize for something that happened earlier at Chip's party."

"What was she doing at Chip's party?"

I rubbed the back of my neck. "Turns out she's his cousin."

He laughed. "Small towns, man. So what happened there you had to apologize for?"

I told him about the incident in her bedroom, and he laughed so hard he wheezed. "That's fucking amazing. Jesus, how did you hold it together?"

"I don't know," I said seriously. "I was in firefighter mode. Plus, the kids were there. Then at the party, Chip was introducing us, and Luna shouts out, 'We know her! We saw her bum!' And the whole place went dead silent."

Justin's eyes went wide. "What did she do?"

"She handled it fine, but I felt bad. Then Luna had an allergic reaction to something she ate, so we had to leave early, and I never got a chance to talk to her. Later, when I saw her come out to her patio, I went over to say sorry and we ended up having a beer together and talking for a while." Exhaling, I let my shoulders slump. "And then I fucked up."

Justin leaned back against a cabinet full of cleaning supplies and cocked his brow. "What did you do, keep her out past curfew?"

I shook my head. "I fucking kissed her."

"And you feel guilty about it because she's young?"

"Yeah. I mean, I stopped it before it could go any farther, but it easily could have. Then I saw her yesterday at the pool—the girls went and dragged her out to swim with them—and she looked so good, I couldn't stop staring at her or thinking about her naked, and it was pissing me off. So I basically announced out of nowhere that I wasn't interested in her. That kissing her had been a stupid mistake."

"Smooth."

"Fuck off."

He grinned. "So what did she say?"

"Nothing. She just grabbed her stuff and left." I ran a hand through my hair. "Then I took the girls home and picked a fight with Naomi."

"You're really on a roll with women, aren't you?"

"Naomi's used to my bullshit, plus she sort of deserved it," I said defensively, "but this girl, Winnie, she didn't."

"So tell her you're sorry."

"I thought about it, but . . . do I have to? It *was* the truth—I'm not interested in dating her. That's all I meant."

"Okay, but you didn't need to say that out loud."

"I thought I was doing her a favor," I argued. "I didn't want her to get the wrong idea after the night before."

"Which was totally *your* doing. You kissed her, right? Not the other way around?"

I didn't answer.

"It's like you took a bite of her dessert without being offered a taste, and then told her you didn't really like it anyway." Justin shook his head. "Dick move."

"I did like it," I muttered. "I'm just too fucking old for it."

"She doesn't know what's in your head. Trust me, dude. I've got four sisters and a wife, and I know how women think. You insulted her, and you should apologize."

I exhaled, afraid he was right. "I don't even want to face her."

"You live right next door to her. You can't avoid her forever."

"Why not? I lived in the *same house* as Naomi for years, and she claims I was excellent at avoiding her."

"Just knock on her door tomorrow and get it over with."

"Couldn't I just leave her a note?"

"I guess you could. But that seems pretty chicken-shit."

"I'm not chicken-shit," I said, puffing out my chest.

"Then be a man and knock on her door, asshole." He punched my shoulder as he left the laundry room. "Don't forget the fabric softener."

I spent all day Tuesday unpacking, organizing, and making a final few runs from my old place to the condo. After the apartment was completely empty, I turned in my keys to the management office and drove away from the Luxury Harbor Complex for the last time.

After emptying the final box, I grocery shopped, ran to a home improvement store to pick up some inexpensive plastic furniture and a little charcoal grill for the patio, and took a nap. After a shower and a frozen dinner, I called the girls to say goodnight, since I didn't have them during this stretch of days off.

Both of them asked me if I'd seen Winnie. I said no and quickly moved on to other things, but when I hung up, I was still thinking about her.

I'd been fighting the idea of an apology for two days, but I realized if I ever wanted a good night's sleep again, I was probably going to have to say I was sorry.

That thought was confirmed when I got a text from Justin that said, **Did you do it?**

When I didn't answer, he followed up with a chicken and poop emoji.

"Dickhead," I muttered.

Then I grabbed my keys and hustled out the door.

Ten

Winnie

B Y NINE O'CLOCK ON TUESDAY NIGHT, I WAS ALREADY IN MY pajamas, curled up on the couch with Piglet watching *When Harry Met Sally* for the one millionth time. I sighed heavily as I stroked her fur and watched the love story unfold in glorious autumn colors.

"That should be me right now, Piglet," I said mournfully. "Walking the streets of New York City in a cute hat with someone who adores me, our feet crunching in the fallen leaves, our hearts destined to beat as one forever and ever . . ."

Piglet yawned.

"Listen. I'm feeling down about myself, okay? I've had a couple tough days, so just let me have tonight to wallow." I grabbed a tissue from the box on my coffee table. "Tomorrow I'll get out of my funk."

As I was weeping my way through the final scene, a knock at the front door sent Piglet running for the pantry. Figuring it was Ellie, who'd said she might drop by after work so we could start planning our collaborative wine tasting dinner, I wadded up my current tissue, tossed it on the table, and hit pause.

However, when I pulled the door open, it wasn't Ellie on the porch.

It was Dex, and he had a chocolate Frosty in his hand.

"Oh," I said, touching my hair. "It's you."

He held out the Frosty. "I brought you something."

"Why?"

He looked uncomfortable. "I don't know. Because you said you really liked them the other night."

I stood a little taller, wishing I wasn't in bare feet and pajamas. "You didn't have to do that."

"You don't want it?"

Of course I wanted it. I wanted him too. He looked hot as hell standing in my doorway in his jeans and T-shirt, his hair freshly combed, his scruff trimmed back.

But I didn't want him to know that.

So I shrugged. "I'm not hungry. You can give it to the girls."

He lowered his arm. "They're not with me this week. I won't see them until Saturday."

It softened me a little, hearing the sadness in his voice. "You miss them when they're not with you?"

"Yeah," he admitted. "But I try to make the best of the time we do have together. Be the best dad I can two days a week. I still make mistakes though." He hesitated. "And I made one the other day with you."

"Yes, you told me already," I reminded him. "Kissing me was a stupid mistake. I heard you loud and clear."

He shook his head. "I meant that what I *said* was a mistake. I was mad at myself and I took it out on you. I'm sorry."

His face was hard to read in the dark, but he sounded genuinely contrite. Sighing, I opened the door a little wider. "Do you want to come in?"

He glanced at the Frosty. "Will you accept my frozen chocolate apology in a cup?"

"I suppose." I took it from him and braced the door open with my back. "Thank you."

"You're welcome." Once the door was closed behind him, he followed me down the hall.

"Should we sit out on the patio?" I asked.

"Sure."

Stopping in the kitchen, I grabbed two spoons from a drawer. Dex went ahead to the living room and paused in front of the television, where Harry was frozen in the middle of his big speech. "My sister loves this movie."

"Doesn't everybody?"

"I prefer thrillers." He gestured at the soggy tissues on my coffee table. "You cry at this movie?"

"Yes."

"But it's a comedy."

"I know, but it's got that scene at the end where he's walking and thinking about her, and then he starts running through the street to get to the party, all because he finally realized that he *loves* her, despite all her quirks, and he can't go another minute without telling her how he feels . . ." My voice caught, and I had to stop and take a breath.

Dex looked at me like I was nuts.

I raised my chin defiantly. "I like a big romantic gesture, that's all. Can you get the door please?"

He pulled the sliding door open, and we went outside.

It was a warm, humid night without much of a breeze, and the air felt thick and heavy. I placed the Frosty and spoons on the table and lit the citronella candle as he lowered himself into a chair.

"We can share," I said, sitting down next to him and pushing a spoon his way.

"That's okay. I brought it for you."

"I might need the whole thing with the week I'm having. Want a beer or something?"

He shook his head. "No, thanks. You're having a bad week?"

"It's not really *bad*." I picked up a spoon and took a bite. "Just some long days at work."

"Where do you work?"

"At Cloverleigh Farms, in guest services."

"What's that mean?"

"It means I don't really have a *specific* job—I sort of float around and help out wherever needed. This week, I'm filling in at the front desk and guests are just being extra cranky about everything."

His eyes followed the spoon back and forth from the Frosty to my mouth with every bite. "Like what?"

"Oh, they're mad they can't get the dinner reservation they want, or the people in the room next to them are loud, or they want an upgrade—which isn't even something we offer. Then there was a double-booking mistake, which I hadn't made, but of course I had to deal with. We had no available rooms, and I had to find somewhere to put this anniversary couple."

"Fuck. What did you do?"

"Luckily, Abelard Vineyards, which is owned by my friend Ellie's family, happened to have a cancellation. We paid for the room there, offered the couple a free meal in our restaurant, and apologized profusely, but they were still pissed. And I get it." I shrugged, turning the spoon over in my mouth and sucking it clean. "We fucked up."

"You tried to make it right. That counts for something, doesn't it?" He seemed distracted by the spoon in my mouth for a moment. "Uh, on second thought, maybe I will have a beer. But I'll grab one from my house."

"Suit yourself."

While he was gone, I was tempted to run in and change—I had on drawstring silk shorts in turquoise with a matching camisole top, no bra underneath. I wasn't terribly well-endowed, so it's not like I was hanging out of it, but it wasn't exactly an appropriate outfit for receiving company.

But then again, he'd come over to *my house* at nine o'clock at night on a Tuesday after making it abundantly clear on a Sunday that he did not find me all that attractive.

So screw it—I was going to sit here in my little pajamas and eat his apology with a spoon.

He came back a minute later with a beer and sat down again, taking a long swallow. "So do you like your job?"

"Yes," I said. "I love Cloverleigh Farms. I practically grew up there. It's where my dad has worked my whole life, and my mom's family owns it."

"I met your mom the other day at the bakery."

I smiled. "I heard."

He took another drink. "Did I tell you the girls raised prices for the swear box on Sundays?"

That made me laugh. "Did they?"

"Yes. Because of Jesus. I now owe a buck-fifty if I say the F word on Sundays."

"Smart girls." I licked the spoon again, a little more seductively than necessary.

"Listen, Winnie, I need to tell you something." His knee was bouncing up and down like he was nervous.

"Okay."

"It's not that I didn't like the taste of your dessert."

I tilted my head. "Huh?"

"I mean, it's not that I didn't like what happened the other night," he said, agitated. "Between us."

"Oh."

"It's just that I don't date. And I didn't want to mislead you. You're so young, I felt bad that I—"

"You thought I might be too young to understand that just because you kissed me, you're not my boyfriend now?"

He laughed sheepishly. "Kind of."

"Well, you can relax." After cleaning off the spoon once more, I stuck it in the Frosty and left it. "I'm actually not looking for a boyfriend at the moment. In fact, I'm doing the opposite—I'm purposely staying single for the rest of the year."

"Oh yeah?" Slightly more relaxed—his leg had stopped the bouncing—he took another drink. "Why's that?"

"I'm sort of a love junkie. I'm rehabilitating myself."

"A what?"

I laughed. "A love junkie—someone who's addicted to love. But the problem is, I get all caught up in the rush of a new relationship and ignore red flags. And the type of guy I'm usually attracted to comes with a lot of them."

"What type of guy is that?"

"Handsome, smart, Prince Charming types. Confident to the point of arrogance. The guy every girl wants and every guy wants to be."

"So you date a lot of selfish assholes?"

"Indeed, I find their narcissism irresistible."

He laughed, shaking his head. "How is that possible?"

"I don't know. I guess I like capturing their attention. I think to myself, 'This guy could have *anyone*, and he wants me.' Something about that feels good. But . . ." I looked at my left hand, fingers spread. "It doesn't last, and I wind up disappointed."

"Were you married or something?" He gestured toward my hand.

"Engaged. Very briefly."

"To who?"

"To a very handsome and charismatic asshole named Merrick, who now lives in Manhattan where I imagine he is joyfully banging an array of hot models, which was what he told me he'd rather do than be with me."

"Got it." He took another drink. "So this stretch of being single—it's going to cure you of your taste for those guys?"

"Hopefully." I shrugged. "But if not, I will at least prove to myself that it's possible to be happy without being in love."

He gave me one of his signature grunts. "It's definitely possible."

"Oh, that's right," I said, amused. "You don't believe in happily ever after."

"Who told you that? Wait, never mind." He shook his head. "Those two cannot keep their mouths shut."

"So it's true?"

"Yes."

"Was your divorce that bad?"

"My *marriage* was that bad."

"Ah." A hot gust of wind ruffled my hair, and I tucked it behind my ear. "I'm sorry."

"Don't be. I wouldn't change anything. I got Hallie and Luna out of it, and I can't imagine my life without them, so I figure this was always how it was supposed to be."

I tilted my head. "You think you were destined to be unhappily married?"

He took another sip. "I think I was meant to be a father, but not a husband."

"Got it." I looked up at the sky. It was too cloudy to see stars tonight. "I think I was meant to be a wife and a mother."

"You're young. You've got plenty of time."

I chewed my bottom lip a moment. "Can I ask you something kind of personal?"

He gave me a wary sideways glance. "Okay."

"Did you leave your marriage? Or did she?"

"She asked me to leave."

"Oh." A minute ticked by in silence, while my mind wandered between the past and the present. "My mom left us when I was two."

He was silent a moment. "That must have been tough."

"I think it was harder on my sisters. I was so young, I don't even remember her living in the same house with us. I grew up hardly knowing her."

"You didn't visit her?"

"At first we did. She moved down to Georgia after she left, and my sisters and I would visit her there during the summer for a couple weeks, but we never loved it."

He sipped his beer again. "I used to go really long periods of time without seeing my kids—months and months, when I was deployed. I dealt with it because I had to. But now I can't imagine it. I fucking miss them when I don't see them for five *days*."

"She used to make promises about coming up to see us, but she rarely kept them. After a while, we stopped believing them." I paused. "And eventually, she didn't even make them anymore."

Dex looked at me, then reached over and touched my wrist. "You deserved better."

Surprised, I glanced down at his hand, which must have made him self-conscious because he removed it. "Anyway," I said, trying to lighten my tone, "I'm hoping my declaration of independence will prevent me from making the same relationship mistakes I've made in the past. Or at least help me learn to be a better judge of character."

"So if I see any selfish-looking pricks on your doorstep, should I tell them to fuck off? I think I'm an excellent judge of character."

"Oh yeah?" I asked, smiling as I imagined him lurking on his doorstep, giving the next Merrick a menacing growl.

He nodded. "I can spot a narcissistic asshole a mile away. I was raised by one."

"Oh." My smile faded.

"It's fine. Believe it or not, his shitty example taught me a lot of valuable lessons about the kind of man and father I want to be."

"That's good, I guess. Silver lining and all."

"Exactly." As he finished off his beer, lightning flashed in the sky. He rose to his feet. "I better get going."

"Okay," I said, wishing he didn't have to leave. But I stood up too. "Thanks for coming over. And for the Frosty."

"You're welcome. And I'm sorry again for what I said."

I shrugged. "No hard feelings."

Once more we stood almost chest to chest, just like we had the other night, the candle flickering next to us in the dark. In the distance, thunder rumbled softly.

Dex glanced out to the left. "Storm coming."

"Yes."

He met my eyes again, then dropped his gaze to my lips. I held my breath, waiting for him to make another stupid mistake and kiss me again. Hoping he would.

But instead, he lifted his beer bottle and slowly rubbed the mouth of it along my lower lip, watching intently. I opened my mouth slightly, and he eased the bottle in a little deeper. I slid the tip of my tongue along the rim. My nipples stiffened beneath the silk of my top.

Exhaling, he lowered the bottle.

"Dex," I whispered.

But he turned around and walked away, leaving me alone in the dark.

Lightning flashed again, and I put a hand over my stomach. My legs felt wobbly, and as the thunder reverberated through the sky, I felt it in my bones. My skin prickled with goosebumps, as if the air was charged with an electrical current.

I could barely breathe.

Eleven

Winnie

THE FOLLOWING NIGHT I DROVE OVER TO ABELARD Vineyards to meet with Ellie about our wine tasting dinner, which was going to be at Cloverleigh Farms in mid-October. Henry DeSantis, the head winemaker at Cloverleigh Farms, was a good friend of Ellie's dad and loved the idea. I'd put it on social media this morning, and already we'd received several calls from people inquiring about tickets.

Ellie answered the back door with a scowl on her face.

"What's wrong?" I asked, following her into the large, French-country inspired kitchen.

"He's here," she said bitterly, taking down two globe-shaped wine glasses from an open shelf.

"Who's here?" I sat down at the marble-topped island, setting my laptop bag on the stool next to me.

"The scoundrel. The rake. The bane of my childhood." She attacked a bottle of wine with an opener, taking out her anger with vicious twists of her wrists as she drilled into the cork.

"Gianni Lupo?"

"Shhh." She glanced over her shoulder toward the hallway that led to the main part of the house. "I don't want him to know I'm here."

"Is he being interviewed for the head chef position?"

"Yes." Setting the corkscrew aside, she poured us each a glass of ruby red Gamay from Abelard. "Tell me you mentioned the position to your sister."

Guilty, I bit the tip of my thumb. "Shoot. I forgot."

She stopped pouring and pinned me with a fiery look. "If he gets this job, you are dead to me."

"I'm sorry," I said. "It's been a crazy week. My mind was all distracted."

"With what?" She picked up her glass and swirled the wine before sticking her nose in it and inhaling.

"I don't know." I slid my glass a little closer to me. "Work. Family."

"Hot grumpy neighbor."

"Hot grumpy neighbor," I admitted, figuring there was no point in lying to her. "He came over again last night."

"Oh yeah? What happened this time?" Her brown eyes danced. "Did he accidentally take your pants off?"

"No," I said, like I was offended. "He brought me a Frosty."

Her eyebrows went up. "How did he know you like them?"

"I guess I mentioned it the other night."

"That was thoughtful of him, to bring you a little gift," she said with syrupy sweetness before she took a sip of her wine.

"It was an apology, not a gift," I explained. "He felt bad about what he said the other day at the pool."

"He should. That was a dick thing to say." Ellie swirled her wine again. "But I still think he doth protest too much. I think he *is* interested in you, and he was just trying to play it cool."

"He said he was mad at himself and took it out on me."

"Mad at himself for what?"

"Making a move on me, I guess. He thinks I'm too young. And he doesn't date anyway."

"He announced all those things?"

I shrugged. "Kind of."

She nodded shrewdly. "More protesting too much. This dude is into you. He kiss you again last night?"

"No," I said quickly, dropping my eyes to the marble counter. "He didn't kiss me."

"But he did something."

"Sort of. Maybe."

"What?"

I peeked up at her. "He—he kind of, uh, penetrated my mouth with his beer bottle."

Ellie nearly choked on her wine. "*What*?"

"He stuck his beer bottle in my mouth," I said, enunciating more clearly.

Unfortunately, right at that moment, the door from the hallway swung open, and Gianni Lupo strode in like he owned the place. "He stuck his *what* in your mouth?"

"What are you doing here?" Ellie snapped. "This is the private part of the house. Family only."

"Good thing your parents just told me I'm family, and that's why they hope I'll accept their job offer." He gave Ellie one of his cocky grins and turned his attention to me. "How are you, Winifred? Long time, no see."

I hadn't seen him since graduation, but he'd hardly changed. Same wavy, floppy dark hair that somehow looked styled and messy at the same time, same blue eyes that girls used to sigh over, same finely chiseled jaw, only now it held a thin layer of scruff. His nose was slightly crooked—if I recalled correctly, it had been broken by one of his brothers in a fight. But it took nothing away from his looks or his confidence in them.

I smiled back. "I'm good, Gianni. How've you been?"

"I can't complain."

"Can you leave?" Ellie asked.

"In a minute," he said, picking up Ellie's glass and tasting her wine. "But first I want to hear the story about the beer bottle."

Furious, Ellie took her glass back and moved it out of his reach. "No. This is a private conversation, asshole."

Gianni looked at me. "I don't know about these work conditions. I might have to document this as harassment."

"So are you taking the job?" I asked.

"I'm thinking about it. I love the concept, and the setting is perfect. I'd have input on finishing the kitchen, which I like. And hiring staff, which is important because I like things done a certain way." He grinned again, glancing at Ellie. "And I love the idea of collaborating on the menu with the winemakers here. They're so friendly."

Ellie glared at him.

"Except maybe this one." He jerked a thumb at her. "Why's she always so mean?"

I smiled. "I think you bring it out in her."

"You'd think she was the one who took seven pies in the face."

"Eight," said Ellie. "I threw eight pies in your face. Because you dunked me like fifty times in that stupid tank."

"I know." He chuckled. "I couldn't resist. You looked so dry and comfortable sitting up there in your little crown and that Cherry Princess sash over your bathing suit. I spent every dollar I had on your booth, and then I borrowed some more. I was in debt for months. You should've been flattered."

"They put my picture on the front page of the news looking all soggy and gross, thanks to you."

"But just think of all the money you raised for our senior class," he said. "We probably wouldn't have been able to have that chocolate fountain at the Prom if it wasn't for me. Anyway, thanks for inviting me to stay and hear the rest of the story, but I have to get going. Another time."

"Bye, Gianni," I said.

As he moved past a stone-faced Ellie, he planted a kiss on her cheek before she had a chance to duck.

"Ew, don't!" She rubbed her cheek as if trying to erase the imprint of his lips.

While she was distracted, he stole another sip of her wine. "You know what? That's really good. I'm excited about this job."

She pointed at the door. "Get out and stay out!"

When we were alone again, she took a big gulp of her wine and poured some more. "I'm going to kill my parents."

"Come on, he's not that bad."

"He is. You have no idea."

"What the hell happened in that closet anyway? Are you ever going to tell me?"

"Nothing," she said quickly. "Nothing happened."

"You two were in there for a full seven minutes, and you're telling me *nothing* happened? He didn't even kiss you?"

"Nope. He didn't kiss me." She took another drink of her wine. "We spent most of those seven minutes fighting. Now let's talk about this beer bottle situation."

"I'm probably making a big deal over nothing, but . . ." Bringing my fingers to my lips, I remembered his eyes on my mouth and the light-bellied feeling it gave me. "It felt kind of dirty. In a good way."

Her eyes gleamed. "So now what?"

"Now nothing. Even if he is interested, he won't act on it."

"So maybe *you* need to act on it."

I shook my head. "No way."

"Why not?"

"Because I'm off men, remember?"

"You're off *relationships*. You're off falling in love. You don't have to be off the fun stuff."

"That's not what you said the other day," I reminded her.

"You said I couldn't handle doing the fun stuff without falling for him."

"Well, I changed my mind. I think this could be good for you. A test of sorts. You can prove to yourself—and to me—that it's entirely possible to mess around with someone without falling in love with him. A sort of neighbors-with-benefits arrangement."

"Won't that mean I've lost the bet?"

"No. As long as you keep things casual, you haven't lost." She hesitated. "But if you can't keep your feelings out of it, then don't do it."

"I think I can," I said. "I mean, it's not like I'm in danger of mistaking his intentions. I know exactly how he feels. Love would never even enter the picture. It would just be for fun. A good time."

"There you go."

"I'd still be independent."

"Exactly, you're just adding a dick and some orgasms."

Laughing, I fidgeted nervously on my chair. "But how do I let him know that I'm up for it? I've never made the first move before."

"Easy." She snapped her fingers. "Get naked and set off your smoke alarm."

I set my glass down and pulled out my laptop. "Very funny."

"Just go out on the patio when you get home tonight," she said with a shrug. "If he's out there again, he's definitely into you, and you should be brave and make a move. Sit in his lap."

"I'll think about it. Now let's get some work done—I talked to Henry, and he's totally cool with whatever we want to do. I also spoke with our chef briefly today, and she's got some great ideas. What do you think about bourbon braised pork belly?"

We went over the ideas for each course, and Ellie took

notes on what wines from each vineyard she thought would pair well with every dish. At one point, her mom and dad came in and said hello, offered a couple suggestions, and said how happy they were about the event.

We talked about how many tickets we should sell in order to keep it intimate, and what our roles would be that evening. Both of us agreed we wanted to keep it small and exclusive, a little pricier than we were comfortable with but not so expensive it was prohibitive. Ellie would talk about the wines, I'd talk about the food, and we'd oversee the servers together.

"I wonder if we could do it outside in mid-October," Ellie said. "Do you guys have a tent? Some heaters?"

"We have a tent for the stone patio that overlooks the vineyard. We had to use it a couple times this summer because of rain. But I don't know about heaters," I said, making a note. "I'll find out."

"Why don't I come by Cloverleigh tomorrow and we can scout out some possible locations?"

"Sounds good," I said, pulling up my calendar. "I have a meeting with Millie at ten and then I'm at the front desk after lunch."

Ellie checked her phone. "I don't have any tastings until two. I'll come around eleven?"

"Perfect."

On the drive home, Dex refused to leave my mind. Could I really seduce him? What if he turned me down? What if he laughed at me? What if I made things so awkward between us we could never look each other in the eye again? Was it worth the risk?

Was I confident enough in myself to go after a man like Dex?

A man with experience. A man who looked at me and saw a young, innocent girl. A man who'd made my nipples hard with a look and a glass bottle.

My pulse quickened as I turned into my driveway and looked at the darkened windows of his place. It was after nine. Was he in bed already?

"I'll just go out on the patio for one minute," I said as I pulled into the garage. "If he's not there, that's that. If he is, that will be a sign from the universe that Ellie is right and I need to be brave."

I let myself into the house and gave Piglet some love, warily eyeing the glass door to the patio. After giving her a snack, I went upstairs to change.

Brave would be easier in a cute dress.

And sexy underwear.

Twelve

Dex

THE NUMBER OF TIMES TODAY I'D THOUGHT ABOUT RUBBING that beer bottle on Winnie's lips last night was obscene.

Fuck, it was obscene that I'd *done* it.

Even more obscene that I'd gotten into bed and jerked off afterward, fantasizing my cock was that bottle.

I'd been mad at myself all day. I'd gone over there to fucking apologize for being a dick, and somehow I'd ended up being one again, even without putting my hands on her or saying a goddamn thing.

And what the hell was I doing out here on the patio again?

What, argued a voice in my head. *Can't a guy have a beer on his patio without feeling guilty about it?*

I frowned. Sure, he could. But why did I keep thinking about her? Glancing over toward her place? Listening for her to come home after work?

It was late—where was she? Meeting some selfish prick for dinner or drinks? Would she bring him back here and share a cupcake with him ten feet from me?

Don't mind him, I imagined her saying to some twenty-five-year-old pin-dick fuckwit who owned a Rolex and multiple pairs of plaid shorts. *That's just the grouchy old man next door. He's harmless.*

I took another long swallow to wash down the jealousy. *I'll finish this beer*, I told myself, *and if she doesn't come out here, I'll go inside and forget about her for good.*

Realistically, I knew I'd probably go in and get myself off thinking about her again, but whatever.

A moment later, the light came on in her place, her sliding door opened, and she stepped outside holding a plastic pitcher. After closing the door behind her, she began to water her plants. She wore a dress tonight, something short and flowery with skinny straps that showed off her shoulders, and her hair was up. Her feet were bare, and I wondered if she'd taken off her high heels after a date.

"Hey," I said, standing up from my chair.

"Oh, hey," she said, giggling nervously. "I didn't see you there."

"We need to stop meeting like this," I joked.

"Nah. It's always a nice surprise." She gave me a smile that tightened my chest. "How was your day?"

"Good. How was yours? Any double bookings?"

"No, thank heavens. It was a perfectly boring day at reception."

"Glad to hear it." I leaned against the brick wall. "Do you always work this late?"

"No, I'm not coming from work just now. I was at Abelard meeting with my friend Ellie about an event we're planning together. I'm really excited about it."

"Tell me," I said, happy she hadn't been out with a guy.

She laughed nervously as she emptied the pitcher. "You don't want to hear about that."

"I asked, didn't I?"

Straightening up, she turned toward me. "Okay. Want to sit down?"

I knew I should say no and get the fuck inside. But I heard myself say, "Sure. Why don't you come sit on my patio this time? My furniture isn't as nice as yours, but it's my turn to host."

She laughed and set her watering can down on the table. "Okay."

"Can I get you a beer?"

"No, thanks." She stopped at the edge of my little patio and gasped. "You decorated!"

"Hardly." I glanced at the insect repellent candle. "But it's so muggy out here after the rain last night, I knew the mosquitoes would be bad."

"Let me turn off my light so it won't attract them." She hurried back to her place, switched off the light, and returned. The lights in my living room were already off, so it was completely dark except for the small yellow flame flickering on the table. I took a sip of my beer, and she crossed her legs in my direction.

"So what are you and your friend planning?"

"A wine tasting dinner," she said, and proceeded to tell me all about it.

I listened, but I couldn't have repeated one thing she said, because I was so conscious of her body and how close it was to mine. The way the candlelight brought out the gold in her hair. The way it might feel in my hands or trailing across my chest. I finished my beer and stared at the mouth of the bottle, wondering about the sounds she might make if I buried my tongue between her legs.

"Dex?"

I realized she'd asked me something, and I looked at her quickly. "Sorry, what?"

"God, I've been talking too much. I probably just bored you to pieces."

"Not at all," I told her. "I just got distracted for a minute."

She glanced at the bottle in my hands. "What were you thinking about?"

The words came out before I could stop them. "Something I want to do but can't."

"Can't?"

"Shouldn't."

A moment passed in complete silence, and I thought I'd gone too far. She stood up.

But instead of walking back to her place like I thought she might, she blew out the candle and stood in front of me. Then she reached for the bottle and set it at my feet.

I looked up at her. Without saying anything, she climbed onto my lap, one knee on either side of my thighs. I held my breath and gripped the arms of the chair.

She placed her palms on my chest. Locked eyes with me. "Something like this?"

My voice was nowhere to be found.

She leaned over and pressed her lips to the side of my neck. "Or like this?"

My cock was surging to life beneath her.

She moved one hand down to my crotch and rubbed the bulge in my jeans as her mouth swept up to my ear. "Or maybe like this?" she whispered.

My fingers curled around the edges of the plastic chair arms. "You should stop."

"Why?"

"It's dangerous to play with fire. And with firefighters."

She laughed softly, switching her mouth to my other ear, nipping my earlobe with her teeth. "But it might be fun."

I groaned as my cock continued to swell under her hand, my strength depleting with every stroke.

She kissed my cheekbone, my temple, my jaw. "Do you want me to stop?" she asked, her breath soft on my skin.

"What I want isn't the point."

"Then let's focus on what *I* want." She reached for the button on my jeans and I grabbed her wrist.

"Don't."

"Why not?"

"Because you're too fucking beautiful to resist and too damn young for me to touch."

"Dex." She took my hand and brought it to her breast. "I want you to touch me."

Beneath the thin material of her dress, her nipple was temptingly hard. I teased it with my thumb and she sucked in her breath.

With my other hand I cradled the back of her neck and pulled her mouth to mine. I slid my fingers into her hair and clenched my fist, making her gasp.

I let go of her breast and locked my arm around her waist like a thick iron chain. "This is what it's like to be with me," I warned her, my lips hot against hers. "I'm not gentle."

"I don't care," she panted. "I want this."

Without another word, I put my hands beneath her and stood up, taking her with me. She locked her legs around my waist and I moved quickly for the door.

Inside, I was too impatient to take her upstairs to my bedroom, so I lowered myself onto the couch. She straddled my legs again, and this time I put my hands under her dress, sliding them up her thighs and gripping her ass.

She put her hands in my hair and her tongue in my mouth and rocked her hips over mine, grinding against me. Inside a minute, she was attempting to lift my shirt over my head and I took my hands off her just long enough to whip it off and toss it aside.

"Oh, God," she murmured, running her hands over my bare chest. "You feel exactly like I thought you would."

"Hairy?" I pushed her dress up her thighs.

She laughed and reached between my legs. "Hard."

This time when she undid my pants, I didn't stop her. When she slipped her hand inside and freed my cock, I didn't stop her. When she wrapped her fingers around me and stroked me from root to tip, I didn't stop her.

And she didn't stop me from easing my hand inside the edge of her underwear. Or softly rubbing my fingertips over her clit. Or slipping one finger inside her as deeply as I could. She was warm and wet, and when she began to move over my hand, my patience ran out completely. I had to get inside her.

Yanking my hand from her underwear, I grabbed her by the waist and set her down beside me on the couch. "Don't move."

Racing up the stairs to my bedroom, I prayed to God I still had a condom somewhere, and that it wouldn't take me all night to find it. I panicked when a frantic rummaging through my nightstand drawer turned up nothing, but luckily, I found a stray one in the second place I looked—my bathroom travel bag. Snatching it up, I bolted back down the stairs three at a time.

She was sitting exactly where I'd left her in the dark, but suddenly I had a fierce longing to *see* her, to watch her come undone beneath me. I pulled the vertical blinds across the sliding glass door and switched on a lamp.

Her cheeks, already flushed, grew even more pink. She looked up at me and smiled tentatively, looking so young and beautiful I almost couldn't go through with it.

Almost.

I dropped to my knees at her feet, reached beneath her dress, and removed her underwear. Slipping my hands under her legs, I pulled her toward me and pushed her knees apart. She gasped. "What are you doing?"

"That thing I was thinking about earlier? It was fucking you with my tongue."

Her jaw dropped, and I lowered my head between her thighs.

She moaned as I caressed her pussy with my tongue, long slow strokes that had her hands clawing the edge of the cushions. Her taste was pure sweetness, and I devoured her like I was scared someone would take my plate away before I was finished.

"Oh my God," she whimpered as I sucked her clit. "That feels so good. The room is spinning."

As her sounds grew more needy, her hands moved into my hair. I slipped two fingers inside her. My cock ached with jealousy as her body tensed up and she grew even wetter. Her fingers curled into fists and she cried out with abandon as the climax shuddered through her.

The moment her hands unclenched in my hair, I stood up, shoved my pants down my legs, felt around on the floor for where I'd dropped the condom, and tore it open with my teeth. She watched me roll it on, her breath coming hard and fast.

Dropping to my knees again, I roped an arm around her waist and hauled her onto the floor. Stretching out above her, I positioned the tip of my cock at the warm, wet place between her thighs and eased inside her. She gasped and clutched at my shoulders.

I threw her arms above her head, pinning her wrists to the rug. "Told you I wasn't gentle," I growled, rocking my hips in slow but deep, hard thrusts that made her cry out with shock or pain or both.

She fought back a little, struggling to get her arms free, but I was bigger and stronger, and I took pleasure in overpowering her. I hadn't even taken the time to get her naked, but somehow her little flowered dress only made my blood run hotter and my instincts dirtier. Had she worn it on purpose, knowing I'd be unable to resist her? For a second, I imagined coming all over that pretty dress—so that she'd never wear it again without thinking about what I'd done to her.

This was all her fault.

"You knew what you were doing." I moved over her in a rough, unceasing rhythm.

"Huh?" She sounded breathless and confused.

"You knew just how to do it." I changed the angle, plunging even deeper inside her. "How to make me want you this way. How to make me this hard."

"Oh, God, Dex." She struggled to speak. "You're so big, it hurts."

"Good." I wanted to punish her for making me give in, for stealing my strength. "Maybe next time you'll think twice before coming over here in a pretty little dress and putting your hands on my cock."

I knew I was taking a risk talking to her like that—she was so fucking young and probably not that sexually experienced—but I couldn't help it. If she slapped my face when it was over and told me she never wanted to fucking see me again, fine. I'd deserve it.

But actually, she seemed to like it. As she got used to my size, her body relaxed and she wrapped her legs around me, rocked her hips beneath me, whispered her own dirty little words.

Yes. Fuck me. Right there. So deep.

And my favorite—*I'm not sorry.*

She felt so fucking good. I couldn't even remember the last time I'd wanted someone this much, or needed the release so badly.

My skin was on fire. My muscles were tense. My body moved inside her with abandon, the heat gathering at the base of my spine. She called out my name, her voice breaking, her hips bucking up beneath me. The storm broke, crashing over me in roaring waves that made my world turn silver, my head echo with thunder, and my cock surge and throb as I released all the pent-up tension within.

When I could see again, I stared down at her, breathing hard. Her expression was something between exhilarated and shell-shocked. Releasing her wrists, I braced my hands above her shoulders. "Fuck. Are you okay?"

"I think so." She laughed softly. "I can't feel my arms. Are they still attached to my body?"

"Sorry I got so carried away."

"You warned me it wouldn't be gentle." She smiled. "You were right—partly."

"Partly?"

Her eyes gleamed wickedly. "You were gentle with your tongue."

At the memory of her thighs open before me, my heart skipped a beat. Immediately I wondered when I could taste her again.

Withdrawing from her body, I stood, yanked up my jeans, and offered her a hand. She took it and rose to her feet, pushing her dress down. Her hair had come loose. "Could I use your bathroom?"

"Sure."

She scooped up her underwear from the floor and disappeared into the small half-bath across from the kitchen, rubbing one wrist. Closing my eyes a second, I exhaled, hoping she wouldn't wake up with bruises tomorrow. What the hell would she say if someone asked about them? Locating my shirt across the room where I'd flung it, I pulled it over my head and went upstairs.

In the master bathroom, I disposed of the condom, washed my hands, and put myself back together. When I came down again, she was sitting on the couch, her hair falling in soft waves around her shoulders. One arm was raised, and she was examining something on the side of her dress.

"Fuck," I said, spotting the hole. "Did I rip your dress?"

"Yes, I think you did."

I groaned. "God, I'm a dick. I'm sorry."

"It's fine—it's on the seam, so it can easily be stitched up."

"Let me do it."

She looked up at me in surprise. "Huh?"

"I'll do it right now." I headed for the stairs again. "Give me one minute to find a needle and thread."

"You *sew*?"

"Yes, I *sew*," I said, heading up the steps. "And I'm offended at your tone."

She burst out laughing. "Sorry! You caught me by surprise, that's all."

It took me a few minutes to remember where I'd put the box my mother had given me with a tiny sewing kit in it, but I finally found it on the shelf in my closet. Tucking it under my arm, I grabbed a TCFD T-shirt from my dresser—sniffing it to make sure it was actually clean—and headed back downstairs.

"Here," I said, handing her the shirt. "Give me the dress and put this on."

She presented me with her back, lifting her hair off her neck. "Can you unzip it for me?"

I tossed my shirt on the couch and did as she asked, the intimate task sending a bolt of heat to my crotch. "I probably should have done this an hour ago, huh?"

"I mean, it might have saved you the trouble of sewing the rip, but then you wouldn't have gotten to impress me with your hidden talent." She grinned at me over one shoulder. "Although I'm learning you have several of those."

Another bolt.

"Okay, you're unzipped."

Without turning around, she lowered the dress to her feet and stepped out of it, handing it over to me. But I stood there dumbfounded for a few seconds, distracted first by the gigantic faded bruise on her hip, and next by the barely-there, strappy black underwear she had on. I'd been so eager to get them off her, I hadn't noticed them before.

"Jesus," I said, staring like a schoolboy. "Do you always have things like that on under your clothes?"

"I'm not telling you," she teased, pulling my T-shirt over her head. "You'll just have to wonder about it every time you see me."

I growled like a hungry bear. "Not. Fair."

"Pretend you don't see the bruise, okay?"

"Is that from your fall off the suitcase?"

"Yes."

I touched her hip gingerly. "I'm sorry. I feel responsible."

"You should." She smoothed the front of my shirt over her chest. "Hey, you were wearing this shirt the day you moved in."

"Was I?"

"Trust me on this." She dropped onto the couch, tucking her legs beneath her. "I spent a ridiculous amount of time staring at your muscles out the front window. Now come on. I want to see you sew."

Sitting down next to her, I opened the box. The dress had a black background, so I dug around for some black thread. It took me a few tries to get it through the eye of the needle, and Winnie giggled.

"Hey, listen," I grumbled, tying a knot the way my mother taught me. "This isn't easy for someone with big hands, okay?"

"You do have big hands," she said, rubbing my leg. "But I like them. And I'm sorry I laughed. You're just concentrating so hard, it's adorable."

I gave her a dirty look before turning the dress inside out. "*I* am not adorable. I am manly and tough. Even when I'm sewing."

"You are. And this is one hundred percent the hottest thing a guy has ever done for me."

"Oh yeah?" I grinned as I began carefully mending the ripped seam with tight, even stitches.

"Definitely. Nothing else even comes close." She watched me finish the job, tie a knot, and snip the thread.

Nervous, I turned the dress right side out and checked my work—probably not as good as my mother would have done, but the hole was gone and I couldn't see evidence of crooked stitches.

I handed it over. "There you go. Sorry I ripped it."

She took the dress from me and grinned. "Liar."

"You're right. I'm not sorry." And she looked so cute in my shirt, I couldn't resist pulling her onto my lap so she straddled my thighs once more. "In fact, put it on and I'll rip it again. I'll tear it to pieces this time. With my teeth."

She laughed. "Easy, killer."

"This is probably one of those red flags you were talking about, huh?" I slid my hands beneath the shirt to the sides of her ribcage.

"I don't know," she said, putting her hands on my chest. "No one's ever torn my clothes before. Or pinned me down that way. Or said those kinds of things."

"I guess even selfish assholes have better manners than me."

She smiled. "I guess so. But it's okay, because I'm not looking for a boyfriend this time, remember?"

"That's right." I recalled what she'd said last night. "You're in rehab for your love addiction."

"Exactly. So you can go right ahead and rip my clothes and pin me down and say all kinds of filthy things to me."

I growled again, gripping her sides. "Don't tempt me, little girl."

"I'm serious." She slid her palms to the back of my neck.

"You can do all that and more, but don't call me baby, don't start believing in happily ever after, and *definitely* don't bring me any more Frostys."

"Never? Not even on your birthday?"

She shook her head. "Especially not on my birthday. Because then I would have to grow old with you, and neither of us wants that."

I scowled. "Fuck that bullshit."

"Then we agree. All in fun." She smiled and leaned forward, kissing my lips. "I should go."

I didn't want her to leave, but I didn't want to ask her to stay either. Like she said, this was all in fun—and as much fun as it would be to throw her over my shoulder, take her upstairs, and have my way with her in bed, spending the night together was something people in relationships did. This wasn't that.

Thank God we were on the same page.

She stood up and traded my shirt for her dress, turning around so I could zip it for her. Again, she held her hair out of the way, and once the dress was zipped, I was tempted to press my lips to the back of her neck. Wrap my arms around her waist. Bury my face in her golden hair and breathe in deep.

But this wasn't that.

This was never going to be that.

"Thanks," she said, facing me again.

"No problem. I'll walk you back."

She laughed. "Dex, I live like fifteen feet away."

But I followed her outside anyway. "I told you before, I'm a firefighter and a dad. Keeping people safe is my thing."

On the patio, she gave me a quick hug. "Sleep tight."

"See you," I said, careful not to hold her.

She walked over to her place and slid the door open, then gave me a wave. "Night."

"Night." I watched her step inside and called out. "Hey."

She leaned out and looked over at me. "What?"

"I had fun tonight."

"Me too."

"But I don't love you."

She burst out laughing. "I don't love you either."

"Good. Now stay off my patio or else."

She blew me a kiss and disappeared inside.

I stood there for a moment, listening to my heart thump a little louder than it should.

Grabbing the empty beer bottle from the ground, I smiled as I remembered the way she'd taken it from me and climbed onto my lap.

She was trouble, all right.

But nothing I couldn't handle.

Thirteen

Winnie

"**Y**OU'RE IN A GOOD MOOD TODAY." MY SISTER MILLIE'S voice was pleasant but slightly suspicious.

Seated across from her at her desk, I looked up from the notes I was taking about a wedding we'd just booked. "What makes you say that?"

"You keep humming."

"I do?"

"Yes. At least I think it's humming—with you it's hard to tell."

"Very funny." My awful singing was a running joke in our family. I was completely tone-deaf and had a voice like a squeaky door hinge.

Millie eyeballed me curiously as she took a sip of coffee. "So what's up?"

"Nothing," I said quickly, dropping my eyes to the list of vendors I was compiling. "Hey, what do you think about suggesting Cece Carswell as videographer? The bride said she wanted a more cinematic feel, maybe not perfectly linear."

"I think she'd be a great fit."

"Cool. I'll send the bride her contact info." I stood up to leave, but Millie held up a finger.

"Not so fast. Something is going on with you and I want to know what it is. You are not a hummer."

"I *hum*," I said. "It's off-key and terrible, but I hum. Everyone hums."

"I know you, Winifred MacAllister. Out with it."

Sighing, I dropped into the chair again. "Okay, but don't get all crazy about this. It's not a big deal."

"What's not a big deal?"

"What I did last night."

Her eyes went wide just as someone rapped on her open office door.

"Knock, knock," Ellie said as she walked in. "There you are. I just saw your dad in the main office and he said you were over here."

"We're just finishing up," Millie said. "Come in and take a seat. Winnie is about to tell us what she did last night."

Ellie raced for the other chair across from Millie's desk, vaulted it, and dropped onto the seat. "Oh, I am *here* for this. Did you seduce the older man?"

"What older man?" Millie squealed.

"The hot single dad that moved in next door to her last weekend," Ellie announced breathlessly. "He's going to be her neighbor-with-benefits while she's on a break from relationships."

Millie set her mug down with a thud. "Wait, what about the bet? Doesn't that mean she lost?"

Ellie shrugged. "I sort of gave her a hall pass for this guy."

"That was nice of you."

"Well, she deserved it after what she went through with Merrick. And she understands that this is strictly a sex thing. No feelings allowed."

"Are you going to tell the story or am I?" I asked impatiently.

"You." She crossed her legs, parked her elbow on her knee and her chin in her hand. "Tell us everything."

"Well, when I got home from your house last night and went out to the patio to water my plants, he was out there having a beer."

Ellie's eyes lit up. "Nice move with the plants."

"Thank you, I thought so too." I tucked my hair behind my ears. "So he'd bought some furniture for his patio, and he invited me to come over and try out his new chairs . . ." I paused. "Long story short, I sat on his lap instead, just as you suggested."

Ellie clapped her hands. "And then?"

"Then we went inside and things happened."

"In his bedroom?"

"Uh, no." I laughed, shaking my head. "We only made it about three feet inside the door."

"Oh my," Ellie said appreciatively. "So how was it?"

"*Hot.*"

"How hot?"

"He threw me down and ripped my dress."

"Oh my God!" Ellie's jaw dropped. "Your grumpy old man crush is a beast."

"He's not a *total* beast—he sewed up the rip afterward."

Millie, who'd been stunned silent this whole time, made a T with her hands. "Wait a minute, wait a minute. Time out. Who *is* this guy?"

"He's my new neighbor," I said. "He moved in last Saturday."

"Why is he grumpy?"

"He's not always grumpy. He just . . . looks serious a lot. He has a resting grump face."

"And he's old?"

"He's thirty-four," I said. "He graduated with Chip—they were good friends in high school."

Recognition flickered on her face. "Is this the guy who was at Chip and Mariah's engagement party? The one with the two little girls?"

"Yes," I said. "He's divorced."

"He's also a former Navy SEAL," Ellie added.

"I met him briefly at the party." Millie smiled. "Seems like a nice guy. And his girls are adorable. They were telling me about the swear box they made because their dad curses so much, and how they're saving for a cat."

"He does swear too much around them," I said, "but he's a really good dad."

"Well, good for you. I think it's—" Suddenly my sister stopped talking and burst out laughing.

"What's so funny?" I asked.

"Oh my God, you don't see it?" She shook her head, her eyes tearing up. "You have a crush on *Dad*, Winnie!"

My spine snapped straight. "I do not!"

"Yes, you do—ex-military, divorced single dad with daughters, swears too much." She leaned back in her chair and kicked her feet. "It's totally Dad. And you're Frannie, complete with gigantic age gap! Just don't let his daughters find you guys making out in the closet like we caught them."

"This is not that situation at all," I argued. "Dad and Frannie were in love. They had a real relationship that they tried to hide. Dex and I are just friends."

One of Millie's eyebrows peaked as she picked up her coffee. "Sounds like it. My friends throw me down and rip my clothes all the time. And then offer to sew them."

Rolling my eyes, I stood up. "Just forget it. I told you it wasn't a big deal. I don't even know if it will happen again."

"Why wouldn't it?" Ellie asked.

I shrugged. "Maybe it was just one of those things we had to get out of our systems, you know?"

"Uh huh." Millie smiled knowingly. "And does it feel like that this morning? Is he out of your system?"

Of course he wasn't.

I hadn't been able to think about anything else since I left his place last night—I'd barely even slept.

My face grew hot.

"That's what I thought." My sister's grin was smug. "Good luck keeping this thing casual."

"I don't need luck," I said, hugging my notebook to my chest. "Because I am the boss of my feelings."

"Of course you are." She started singing the song I'd been humming before, except that she could actually sing. *"L is for the way you look at me . . ."*

"Come on, Ell," I said. "Let's go take a look at the patio."

"Okay. Bye, Millie." Ellie got up and followed me to the door.

We heard my sister crooning all the way down the hall.

Later that afternoon, there was a lull at the front desk, and I took a minute to check my email. Most of it was junk, but I also had a message from a woman named Sandra Elson, who'd interviewed me last spring for a position in a Manhattan hotel. I hadn't gotten the job, which turned out to be just as well, but afterward, she'd sent me a nice note saying that while I'd been a very strong candidate, the position had been filled internally.

Her return email address indicated she was now working for a new hotel, and the subject line said, **Following Up —New Opportunity**.

Curious, I opened it.

Dear Winifred,

Hello! I hope you are well. I wanted to reach out to you about a job opportunity at The Alexander, a boutique hotel in a former summer home in Newport, Rhode Island. I recently took a job here as manager, and I'm looking for an event planner to coordinate large gatherings, such as corporate retreats and wedding receptions, but also smaller events for our guests.

The Alexander is an elegant inn, just twenty-two rooms, in a nineteenth century mansion built by a silver heiress and her literary novelist husband. They threw famous parties here in the twenties and thirties—Harry Houdini performed at one!—and the home has been featured in a few Hollywood films. The grounds boast a gorgeous rose garden and spectacular ocean views.

There are several spaces ideal for weddings and receptions, including a luxurious Gilded Age ballroom, terraces overlooking the gardens, and interior rooms for more intimate occasions. When I first saw the possibilities, I immediately thought of you. As you know, your portfolio and personal interview made quite an impression on me.

If you're interested in talking about the job, please do give me a call. I think you'd enjoy the atmosphere and creative freedom, and I will make it worth your while.

Sincerely,
Sandra Elson

Below her email signature was a telephone number as well as a website for The Alexander. I immediately clicked on the link, eager to see what she'd described.

When the site came up, I gasped. Sandra's words had hardly done it justice—I wasn't surprised it had been featured in Hollywood films because it looked like a movie set. I could imagine Rhett Butler carrying Scarlett O'Hara up the wide stone staircase, or Grace Kelly gliding across the elegant living room floor with a martini in her gloved hand, or Fred Astaire and Ginger Rogers twirling madly in the cavernous ballroom, an orchestra at one end.

The rose gardens were breathtaking, the decorating sumptuous and deliciously over the top. There were marble fireplaces and velvet loveseats and ceilings carved with murals and friezes. The entire place reverberated with the glamour and romance of a bygone era. Perusing the website, I was inundated with ideas for wedding ceremonies and grand receptions and cozy, intimate wine dinners. Designing events for a place like this would be a dream job for me.

Immediately I typed a reply, thanking her for thinking of me and letting her know that I'd love to chat more about the opportunity—but I couldn't bring myself to hit send.

I stood there staring at the screen as the minutes ticked by, and my fingers wouldn't tap that blue button.

It was an unbelievable offer, one I should jump at.

What was holding me back?

When my shift at the front desk was over, I poked my head into my dad's office. "Hey."

He looked up and smiled, his deep blue eyes crinkling at the corners. "Hey, sweetheart. Working late?"

"I'm done now." I wandered in and dropped into a chair in front of his desk. "Got a minute?"

"Sure." He closed his laptop. "What's up?"

I told him about the email I'd just gotten from Sandra Elson.

"That's awesome, Win. You must have really knocked her out in that interview. Did you reply?"

"Yes. I told her I was interested." I shook my head. "But I didn't send it."

He leaned back in his chair. "Why not?"

"I don't know for sure. Maybe because it's so far away?"

"You were going to move to New York City, weren't you?"

"Right, but that was different. I was moving with someone I knew. I wouldn't know anyone in Rhode Island."

"I have no doubt you'd make friends instantly. You've always had that gift."

I rolled my eyes. "Stop."

"I mean it, Win. Your teachers always used to remark on how friendly you were to everyone. They always put the new kids in the desk next to yours because they knew you'd be kind and welcoming. And remember the Buddy Bench at elementary school? You wouldn't let someone sit on that thing for a minute without running over and asking them to play."

"Yeah." I smiled at the memory. "It used to break my heart when kids would go sit there alone."

"Because you're a people person. You like making people happy—and that draws people to you. It's what makes you such a natural in this industry too."

"So you think I should tell her I'm interested, huh?"

"I think you should make your own decision and not be afraid." He held up his hands. "And even though I'd miss you and Mom will probably wring my neck for encouraging you to move away, I think you have to do the thing you were meant to do. If that takes you away from home, so be it."

"Don't tell her yet, okay? I just want to catch my breath and think." My eyes scanned the shelves behind him, where familiar old photos were perched among books and vacation souvenirs and other little things my sisters and I had given him over the years. I spotted a framed picture of my older sisters and me with our dad that had been taken almost twenty years ago. I was sitting on his shoulders, and Millie and Felicity each hung off his biceps. It reminded me of something Hallie and Luna would do to Dex. I laughed a little. "God, that picture is so old."

My dad glanced behind him to see what I was talking about. "*I'm* so old. I didn't even have gray hair then. And I was in such good shape."

"You're still in good shape, Dad." It was true—even in his mid-fifties, my dad still worked out almost every day. "I bet you could still put me up on your shoulders."

"But I wouldn't get very far."

I laughed. "Was that at a Cloverleigh Farms staff picnic?"

"I think so. I'm pretty sure Mom took that before we were married."

"When you were sneaking around and hiding in closets?"

"Probably."

I shook my head. "You guys were so obvious. Millie and I were just talking about it earlier today."

He chuckled. "Yeah."

"And then you tried to break it off, remember? And we had to call a family meeting to give you the hard words."

"I remember." He studied the picture a moment longer and looked at me again. "Good thing I had you three to tell me I was being an idiot."

I laughed. "We didn't say it like that."

"Oh yes, you did. I distinctly remember Millie saying those exact words."

"Well, it was true. And we didn't want you to make a huge mistake. Just think, maybe you wouldn't have gotten married and had Emmeline and Audrey if it wasn't for those hard words."

"I'm definitely the luckiest guy in the world," he said. "Everything I needed to be happy was right there in front of me."

"That is lucky," I said softly.

"But I had to make choices leading up to that point that weren't easy to make." He looked at me intently. "Don't be afraid to do things that seem scary. Even make mistakes. It's how you grow and learn."

I smiled. "Spoken like a true dad."

"Hey. At heart, we are who we are."

Rising from the chair, I came around and kissed his cheek. "I'd miss being able to come in here and bug you while you're trying to work if I left."

"I'd miss that too."

Heading for the door, I gave him a wave. "Bye, Dad. See you tomorrow."

"Bye, Win."

After work, I went to Pilates class, then headed home. I kept wracking my brain for any valid reason I shouldn't hit send on that reply to Sandra and coming up short. The pros were obvious, and any possible con was based solely in fear, and I didn't want to be the sort of person who failed to chase a dream because she was scared.

But pretty soon, my thoughts strayed to Dex. As the water ran down my body, I thought about him in the shower. I wondered what he looked like naked. What his hands would feel like on my skin if he were here right now. What things he might do to me or say to me.

The water was hot, but I shivered.

I still couldn't believe I'd had the nerve to get on his lap like that, to flirt with him and kiss him and provoke him. I'd felt so strong and brave and sexy. And no, he wasn't gentle—but every time I thought about him sewing my dress, my heart melted. And I'd been smiling all day about the way he said goodnight, making sure to tell me he didn't love me.

He was good at making me laugh. Being with him was so easy.

I got out of the shower, aimed the blow dryer at my head for five minutes, and threw on a cropped sweatshirt and shorts. Downstairs, I was hunting in the kitchen for a dinner idea when someone knocked on my door.

My pulse quickened.

Despite the fact that I was supposed to be playing it cool, I pretty much *ran* toward the door. With my hand on the knob, I forced myself to take a breath and assume a casual expression. Then I pulled it open.

"Hi," he said, looking unbelievably sexy. His hair was damp and messy, like he'd just gotten out of the shower but hadn't bothered to comb it. His eyes immediately went to my bare midriff.

"Hey."

"Don't worry, I didn't bring you a Frosty."

I laughed and wagged my finger at him. "Good."

"I was wondering if you had any smoked paprika."

"Smoked paprika? I'm not sure, but come in and I'll look."

He followed me back to the kitchen, sending Piglet running for her life. "I decided to test out my new grill with some burgers. The paprika is for the seasoning."

"That sounds good." I opened a cupboard door and shuffled some dried herbs and spices around. Spotting some smoked paprika in the back, I grabbed it and set it on the counter. "There you go, neighbor."

"Thanks. Have you eaten yet?"

"No, I was just about to make dinner."

"Want to come over? I have plenty. I bought a pound of meat."

"Come on, you can eat a pound of meat, no problem." I poked him playfully in his stomach, which was rock hard.

He swatted my hand away and grabbed me by both arms,

twisting them behind my back. "What I *can* do and what I *should* do are sometimes two different things."

A hot little spark zipped up my spine. "Oh, are we playing this game again?"

"Does it feel like a game?" His hips anchored mine to the island.

"It feels like you came over here for something other than smoked paprika."

"Maybe I did."

"It also feels like I'm being arrested."

"I'm not a cop." Clamping one hand around my crossed wrists, he slid the other around to my belly and up the front of my sweatshirt. I wasn't wearing a bra, and his palm covered one breast. "Right now, I'm not even sure I'm one of the good guys."

My nipple tingled as he teased it with his fingers, pinching it hard enough to make me gasp. Heat began to pool at my center.

"I've been thinking about you all fucking day," he growled, moving his hand down my shorts, inside my underwear. "About the way you taste. About the way you move. About the sounds you make when I put my tongue right here." He brushed his fingertips lightly over my clit, and I moaned softly. "Yes," he whispered. "Like that."

"What else?" I asked breathlessly. "What else did you think about?"

He eased his fingers inside me. "I thought about how wet you were last night. About my cock inside you. About fucking you."

My legs were trembling as he moved his fingers in and out of my body, rubbing slow, decadent circles over my clit. I pushed my ass back against him, and he laughed, low and gravelly.

"You want my cock again?" He put his fingers back inside me. "Right here?"

"Yes," I breathed.

"You have to say it."

I chewed my lip a second. Could I?

"Say it," he demanded, his hand going still. "Or I won't give you what you want."

"I want your cock again."

"Say please." He began to stroke me again.

"Please," I panted.

"Good girl." He rubbed me a little harder and faster in just the right spot. "But first you're going to come—just like this." He released my arms and I fell forward over the island, my palms flat on the counter. With his free hand, he gathered up my hair in his fist and tightened his fingers, holding my head still. I winced as pain prickled across my scalp, but it was a delicious contrast to the fluttering pleasure building between my legs. The muscles in my lower body began to hum and my core muscles pulled tighter and tighter, the tension thrilling and delicious. My knees buckled as the orgasm pulsed through me.

A moment later, he was yanking my shorts and underwear down. Straightening up, he spun me around and began to unbutton his jeans.

Then suddenly he closed his eyes and scowled. "Fuck!"

"What?" Still breathless, I blinked at him.

He inhaled. "I don't have a condom."

"Oh."

"I don't suppose you . . ."

I shook my head.

He took another deep breath and did up his pants. "Okay. Game over."

"Well, wait a minute. It doesn't have to be over." I dropped to my knees in front of him and released the button on his jeans again.

"Hey." He put his fingers under my chin.

I looked up at him, eyes wide with phony innocence as I unzipped his jeans. "What?"

"You don't have to do this."

"You don't want me to do this?" I pushed his hips back against the counter and tugged his jeans and boxer briefs to his knees. His cock sprang free, tall and thick and hard.

He braced the heels of his hands on the edge of the granite. "I didn't say that."

"I didn't think so." Taking his impressive erection in both hands, I licked my lips, then swept my tongue along the crown. He was warm and smooth, and I liked the way his breath came faster as I circled the head, slid my hands up and down the length of his shaft, allowed just an inch between my lips and sucked gently.

"Fuck, that feels so good." His voice was raw with arousal, and I felt his cock swell and throb once against my palms. I moaned as I licked a salty droplet from the top. He continued to groan and growl and curse as I slowly licked him from root to tip, purposely not taking him deeper into my mouth. As I teased and played, I could sense the restraint in his body—how hard he was working to maintain control and not hold my head still so he could shove his dick to the back of my throat. Whenever he flexed his hips, I pulled back, laughing softly.

Finally, he put his hands on my head, threading his fingers into my hair and forcing me to meet his eyes. "Are you fucking messing with me?"

"I don't know what you mean," I said, looking up at him with delight.

He clenched his jaw, torn between lust and fury. "Winnie."

"What?"

"You know what I want."

"I might," I said coyly as his dick pulsed in my hands once more. "But you have to say it."

His dark eyes gleamed with understanding. "You're getting me back."

"I'm just playing the game you started." I grinned seductively. "So go on. Tell me what you want."

For a second, I thought he wasn't going to do it. I could see in his face the reluctance to get rough with me in this situation—I knew all he could think about was how much younger I was. But I also knew how badly he wanted this, and it gave me confidence to stand my ground.

Or kneel on it, anyway.

"I'm a big girl, Dex." I licked him again. "I can take it."

His hands tightened in my hair. "I want my cock in your mouth."

I took him between my lips, the sensitive crown gliding over my tongue, and moved my hands to his muscular thighs.

"I want to watch you take it in deep. I want to see you suck it like you can't get enough. I want to fuck your mouth until I come." He went slow at first, pushing in and pulling back, forcing me to take him a little farther each time, until finally the tip reached the back of my throat. I panicked a little because I couldn't breathe, and pushed back on his legs slightly.

He withdrew a couple inches, but not all the way. "What's the matter, big girl? Can't take it?"

Determined to prove I was worthy of his fantasy, capable of fulfilling his desires, I caught my breath and moved my hands to his hips, gripping them hard and sucking him with loud, greedy noises. He groaned and stayed still a minute, watching me working my mouth up and down his cock, which grew even harder and thicker. I could taste how close he was.

He took over then, thrusting deep and hard and fast, cursing and snarling, his hands holding my head in place while he fucked my mouth like he wanted to. I held on for dear life, trying not to choke or gag, desperately hoping I could last until he couldn't.

"Fuck, I'm gonna come," he growled, giving me a warning.

But I wanted him to finish just like this, so I stayed right where I was and moved one hand between his thighs, sliding my fingers along the crease and wrapping them around his balls. They tensed up as his body ceased moving, and within seconds I felt the quick throb and hot stream of his climax, heard the sudden inhalation of breath and then the low, prolonged moan of his pleasure.

When the pulsing subsided, I fell back onto my heels and gasped for air, wiping my mouth on my sleeve.

"Jesus Christ." Dex looked dazed, maybe a little frightened. "That was insane."

"But good?"

He stared at me. "Yeah. You won the game."

I laughed triumphantly as I rose to my feet. "What do you say we call it a draw?"

"Works for me." He zipped up his jeans and I went to grab a bottle of water from the fridge, but he caught my arm. "Hey."

"Yes?"

"One of these days, I will actually get all your clothes off."

I smiled. "We'll see."

Fourteen

Dex

I LEANED BACK AGAINST THE ISLAND IN MY KITCHEN, WATCHING as Winnie formed three hamburger patties from the mixture in the bowl. "I promise I didn't invite you over for dinner tonight just so you would make it."

"Ha."

"You think I have ulterior motives?"

She laughed. "I think we have already established what your motives were when you came knocking at my door."

Coming up behind her, I locked an arm around her neck. "Hey. I just came over to borrow some paprika. It was your fault things turned sexy."

"My fault!" She placed the last burger on a plate. "How's that?"

"You answered the door in this little outfit." I put my other hand on her belly. "How was I supposed to resist?"

She playfully elbowed me in the gut. "Let go of me, you brute. I'm hungry. And I'm really not in the mood to lecture you about why a woman's clothes should not be blamed for a man's behavior."

"Fine." I let go of her and held up my hands. "I'll take the blame."

She handed me the plate and a wood-handled metal spatula. "Good thing I enjoyed it."

"Then I'll take the credit too."

She turned me around by the shoulders and gave me a shove toward the patio. "Go put those on the grill for three minutes and then flip them over."

"That's it?"

"Yes. I'll be out in a sec with cheese." She glanced at the oven timer. "The French fries will be done in a minute, and as soon as I pull them out, I'll stick the buns in there to warm them up. Do you like lettuce and tomato on your cheeseburgers?"

"Yes. Do I have any?"

She laughed and pulled the fridge open. "No. But I do. I'm going to run back home real quick while you get those burgers on the heat."

I went out to the patio and did what she said, carefully timing the three minutes with my phone, then turning them over. Winnie came through the sliding door a minute later and placed a slice of bright orange American cheese on each of them.

"Sorry I don't have anything fancier," I said. "You probably eat your burgers with Brie or something. And make fries with real potatoes instead of from a bag in the freezer section."

"Listen, you're talking to a girl whose favorite dessert is a Frosty."

I smiled at her. "True."

She lifted her hair off her neck as if she was warm, and I noticed how the sunset gave it copper-penny highlights. I recalled my hands tangled up in it, my cock sliding between her perfect pink lips, and my stomach muscles contracted. I wanted her again tonight, and it wasn't a good idea.

Quickly, I looked out toward the pool.

Dropping her arms, she fanned her face. "Whew. It's hot out here, isn't it? Want something cold to drink?"

A beer would have tasted good and maybe numbed some of what I was feeling, but I had to work in the morning. "Just water, I guess."

"Okay." She put a hand on my shoulder before heading inside, and it took a lot more strength than I'd have liked for me not to grab her arm and pull her back to me for a kiss.

I felt like a fucking teenager.

We ate side by side at my kitchen island.

"So the girls will be here this weekend, huh?" she asked.

I nodded. "I'll pick them up on Saturday morning, right after my shift ends."

"That'll be fun. Last weekend before school starts, right?"

"Yes. I take them back to their mom Monday, and they start school Tuesday."

"What's your plan for the weekend?"

"Plan?" I picked up my water glass and took a drink.

"Dex! You have to do something fun for the last weekend of summer!"

"We'll have fun." I shrugged. "I'll take them swimming. We'll go for ice cream."

"That's fine, but you need something more than that." She thought for a second, munching on a fry. "I know! Bring them over to Cloverleigh Farms for horseback riding. My dad used to take us when we were kids and it was the best."

I gave her a look. "Whose horse?"

"We have a few there that belong to family. My cousin Whitney has one, my cousins Sawyer and Elsa have one, and the farm itself usually keeps at least two. We do hayrides in the fall and sleigh rides in the winter." She grew more animated as she talked. "Do they like horses?"

"They like all animals." I took a bite of my cheeseburger, which was definitely the best one I'd ever made. Too bad the girls weren't here for this meal. "They're still after me about a cat."

Winnie laughed. "Just get the cat. I told you, I'll feed it on your work days. It's not a big deal."

"I'll think about it."

"I think it's good for kids to have a pet," she went on. "It teaches them responsibility and respect for living things."

"You sound like Hallie. Just older—barely," I teased.

She nudged me with her leg. "It's all true. Your daughter is smart. She's probably done the research."

"She does love research," I said. "Asking questions is her favorite activity."

Winnie picked up her water glass. "What does she do with all her knowledge?"

"She writes stories. You should see all the notebooks she's filled."

"I love that. A curious, creative soul who loves to learn."

"Almost as much as she loves socks."

Winnie laughed. "I saw her swimming with her little aqua socks on. She really hates being barefoot, huh?"

"She really hates it. Just makes her too anxious to enjoy herself."

"Hm. I wonder what she'd do if I offered to paint her toes for the last weekend of summer."

I shrugged. "Not sure. I've never offered that before."

"So let's try it. I have to work Saturday evening—I'm helping Millie with a wedding—but I'll be around earlier in the day. And I have tons of colors she can pick from. Maybe if she was excited about showing off her fun polish, she'd be less anxious about going barefoot?"

"Maybe. But don't be hurt if it doesn't work."

"I won't at all, I promise. Let's try it."

I was touched by her offer. "Thanks. That's nice of you."

"My little sisters used to let me give them pedicures all the time. I'll give Luna one too." Then she laughed. "You want one?"

"No," I said firmly. "I have big ugly man feet and they're going to stay big ugly man feet."

She laughed. "Fine, be that way. And if you're too busy, it's not a big deal."

"I'm sure if I mention it to them, they will be knocking on your door at eight a.m. Saturday morning."

"Perfect," she said. "I like getting up early. And if you want to bring them over to the barn this weekend, we can do that too." She ate her last French fry. "Maybe Sunday would be good for that. Let me check with my cousin."

Although Winnie offered to help me with the dishes, I refused to let her, since she'd done most of the work getting dinner together.

"I've got this," I told her, placing both our plates in the sink.

"Are you sure?" She finished her water and set the glass down. "I don't mind."

"I'm sure. I'm used to it—at the station, they don't let me near the food because I'm such a bad cook, so I'm always on clean-up duty."

She laughed, leaning her lower back against the counter next to the sink. "I think a man who cleans is just as sexy as a man who cooks. Maybe even sexier."

"I don't think the guys at the station give a fuck about that," I said wryly, turning on the faucet. "They just won't go near anything I make."

"It's okay. Your talents lie elsewhere."

I glanced over to find that wicked little grin on her face, the one that made the crotch of my jeans go tight. "Thanks."

"You're welcome." She touched my arm. "Well, I should head out. Thanks for—oh! I forgot to tell you about my job offer."

"Job offer?" I rinsed our plates and put them in the dishwasher.

"Yes. For a position as event designer at a boutique hotel in Newport, Rhode Island. I got an email today from the new manager there—she interviewed me in New York last spring and remembered me."

"Nice." I dumped the ice from her water glass and put it in the top rack. "You gonna take it?"

"I'm—I'm not sure yet. But I'm definitely interested. I just have to reply to her email and tell her so."

I nodded, unnerved by the way my gut twisted thinking about her moving to Rhode Island. Why should it make any difference to me? "Cool. Congratulations."

"It's too soon for congratulations, but I'm kind of excited." She laughed self-consciously. "And maybe a little nervous."

"Why?"

"I've been asking myself that all day, and I think it's just because it's so far from home."

I faced her, drying my hands on a kitchen towel. She looked so young with that apprehensive expression on her face. "Leaving home was the best thing I ever did."

"Was it?"

"Yeah. I was restless. I felt cooped up here. I wanted to push myself, see what I could do." I shrugged. "I had to prove myself."

"Yeah." She bit her lip. "I'm not sure I have that same kind of cooped-up feeling, but I do feel restless sometimes."

"You should go for it. Don't hold yourself back."

"Thanks." Smiling, she pointed a thumb toward the patio door. "Should I go out the back?"

"I'll walk you," I said, tossing the towel aside.

"Dex, I'm not a kid."

I glared at her and headed for the back door. "Don't argue with me. It's dark. You know how I am."

She sighed, but she followed me outside.

"Night," she said, giving me a little wave. "Thanks for . . . everything."

I folded my arms over my chest, wishing I had a reason for her to stay longer. Or at least touch her again. "You're welcome for everything. Night."

She headed across the small patch of lawn between my patio and hers. After I made sure she got in, I went back to the kitchen to continue cleaning up. That's when I spotted her smoked paprika on the counter. Without thinking, I grabbed it and hurried out again.

Ten seconds later, I knocked on her sliding door. I could see her checking her phone in the kitchen, and she looked up in surprise before coming over to open it.

"What's up?"

"You forgot this." I handed over the spice.

"Oh—thanks." She shook it and laughed. "Now I'll always think of you when I use it."

"Good." We stood there for a moment, then I leaned in and kissed her softly. "Night."

"Night." She looked up at me, her expression a little bewildered, as if the gesture had taken her by surprise.

It had taken me by surprise too, and I quickly turned and walked toward my place.

Before I got there, she called out. "Hey, Dex?"

"Yeah?" I turned around, terrified she was going to ask me if I wanted to come in and knowing I'd say yes.

She was leaning out her doorway, a playful grin on her face. "I had fun tonight."

"Me too." And then I relaxed, because I knew what was coming.

"But I don't love you."

I grinned back. "I don't love you either."

Then she disappeared, and I could breathe again.

"So? Did you apologize?" Justin asked, climbing onto the stationary bike next to the treadmill as I approached my third mile.

"I did."

"And?" he said, starting to pedal.

"And it was fine."

"Fine?"

I shrugged. "I brought her a Frosty. She forgave me."

"And that's the end of the story?"

Increasing my speed slightly, I didn't say anything.

"Because that doesn't seem like the end of the story."

"There may have been an additional chapter," I admitted. "What do you call those things at the end of a book?"

"An epilogue?"

"Yeah. There may have been an epilogue."

Justin laughed. "What happened during the epilogue?"

I wiped sweat off my face with the bottom of my T-shirt. "Pretty much everything."

"*Everything*?"

"Yeah."

"Because I'm imagining a lot of things."

I nodded. "They probably all happened."

"Well, fuck."

"We did."

He laughed. "So did you change your mind about her?"

I crossed the three mile threshold and slowed my speed to a walk. "What do you mean?"

"You said you weren't interested in dating her because she was too young."

"She's still too young, and no—I didn't change my mind. I'm not interested in dating her." I wasn't, was I? How come the answer felt a little muddy in my brain? Was it the blowjob?

"Oh." Justin was quiet for a minute. "And she's cool with that?"

"Totally. She's not interested in dating me either. In fact, she made it very clear she is only interested in me on a physical level."

"Seriously? So is this like an ongoing thing?"

I gave him the side eye. "Mind your own fucking business."

"I can't. This girl has you messed up. I want to meet her."

"No fucking way." I stopped the treadmill and jumped off. "Were you even listening to me? We're not a thing, Justin. I'm not introducing her to my family. That would give her the wrong idea—and you guys too."

"But you already know some of her family, right? Your friend turned out to be her cousin?"

"That happened by accident. It was a coincidence." But I frowned, thinking about Chip and wondering how he'd feel about me messing around with Winnie.

"Still coming over Monday for a cookout?" Justin asked.

"Yeah," I said distractedly. "We'll be there."

"Feel free to bring a friend."

I rolled my eyes and headed for the door. "Fuck off."

"What? I said friend, not date! I just want to see this girl."

"*No.*" If my sister and Justin saw how young she was, I'd never hear the end of it. I did *not* need to bring her around my family.

Better to keep her separate from the things that mattered.

Saturday morning, as I pulled up in Naomi's driveway, Hallie came racing out to meet me.

"Daddy!" she shouted, throwing her arms around me as I tried to get out of my car. "You're here!"

"I'm here."

"We're hungry." She tossed her head back and looked up at me. "Can we go to that bakery again? Where Winnie's mom works?"

"Maybe. Go get your stuff."

As she went back in, Luna came hurrying out, dragging her little suitcase on wheels. "Hi, Daddy."

"Hi, Loony Toon. Let me take that." I grabbed the handle of her suitcase with one hand and scooped her up with the second, rubbing my scratchy jaw on her cheek. "How are you?"

She giggled and squirmed in my arms. "Good. Can we go swimming today?"

"Sure."

"With Winnie?"

"We'll see."

Naomi came out, already dressed for work. "Hey. Got a second?"

I set Luna down, opened the back door, and told her to get in the car. After stowing her suitcase in the back, I faced my ex again. "What's up?"

"I wanted to talk about October twenty-third. It's technically your Saturday, but I wondered if I might keep the girls that night."

"Why?"

"Bryce and I have decided to get married that day."

"So?" I said, just to be difficult.

"Dex, come on. I want the kids there."

"I thought you were getting married next summer."

"We decided we didn't want to wait." She frowned at me. "And what do you care?"

"I don't. You two can get married tomorrow if you want. But why should I give up one of my nights with my kids?"

"Really, Dexter?" She tilted her head. "You can't do me this *one* favor? On this *one* Saturday night?"

I crossed my arms over my chest. "That's not what this is about. It's about respecting the time I have with them— and you don't."

Her expression softened, and she nodded. "I'll try to be better about that."

"No more phone calls checking up on me. No more lectures about allergies or meals or how things need to be done. When they're with me, they're mine."

She took a breath, briefly closing her eyes. "Okay."

"Seriously? Okay?" I wasn't sure I believed her. "If I say yes to the wedding day, no more micromanaging from afar?"

"You have my word." She held out a pinky and offered a tentative smile.

Reluctantly, I hooked mine through it. For a second, I remembered good times with Naomi, and it eased some of the resentment and anger in me. "Thank you. I know I'm not perfect, but I'm trying."

"I know you are." She tucked her hands into her back pockets. "And they're so crazy about you. Honestly, it gets to me. I have to be the mean parent, and you're the fun one. I take them to get flu shots and school shoes and teeth cleanings, and you take them for donuts and swimming and fire station visits."

"So give me some of those responsibilities, Naomi," I said. "I can handle them. Sometimes I feel like you hoard all that shit just so you can complain about me."

She nodded. "Okay. I'll make more of an effort to go fifty-fifty on that stuff."

"Good." I managed a half-smile. "And maybe let them have a fucking donut every once in a while. It won't kill them."

Laughing, she shook her head, her eyes wandering over my body. "I don't understand how you eat that way and stay so fit. It's not fair."

"Have a good weekend," I said, opening the driver's side door.

"What are you going to do with them?" she asked.

I gave her a warning look, and she put her hands up.

"I'm just asking out of curiosity! I'm not micromanaging."

"I'm not sure. We'll go swimming, probably, and I might take them over to Cloverleigh Farms to go horseback riding."

She looked surprised. "I didn't know they had horseback riding there."

"I don't think it's open to the public. Winnie invited us. She works there."

"Winnie invited us where?" Hallie said, who'd come out with her bag in one hand, Rupert the penguin in the other.

"Horseback riding," I told her, taking her bag. "Hop in."

Hallie jumped into the back seat and immediately she and Luna started squealing with excitement.

"The girls talked about Winnie a lot this week," said Naomi. Then she laughed. "It's funny, when you first mentioned her, I pictured an old lady. Such an old-fashioned name."

"She's not old." I went around to the back of my SUV and stuck Hallie's bag next to Luna's.

"I know that now. Hallie says she's twenty-two."

"Sounds right."

"And very pretty."

I shrugged.

"I hear she came to the pool with you guys."

"Bye, Naomi. See you Monday." I got in the car and shut

the door. My ex-wife was the last person on earth I wanted to discuss Winnie with, and an excellent reminder of why I did not do relationships.

"Bye, girls!" Naomi blew kisses to Hallie and Luna. "I love you! Have fun!"

I backed out of the driveway and turned on the Dad station, which happened to be playing "Bohemian Rhapsody."

"Oh, I love this song!" Hallie said.

In the rearview mirror, I caught them both bopping their heads along to the music, and smiled.

I could feel a ten coming on.

Fifteen

Winnie

ABOUT EIGHT-THIRTY A.M. SATURDAY MORNING, I WAS sitting at the island with a cup of coffee when I heard knocking on the sliding glass door.

I looked over and saw Hallie and Luna on my patio grinning excitedly. Hallie waved and Luna bounced up and down as I opened the door. "Good morning, girls!"

"Good morning!" they chorused.

"What a beautiful day, huh?" I looked behind them at the sunny, cloudless sky.

"Yes. Daddy says maybe we're going horseback riding this weekend!" Luna said breathlessly. "Is it true?"

"Sure," I said. "Tomorrow, if that works for your dad. My cousin can meet us there in the morning. She has a horse you can ride."

"What's the horse's name?" Hallie asked.

I laughed. "I'm not sure, but I'll find out. Hey, would you girls like a pedicure this morning?"

"Yes!" Luna shouted. "What's a pedicure?"

"I'll paint your toes." I stuck one bare foot out. "Like mine. See?"

"Can you paint mine red like yours?" Luna asked.

"Sure." I glanced at Hallie, who was looking down at her sneakers. "What do you think, Hal? Red? Purple? Blue?"

She smiled. "You really have blue?"

"I really do."

"Okay." She looked a little anxious about it, but she nodded. "I want blue."

"Great. Then maybe we can show off our toes at the pool today. Why don't you go tell your dad we're going to play salon over here, and I'll get everything set up?"

"Okay!"

"And when you come back, just wear flip-flops, okay? Or bare feet. You won't be able to put on socks and sneakers."

They joyfully skipped back toward their place, and I headed for the upstairs bathroom to get all my supplies.

As I went up the steps, I wondered if Dex would come too. If I'd had his number, I'd have texted him an invite. When I got back downstairs, I set the nail polish bottles on the counter and decided to go over and knock on his door.

I went to the front this time, and he opened it with a cup of coffee in his hand. He wore gray sweatpants and a US Navy T-shirt. His mouth curved into something close to a smile, making my heart flutter faster. "Morning, neighbor."

"Morning. I came over to ask for your number."

He took a sip of his coffee. The mug had a firefighter's boot on it and read My Dad is My Hero. "Why?"

"I think my place needs a fire inspection. I thought maybe I'd call you to schedule one." I grinned. "I know how you are about safety."

"Ah." He sipped again, his brown eyes dancing. "Then I suppose I could give it to you. For safety reasons."

"Why don't you come over with the girls and we can exchange information?"

"Just information?"

I laughed. "This time, yes."

"I could come over," he said, like he was doing me a favor. "Have you eaten breakfast?"

"Not yet. Just coffee."

"I'll bring you a monkey bread muffin."

My eyebrows lifted in surprise. "Were you at Plum & Honey already this morning?"

"Yes. The girls insisted." He paused. "And I *might* have asked your mom what your favorite muffin was."

"Look at you being a nice guy."

"I know." He put his grump face back on. "Don't fucking tell anyone."

I zipped my lips. "Your secret is safe with me. See you in a few." As I headed across his driveway toward my place, he called out.

"Hey!"

"Yes?" I turned around.

"Did you hear back about the job in Rhode Island?"

I smiled, pleased that he remembered. "Yes. We're going to talk by phone next week. I'm really excited."

He nodded. "Good."

That evening, I headed over to Cloverleigh Farms to help Millie with a large wedding reception. Usually, our Aunt April was on hand to help with big events, but she and her family had gone down to Chicago to see one of Chip's games.

It was a long night, and by the time the wedding party went back to the bar at the inn to keep the celebration going, it was after eleven. Millie and I left the staff to break down the room and retreated to her office, where I dropped onto her couch and kicked off my shoes.

"Shot of whiskey?" she asked, taking a bottle from a shelf behind her desk.

"Yes, please." I stretched my legs and feet. My red toe polish reminded me of giving the girls pedicures this morning. It had been so much fun, and Hallie had been excited enough about her blue toes that she'd forgone her water socks and gone barefoot at the pool—at least for the ten steps between where she'd left her flip-flops on the cement and the shallow end.

But Dex had called it progress and thanked me with a secret smile that made my heart threaten to burst.

Millie poured a little whiskey into two old fashioned glasses and brought them over to the couch. "Sorry I don't have ice."

"It's fine." I took the glass, scooting over so she could sit next to me.

"Cheers." She tapped her whiskey against mine. "Thanks for the help tonight."

"My pleasure." I took a sip, enjoying the way the fiery liquid warmed my throat.

"So what's new with your dad crush?"

I rolled my eyes. "He's not my dad crush. He's just my neighbor."

"So you haven't fooled around with him again?"

I took another sip. "I didn't say that."

My sister laughed, kicking off her shoes and tucking her legs beneath her. "Tell me everything."

"There's not much to tell. We hung out on Thursday night and . . . stuff happened. But we hung out all day today, and nothing happened."

"What did you do today?"

I told her about playing salon with the girls. "I painted their toes and they did my hair, which was—interesting."

Millie laughed. "Remember when we played salon and Felicity cut her bangs so they were like an inch long?"

"Yes!" I howled at the memory. "Dad was so mad at us.

There were no scissors involved today, but there were a *lot* of accessories. They brought over a bag of hair bows. I looked like I'd been gift-wrapped by a toddler."

"Where was their dad during all this?"

"He was there, drinking coffee and laughing at me. Then I suggested he let them do *his* hair, and when they begged and pleaded, he couldn't say no." I giggled at the memory. "They stuck a headband with pink cat ears on his head and he caught me taking a picture with my phone."

"Let me see!"

I dug through my purse and found my phone, then brought up the picture of a scowling Dex to show her.

She burst out laughing. "That is one furious feline. But damn, he's hot."

"He was so mad when I wouldn't delete it." I dropped my phone back in my purse. "He threw me in the pool later, even though I told him I didn't want to get my hair wet."

Her eyebrows arched. "Sounds like a fun day."

"It was."

She sipped again. "I know you said you guys are not Dad and Frannie, but something about all this seems very familiar."

I sighed in exasperation. "I swear it's not like that with us. Dad and Frannie were in love. Dex and I are not. In fact, that's one of our inside jokes. We both agreed that this thing between us should stay casual, so every time we say goodnight, one of us is like, 'I had fun tonight, but I don't love you.'"

My sister pressed her lips together.

"Stop looking at me that way," I said. "We just have a good time together. He makes me laugh and has a nice dick, okay? Let me just enjoy it."

"Okay, okay." Sighing, she unfolded her legs and stretched them out. "Will you see him tonight?"

"No."

"Why not?"

"Because his kids are there." I tossed back my last swallow of whiskey. "We don't want them to suspect anything. And I don't think it's a good idea to mess around with him too often, you know? If you're going to keep something casual, it should probably be something that only happens now and then."

"True. Especially for you."

I'd sort of been hoping for tacit permission to at least sext him later, now that I had his number, but hearing Millie confirm what I'd said, I knew I shouldn't.

"I should get going," I told her. "I told the girls I'd bring them horseback riding tomorrow. Whitney is meeting us at the barn at nine."

"That'll be fun." She paused. "Dex coming too?"

The question shouldn't have felt so loaded.

"Probably." Avoiding her eyes, I stood up, slipped my heels back on, and set my empty glass on her desk. "Thanks for the drink."

"Anytime. Drive carefully."

The next morning, we drove together to Cloverleigh Farms and walked over to the barn. I introduced Dex and the girls to my cousin Whitney, who'd spent years working in the stables and had always loved horses.

The girls promptly fell in love with Buttercup, a gentle, chestnut-brown Quarter Horse, and quietly listened as Whitney showed them how to feed her, brush her coat, and get her ready to ride.

It was another beautiful day, warm and sunny with just enough of a breeze to make the heat bearable. Dex and I stood off to the side near the split-rail fence as Whitney patiently let each girl have a turn in the saddle, carefully leading Buttercup around the paddock. They begged to do it again and again.

"This is so nice of you and your cousin," Dex said. "I really appreciate it."

"Of course. Whitney said she was thrilled to do it, and she doesn't have to be at work until one."

"She's Chip's cousin too?"

"Right. Whitney is my Aunt Sylvia's oldest. She's about Millie's age—or close to it, maybe around thirty—and works for her stepdad, my Uncle Henry. He's the winemaker here." I gestured back toward the winery. "But Whitney manages the tasting rooms in Hadley Harbor and Traverse City, so she's not here every day."

Dex was quiet a minute. "Pretty soon my girls will have a stepdad."

I looked over at him. "My mom mentioned something about Naomi being engaged. When is she getting married?"

"In October."

I smiled at Luna, who was waving to us from Buttercup's back. "Is he a good guy?"

Dex shrugged. "He's okay."

"Are you . . . upset about her remarrying?"

"Fuck no," he scoffed, as if I'd offended him.

I glanced at him. His jaw was set hard. He wore sunglasses, so I couldn't see his eyes, but I had a feeling they were stony. Something about the situation clearly bothered him, but I wasn't going to force him to admit it. Wordlessly, I focused on Luna again.

"Sorry. I didn't mean to snap at you." His tone was grudging but softer. "I don't have a problem with Naomi remarrying. I just don't like the idea of someone else thinking he can be their dad."

Aha. "That's understandable."

"They're going to live in his house, take rides on his sailboat, go on his vacations. He's got money. He'll be able to give them things I can't. That—that sticks in my craw."

"But you're their dad—the only one they've got—and they love you beyond the moon. It won't matter what he buys them, Dex. They'll always want to be with you."

He didn't say anything, but his throat muscles remained taut.

"My sisters and I could have cared less about things like money or stuff," I told him. "What we loved more than anything was the time we got with our dad. The way he made us laugh and feel safe. The way he showed us he loved us." I put my hand on his arm. "I promise you, no one will *ever* replace you in their eyes. Someday when they're older, some guy is going to come along and try, and—"

"Fuck that guy." Dex stood taller and puffed out his chest. "I'll kick his ass."

I laughed, rubbing his forearm. "Easy. It's okay. They're only eight and five. You've got time before boyfriends."

He still looked alarmed. "I'm not going to be good at that."

"My dad wasn't either. But we knew it was because he loved us, and he was protective."

Taking a deep breath, he exhaled. "Yeah. Thanks."

"You're welcome." I didn't want to stop touching him— his skin was warmed by the sun and he smelled good. I sort of wished I could loop my arm through his and press my cheek against his bicep . . . but I didn't. "I'm always here to listen. And I understand how complicated divorces and remarriages and single parenting can be."

"Thanks." He watched as Whitney lifted Luna down and helped Hallie into the saddle. "I don't usually spill my guts about that stuff."

"I know. You just grunt and go about your business."

He elbowed me and stayed close enough that our arms remained touching. "I was trying to say something nice to you."

"You were?" I feigned surprise. "I must have missed it."

"I was working up to it."

"Keep working."

He nudged me again. "It's easy to talk to you. You *make* it easy. Somehow."

I smiled, my heart swelling at the compliment. "Thanks."

A minute or two went by, a soft breeze ruffling our hair. Several times, I thought I saw Dex open his mouth to say something, but he never spoke up. Closing my eyes, I tilted my face to the sun, enjoying the warmth on my skin.

Then I heard his voice.

"What are you doing tomorrow?"

"Working in the morning. Off in the afternoon."

"If you're not busy after work, would you like to come to a cookout?"

Sunday evening, I went over to my parents' house for dinner, as usual. Because it was the last night of summer, my two younger sisters ate as fast as humanly possible and raced out the door, eager to eke out the last bit of fun before they started their junior year.

Millie and I lingered at the table out on the deck for a while with our mom and dad, drinking wine and chatting about last night's wedding, the wine tasting dinner Ellie and I were organizing, and the new restaurant opening at Abelard.

"I can't wait to try it," my mom said. "I hear they hired one of the Lupo brothers to be head chef."

"Gianni," I said.

"He graduated with you, right?" my dad asked.

"Yes, and Ellie's losing her mind." I laughed, recalling the scene in the kitchen with them. "She can't stand him."

"He's worked in some pretty famous restaurants though," Millie said. "In New York, Rome, San Francisco. I just read an article about him. He's supposed to be really talented. Kind of cocky for his age, but talented."

"I thought he was on some Hollywood reality show." My mom poured herself some more wine. "The same one his dad was on years ago."

"He was, but he's back." I slid my glass over, and she poured more for me too. "I saw him at Abelard the other day."

"Those Lupo boys were always a handful in school, weren't they?" My mom laughed. "Little devils. But so cute."

"Don't say that in front of Ellie," I told her.

"I ran into Mia last week," my mom said. "She told me the delays with the restaurant have been a big headache, especially because they were hoping to live in France for a while."

"They're moving?" I paused with my glass halfway to my lips. "Ellie didn't mention that."

"I don't think it's for sure, but she said she's always wanted to spend extended time there, and now that their youngest is off to college, they're considering it."

"Interesting," my dad said. "I wonder if they're hiring someone new to manage Abelard."

"You should apply if they are, Winnie," said Millie. "You'd be perfect for that job."

I smiled at her. "Thanks. But actually, I think I have an offer somewhere else."

"You do?" My sister reached over and slapped my arm. "Why didn't you tell me already?"

"Because it's not a sure thing yet." I described Sandra Elson's email and the position at The Alexander. "I'll know more next week. She's going to call me Tuesday."

"That's so exciting," my sister said. "Will you take it?"

"I might, if the offer is right. It sounds like a dream job." I hesitated, taking a sip of wine. "It's just far away from home."

"But you have to follow your passion," my mother surprised me by saying. "You can't be so scared of the unknown

179

you let it keep you from taking a chance on something that could change your life."

"I thought you'd hate the idea of my leaving," I said with a chuckle. "And here you are telling me to go."

"I *do* hate the idea of you leaving." My mom laughed too, but her eyes misted over. "And I *will* miss you. But Dad told me about this the other day, so I've had time to rehearse my reaction and not say the selfish things I'm feeling."

"Dad!" I thumped his shoulder. "I asked you not to say anything yet."

"And I was careful not to make that promise. I tell her everything, I can't help it." My dad slung his arm around my mom's shoulder and kissed her head.

It's easy to talk to you. Dex's words from earlier echoed through my head.

"Anyway," I said, "it's premature to talk about leaving yet. I want to hear the details from Sandra, and then I can make a decision."

Later, Millie and I walked out together. "What are you up to tomorrow?" she asked.

"I have to work reception in the morning. Then I'm heading over to Dex's sister's house for a cookout."

Millie laughed.

"What? It's just a cookout," I said defensively.

"I talked to Whitney today. She said you guys were at Cloverleigh all morning."

"We were. She was awesome with the girls. I owe her one."

"She said they were adorable."

"They *loved* it. They didn't stop talking about it the whole way home."

"She also mentioned you and Dex looked pretty cozy together," she said suggestively.

I shrugged. "I don't know what made her say that."

"I think it was just a feeling that you seemed comfortable with each other—like old friends," Millie said. "She was surprised that you guys met recently."

"Yeah. We clicked fast. Good chemistry, I guess." I played with my keys. "But you can tell Whitney—like I keep telling you—there's nothing serious between us."

I didn't have trouble meeting her eye, because it was the truth.

But damn.

Being the boss of my feelings was getting harder every day.

Sixteen

Dex

"**W**ANT TO HEAR ABOUT THE NEW STORY I'M writing?" Hallie asked Sunday night when I went in to say goodnight to the girls.

"Yes." I sat down on the edge of her bed.

She hugged Rupert the penguin tight, resting her chin on his head. "It's about a princess."

"Oh yeah? What's her name?"

"Her name is Minnie."

"Princess Minnie." Leaning back on my elbow, I pretended to consider the name. "And what does she look like?"

"She's very beautiful, with long golden hair. She lives in a little cottage in the forest. And she has a cat."

"What's the cat's name?" Luna asked, turning onto her side to face her sister's bed.

Hallie thought for a moment. "Tigger."

"Interesting," I said.

Luna giggled and tucked her hands beneath her cheek.

"Princess Minnie is very sad when Tigger runs up a very tall tree and won't come down," Hallie went on. "And she has no one to ask for help."

"Aren't there some townspeople about?" I asked.

"No." Hallie's tone was solemn. "Minnie cannot go to

town because she's *hiding* in the forest. Her parents are cruel and they want her to marry a mean prince."

"Well, that sucks."

"There's only *one* person she can ask—he lives near her in the forest, and she sometimes sees him through her window." Hallie took a breath. "But she's scared of him."

"Why?"

"Because he's an ogre. A big hairy ogre."

I frowned, cocking one brow. "And what's the big hairy ogre's name?"

"Rex."

"You don't say."

"Every night she hears Rex snoring really loud and making other scary ogre noises. The ground trembles when he walks."

"Because he has giant muscles?"

"Because he has giant *feet*."

I sighed. "So does the princess overcome her fear and knock on his door?"

"I don't know yet. That's as far as I've gotten."

"What?" I swatted her leg through the covers. "You're just going to leave Luna and me hanging there? With poor Tigger up a tree and Princess Minnie all alone and scared?"

Hallie smiled. "It's a good story, right?"

"Yes. You need to finish it." I slid off the bed and kissed her forehead. "Tell me something—is the ogre really a prince under some kind of evil spell?"

She shook her head. "No, he's really an ogre."

"Figures." I kissed Luna's temple and turned off the light. "Goodnight, girls. See you in the morning."

"Daddy?" Hallie yawned.

"Yeah." I paused in the doorway.

"Today was another ten."

I took a bow. "Thank you, I agree."

"Can we ride horses again tomorrow?"

"No. We're going to Aunt Bree's tomorrow."

"But Winnie is coming, right?"

"She might. Go to sleep."

Leaving the light on in the hall for them, I went back downstairs to clean up the mess we'd left in the kitchen. We'd made our own pizzas for dinner, and there was sauce and shredded cheese everywhere. Afterward, I opened a beer and sat on the couch with the television on, not really noticing what was on the screen.

It was torture to glance at the sliding door and wonder if Winnie was out on her patio. Should I go out there? If she was sitting at her table, should I invite her over? If she accepted my invitation, could I keep my hands to myself?

Frowning, I took a long swallow from the bottle and picked up a couch pillow, holding it to my chest. It bothered me how badly I'd wanted to keep touching her today. How often I'd caught myself staring at her mouth. How many times I thought about inviting her over for dinner tonight.

But it was bad enough I'd impulsively invited her to come to Bree's tomorrow. After what I'd said to Justin, he was going to give me a whole bunch of shit for bringing her—and I'd deserve it. But I liked being around Winnie. She was always upbeat and she made me laugh. She called me out on my bullshit and I could say things to her I couldn't say to anyone else. I felt like she understood my situation because of the way she'd grown up, and she didn't judge me when I got frustrated or angry. She had no stake in it—she wasn't going to use anything against me later. She just listened.

And I liked listening to her too. She got so excited when she talked about the dinner she was planning with her friend or ideas she had for events at her potential new job. I liked hearing stories about her family too—it was obvious she was close to them and that she'd had a happy childhood despite her real mom leaving when she was so young. I found my-self curious about her dad and kind of wanted to meet him.

Not to mention how damn good she was to my girls, and how they'd taken to her like she was a long-lost aunt or something.

Plus, she had those lips and that tongue and the sweetest curves known to man.

Yes, she was young, but I even liked the things that re-minded me of her age—like her adorable laugh or the bounce in her step or the way she and the girls used slang words or talked about songs or celebrities I'd never fucking heard of.

I took another sip and stood up. Moving slowly, like I wasn't even sure where I was heading, I went out on the patio. Standing there for a second in the dark, I drank again and then looked over to the right.

She wasn't out there, and her lights were off.

Disappointed, I went back inside.

The next day, I sent Hallie and Luna over to knock on Winnie's door while I backed the car out of the garage. She came out a minute later carrying a brown paper bag. She was wearing a yellow crop top, denim shorts with daisies on them, and white sneakers. Her hair was in a ponytail. She looked sexy and sweet, even younger than usual. My heart revved like an engine.

They piled into the car and buckled up. "Hi," she said, setting the bowl and bag at her feet.

"Hey. You didn't have to bring anything."

"It's just some guacamole and chips. Nothing fancy."

"But I'm not bringing anything. You're making me look bad."

She laughed. "You're bringing me. I got you."

When we arrived at Bree and Justin's house, we walked around to the yard, where they were sitting on the deck with some other friends, watching their kids run around on the lawn with squirt guns and water balloons.

Hallie and Luna immediately ran out to join them, while I introduced Winnie to the adults. My sister jumped up to get her a drink, and Justin, who was holding the baby over his shoulder, grinned at me knowingly.

I resisted the urge to flip him off.

While Winnie set the guacamole and chips on the table, I went inside to grab a beer and found my sister pouring a glass of wine.

After prying the cap off the beer bottle, I stole a cherry tomato from a big bowl of pasta salad on the counter.

"Hey." She slapped my knuckles. "Keep your hands out of the food."

"I'm hungry."

"We'll eat soon. What time do you have to have the girls back?"

"Six. But I'm sure Naomi will be texting me by four that it's their first school night of the year and I should have them back sooner."

"You guys getting along okay these days?"

"Yeah." I shrugged and tipped up my beer. "She's getting married next month."

"I heard." She put the bottle of wine back in the fridge. "Does that bother you?"

"Nah. Bryce is decent enough. He's good to the girls, and they seem to like him."

"Winnie seems nice." My sister leaned back against the counter. "Justin mentioned you had a new friend. That's her?"

I wasn't fooled by her casual tone. It was obvious she knew what I'd been up to. "That's her."

Bree didn't even bother to hide her smile. "She's *super* cute."

Frowning, I gave Bree the finger I hadn't given her husband.

"What?" She laughed. "I think it's great. She'll keep you young. What are kids these days into, anyway?"

"She's not a kid—she's twenty-two. And she's not just cute, she's cool and she's funny and she's great with the girls."

"Wow." Her eyes lit up. "Lucky you, moving in next door to someone like that."

"She's moving out soon," I said quickly.

Bree's face fell. "Oh. How come?"

"She got a job offer in Rhode Island."

"Well, shoot." Bree sighed. "I guess that's that."

"That's that. Come on, let's go outside."

"Okay, but I have to tell you one thing." Her expression put me on edge.

"What?"

"Dad called me."

I scowled. "For money?"

"No. He's sick."

"Tough." I took another drink. "With what?"

"Lung cancer. It's terminal."

Something like pity tugged at my heart, and I shut it down immediately.

"He asked to see us. And his grandkids." She hesitated, took a breath. "I'm thinking about it."

"Well, I don't need to think. My answer is no."

"Dexter," she said softly. "He's our father, and he has terminal cancer. Don't you think we should be there for him?"

"The way he was there for us or for Mom, when she was sick?" I asked pointedly.

She pressed her lips together. "I know he's not perfect. *He* knows he's not perfect. He understands he's made mistakes."

"This is what he does, Bree. He makes you believe that he's sorry and he's changed, but in the end, he's the same guy he always was, and that guy sucks." I shook my head. "I don't need to say goodbye."

"Did you know he got married?" She looked up at me with hope in her blue eyes, and it killed me to see it—she looked like our mom did every single time he came back.

"No."

"Last year. He met her at AA, I guess. Her name is Gloria, and she sounds nice. They live about two hours away."

"You talked to her too?"

"She wrote me a letter, asking if it would be okay for Dad to call. She said from the moment they met, he's talked about all the regrets he has about his kids. She told me about his cancer and begged me to consider reconciling with him before it's too late."

I steeled myself. "You can. I won't. And he's not coming near my kids."

She moved closer, placing a hand on my arm. "Please just think about it. For me. I don't know if I can do it without you."

Swallowing hard, I forced myself to keep those walls in place. She was my baby sister, and my instinct was to protect her, but I couldn't if she chose that path. "Sorry, Bree. I can't."

The rest of the day was ruined by my conversation with my sister. I sat outside with everyone, but I didn't talk, I didn't laugh at anyone's jokes, and I avoided meeting Winnie's eyes. She could tell something was up with me, and a couple times she asked if I was okay, but I brushed her off. Mostly I just looked out onto the lawn where the kids were playing, determined not to let anyone hurt my girls, ever—especially not my father. He'd done enough damage. And I didn't care if he was sorry now. It was too late—he didn't deserve them.

The guy is dying, asshole. Are you that devoid of compassion?

But all it took was thinking about my mother alone in her hospital room, her body weak from two years of chemo and radiation that hadn't cured her, her shaky voice asking if we'd heard from him, to harden my resolve. He hadn't been there for her in the end. I didn't have to be there for him. If that made me a heartless bastard, so be it.

At one point, I went into the house to use the bathroom, and as I was coming back through the kitchen, Winnie was coming in. "Hey," she said, looking at me with concern. "Are you sure everything is okay?"

"I already said it was," I snapped.

"I know, but you don't seem like you're having much fun."

"Well, you don't know me."

Her expression went from worried to hurt. "Dex, I just—"

"Look, just because we fucked doesn't mean I have to tell you everything. Leave me alone." Hating myself, I shouldered by and went back outside.

When she came out a few minutes later, the color had drained from her face, and her nose looked a little pink, like maybe she'd been crying. She didn't sit next to me like she had been before—instead she took a seat next to my sister and asked if she could hold the baby.

Furious and having only myself to blame, I slouched lower in my chair like a toddler in time-out and ignored everyone.

I was in such a shitty mood, I didn't even stay as late as I could have, despite the fact that Naomi never sent a pestering text. Around four, I collected the girls, who complained about leaving and crabbed the whole way home, which only made me crankier. I yelled at them to stop fucking whining, which made Luna cry and Hallie give me the evil eye in the rearview mirror.

"You don't have a ten anymore, Daddy. You have a one."

Next to me, Winnie sat with her palms pressed together between her knees, totally silent. When we pulled up in my driveway, she barely waited before the car was in park before getting out. "Bye, girls," she said, giving them a quick wave before going into her house.

"Is Winnie mad at us?" Luna asked tearfully.

"No. She's mad at me."

"Why?"

"Don't worry about it," I snapped before taking the edge off my tone. Pinching the bridge of my nose, I exhaled. "Please just go in the house and pack your bags."

After returning the girls to Naomi—they gave me hugs good-bye I didn't deserve—and telling them to have a good first day at school tomorrow, I went home and threw myself facedown on the couch. I had laundry to do and dishes to put away and bathrooms to clean, but I didn't feel like doing any of it. I just wanted to stew in my anger and self-righteousness.

Because I was fucking right, wasn't I? Bree was wrong, and I was right. It was like she'd erased all the horrible memories of what it was like every time he decided to show up in our lives. It was bad enough that we'd gone through it—why would she want to subject our children to the same bullshit? And what for? So they could learn they had a grandfather just to watch him die? What kind of stories were we supposed to tell about him?

Still . . . I know I shouldn't have spoken to Winnie like that.

Hallie was right. I was an ogre.

Flopping onto my back, I draped an arm over my fore-head. Every time I thought about the hurt expression on her face when I'd snapped at her, or her pink nose when she came outside and didn't want to be near me, my chest caved. But apologies didn't come easy to me—mostly I was the kind of guy who'd rather dig his heels in and claw at the dirt than admit he was wrong or at fault.

And really . . . was I all *that* wrong? What was so bad about what I'd said? It was the truth! It's not like we were dating. But it reminded me of the guilt I felt after Naomi would accuse me of shutting down or pushing her away. "You make it painful to love you," she'd say. "Why won't you let me in?"

I scowled, the old resentment bleeding fresh. I'd never asked her to love me. This was why I was better off alone. I didn't want to owe anyone an explanation or an apology. I didn't want to be responsible for someone else's feelings. I couldn't be trusted with them.

In the end, I lay there so long I fell asleep. When I woke up, it was dark, and I sat up, groggy and disoriented. Checking my phone, I discovered it was after nine o'clock. I also discovered I'd missed a call from my sister and a text from Justin asking if I was okay.

But I didn't feel like talking to anyone. Exhaling, I set my phone aside and rubbed my face with both hands. There was a gaping pit in my stomach, and my head was throbbing.

I turned off all the lights and went upstairs to bed.

Seventeen

Dex

I WAS PREPARED FOR JUSTIN TO GRILL ME AT WORK THE NEXT morning, but he didn't. In fact, he said nothing to me at all, which made me feel even worse.

Naomi sent me some photos of the girls' first school morning, and their joyful smiles tugged at my heart. I felt terrible for yelling at them yesterday. None of this was their fault.

I went through the motions of my shift, which was uneventful. On one level, this was a good thing, since it meant there were no dire emergencies. But it left me with a lot of free time and headspace to think about things—Winnie, my father, my sister, my kids, my behavior—and none of it made me feel good about myself.

After dinner, I finally broke down and sought Justin out in the dorm room where he slept. He was seated at the desk flipping through a binder.

"Hey." I leaned on the doorframe.

He barely glanced up. "Hey."

"Aren't you going to ask me about yesterday?"

"No."

"Why not?"

"It's not my business." He shrugged. "And Bree told me not to."

I frowned. "Is she mad at me?"

"No, I wouldn't say she's *mad*. I think she's hoping you'll change your mind, but she understands why you feel the way you do." He flipped a page in the binder. "She knows you."

I hung around in the doorway another minute, scratching at a nick in the frame. "I was a dick to Winnie yesterday."

"I figured something must have gone wrong."

"It did." When he didn't ask me what it was, I kept going. "She knew I was upset about something, and when she wouldn't leave me alone about it, I jumped down her throat."

He nodded. Turned another page.

"I was mad at my dad and at the situation, and maybe even at my sister for being so trusting, and I took it out on her." I cringed. "I said something real fucking shitty to her, and I'm sorry about it."

Justin finally looked up. "Maybe you should be saying this to her, man."

I exhaled. "Yeah, I know."

After leaving the station Wednesday morning, I ran some errands and spent the afternoon painting the girls' bedroom as a surprise for them—the wall behind Luna's bed pink, the one behind Hallie's bed lavender.

Dad guilt in all its pastel glory.

I looked at my phone a hundred times, but with every hour that went by, it just got harder to reach out.

Around seven, I called the girls, who told me all about their first couple days at school. Hallie was excited about a new friend she'd made, Luna adored kindergarten so far, and neither of them said a word about Winnie or my grumpy mood the other day—it was like they didn't even remember it.

But I was sure Winnie hadn't forgotten a thing.

Finally, just after eight o'clock, I sat down at the foot of my bed and sent her a text.

Sorry about Monday. I was a jerk.

I sent that, and while I was wondering if I should offer an excuse, she replied.

You were.

Exhaling, I texted her again. **Can I explain?**

You can try.

I don't want to do it over text. Can I come over?

She didn't respond right away.

I just got out of the shower.

Give me five minutes.

But I was so anxious to get the apology off my chest, I only gave her three—I didn't even put shoes on, I just ran over there in bare feet, gray sweatpants, and a white T-shirt.

She answered the door in a short robe that tied at the front, her hair wet and uncombed, and a brush in her hand. She looked so young and pretty without makeup, my breath hitched. But her expression was anything but friendly.

"Come in," she said tonelessly.

I followed her into her living room. When she sat on one end of the couch, I sat on the other. Rubbed my hands over my knees. Took a breath. "I owe you an apology."

She began brushing her hair. Pinned me with cool, detached eyes. "Yes. You do."

"I'm sorry for the way I treated you. You didn't deserve it."

"You really hurt my feelings."

"I know." I swallowed hard. "I could tell."

"I was just trying to make sure you were okay. As a friend."

"I wasn't okay. But that's no excuse for the things I said." I took another deep breath. "You didn't do anything wrong, Winnie. I was angry about something else and lashed out at you. I sincerely apologize."

"Apology accepted," she said, tugging at tangles at the back of her head.

Relieved—and grateful she was so understanding and sweet—I leaned over and reached for the brush. "Let me."

"Huh?"

"Come sit here." I moved toward the middle of the couch and widened my knees, patting the cushion between them.

She looked a little dubious, but she did as I asked. "You're going to brush my hair?"

"Yes," I said, starting at the bottom. "I have to make up for being a jerk to you. And besides, I'm good at this."

She was silent as I combed through her hair with slow, smooth strokes. It smelled delicious—like coconut.

"How was your interview?" I asked.

"Good."

"Did she offer you the job?"

"Yes."

"Did you accept?"

She hesitated. "Yes. I did. But I haven't even told anyone yet. You're the first."

"Congratulations," I said, even though my heart sank at the thought of her leaving. "You must be really excited."

"The hotel is undergoing some renovations, so I won't go until early October, but yes—I'm excited. I think it will be good for me." She paused. "I think maybe I need a change."

"Change can be good." Her hair was all combed out, but I kept brushing it. "Bree said my father wants to see us. He's got terminal lung cancer. That's what upset me on Monday."

"Oh." She put a hand on my leg. "I'm really sorry, Dex."

"The last time I saw him was at my mother's funeral. That was seven years ago. He hadn't been around before that in years—she had breast cancer and went through treatment alone. Then he showed up all sad and somber, like he gave a fuck."

She didn't say anything. Her silence was inviting, and the fact that I could talk without eye contact helped too.

"I guess he's sober and remarried now. Bree is in touch with his new wife. She asked if we'd consider reconciling with him."

"That's got to be a tough decision."

I exhaled. "Bree feels bad for him. I don't know if I do or not. What does that say about me?"

"It says you were very hurt by him as a child. And that your feelings are complicated."

"Yeah." I watched the bristles slide through her hair. "Bree has always been more forgiving than me. She's like our mom was."

"You make being forgiving sound like a bad thing."

I frowned. "It is where my father is concerned. You can't trust him to mean what he says. How do we even know he really has cancer?"

"Dex," she said softly.

But I dug in deeper. "I will never allow him near my children. He forfeited that right years ago."

"He wants to see the girls too?"

"Yes. And Bree's kids. She said she's thinking about it." I dropped my arms. "But I can't. And I won't feel bad about it. I'm protecting them."

"That's your right as a father."

I sighed, tipping my forehead against the back of her head. How did she know exactly what I needed to hear? Again, I was really fucking sad she was moving away. And I didn't want to think about my family anymore.

Winnie took the brush from my hand and set it aside, then surprised me by circling my wrists and wrapping my arms around her like a blanket. "You're a good dad, Dex."

"But I'm a shitty friend."

"Oh, I don't know. This was a pretty nice apology."

"I had to make things right with you. Your face was haunting me."

She laughed gently. "Good."

Her hair smelled so nice, I couldn't resist burying my nose in it and inhaling. Or sliding one hand inside her robe. Or pressing my lips to her shoulder. "So have I?"

"Have you what?" she whispered as I moved her hair aside and kissed the back of her neck.

"Made things right."

"I mean, you're on the right track . . ." She tilted her head, allowing me to devour one side of her throat. "But it might take some more effort."

"Yeah?" I pulled the belt on her robe loose and moved both hands to her breasts. She arched her back, pushing them into my hands.

"Dex," she whispered. "Do you want to come upstairs?"

Without hesitation, I stood up, sweeping her into my arms and heading for the stairs. "How's this for effort?"

She gasped and looped her arms around my neck. "This is *such* good effort. Don't stop."

I carried her up the stairs. "Last time I came up here, your smoke alarm was going off."

"This time there's a real fire," she murmured, kissing the side of my neck.

I entered her bedroom and placed her on the bed, then opened up her robe and slid her underwear off. Her blinds were open, and moonlight spilled in through the windows, bathing her skin in silver. "Finally. God, you're beautiful."

"Thank you."

I took off my shirt and ditched my pants in record time. Then I climbed onto her bed and stretched out above her, my cock thick and hard between us. "I've been thinking about this for days."

"Me too." She wrapped her legs around me and slid her

hands into my hair. "I would lie here at night and think of you one wall over, and wish you were here. Of course, that was before I got mad at you."

"I'm here now," I told her. "And I won't leave until we're friends again—no matter what it takes." Then I stopped moving. "Fuck!"

"What?" She realized before I even said it. "Oh—no condom."

"No condom." I started to pull back, but she held on to me.

"Wait," she said. "I'm okay if you are. I'm on the pill."

"I haven't been with anyone since my divorce—and actually a while before that."

"Then don't stop," she whispered, kissing my jaw as she tightened her legs around me. "We're not quite friends yet."

Eighteen

Winnie

THAT NIGHT, DEX WAS SURPRISINGLY TENDER.

I wasn't sure if it was because he was still trying to make amends or he was just revealing another side of himself, but either way, it was different than it had been before.

He used his mouth on me first—kissing his way from my toes all the way up the backs of my legs and along my inner thighs. He licked me slowly and softly, gently sweeping his tongue over my clit or tracing little circles around it, barely using any pressure at all. He used his fingers too, but didn't push them in deep. Instead, he teased me with light, shallow strokes, ignoring my impatient wriggling beneath his touch. And he brought his hands to my breasts, brushing his thumbs over my nipples as I arched and writhed, trying to get him to give me what I wanted.

"Dex," I whimpered, sliding my fingers into his hair. "Don't tease me."

He laughed gently, but moved his tongue faster and harder, pinching my nipples, sucking my clit into his mouth.

I came so hard I saw stars, and before I could even breathe again, I was reaching beneath his arms to drag him up my body, frantic with the need to feel him driving into me the way he had before—uncontrollably, desperately, ferociously—but this time with no barrier between us.

But he refused to rush, easing inside me with deliciously slow, measured strokes, giving me a little more each time. When he was buried to the hilt, his eyes closed, like this was heaven to him and nothing had ever felt so good. I inhaled deeply, drunk on the scent of his skin and the way he filled me and the masculine weight of his hips between my thighs. Running my hands down his back over his round, muscular ass, I pulled him in deeper. He groaned and crushed his lips to mine, kissing me passionately before he began to move.

There's nothing between us, I thought blissfully. *We're as close as two people can possibly be.*

And I felt myself unraveling in a way that wasn't just physical.

Instantly on alert, I spanked him playfully. "What's with being so gentle?"

"I'm trying *very* hard tonight," he replied, his voice tight with the struggle.

"Dex." I urged him to move faster with my hands and my hips. "Don't hold back. I want to make you come."

"Fuck. You don't know what it does to me when you say that stuff."

"When I tell you I want your cock?" I said breathlessly. "When I tell you how good it feels inside me?"

He growled angrily, getting rougher. Faster. Harder. Deeper. It was exactly what I needed to keep my feelings locked up where they belonged. This wasn't about being close to him.

This was about heat. Friction. Desire. Chemistry. Sweat.

His body on mine. His thick, hard cock pumping inside me, rubbing against me, taking me higher, making me gasp and bite and cry out and dig my nails into his muscles. A moment later, he was pouring himself into me, groaning long and loud as my body tightened and pulsed around him.

"Okay," I panted. "Okay, we're friends again."

"Are you sure?" His breathing was ragged and quick. "Because I could come back tomorrow and keep trying to win you over."

I paused. "Right. Good point. I take it back."

Laughing, he lifted his chest off me and looked down. "You do?"

"Yes—you're still a jerk, and you need to go home and think about what you did."

"Oh, I will." He pressed his lips to mine. "You can be damn sure of that."

A little later, I walked him down to the door. "How was the girls' first day at school? I was thinking about them yesterday."

"Good. I pick them up Sunday after church. I'm sure they'll be on your doorstep soon afterward."

I laughed, pulling my robe closed tighter around me. "I'd like that."

"They'll be sad to hear you're moving."

"I'm sad to move away too, but the offer is too good to pass up." I'd been telling myself that for two days.

He nodded. "And you leave when? Early October?"

"Yes. I have to fly back a couple weeks later for that wine tasting dinner I'm co-hosting with Ellie, but the woman who hired me said that was no problem."

He thought for a moment. "So you have about a month here."

"Right." I gave him a flirty grin. "Think you can fully redeem yourself in thirty days?"

"I don't know," he said seriously, scratching his head above his right ear. "I mean, you're pretty hard to please."

"It's the new me." I stood taller. "I'm setting higher standards for myself."

He took my forearm and pulled me toward him, wrapping me in his arms. "Good. You should."

With my cheek against his chest, I snuggled against his warm, hard body and waited for him to make another joke, but he didn't. Tucked in the shelter of his embrace, I felt safe and content—so safe and content, I quickly grew uneasy.

"Okay, time for bed." Gently, I pushed against his chest and stepped back. "See? This is me being independent. The old me would have asked you to stay the night."

"And the new you is kicking my ass out?"

I nodded. "Straight to the curb."

"Good." He pulled the door open and glanced over his shoulder. "I'll talk to you tomorrow."

"Night."

Then he was gone, pulling the door closed tight behind him. I was still standing there looking at it when two soft knocks made me jump. I pulled it open.

"I forgot to tell you I don't love you." He shrugged. "Given how nice I was tonight, I didn't want you to get worried or anything."

I laughed. "Thanks for the reminder. I don't love you either."

But as I went up the stairs, I couldn't help thinking it was a damn good thing I was moving away soon. Because I might not love him now, but I could.

I easily could.

Around one the following afternoon, I knocked on my Aunt Chloe's office door.

She looked up from her computer and smiled. "Hey, Win. What can I do for you?"

"Got a minute?" I asked.

"Of course." She closed her laptop. "Take a seat."

I perched on the edge of one of the chairs in front of her desk and looked around. Her office was bigger than my dad's, but just like his, the shelves were full of family photos—a wedding picture of her and Oliver; school photos of their teenagers, Sawyer and Elsa; a professional family photo of them on the beach in coordinating khaki pants and white button-downs.

She followed my line of sight and laughed. "Oh God, that picture. I fought Oliver so hard on those stupid matching outfits, but apparently it's some sort of Pemberton family tradition."

"It's a nice shot," I said. "Your family is so beautiful. Elsa looks just like you."

Her sigh was wistful. "Hard to believe she's in high school now. Time flies."

I nodded, my fingers twisting together. "I wanted to talk to you about something."

"Shoot."

"I was offered a job as head of events at an inn in Newport called The Alexander."

Her eyebrows rose. "Good for you. Did you take it?"

"I did," I said, "but it doesn't start until October, so I'll be here at least three more weeks. I can help you find someone to replace me, if you'd like."

She waved a hand in the air. "Don't worry about that. I'm excited for you! Tell me about the job."

Relaxing, I described the position to her, and she eagerly opened her laptop and checked out the Alexander's website.

"Oh, Winnie, it's gorgeous—that architecture! The setting!" She clucked her tongue. "You're going to love it. And they're so lucky to get you."

"Thanks."

She closed her computer again. "Have you told your folks?"

"They know about the offer, but I haven't told them I accepted yet."

She grinned ruefully. "Frannie will cry buckets just like she did when Felicity moved to Chicago."

I laughed. "Well, she knew it was a possibility."

"This is so great, Winnie. I'm thrilled for you. And of course we'll miss you around here, but I completely understand wanting to broaden your horizons."

"Thank you." I paused. "I really do love it here. Cloverleigh Farms has always felt like home to me."

"Sometimes we have to leave home to chase our dreams." She sighed, looking around. "And sometimes we find ourselves right back where we started, and that's okay too."

I laughed. "Thanks, Aunt Chloe."

"You're welcome, darling." She blew me a kiss as I rose to my feet. "I'm always here if you need anything."

I'd just gotten home from Pilates that evening when I heard a knock at my door. I pulled it open to find a grouchy-looking Dex on my porch.

"So where can I adopt a cat?"

I laughed. "You want to adopt a cat?"

"Fuck no." He exhaled loudly and held out a folded piece of paper. "But the girls won't leave me alone about it. I just found a note in a dresser drawer they must have written last time they were here."

I took the note and unfolded it. It was written on lined paper that had been torn out of a notebook. The print was round and childish but neat.

Dear Daddy,

We think we should be aloud to have a cat here. We will take good care of it. You can hug it when we are not here. You need more hugs so you do not turn in to an oger.

Love,

Halsy Pal and Loony Toon

I smiled and looked up at him. "An ogre?"

"Yeah. Did I tell you about the story Hallie is writing?"

"No. Is there an ogre in it?"

"Yes. Named Rex. There's also a princess named Minnie."

I clapped a hand over my mouth. "Not too subtle, is she?"

"Nope. Anyway, a cat isn't a sailboat or a fancy vacation or even a horse, but it's something they'll love." He sighed, closing his eyes. "And I'm a sucker, just like you said."

"I think it's great. I'll get you the name of a few adoption places. And my offer still stands to feed the cat while you're at work." I paused. "At least until I move."

"Thanks."

"I can probably help you find someone in the complex willing to swing by and feed it. There's a widowed lady who lives one building over that's really nice."

"Sounds good." He reached for the note. "Have you eaten dinner yet?"

"No. I just got home." I pulled my sticky shirt away from my body. "I worked out, so I was going to shower before I thought about food. I'm sweaty."

"I was just going to order some takeout. Want to come over and eat with me?"

"Sure."

"Do you like Thai food?"

I rubbed my belly. "Love it."

"Okay. I'll order some different things, and we can share."

"Perfect. I'll be over in about half an hour."

"Cool." He put a hand on the door, pushed it wider and stepped over the threshold, staring me down. "This isn't a date."

"Thank God."

"But if you want to wear the sexy black underwear, I won't be mad."

Laughing, I turned him around and shoved him out the door.

"How did you even find this show?" Dex asked me a couple hours later. After dinner, we'd decided to veg out on the couch and watch TV. I'd convinced him to watch a few episodes of *Bewitched*.

"I don't remember. I think my grandmother liked it, and we'd watch it when she'd come to visit us." We sat side by side, our legs propped on the coffee table. Beneath my shorts and oversized sweatshirt, I'd worn the lacy underwear he liked, but he didn't know it—yet. "I loved the idea of being able to wiggle your nose and cast a spell, and no one would know it was you."

He snorted. "I bet you tried it."

"All the time. But it only worked once."

He put an arm around me. "What was the spell?"

"I made my dad fall in love with our nanny."

Dex laughed. "Of course you did."

"I never told a single soul, either. I just wiggled my nose and went about my business, but when it happened, I wasn't a bit surprised."

"Magic," he said.

"Magic."

"I'm gonna try. Am I doing it?"

I looked up to see him concentrating hard at twitching his nose. "Sort of. Now think about something you want to happen."

He closed his eyes. Ten seconds later, he opened them again. "It didn't work."

"What did you wish for?"

"A blowjob."

"Dex!" I spanked his leg. "Magic doesn't work that way."

"Too bad." He flipped me onto his lap so I straddled his thighs. "But it's fine. There are plenty of other things I'd like to make happen."

I whipped my sweatshirt off, revealing my skimpy black bra, gratified when his jaw dropped open. "Like that?"

"Exactly." He pulled me closer and rubbed his face against my breasts. "You just made a believer out of me."

He carried me into his bedroom with my legs wrapped around his waist. After tipping me backward onto the bed, he yanked off my shorts, leaving me in the black bra and panties. "Those stay on," he ordered when I hooked my thumbs in the waistband of the underwear.

He whipped all his clothes off and climbed over me, his eyes hungry and dark—which was when I took him by surprise and flipped him over. It required all my might, and when I had him beneath me, I laughed triumphantly.

"What's this?" he asked.

I grabbed his thick wrists and pushed them to the mattress like he always did to me. "I want to be on top."

"Oh yeah?"

I nodded, slowly rocking my hips, grinding against his hard, swollen cock. "Got a problem with that?"

He growled, his hands curling into fists, then spoke through clenched teeth. "No."

"Good. Now listen to me." Talking to him like this, seeing him beneath me on the bed, had my heart racing and my panties wet. "I'm in control tonight. You don't touch me unless I allow it. You don't come until I say you can. Understand?"

He gave me his angry-bear scowl and lifted his wrists off the bed, letting me know I was only on top because he was permitting it.

I stopped moving. "Understand?"

Beneath me, his massive erection throbbed like it wanted to answer for him. He dropped his wrists again.

"There, see? You're going to like this." Smiling in satisfaction, I leaned forward, brushing the curve of my breasts against his chest, his jaw, his mouth. His arms twitched with the urge to get his hands on me. But since that wasn't allowed, he lifted his head and used his tongue, stroking my nipples through the satin and lace.

"Take it off," he commanded.

I laughed throatily. "Nope. You wanted to leave it on, remember?"

After a string of curses, he used his teeth to drag the thin bra cup beneath one tingling peak and quickly sucked it into his mouth before I could stop him. But truthfully, it felt so good, I arched my back and moaned with pleasure and let him do the same to the other breast while I rocked my hips over his rock-hard abs.

I could feel the impatience growing within him, his body tense and trapped beneath me. I lifted my chest and stared down at him. "Your hands stay right here, or I won't let you come while I ride you."

He didn't answer. His breathing was labored and ragged. I tested him, letting go of his wrists—he left them on the mattress.

Smiling, I shimmied down his body. He inhaled sharply as I fisted his huge cock with one hand and gave it a few tight strokes. He propped himself up on his elbows.

I stopped moving my hand.

"I just want to watch," he said.

"I suppose I could allow that." Kneeling above him, I pulled my panties aside and positioned the tip of his dick between my legs. Then I slid down his length, inch by inch.

Finally, my body rested on his, and he filled me completely. His cock twitched. I smiled, swiveled my hips, and it happened again.

"Fuck this," he growled. "I have to touch you."

"I wouldn't if I were you," I warned, starting to undulate seductively. I lifted my hair and held it on top of my head as I moved above him in slow, sinuous motion. "Not if you want to come tonight."

"I'm about to come right this second."

I laughed. "Not yet, please. I'm just getting started."

He cursed again. "You're going to torture me until I break, is that it?"

"I'm going to fuck you until I come, is that the same thing?" I was already close, but I didn't tell him that.

"Yes," he rasped.

I circled my hips a few more times before putting my hands on his chest and pushing him down again. "Then you'll just have to lie back and take it."

"The day we met, I thought you were so innocent and sweet." He struggled for control as I continued to ride him.

Leaning forward, I grazed my tongue along his bottom lip. "The day we met, I thought about biting you."

"Fuck. Who *are* you?"

Delighted, I took his lower lip between my teeth and tugged, clenching my core muscles at the same time. "Just the girl next door." I laughed. "Are you sorry you invited me over to play?"

"No." He brought his hands to my ass. "But goddammit, you're making me crazy."

I let him keep his hands on me because they felt good, and I moved over him harder and faster, my body tightening around him. My breath was quick and shallow. "God, you feel so good. I want to come on that cock."

"Jesus." His body tensed. His fingers dug into my skin and his hips bucked up beneath me. "Fuck. I'm gonna—"

"Not yet," I told him, nearly delirious with the need for release and the thrill of bossing him around. I was torn between wanting to let go and hang on.

"Come for me," he growled. "Right fucking now."

Unable to hold back any longer, I cried out with every pulse as the orgasm burst open inside me, and a moment later felt his climax surging from his body into mine. I rode it out until I was sure I'd wrung every last drop from him—his low, guttural moans accompanying my high-pitched sighs.

"Fuck, that was mean," he said after I collapsed onto his chest. His heart was thumping hard.

"I quite liked it," I panted. "I felt very powerful."

"Witchcraft." He pinched my ass.

I smiled. "Babe, I had the sexy black underwear. I didn't even need witchcraft."

He laughed, and I realized how much I loved the sound. "But will you take it off now?"

I picked up my head, surprised. "Okay."

He watched as I slipped the lingerie from my body, then reached for me, pulling me down so I lay atop him, head on his chest.

We stayed like that for a moment, our breath still returning to normal, our pulses slowing. He began to run his palms up and down my back. As I stared at the moonlight slanting through his blinds, a childhood memory surfaced.

"When I was young, I hated nighttime," I confessed. "I thought there were monsters under my bed."

"Yeah?"

"I was so scared of them. I'd lie there frozen with fear, too scared to even go get my dad, because I knew for sure that as soon as I put my feet on the floor, that monster would grab my ankles."

Dex kept rubbing my back with slow, reassuring strokes.

"Sometimes, if I worked up enough nerve, I'd stand up on the mattress and take a running jump as far away from the bed as I could and go racing for my dad's room, which was all the way on the first floor of our house—this was before he even got remarried."

"And what would he do?"

"Sometimes it was enough for him to just check and make sure nothing was there. Sometimes he would lie down with me until I fell asleep." I chuckled at a memory. "Sometimes he'd bring the 'monster repellent' and spray it under my bed."

"That's fucking smart."

"It was. He was a great dad, just like you are." My smile faded. "Eventually I outgrew the fear of monsters under my bed. But I guess I never stopped hating the feeling of being left alone at night. Later, my therapist helped me unpack that a bit. She thought it was related to being abandoned by my mom so young. I was afraid everyone I loved would leave me that way, and I didn't feel safe."

His arms closed around me. "I'm sorry. That makes me want to go back and give little Winifred a hug."

"Grownup Winifred likes hugs too." I smiled again, even though my throat felt tight. "In fact, little Winifred grew up craving affection and attention so much that she became a love junkie. When someone made her feel special, she grasped it like a lifeline so she wouldn't drown in her worst fear."

Dex's hands stopped moving. "What was her worst fear?"

"That deep down, she was unlovable." I took a breath. "But now she knows that isn't true—or at least, she's working on it."

"I hope so," he said quietly.

I picked my head up so I could look at him. "Honestly, it's much better than it used to be. I've had a lot of therapy, and I understand myself so much better than I used to. I still make terrible romantic choices sometimes, but I know I deserve to be with someone who makes me feel good about myself and not just lucky to be with them."

"Fuck yes, you do."

"And I'm not scared of monsters under my bed anymore." Then I laughed. "But there *is* this one ogre who likes to mess with me . . ."

"Ha."

I gave him a quick kiss. "I'll be right back. Can I use your bathroom?"

"Sure."

When I came out, Dex was right where I left him, lying on his back in bed, but covered to the waist. His eyes were closed and his breathing was deep and slow, as if he was asleep.

Not wanting to wake him, I tiptoed around, hunting for my clothes.

"And where are you sneaking off to?"

I looked over at him. "I'm not sneaking. I just didn't want to wake you."

"Don't go."

My heart skipped a beat. "Huh?"

"Don't go yet."

"Why?"

He threw a pillow at me. "Because I'm not done messing with you."

Laughing, I scooped up the pillow and brought it back to the bed. "I thought maybe it was against our rules to stay over."

"Listen," he said, taking my arm and pulling me under the covers. "Ogres don't follow any fucking rules. When they want a princess in their bed, they just grab one."

"Any one?"

"Their favorite one," he clarified, flipping me beneath him. "And my favorite happens to be Princess Minnie."

I laughed. "You never told me about the end to the story Hallie wrote."

"It's not over yet. She left me on a terrible cliffhanger."

"What was it?"

"Princess Minnie's cat, Tigger, ran up a tree, and she needs to ask Rex the Ogre for help to get the cat down, but she's scared of him." Dex lowered his head to my chest and kissed by breast, my collarbone, my throat.

"She doesn't know him," I said. "I'm sure he's not that scary once she gets past his hideous, grotesque appearance."

He bit my shoulder for that. "I asked if the ogre was really a prince in disguise."

"And is he?"

"Nope. He's really an ogre." He kissed his way across my collarbone.

"Well, you know, princes are overrated."

"Yeah?"

"Yeah. They're handsome and rich, but they know it. They don't even have to work to get the girl—girls are lining up at the castle door for them. But an ogre . . . an ogre has to woo his lady."

He picked his head up. "*Woo* his *lady*? That sounds hard."

"It is." I wrapped my legs around him. "But you're doing a good job so far. Don't stop."

I woke up with Dex's naked body curled around mine, his arm wrapped around my waist, strong and solid. It was still dark, but I had no idea what time it was—I didn't even want to look. Inhaling deeply, I let the scent of him swim around in my head, reluctant to move.

Again, I had second thoughts about leaving. Maybe we could have made this work. Despite the age gap, we were good together. I loved that he was gruff on the surface but had a soft side he kept hidden. I understood that—no one wants the world to see their weak spots or scars.

Although I'd shown him mine, hadn't I?

Which was funny, really. I'd never even told Merrick about the monsters under my bed, or my mother abandoning us, or my fear of being unlovable. But something about Dex made me want to be vulnerable with him. I felt safe and—

A tiny frisson of worry snuck up my spine.

Gently disentangling myself from his embrace, I sat up and swung my legs over the side of the bed.

"You leaving?" Dex's voice was raw with sleep.

"Yeah. I should go home. I have to be at work early. My alarm is set." Moving tentatively across the room, I felt around on the floor for my bra, finding it over by his dresser. Once it was hooked, I turned around, surprised to see him getting out of bed. "Dex, don't get up."

He said nothing, just pulled open a drawer and tugged on some sweats.

"Guess I left my clothes downstairs."

He laughed. "Wait here. I'll get them."

A few minutes later, he walked me across the driveway

in the dark to my door. Rising on tiptoe, I gave him a hug. "Thanks for the Thai food. And the woo."

"You're welcome."

"Tomorrow I'll text you the names of a couple pet adoption places."

"Thanks."

I unlocked the door. "Night."

"Night."

It wasn't until I was halfway up the stairs that I realized we hadn't said our usual parting lines to each other. I stopped and waited, expecting him to knock again so he could tell me he didn't love me.

But the house stayed silent.

Nineteen

Dex

I RAISED MY ARM TO KNOCK ON THE DOOR LIKE I HAD LAST NIGHT, ready to make the joke again—tell her I didn't love her.

But I couldn't do it.

After what she'd told me tonight, I couldn't do it. Lowering my hand, I stepped off her porch.

She didn't need to hear those words tonight, not even as a joke. She'd trusted me with something fragile, and I didn't want to trample on it. In fact, it was the opposite. I felt even more protective of her than I had before.

Back at home, I stopped in the kitchen for a glass of water. As I drank it, I thought about Winnie being abandoned by her mom so young, about my daughters being shuttled back and forth between their parents, about my own youth spent watching my dad be a husband and father only when he felt like it.

Fuck, did anyone survive childhood without wounds?

Upstairs, I crawled back into bed and caught the scent of Winnie's coconut shampoo. Turning onto my side, I grabbed the pillow she'd used and buried my face in it, inhaling deeply. My entire body warmed, and I wished she was still next to me.

But part of me knew it was a good thing she wasn't.

I didn't want to get used to her. She wasn't mine to protect.

The following day, while I was driving home from the grocery store, I got a call from a number I didn't recognize. I let it go to voicemail and listened to the message once I pulled into the garage.

"Hey Dex, this is Tyler Shaw. I wanted to reach out to you because Chip mentioned that you might be looking for an extra gig, and I could use another conditioning coach at Bayside Sports. It's mostly baseball training for high school kids in the off-season, but I think a lot of these guys would think it was pretty badass to be coached by a Navy SEAL, and who knows? Maybe you'd find the Navy some new recruits. Anyway, give me a call if you're interested. Thanks."

I dialed him back right away. The job sounded great—I enjoyed physical training, and it would be cool to work with high school kids. The extra income would be welcome too.

And the distraction from Winnie.

"Hello?"

"Hey, Coach."

Tyler laughed. "Matthews, I haven't been your coach in what, sixteen years?"

I grinned. "Doesn't matter. You're still Coach to me."

"You get my message?"

"I did, and I'm really interested, but I'm not certified or anything."

"That's okay. You'll be covered by the facility's insurance policy, and I'm just looking for someone that can work on endurance, strength, and mental mettle. I remember that being your superpower as a baseball player, and I figure you probably got a lot of that in your SEAL training."

"Uh. Yeah." I shook my head at the memories of grinder PT. "I can put them through hell if you want."

He laughed. "Just put their attitudes in check and make them better athletes."

"I think I can do that. My only hesitation is my availability." I told him about my twenty-four-hours on, seventy-two-hours off schedule at the station. "I have my daughters during those seventy-two hours off every other week, so the days are always shifting around. But I wouldn't be able to coach while I had them."

"Understood. Why don't you come over here on your next day off and look around, see the facility, the equipment and all that, and we can talk about getting some sessions on the books that work for you?"

I glanced at the time. "I'm off today if you're going to be there for a bit."

"I'm here until five o'clock. Come any time you like."

After wolfing down a sandwich for lunch, I headed over to Bayside Sports, a huge complex just outside of town. The guy at the desk directed me to Tyler's office, and I knocked on the open door.

He looked up from his desk and smiled as he rose to his feet. "Hey, Dex."

"Hey, Coach. Nice place here."

"Thanks." He came around the desk and shook my hand. "Let's have a look around."

He gave me a tour of both the indoor and outdoor facilities, and I was thoroughly impressed with the size, the amount of equipment, and the quality of the machines. We talked about the kind of sessions I might do, how we could schedule them, where they'd fit into an athlete's overall training regimen. He asked if I'd be interested in doing private fitness coaching since he fielded quite a few inquiries from parents looking to give their kids a leg up on the competition, what I'd charge for both group and private sessions, and what my schedule was like through the fall and winter. I told him I was up for helping out wherever I was needed, as long as he could work with my availability.

We went back to his office, where I filled out some paperwork and gave him my schedule for September and October.

"This is totally workable," he said. "I'm going to put a few group sessions on the website for September, and send out an email that we've got a new trainer—a firefighter and ex-Navy SEAL—but his time is limited so if you want to get in, you have to act fast. I'm positive they'll be full in a week."

"Sounds good." While he typed something on his computer, I glanced around his office. He had a lot of photos and memorabilia from his MLB days, but also pictures of his family. I recognized his wife April—Chip's birth mom—and their two younger kids. He also had a big picture of Chip framed on the wall—standing on the mound, looking fierce and ready for battle. It looked like it had been taken in the early days of Chip's Major League career, and I could easily see the resemblance between father and son.

It made me think of my own father. What did he look like now? Was he still tall and wiry? Did he still have dark hair? Mean eyes? Were his knuckles still scarred?

Or would he be old and frail now? White-haired and stoop-shouldered, just another old man shuffling toward death, burdened by the weight of regret. Maybe I wouldn't even recognize him.

Tyler frowned at his computer screen. "Can you text me a short bio by the end of the day?"

"Sure." Maybe Winnie would help me with that.

"Thanks. Before you go, I'll take your picture."

"Okay." I ran a hand over my hair. Had I even brushed it today?

"Don't worry about your hair, Matthews. They're all going to be looking at those guns." He grabbed a shirt from a file cabinet drawer and tossed it at me. "Here. Put this on. It's a medium, so it's probably going to be a little tight, but that's the idea."

I laughed. "Okay."

After the guy at the desk took a picture of me in a very fitted Bayside Sports T-shirt, I shook Tyler's hand, thanked him, and told him I'd get the bio to him later tonight.

"Perfect," he said, giving me a smile. "Welcome to the team."

On my way home from Bayside, I stopped by my sister's house. I hadn't spoken to her all week, and I felt bad about it. She and I were close, and even though I had no intention of changing my mind about seeing our dad, I didn't want that to come between us.

I let myself in her side door just as she was coming into the kitchen. Her eyebrows rose in surprise. "What are you doing here?"

"I don't know." I ran a hand over my hair. "I was in the neighborhood, thought I'd stop in and say hi."

She glanced over her shoulder. "I just got the kids down for a nap. Let's go outside."

"Okay." I went out to the deck and dropped into a chair, slipping my sunglasses on. Bree came out a minute later with a baby monitor, setting it on the table before she sat next to me.

"Justin around?" I asked.

"No. He's at a dentist appointment."

I nodded and looked around their yard. "Tell him I said he should mow the lawn."

She nudged my leg with her foot. "Tell Hallie I said you should stop wearing her clothes."

Glancing down at my ridiculously tight shirt, I chuckled. "My new uniform."

"You got another job?"

"Just part-time. I'm going to do some conditioning sessions over there. Give them a little taste of boot camp."

She laughed. "I'm sure they'll love it."

We sat in silence for a moment. On the monitor, Prescott made a few fussy noises, but settled again.

"How's the first week of school going for the girls?" Bree asked.

"Good." The tension in my jaw eased a little. "They really like their teachers, and Naomi says Hallie hasn't had any anxious mornings."

"Oh, that's wonderful."

"Did I tell you they conned me into getting a cat?"

Bree laughed. "How'd they manage that?"

"They ganged up on me. Sneak attack. But it turns out a cat will be fine alone for twenty-four hours, so I won't need anyone to feed her while I'm at work." I paused. "Although Winnie offered to feed her."

My sister glanced at me. "How's that going?"

"Fine."

"Justin said you were going to apologize to her for something you said."

"Justin has a big mouth," I muttered.

"Well, it was obvious something was wrong on Monday. I didn't need to be told that. I just wondered what it was."

I exhaled. "I was a dick. I said I was sorry. It's done."

"What were you a dick about?"

"None of your beeswax," I said.

"Let me guess." Lifting herself on the arms of the chair, Bree tucked her legs beneath her. "She noticed you acting like a bear with a thorn in his paw and asked what was wrong, and you gave her the finger and told her to mind her own beeswax."

"Something like that," I said with a one-shouldered shrug.

"You know, it wouldn't kill you to tell the truth every once in a while when someone asks if you're okay."

I clenched my jaw again. "I made it right with her."

"Good. So when will you get this cat?"

"Not sure. I don't know how long the adoption process is or even where to go, but Winnie knows a few places." Her name was out of my mouth before I could think.

My sister shook her head. "You're really gonna be lost without her when she moves away, aren't you?"

"I'll be just fine." But I shifted in my chair, and the silence that followed bothered me.

"So what was it you wanted to talk about?"

"Dad, I guess. Did you see him?"

"Not yet. But we spoke again on the phone."

I kept my focus straight ahead and said nothing. Part of me was curious about the conversation, but I refused to ask.

Bree sighed. "I've decided I'm going to visit him next weekend. But you don't have to see him, Dex. I know he was much harder on you, and your memories are different than mine."

"I know I don't have to see him," I said. "But I'm having a hard time letting you do this alone."

From the corner of my eye, I saw her smile. "Aw. You love me."

"Occasionally," I grumbled.

"Well, that's sweet. But I thought about it and talked it over with Justin, and I decided if I'm going to do this, I'm not going to do it hiding behind my big brother."

"And you're ready to forgive him for everything?"

"I don't know, Dex. But it doesn't do much good to keep hanging on to this shit, does it? Why not let it go before he's gone forever and you lose the chance?"

"I just don't think I can," I said stubbornly.

"Well, I need to at least try. But I can handle this on my own. You don't even have to hear about it if you don't want to."

"Fine."

I stayed just long enough to see the kids when they woke up and give Justin shit about his long-ass lawn—he was equally relentless about my tight shirt—and then I headed home.

Feeling restless and agitated, I decided to take a run. It didn't sit right with me, the way my sister seemed able to stare down demons I couldn't. I didn't like thinking of myself as the kind of guy who avoided a challenge. Tyler had mentioned my tough mental mettle from my days on the high school team, and it was true—I'd learned to put my feelings aside and focus on the game. I never brought any bullshit onto the field. That kind of machine-like ability to focus on the job at hand—show up, get it done, and get out—had served me well as a SEAL too. And now as a firefighter.

Five miles later, I returned home and put myself through some strength and core exercises on the lawn just beyond my patio. Pushing myself hard felt good.

After my final push-up, I collapsed on the grass, rolling onto my back. The late afternoon sun was bright in my eyes, and I closed them, breathing hard. A few seconds later, a shadow fell over my face. I opened my eyes, shading them with my hand.

Winnie stood there with a bottle of water. "Thought you might need this."

"Thanks." I sat up and popped to my feet, although I groaned while doing it. "These old bones just took a beating."

She laughed. "I saw. I was sweating just watching you."

I uncapped the water and chugged half of it down. "Did you just get home from work?"

She nodded, glancing down at her dark green Cloverleigh Farms polo and khaki pants. "Yes. I escaped early."

"Nice." I drank the rest of the water. "Guess what I did today?"

"What?"

"Got a side job doing some fitness coaching at Tyler Shaw's sports complex."

Her mouth fell open, and she clapped her hands excitedly. "That's amazing! How'd that happen?"

"He reached out this morning, and I went over there this afternoon."

"Want to train me?" She flexed her biceps, and I gave one a squeeze.

"Yes. You need it."

Sticking her tongue out, she gave my chest a shove. "I'll have you know, I can hold a plank for two solid minutes."

"Sorry," I said, chuckling. "Let me make it up to you. Want to go grab some dinner?"

Her face fell. "I can't. I'm actually just home to change real quick, and then I'm meeting Ellie for dinner downtown."

"Oh. No big deal," I said, even though I was disappointed that I wouldn't get to see her tonight. Tomorrow I worked, and then I'd have the kids.

"I won't be late," she said suggestively, playing with the braid trailing over one shoulder. "Maybe we could hang out when I get back? I could text you?"

"Whatever," I said, like I wouldn't be waiting by the phone. "I'll let you know when I'm home."

"Okay. Have fun." I watched her walk back toward her house, giving me a little wave over one shoulder before she slipped inside the sliding door.

Exhaling, I thumped the empty plastic water bottle against my leg for a moment, annoyed that she had me missing her when she wasn't around. That wasn't part of the deal.

I headed back inside, determined to do a better job keeping those feelings in check.

Twenty

Winnie

"**I** CAN'T BELIEVE YOU'RE ABANDONING ME," ELLIE MOANED, taking a big gulp of her cocktail.

I laughed. "I'm not abandoning you."

"You are. You're abandoning me with my mother and Gianni Lupo, and you're going off to Rhode Island just because someone offered you your *dream job*." She made a face. "Rude."

"That's how I felt when you went off to France without me," I reminded her, taking a sip of my vodka martini. "And maybe you should keep your voice down, since we're in a Lupo restaurant."

"This isn't his restaurant. It's his dad's. I like his dad just fine. And France was different. It was temporary." She sniffed. "This is permanent. You're really leaving me."

"So come with me," I urged. "I'm sure there are wineries near Newport. Can't you find a job out there too?"

Ellie sighed. "I can't. I'm stupidly attached to Abelard. It's always been my dream to work there."

"I understand. It's home to you." I played with the stem of my glass. "It's hard for me to leave home too."

"Are you having second thoughts?" Ellie's eyes widened.

"No, not exactly. I'm committed to the job, it's just . . ." I glanced at a table to our left, where a family was celebrating a fiftieth anniversary. *"Actually, it's nothing. Nerves."*

She eyed me shrewdly as she sipped her gimlet. *"Except that's not your nerves face. That's your I'm-trying-to-keep-from-admitting-the-truth face."*

I tried to hide behind my martini glass while taking a sip. Setting it down, I shrugged. *"I'm . . . I'm kind of into the guy."*

"The neighbor?"

"Yeah. But that's why it's better that I'm leaving, right?"

Ellie studied me with pursed lips. *"I don't know. I mean, it's only been a couple weeks, right?"*

"Right." I sat up taller and told myself to stop being foolish. *"I'm being silly. He's just really cool, and we have a good time together. But it's not serious."*

"Are you guys seeing a lot of each other?" she asked casually.

"Not really." I looked left again. Someone had tied balloons to the backs of their couple's chairs—one said *"50 Years"* and the others were shiny gold hearts. *"Just the nights he doesn't have the kids or work."*

"Every night he doesn't have the kids or work?"

"Um, yeah. So far." I picked up my martini and sipped. *"But we're still just friends with benefits."*

"It's just that you're really digging those benefits?"

I laughed. *"Yeah."*

"Well, maybe you'll meet a hot guy in Rhode Island who can offer you all those benefits but comes with less baggage." She tipped up her gimlet. *"Although if you fall in love with him before Christmas, you still owe me the thing."*

"How are you even going to collect if I live in another state?"

"You'll come home for the holidays at some point, right? You'd never stay away from your family for too long."

"Maybe I won't *tell* you about falling in love with the hot Rhode Island guy," I said teasingly.

Ellie held up one hand. "Please. You are incapable of holding back your feelings. Some people bury them, Win, but you toss them in the air like confetti."

Our server appeared and set down a plate. "Ladies, the grilled peaches and burrata with prosciutto and arugula."

"Did we order this?" I looked at the dish, my mouth watering.

"I don't think we did, but it looks amazing." Ellie smiled at the server. "Some other table is probably waiting for it."

The server shook his head. "The chef sent it out for you."

"He did?" Ellie laughed. "Is it Mr. Lupo?"

"Yes," the server replied.

"Please say thank you for us," I said, spreading my napkin on my lap.

The server nodded. "Enjoy."

Throughout the rest of the meal, extra dishes were sent out to our table—tiny, single-bite amuse-bouches that surprised and delighted us every time. A sautéed scallop dusted with walnut crumbs, a pâté topped with fig and apricot, a roasted baby beet with goat cheese and mint. Our entrées, veal for me and stuffed pork chops for Ellie, were delectable. And for dessert, which neither of us had ordered, our server brought two house-made cannoli.

Although we protested that we were too full to eat them, we took one bite and kept going. When there was nothing but crumbs left on the table, our server came over and smiled. "Did you enjoy the meal?"

"Every bite," I said. "But I'm beyond full, so don't bring us any more food."

He laughed. "How about a digestif? Maybe Limoncello?"

Ellie and I exchanged a glance and shrugged. "Okay," she said. "That sounds good."

"I'll be right back." He was only gone for a couple minutes, returning with two crystal cordial glasses of icy Limoncello.

"Thank you. And please tell Mr. Lupo how much we enjoyed every bite," Ellie said. "That was so nice of him to spoil us all night."

The server nodded, placing his hands behind his back. "You must be good friends."

"He's good friends with my parents," she explained, taking a tiny sip of Limoncello. "I grew up calling him Uncle Nick."

He looked confused a moment. "The chef tonight is Gianni Lupo. Not his father."

Ellie's mouth fell open. "Gianni was the chef tonight? Dammit! If I'd known that, I wouldn't have eaten all those things he sent out."

"Right," I said knowingly. "Because we turn down housemade cannoli all the time." I looked at the server. "Please let him know everything was wonderful, including the service. Thank you."

"You're very welcome." He nodded and backed away. Ellie set down her drink and took out her wallet.

"What are you doing?" I asked her.

"I'm getting ready to leave. Any minute now, Gianni will come out here and gloat that we devoured all his stupid amazing food."

"Ellie, you should be happy he's so good. He's coming to work for Abelard."

"Well, I'm not. He bugs me."

"Don't you think it's time to move on from high school grudges?" I picked up my chilled glass and took a sip of the sweet, tangy liqueur.

"I would if he didn't still act like he was in high school and all girls should fall at his feet and everything he does is so clever and cute!"

"Evening, ladies. Talking about me?" Gianni appeared at our table in his white chef coat, looking pleased with himself.

"Thank you so much for everything tonight, Gianni." I smiled at him while Ellie scowled into her Limoncello. "It was delicious."

He bowed slightly. "My pleasure. I'm glad you liked it."

"We loved it."

Gianni looked at a seething, silent Ellie and grinned at me. "I don't think your friend here agrees."

"She does. She just can't find the words to say how good it was."

He laughed. "Well, I should get back to the kitchen, but I wanted to thank you for coming in and let you know everything is on the house tonight."

"No way," snapped Ellie. "We're paying for it. Bring us the bill."

"There's no bill to bring you." Gianni shrugged. "Just tip your server."

"That's really generous of you," I told him. "Please come over to Cloverleigh Farms soon so I can return the favor."

"I'd love to," he said warmly. "I know the chef there, and I think she's great. Really smart and creative."

I smiled. "You're always welcome."

He looked at Ellie, and pointed at me. "See, that's how you treat people, Héloise," he said, giving her name the correct French pronunciation. "I'm beginning to think it's good that you work down in a cellar and not front of house."

"Bye, Gianni," I said, wishing he'd just leave before Ellie lost her cool completely.

"Ciao, ladies. Enjoy the rest of your evening." With one last boyish grin, he went back to the kitchen.

"Okay, he's gone," I said, watching him disappear into the kitchen. "You can stop turning purple."

"I can't help it," she blustered. "He infuriates me."

I sighed and picked up my drink. "Come on, let's finish up and tip our waiter. I don't want to be out too late."

"Why's that?" One of her brows peaked.

"No reason." I tried to sound breezy as I looked left again. The anniversary party was long gone, but they'd forgotten the balloons. "Fifty years. That's a long time to be married."

"It is," Ellie agreed.

"I wonder what the secret is," I said. "Like why does it seem to work for some people and not others?"

"Maybe some people just aren't cut out for that kind of long-term commitment," Ellie mused. "You have to have a lot of patience. And be really forgiving. And be accepting of the other person's flaws or even just the things about them that make you crazy. Because there will be plenty of those."

I smiled. "Are you thinking about your mom and dad?"

"Yes," she admitted with a laugh. "I love my mom, but she's just wired so tight, sometimes I'm amazed she hasn't snapped yet. Or that my dad hasn't snapped. They're so different."

"Yeah, but I feel like your parents have a pretty good time together." I grinned as I took a sip of my drink. "I mean, judging from the box under—"

"Stop," Ellie pleaded, her eyes desperate. "I beg you not to finish that sentence."

I laughed and set my glass down. "Okay. But all I'm saying is, that kind of chemistry matters."

"Is that why you're rushing home tonight?" Her eyes danced with light. "To study chemistry?"

"There are worse ways to spend an evening," I said.

She touched her glass to mine. "I'll drink to that."

Dex's house was dark when I pulled into my garage around

nine, so I figured he must have gone to bed already. Even so, I decided to send him a quick text. **Hey you. I'm home, but no worries if you're already asleep.**

Setting my phone aside, I gave Piglet some food and attention, but she seemed more interested in her dinner than me. I grabbed a bottle of water from the fridge and was unscrewing the cap when my phone buzzed on the counter.

In bed but not asleep.

I smiled and replied. **What are you wearing?**

Not much.

Leaning back against the island, I wondered if I should invite him over. **What would it take to get you naked?**

Also not much.

I laughed to myself. **Do it.**

Alone?

If you like. Or you could come over and get naked with me.

I swear he knocked less than a minute later. I pulled open the door, backed up, and gasped in mock horror. "It's the ogre next door! What shall I do?"

He slammed the door behind him. "Run."

Shrieking wildly, I took off for the stairs, where he caught me around the waist, threw me over his shoulder and took the steps up two at a time. Continuing to howl, I kicked my feet and thumped my hands on his back. Up in my room, he threw me down on the bed and tore my clothes from my body while I did my pretend best to fight back. After ditching his jeans and T-shirt, he crawled over me, both our chests heaving. "Remind me to tell you how to escape a house. You don't fucking run up the stairs."

"Maybe I wanted to get caught."

He shook his head. "Poor little princess. Do you have any idea how loud I'm going to make you scream?"

"And there's no one around to hear me in this dark, deserted forest, is there?"

"Nope." He anchored my arms over my head. "You're all mine to do with what I please."

"Is this payback for last night?"

He laughed, low and sinister.

My entire body shivered.

"Did you have a good time at dinner tonight?" Dex's fingers trailed up and down my back.

"Yes."

"Where'd you go?"

"Trattoria Lupo. The food was delicious." Almost as delicious as lying here in his arms. "And we ended up getting the whole meal on the house because Ellie's family knows the owners."

"Nice."

"What did you do for dinner?"

"Blackened some chicken. Not on purpose."

I laughed. "There was a fiftieth anniversary party at the table next to us."

"Yeah?"

"Mhm." I started tracing his collarbone with a fingertip. "That's a long time, isn't it?"

"Fuck yeah, it is. I don't know how anyone does it."

I bit my lip. "Can I ask what went wrong with you and Naomi?"

He exhaled. "We never should have gotten married in the first place. We did it for the wrong reasons—at least I did."

"What were your reasons?"

"You'll think I'm a shitty person if I tell you."

"No, I won't." Picking up my head, I propped it in my hand, my arm over his chest. "Tell me."

"I cared about Naomi, but we'd been broken up for like six years at that point. I was home on leave and we ended up messing around—she'd just gotten out of a terrible relationship and I'd just served back-to-back tours, my mom had just gotten her diagnosis . . . both of us were lonely and looking for escape, and reliving old times seemed like the answer. It should have ended there, but we got drunk one night and she threw out the idea of getting married. I thought about it for three seconds and said okay."

"That's what you said? 'Okay?'"

"Yeah. Because I'd never had any real desire to get married before, but you know what I did have a desire to do?"

"What?"

"Succeed at something where my dad failed. Prove I was a better man."

I pressed my lips together. "Oh."

"Told you it was shitty."

"I think it's . . . understandable, given your background."

"Maybe. But it's not a good reason to get married."

"No," I agreed.

"We did it fast, before I shipped out again. And she got pregnant with Hallie right away. But the long separations didn't do us any favors, and being married to a SEAL is tough. She hated the absences, the intensity of the job, the questions I couldn't answer. She always accused me of being distant, even when I was there. Said I wasn't a family man."

"So she asked you to leave?"

"Yeah. I probably would have stayed in it for the kids' sake—or to prove I wasn't my dad again—so in a way, it's good that she ended it. Put us both out of our misery."

"Yeah." I put my head down again. "I suppose that took a lot of guts for her to do."

"And it was all for the best. Now she's going to marry Bryce, and *he* has to put up with her nagging. Meanwhile, I get to enjoy my freedom and the occasional romp with the princess next door." He tugged on my hair. "I was lying there thinking about you when you texted."

I smiled. "What were you thinking about?"

"That I wished you were home already, so I could come over and ravage you. You're moving out soon, and what if the next neighbor who moves in isn't as cute as you? I might not want to get naked with them."

Giggling, I slapped his chest. "You're not even going to miss me, are you?"

When I tried to roll away, he caught me from behind and wrapped me up tight in his arms, his erection pushing against my ass. "Ogres don't miss anybody. That's the best part of being an ogre."

"Let me go, I can't breathe," I protested, squirming in his embrace. "Go back to your lonely ogre cave."

"I'm going." He flipped me onto my back and reached between my legs, where I was still warm and wet. "But not yet."

Playfully, I fought back, beating my fists against his chest as he moved between my thighs. After sliding inside me, he pinned my hands outside my shoulders.

I grinned up at him, but he wasn't teasing anymore. His eyes smoldered in the dark as he moved above me, and my smile faded. He didn't kiss me, but his face hovered above mine close enough that I felt his breath on my lips. I dug my heels into the backs of his muscular legs and wove my fingers into his hair. For the first time tonight—maybe the first time ever with us—none of this felt like a game.

Not his body buried deep inside mine. Not the fiery heat between us. Not even the words he spoke as he rocked his hips above me.

"I don't love you." His voice was low and raw, straining with urgency. "I don't love you."

And he crushed his mouth to mine before I could say it back.

Afterward, he rolled out of bed quickly and yanked his jeans on. "I have to work tomorrow, and I pick up the girls on Sunday. Will you be around?"

I tried to keep things light, even though the intensity of our last round had me uneasy. "If you're lucky. So do I have to walk the ogre out?"

"No. That's another good thing about ogres." He pulled his shirt over his head. "We are very self-sufficient. I'll lock the door. I can't have anyone else messing with my princess."

"Thank you."

He came over and kissed the top of my head. "Night."

"Night."

When I heard the door shut downstairs, I flopped onto my back and lay there for a moment starfish-style. My heart continued to pound in a way that scared me, every beat telling me that *this* was something special, *this* was something different, *this* was what love songs were written about.

This was *it*.

I bolted upright.

"No, it's not," I said quickly, scrambling to the edge of my bed and hopping off. "I'm not listening to you, heartbeat. This is not it."

I hurried into the bathroom and drowned out my heart with running water while I washed my face, then the buzz of my electric toothbrush. Back in my room, I sang "Yankee

Doodle" loudly and off-key while I put my pajamas on, because it was the only song I could think of that wasn't about love.

Then I jumped into bed and buried my head under the pillow.

On my nightstand, my phone vibrated, and I sat up to reach for it. When I saw the text, I started to laugh.

What the hell is going on over there?

That's my singing voice.

Jesus.

My choir teachers used to ask me to mouth the words at concerts.

Can't say I blame them. Should I put some earplugs in or is the concert over tonight?

I guess it's over. Unless you have a request.

My request is that you stop singing.

I'm done.

Thank God. Night.

Laughing to myself, I set my alarm and put my phone back on the charger. Wrapping my arms around my pillow and hugging it close, I took a few deep breaths.

Hello, heart? This is brain. We'd like to remind you of the rules on this ride.

In order to stay safe, you must keep your hands, feet, and feelings inside the cart at all times. We cannot be responsible for items that are lost or stolen. In case of an emergency, please use the nearest exit.

But my heart refused to listen.

Late Sunday afternoon, there was a knock on my front door. When I opened it, I saw Hallie and Luna standing on my porch. They wore nice clothes, as if they'd been to church, and Hallie's two French braids were perfect and even—pretty, but I sort of liked Dex's lopsided pigtails better.

"Hi, girls! How are you?"

"Good." Luna beamed. "Daddy painted our room. Pink *and* purple."

"I heard. Do you love it?"

"Yes!"

"But we came to tell you something even better," Hallie said.

"What's that?"

"We're getting a cat!" Luna said excitedly. "We went to the adoption place right after church today and picked him out."

"Yay!" I clapped my hands. "Come in and tell me about him. Does your dad know you're here?"

"Yes," Hallie said as they followed me to the kitchen. They climbed onto the stools at my island. "He said we could knock on your door, but if you weren't home we had to come right back."

"I'll send him a quick text." I grabbed my phone and sent Dex a note letting him know the girls were with me, then set it aside. "Okay, tell me everything."

"He's black with white feet," gushed Luna.

"And he's so soft," added Hallie. "He loves to be petted."

"I can't wait to meet him. When can you bring him home?"

"Tomorrow after school," said Hallie. "So after we change clothes, we're going to the pet store to get food and a bed and some toys for him."

"What are you going to name him?" I asked.

The girls looked at each other. Hallie sighed. "That's a problem."

"Why?"

"Daddy said since we picked the cat, he gets to name him."

I laughed. "What does he want to name him?"

"Here are the choices." Hallie pulled a piece of paper from her skirt pocket and read it solemnly. "Steven Tyler, Freddie Mercury, or Eddie Van Halen."

I covered my mouth with one hand. "Which one do you like best?"

Hallie looked at me like I was nuts. "None of them. Those aren't cat names. Those are man names."

"I like Freddie," said Luna.

"I do too," I told her. "And what if you called him Freddie Purrcury?"

Hallie perked right up. "That's perfect! I mean—*purr*fect."

"Hello?" Dex's voice floated through the screen door.

"Come on in!" I called.

I heard the door open and close, and he appeared in the kitchen a moment later. He was also dressed for church, in charcoal gray pants and a light blue button-down. I'd never seen him in that color blue before, and I liked the way it looked against his skin. My pulse quickened when he smiled at me.

"Hey," I said. "I'm just hearing all about your new cat."

"We'll name him Freddie Purrcury," Luna said. "Is that okay with you?"

Dex groaned. "I guess."

"I think it's a good compromise," I said, patting his shoulder.

"Can Winnie come to the pet store with us, Daddy?" Hallie asked.

"Please," added Luna, clasping her hands in prayer beneath her chin.

"That's up to her," Dex said.

I hated to disappoint them, but I couldn't. "I'm sorry, girls. But my real estate agent is coming over, so I have to stay here."

"What's a real estate agent?" Luna asked.

"It's the person who's going to help me sell my condo."

"You're moving?" Hallie's eyes were wide.

I felt sad, breaking the news. "Yes. I have to, because I have a new job in Rhode Island."

"Where's Rhode Island?" Luna looked from me to her dad. "Is it close?"

Dex shook his head.

"So we won't see you anymore?" Hallie asked, looking like she might cry. "Ever again?"

"Sure, you will. I'll come back for visits." I tried to sound reassuring. "I just won't live next door anymore."

"But who will live here?" asked Luna, her expression worried. "And will they adopt Piglet?"

"Piglet will come with me," I told her with a smile. "And you'll have a new neighbor living here—maybe even some kids. That would be fun."

They didn't look convinced.

"I'm sad," Luna said.

"Me too," added Hallie. "I don't want you to go."

"Hey, listen." Dex spoke up, reaching over to tweak Luna's ear. "How about, 'Congratulations on your new job, Winnie?' Or 'We're happy for you, Winnie?' Or even 'We'll miss you, Winnie, but we'll keep in touch?' Stop making her feel bad. She has to move for work."

"Sorry," Hallie said. "Congratulations on your new job, Winnie."

"We're happy for you." Luna sounded anything but happy.

"Thank you." I smiled, although I didn't feel happy either at the moment. "I'll really miss having you right next door, but your dad is right. We can keep in touch."

"We can email from my iPad, Luna," Hallie said.

"That's perfect." I reached for the pad of paper where I scribbled my grocery list and wrote down my personal email address. "Here. Email me any time."

"Are you leaving before tomorrow?" Luna looked scared. "You won't be able to meet Freddie Purrcury."

"No," I said, laughing. "I'm not leaving until October. I've got a whole month here. And I cannot *wait* to meet Freddie Purrcury."

"Come on, girls." Dex gestured for the kids to get down from their stools. "We have to go change and get to the pet store before it closes. And Winnie doesn't want us in here messing up her place before the agent gets here."

"It's no big deal," I said. "She's just going to give me some advice for showing it and help me come up with a listing price."

"Hopefully, it sells quickly." He shooed the girls toward the front door.

"Yes, hopefully so." I crossed my fingers and held them up, although I felt like hiding them behind my back. "Have fun at the pet store."

It felt strange watching him leave without a hug or our usual jokes, and the place seemed extra empty once they were gone.

Piglet came wandering out, now that the coast was clear, twining around my ankles. When she meowed, I knelt down to pet her.

"Don't scold me, okay? I'm only sad because I like our usual goodbyes. I like his hugs. I like his kisses. That's not the same as being in love with someone."

But it was a slippery slope, and even Piglet knew it.

Twenty-One

Dex

"**W**HERE YOU BEEN, MAN?" JUSTIN ASKED, PEDALING hard on the stationary bike.

"What are you talking about?" I slowed to a jog on the treadmill. "I see you at work every few days."

"You haven't come to the house since Labor Day. That was nearly a month ago."

"I've been busy."

"Busy with your girlfriend?"

"I don't have a girlfriend." I kept my eyes straight ahead but knew exactly what look he was giving me.

"I thought things were going better since you took my advice and apologized."

"Things are fine. She's just not my girlfriend."

Although from the outside, I could see how someone might think that. I saw her every night I didn't work or have the kids. And even when I did have the kids, she often invited them over to paint nails or bake cookies, and we occasionally had her over for dinner. If I had them on weekend mornings, we'd all go to her mom's bakery, and once she gave them a tour of the kitchen there. She fed Freddie Purrcury while I was at work, and I'd bring her a Frosty or a monkey bread muffin the next day to say thanks.

When the girls were around, we were excellent at keeping our hands to ourselves.

When we were alone, it was another story.

There probably wasn't an inch on her body I hadn't kissed, and she could say the same about mine. But even when we weren't naked, I loved being with her. Sometimes she would say something that reminded me of how young she was, and I'd groan. But I'd come to appreciate her youthful optimism and bright-eyed positivity—she saw the best in everything and everyone.

And I certainly enjoyed her boundless sexual energy.

Sometimes I felt so good around her, I'd find myself wishing things could be different with us . . . but I never let myself go too far down that path.

Maybe in another time, another place, Winnie and I could have been something more, but it was pointless to think about that now.

It was October first already—she'd be gone in a week.

Last weekend she'd taken a three-day trip to Rhode Island, during which she'd signed a lease for an apartment, met her boss and co-workers, and saw her new office. She'd loved the hotel as much as she thought she would, and was full of ideas for her new job.

I'd been without the kids and off work all three days she'd been gone, and all I'd done was fucking mope and check my phone for texts from her. I didn't even want to think about what it was going to be like when she left for good.

"I've been busy with my kids," I told Justin. "And coaching."

"How's that going?"

"I really like it." I grinned ruefully. "Most of those cocky teenage assholes think being tough is about how many push-ups you can do—which was exactly what I thought at their age too—but they're learning."

"How are the girls?"

"Great. Now that we have the cat, they have even more things to fight about—who gets to feed him, who he likes better, whose bed he should sleep on. They also drew pictures of him on each other's arms with a black Sharpie. *Cattoos*, they said."

Justin laughed, slowed his pedaling, and wiped sweat from his face. "Well, we miss seeing them. Don't be a stranger too much longer, okay? Life's short."

I fell silent, thinking—as he probably was—about the call we'd responded to earlier in the week. A structure fire with two children trapped in first-floor bedrooms. I'd been in a lot of life-threatening situations in my SEAL days, but I'd never prayed as hard as I did that day as we felt our way through the house on our hands and knees with zero visibility. Thankfully, we'd located them hiding together in the closet and were able to extract them before the roof collapsed. They were going to be okay, but both were in the hospital with serious injuries.

I normally didn't go to the girls' school when they weren't with me, but after my shift ended the next day, I'd shown up at pickup time, needing to see them and hug them and hear their voices. Naomi had understood, and let me have a little time with them that afternoon. She'd even given me a tearful hug, congratulating me on the rescue and telling the girls how proud they should be of their dad.

"Yeah," I said. "I'll give Bree a call."

"Why don't you come over tomorrow night for a few beers? Do you have the kids?"

"Not until Wednesday." Tomorrow was Saturday, but I wanted to spend the evening with Winnie.

Justin guessed what I was thinking. "Bring her with you. We'll play cards or something."

"Maybe," I said hesitantly.

"Come on, you can keep your fucking pants on for a couple hours," he chided.

I slowed the treadmill to a walk. "I'll think about it. But today is her last day at work, and she's still got a lot of packing to do."

"When does she leave?"

"Thursday."

"Oh, wow. I didn't realize it was so soon."

"Yeah." I tried to sound offhand. "Less than a week."

"Did her place sell?"

"Not yet. She's still next door."

"You guys gonna date long-distance once she moves?"

I gave him a look like he was crazy. "No."

"Why not?"

"Because." I switched the machine off and stepped down. "I wasn't even good at a relationship when I lived in the same house as Naomi, let alone when I was gone."

"But you could—"

"No." My tone was final. "But if you get off my ass, I'll ask her about cards tomorrow night."

He held up his hands. "Okay, okay. I'm done."

I was hoping Winnie would rather just have a quiet night in, but she loved the idea of going to my sister's house to play cards. She even made some kind of chili dip to bring. "You think it's okay to use her oven?" she asked on the ride over.

"I'm sure it's fine."

"I just didn't want to heat it up at my place because the cheese would get hard."

"I'm sure it's fine," I repeated.

She glanced at me. "You okay?"

I rubbed the back of my neck. "Sorry. I'm just a little out of it. Haven't slept well this week."

"I won't keep you up late tonight." She reached over and rubbed my leg. "Unless you want me to."

Glancing over at her, I tried to smile. "How was your last day at work?"

"It was really nice. They had a cake for me and everything."

I tried to think of something else to say, but couldn't. I continued to feel slightly ill at ease on the drive, and when we pulled up in front of Bree's house, I turned off the engine but didn't get out right away.

"What is it, Dex? I can tell something is wrong."

I frowned, staring at the steering wheel.

"Talk to me," she pleaded.

"That fire on Monday really messed with me." It wasn't the whole truth, but it was something.

She reached over and took my hand. "I bet. Have you heard any more about the kids?"

"Last I heard, they were still in the hospital, but expected to be okay."

"Good." She smiled. "You're all heroes. Everyone is so proud of you guys."

"I'm not feeling like a hero," I said. "I'm feeling like a coward."

"Why?"

I took a breath and spilled some more. "I haven't asked my sister about her visit with our dad."

"Oh." Winnie shifted in her seat to face me. "I didn't realize that happened."

"It happened last weekend. I didn't say anything about it."

She remained silent, holding my hand and giving me the space she knew I needed.

"I told her I didn't want to know how it went."

"And have you changed your mind?"

"I don't know. Part of me feels like I should get over my anger because it's my father and he's dying, but another part just wants to keep that door closed."

Winnie nodded, then looked down at our hands. "I struggle with those feelings about my mom too. My real mom—Carla. Not that she's dying," she added quickly, "so it's not the exact same, but I sometimes ignore her attempts to reach out. Like I won't text or call her back for days, or even weeks. And I feel guilty about it, because I know she's my mother and she's offering what she's capable of, but it still hurts. I don't want it to affect me, but sometimes it does."

"Yeah."

"It's like I want to punish her, but I'm the one who feels punished." She squeezed my hand. "So I understand wanting to keep the door closed."

"You don't think I'm a shitty, fucked-up person to refuse a dying father's request to see his son?"

"Well, when you put it like *that* . . ."

I managed a brief smile. "Thanks."

"I'm teasing." Bringing my hand to her lips, she kissed my fingers. "No, I don't think you're a shitty, fucked-up person. I think you're protective of yourself and the people you love—for good reason."

It was crazy how well she understood me. It made me want to keep talking, turn myself inside out and admit that I was scared to see my father because I didn't want to feel sorry for him—I didn't want to feel anything for him, because I didn't like things I couldn't control, including that she was leaving and I was scared of being lost and lonely without her. That I was going to miss her so much it hurt. That somehow I'd fallen in love with her, when that had been the one fucking thing I was so sure wouldn't happen. That my feelings were building and growing and spreading like wildfire, and I couldn't contain them.

I swallowed hard. "Let's go in."

I tried to have fun, but it was a struggle. Winnie was enjoying herself, and that made me happy. She grew up playing cards on Saturday nights with her family too, and she got along with my sister so well, it was like they'd always been friends.

Several times, I'd look over at her and my heart would threaten to burst in my chest. Sometimes I'd have to reach over and touch her shoulder or her leg or her arm, just to satisfy the urge to be closer to her.

I couldn't wait to get her alone. Maybe she'd stay the whole night with me tonight. So far, we'd always left one another's beds before the sun came up—we'd never woken up together. I wanted that.

I wanted it way too fucking much.

And I knew that once it happened, I'd want it all the time. My hunger to be with her refused to be satiated—it just fed upon itself and continued to grow.

At the end of the night, she excused herself to the bathroom while Justin put away the cards and I followed Bree into the kitchen.

"That was really fun," she said, setting glasses in the sink. "Thanks for coming over."

"Sure." I leaned against the kitchen doorway, hearing Winnie's voice in my head.

It's like I want to punish her, but I'm the one who feels punished.

I knew exactly what she meant.

"You see Dad last weekend?" I ventured.

"Yes."

"How was it?"

"Hard." Bree began putting leftover party meatballs into a plastic container. "But I'm glad I went."

I took a swig from my beer. "He look the same?"

"No. He's frail and shriveled. He's in a lot of pain."

I wouldn't feel anything. I wouldn't.

"He asked about you."

I drank again. "What did you tell him?"

"Just the basics—you left the Navy, you're a firefighter now, you've got two beautiful girls." She stuck the container in the fridge. "But that's as much as I said and I didn't show him any photos."

"Good." I paused. "Are you going to see him again?"

"Next weekend." She began putting plastic wrap over the dip Winnie had brought. "Winnie is such a doll. I wish she wasn't moving away."

I said nothing.

She glanced at me over her shoulder. "Don't you?"

I shrugged, faking indifference. Trying to get back on an even keel. "What good would it do if she stayed?"

My sister rolled her eyes. "I don't know, Dex. Maybe you'd enjoy a healthy adult relationship?"

"Nah." I finished the last of my beer. "I'm not interested in a relationship. And she deserves way better than me."

"I might be tempted to agree with you on that, but since she's in love with you, it doesn't matter."

"She's not in love with me," I said quickly.

"Dex, she never stops smiling at you. And laughing at everything you say. And you can't stop touching her." Bree shook her head as she put the plastic wrap back in the drawer. "You're just as crazy about her as she is about you. Don't bother denying it."

"Well, she's leaving, so it doesn't matter."

"You know, there are things called airplanes that fly back and forth between Michigan and Rhode Island." She turned around and leaned back against the sink, folding her arms. "Perhaps you've heard of them."

"Perhaps you've heard of my two children."

"What about them?"

"I can't just fly off to Rhode Island when I feel like it. And despite having two jobs, I'm not rolling in money either. I can't afford a bunch of plane tickets."

"Excuses, excuses." She shook her head. "Why won't you admit she makes you happy?"

"They're not excuses, Bree," I said angrily. "I'm not rich. And I'm trying to be a better father than ours was, and that means being there for my kids."

"You're not Dad, Dex." Bree was getting emotional too. "You never have been."

"That took work!" My body temperature rose as my temper flared. "He was the only example of fatherhood I had, and everything I've ever done was to distance myself from that."

"Exactly!" She shook her head. "You were never afraid of becoming Dad. You were afraid of becoming Mom. You still are."

"What?" I glared at her.

"You hated the way Mom loved him and kept taking him back. You thought she was gullible and weak."

"She was!" I exploded. "She let him come back into our lives and hurt her—hurt *us*—again and again. That's what happens when you love someone. You give them the means to hurt you!"

"It's called being vulnerable, Dex, and it's not a bad thing. It's healthy! What's not healthy is keeping your feelings all bottled up inside because you're afraid to love somebody."

"I'm not afraid of anything!" I roared.

She held up her palms and lowered her voice. "Okay, okay. Stop shouting."

But I couldn't stop—it felt like a volcano was erupting inside me. "And besides the fact that Winnie and I have explicitly agreed to keep things casual, I made up my mind when Naomi and I split that I wasn't ever going through that again."

"Not all relationships end badly, Dex. And I never said anything about getting *married*. I just don't see why you'd throw away what you guys have when it's so good."

"We don't *have* anything, Bree," I snapped. "It's just sex. That's it. Sex. So stop trying to put words in my mouth or invent feelings I don't have. I'm not in love with her. When she leaves, we're done."

Bree's eyes went wide, and she pressed her lips into a thin line. Her focus was over my shoulder, and I knew without turning around that Winnie was standing there. My guts churned.

Closing my eyes, I exhaled, my shoulders dropping.

Behind me, I heard her voice, small and hurt. "Um, I'll just wait outside. Thanks for everything, Bree."

When I opened my eyes, I saw my sister with her hands over her mouth. "Think she heard me?"

She nodded.

"Fuck!" I clanked my empty beer bottle on the counter, wishing I could shatter it against the wall—or even better, my stupid skull.

"Hey." Justin appeared in the kitchen doorway. "Winnie just blew out of here like a hurricane. Everything okay?"

"I gotta go." I shouldered past him and headed for the door.

Twenty-Two

Winnie

*D*ON'T CRY, DON'T CRY, DON'T CRY.

Out on the porch, I took a few deep breaths of the crisp October air, trying to keep the sobs from escaping.

I felt like I'd just gotten the wind knocked out of me.

How had this happened? I'd been so careful this time! I'd been so sure I wouldn't wind up hurt as long as I kept my expectations realistic and my feelings in check.

But you didn't do that, did you?

A spiteful voice in my head spoke up.

It doesn't matter what you said you were going to do—it's what you went ahead and did that matters. And you went ahead and fell for this unavailable guy who told you right from the start that he wasn't interested in you like that.

Yes, he was a jerk to say those things. But you're a fool. And only one of you will cry yourself to sleep tonight.

One tear slipped down my cheek, followed by another. Behind me, the door opened, and I swiped at my cheeks, glad for the dark.

"Ready to go?" I asked, proud of how calm my voice sounded.

"Yeah."

We walked to the car, and I waited stiffly while he unlocked the passenger door. When I got in, I was careful not to brush against him, and I pulled the door shut myself.

Worried he was going to apologize or offer an explanation right there at the curb, I was relieved when he started the car and put it in drive. I really didn't want to hear him say he was sorry. Not this time.

The ride home was tense and silent. I gripped the edge of my seat as if it was a life raft in choppy waters. When he pulled into his garage, I was quick to unbuckle my seatbelt.

"Winnie, wait." He reached over and circled my wrist. "Don't go yet."

I froze, one hand on the door handle.

"I need to apologize."

"That's not necessary."

"Yes, it is. I didn't mean what I said."

"I think you didn't mean for me to *hear* it."

He exhaled. "That's true, but what I said came out wrong. It's not just sex between us. I was worked up about things my sister was saying, and I lost my temper."

"It's fine. I'm going now."

But he held on to my wrist. "It's not fine, Winnie. I said something shitty, and you should call me out on it."

"Is that what you want?" Snatching my hand from his grip, I shifted to face him. "For me to get so mad I never want to see you again? For me to say shitty things right back to you so I can hurt your feelings the way you hurt mine?"

His jaw was clenched hard. "Yes."

"Well, that's not how I work. I don't treat people I care about that way."

Exhaling, he pinched the bridge of his nose. "I hate that I hurt you."

"You're not the first, and you won't be the last. I'll live."

He dropped his hand and looked at me. "Winnie." His voice cracked.

"I'm just going to be honest, Dex." I couldn't stop the tears, so I just let them come. "I know this is not what we planned. I tried really hard not to fall for you. I didn't want to. But I did."

"Don't say it," he begged.

"I have to. Maybe I'm a fool, but I'm not a coward. I love you. And I don't want this to end."

"But you're leaving," he blurted. "And I can't ask you to stay."

"Can't or won't?"

He opened his mouth, then closed it again. Swallowed. "Can't."

"Why not?"

"Because it's not what we said this would be. And you have to follow your dream."

"But things change," I wept. "And I have a lot of dreams. One of them is finding someone to share my life with. And if you're willing to try, maybe we could make it work between us. Maybe I don't have to leave."

He shook his head. "It's better this way, Winnie. You go your way, I go mine."

"But not if we have feelings for each other! Doesn't that count for something?" Taking a deep, shaky breath, I forced myself to be brave. "*Do* you have feelings for me?"

He stared straight ahead. His jaw ticked.

"I know what we used to say in the beginning. But I haven't heard you say it in a while. Is it still true?"

It seemed like an eternity passed before he answered. And when he spoke, his voice sounded different.

"It's still true," he said woodenly. He looked at me, his expression completely blank. "I don't love you."

I squeezed my eyes shut, the tears hot on my cheeks.

"Goodbye, Dex." Choking back a sob, I got out of the car, hurried from the garage, and let myself into my front door.

As soon as it was closed, I burst into tears, bawling into my hands, my body shuddering with hurt and humiliation. I wept until my eyes ran dry, and then I went upstairs, scrubbed off the remains of my makeup, and got into bed.

It wasn't long before sadness filled the well again, and I ended up crying myself to sleep, just as I predicted.

But it was my own fault.

The next day was Sunday, so I should have gone to my parents' house for dinner, but I couldn't bring myself to do it. My face was puffy, my eyes were bloodshot, and I didn't feel like explaining to anyone why I looked like a train wreck. Besides, I had a lot of packing to do—the moving truck would be here Wednesday, and I was leaving for Rhode Island on Thursday.

My place hadn't sold yet, but even though my agent had told me it would show better with furniture, I didn't want to leave anything behind. It would feel like more of a fresh start if I didn't have to come back here.

I called my mom and apologized that I wouldn't be at dinner tonight, blaming my stuffy nose on a nonexistent cold that was going around and my absence on the move.

"Don't worry about dinner," she said. "But honey, are you sure you're okay?"

"I'm fine," I said listlessly. "I'm just run down."

"Why don't I bring you something to eat?"

"No, Mom, you don't have to do that. I have things to eat here." I glanced at my fridge with no appetite whatsoever.

"Well, make sure you eat them. And get a good night's sleep."

"I will."

But after we hung up, I felt so lonely I called Ellie. "Hey. Can you come over?"

"Of course. What's wrong?"

"Dex and I ended things last night, and I could use a friend," I said, a sob catching in my throat.

"On my way."

She showed up with tacos and tequila. "So what happened?" she asked as she poured us each a shot.

"Exactly what I didn't want to happen," I said miserably. As I unpacked the tacos from the bag, I told her about what I'd overheard at Bree's house and the final conversation in the garage.

"Ouch." She handed me a shot. "I'm sorry, Win."

"I have no one to blame but myself." I tossed back the shot, grimacing as it burned its way down my throat. "Well, maybe you."

She did her shot and winced. "Me! I didn't tell you to fall for that guy. I just said it was okay to bone him a few times."

"You should know me by now. I can't bone anyone without catching feelings."

She sighed. "You do have that tendency."

"It was so embarrassing, Ell." I sank onto a counter stool and dropped my head into my hands. "I told him I loved him."

"Of course you did."

I peeked at her. "Don't poke fun. I really thought this was different. Am I just that dumb?"

Sighing, Ellie poured us each another shot. "You're not dumb, Win. You just love people easily. It's who you are."

"I guess." I stared at my second shot. "I feel like I'm in that drawing with all the staircases that never go anywhere. I think I'm going up but then I turn and I'm at the bottom. I can't get out."

"I know, babe. And I'm sorry. One of these days you're going to fall for the guy who deserves you."

"Oh, God." I looked at her in alarm. "I owe you the thing now, don't I?"

"I'm thinking maybe I'll give you a mulligan on this one." She shrugged. "Seeing as I did encourage you to bone this guy."

"Thanks. I feel bad enough without adding the weight of that particular humiliation."

"But one is all you get. If you meet Mr. Right in Rhode Island before Christmas, I own you." She picked up her shot glass and held it up.

I clinked mine to it. "Deal."

We did the second shot together and set the glasses down.

"Now let's eat some tacos and get you packed up for your new life adventure," she said with a smile. "Because even though I'll never forgive you for leaving me to deal with Gianni Lupo on my own, you're still my person, and I'm excited for you. Good things are ahead, Win—I can feel it."

"Thanks." I smiled back, grateful for her. "I might have crappy taste in guys, but my taste in friends is impeccable."

Ellie stayed until after midnight, helping me pack, making me laugh, and doing her best to keep my mind off Dex. I loved her dearly for it and hugged her hard when she left. But when I was alone in my bed, all I could do was think about him on the other side of the wall and wonder if he was as miserable as I was or relieved to be rid of me.

Was I just a fun little side dish to him? Had he been able to keep his real feelings locked away? Could I have mistaken all his sweet gestures and perfect kisses and warm, protective embraces for something they weren't? Was this just one more link in the chain of infatuations I'd blown all out of proportion?

I couldn't make myself believe it.

What I felt for Dex was real. What we had together was good.

What we could have been would always make me wonder.

Twenty-Three

Dex

I BARELY SLEPT SATURDAY NIGHT, AND SUNDAY I SKIPPED GOING to church. As much as I liked seeing the girls there, I didn't even feel like I could face them after what I'd done. I was sick to my stomach every time I thought about it.

Instead, I hid out all day in my condo like a criminal—which was exactly how I felt.

I'd done something unpardonable. I'd stolen something valuable. I'd vandalized something beautiful.

And I'd lied to someone who deserved the truth.

But she knew, a stubborn voice in my head would argue. *She knew from the beginning what this had to be. It doesn't matter how I really feel. What good would it do her to hear the words?*

I loved her—of course I did. But that kind of love wasn't stable or dependable. That kind of love wasn't a solid foundation. It felt strong, but that was an illusion. What love did was drain your strength and take away your ability to make good decisions.

And you couldn't second-guess yourself. If I'd learned anything as a SEAL sniper, it was that I had to trust myself to make split-second decisions under the most stressful circumstances imaginable—there was no time for doubt or uncertainty. It was a matter of survival.

I'd saved us both.

There was no way she and I could have made things work, not even if she'd stayed here. She was too young. She had everything ahead of her—marriage and kids and her fucking *twenties*. I was so far removed from that stage of life, where anything seems possible and all your dreams are still alive. And I'd already had my children. What I needed to focus on now was raising them.

She'd been a welcome distraction, but it was over now.

It killed me to think of her hurting, just on the other side of the wall, but I stayed strong.

Someday she'd thank me.

On Monday afternoon, I went to the gym for a few coaching sessions, during which I barked at the guys more than necessary and made them work five times as hard. Usually, they thanked me after training, or stuck around and talked with me a little, but today every single one of them took off as soon as we were done.

Not that I blamed them.

On the way home, I thought about stopping at Justin and Bree's, but I hadn't spoken to either of them since Saturday night and didn't feel like rehashing the breakup. It was too raw.

I knew I owed my sister an apology for yelling at her, and I'd give it, but I wasn't ready yet. If she started coming at me with all that shit about being afraid to love someone, I'd lose it again.

When I got home, I showered and made myself some dinner, but I had no appetite. Stretching out on the couch, I tried to get Freddie Purrcury to sit with me while I watched TV, but he refused.

"What did I ever do to you?" I said as he presented me with his ass and put his tail in the air before walking away.

I looked at my cell phone on the coffee table, tempted for the millionth time to call Winnie and ask her how she was feeling. Did she hate me? Would she leave town without speaking to me again? The thought made my heart sink like a stone.

Maybe I could just send her a quick text. Just check in—as a friend. Make sure she was okay.

But the words got stuck between my mind and my fingers, and I couldn't do it.

Instead, I called the girls to say goodnight. Luna was still in the shower, so I chatted with Hallie for a few minutes. "Are you writing any new stories?" I asked her.

"I'm still working on the one about the ogre and the princess."

"Oh." My heart lurched. "So tell me what's happening."

"Well, the princess was very brave and went to seek out the ogre in the forest. She finds his cave."

"How did she know where to look?"

"She followed the sound of his snoring."

I almost smiled. "Go on."

"So she calls out to him, and he's extra grumpy because she woke him up, but he listens to her story about her cat Tigger running up the tree."

"Does he agree to help?"

"No."

"Why not?" I frowned, annoyed that even in ogre form I was a jerk.

"Because the ogre has a secret he doesn't want her to know."

"And what's that?"

"He's afraid of heights."

"The *ogre* is afraid of heights?"

"Yes. So he won't go up the tree to save the cat, but he

can't tell her the real reason, so he just sort of grunts at her and tells her to leave him alone."

"Does he at least feel bad about it?"

"Yes, because he can hear her crying as she runs back home through the forest. But not bad enough to overcome his fear of heights. He's a very stubborn ogre."

"Clearly." I got off the couch and wandered over to the sliding door. Pulling it open, I stepped onto the patio, feeling like I could use some fresh air. "So then what happens? Does the cat die? Or does the ogre get over himself and help the princess?"

"I don't know yet. That's as far as I've gotten."

I glanced over at Winnie's patio and thought about kissing her the night we'd met. I'd been so drawn to her—I still was. Now I'd never feel those lips on mine again. "Well, let me know how it ends."

"I will. Can I talk to Freddie Purrcury?"

I frowned. "No."

"Why not?"

"He's being rude."

"What did he do?"

"He's ignoring me."

She laughed. "He only likes it when we're there. Want to talk to Luna?"

"Yes. I love you. Goodnight."

"I love you too, Daddy. Night."

Luna came on a few seconds later. "Daddy?"

"Yeah?"

"Winnie's not gone yet, is she?"

I swallowed hard. "I don't think so."

"Okay good, because we want to give her a going-away gift. We saw something *purr*fect at the store," she said with a giggle. "Will you take us to get it?"

"Yeah." I closed my eyes, the ache of missing her already

deep in my bones. "It will have to be Wednesday when I get you. I'm pretty sure she leaves the next day."

"Okay."

We chatted for a few more minutes, then said goodnight. I stayed outside for a little while, watching it grow darker.

If I hadn't broken things off, Winnie and I would probably be together right now. Maybe I'd be helping her pack. Maybe we'd be eating dinner at my place. Maybe we'd be in bed, taking advantage of every last minute we had before she left.

My body warmed thinking about it, and I was tempted to go knock on her door. Apologize. Tell her the truth. Make her understand that I'd only lied to protect her—because that's what I did when I loved someone. I protected them.

But in the end, I couldn't bring myself to do it, and I went back inside alone.

Justin and I arrived at work Tuesday at the same time and parked next to each other. As soon as we got out of our cars, I held up my hands in surrender. "I know, I know. I'll apologize to Bree."

He nodded. "Good."

"Does she hate me?"

"No. She feels bad. She thinks she said things that pissed you off so much, you'll never speak to her again."

"She did piss me off. But only because she knows how to push my buttons."

"Sisters are good at that." We started walking toward the station. "So what happened with Winnie?"

"We broke it off."

"Mutual decision?"

I frowned. "Not exactly. She had it in her head that we could try long-distance or something."

"And you really don't want to?"

"No, Justin! I'm not her fucking high-school boyfriend. She's not going away to college—she's moving to another state. She took a job there."

"Maybe she didn't know you wanted her to stay."

"There was no way I could've asked her to stay."

"Why not?" Justin asked as we reached the building. "I told Bree I was going to marry her on our second date."

"You guys are different." I paused at the door without opening it, staring at my reflection in the glass. "It wouldn't have worked for us. She's too young for me. We're at completely different stages of life. I've already done the marriage and family thing, and I fucked it up. Now I'm trying to be the best possible single dad I can be, and I've got no room in my life for anything else."

"Okay."

"Asking her to give up her dream job just to be with me when I can't offer her the future she wants would have been unfair."

"Okay."

"It's not because I'm scared."

He hesitated. "Okay."

"No matter what my sister says. It's not because I'm scared. It's because I'm strong."

My brother-in-law remained silent.

I kept staring at myself in the glass. "I'm not in love with her. I don't need her in my life. I'll be fine without her." I swallowed. "Eventually."

"Okay, brother." Justin put a hand on my shoulder. "Maybe you should go inside and scrub some toilets or something. It'll take your mind off this."

I grabbed the door handle and yanked it open.

Hallie grabbed the coffee mug off the shelf at the gift shop and held it up. "See Daddy? Isn't it cute?"

It was cute. It had a cartoon of a cat with a thick Freddie Mercury mustache on it, wearing tight pants and a yellow jacket, one paw in the air, one holding a mic stand. Beneath the drawing it said *Don't stop meow*. But I couldn't even smile. "Yeah."

"It's so that she won't forget us," said Luna excitedly, bouncing around and knocking into things on the shelves. "Every day she can use her mug and think of us."

I cleared my throat. "She'll love it. Come on, before you break something."

We paid for the mug and left the shop, wandering down the block toward the car. My feet felt heavy and slow as I dragged them through the fallen leaves on the sidewalk. A small moving truck had been parked in Winnie's driveway all morning, and I'd been fucking miserable watching all her furniture disappear inside it.

"Can we bring it over to her when we get home, Daddy?" Luna asked, scuffing her heels through the crunchy brown and yellow leaves.

"If she's there."

"I hope she is!" Hallie hurried ahead to the car and tugged at the door handle. "Let's hurry."

When we pulled into the complex, we saw that Winnie's garage door was open, and she was loading a suitcase into her trunk.

At the sight of her, my heart caromed in my chest and I nearly side-swiped another vehicle—I couldn't take my eyes off her. She wore jeans and a fuzzy white sweater that looked soft and cozy. Her hair was tucked into a nest on the top of her head. I wanted to wrap my arms around her and hold her close, bury my face in her neck and beg her not to go. Tearing my eyes away, I pulled into our garage and turned off the car. Took a deep breath.

"Can we give it to her now, Daddy?" Hallie was already unbuckling her seatbelt.

"I guess so." Steeling myself, I helped Luna out of the car. They grabbed the gift shop bag and went racing out of the garage.

Slowly, I collected their backpacks from the back seat, stuck them inside the back hallway, and made my way out of the garage. As I walked across to Winnie's driveway, I could hear a delighted squeal of surprise—Winnie's—and childish laughter.

"Oh my goodness, I love it!" Winnie's entire face was lit up as she looked at the mug. "Thank you so much."

I watched as she gave them each a hug, feeling jealous and hating myself for it. She noticed me approaching over Hallie's shoulder, and her face changed immediately, the smile fading into nothing.

"Hey, Dex," she said coolly, placing the mug back in the bag.

"Hey, Win." I stuck my hands in my pockets. "You like your gift?"

"I love it." She looked at the girls before smiling again and holding the bag to her chest. "I promise to use it every day. And I'm so happy you came by, because I have something for you too."

Hallie and Luna exchanged an excited glance. "You do?"

"Yes. Want to come inside?"

They looked at me. "Can we, Daddy?" Hallie asked.

"Sure. I can wait out here."

Winnie met my eyes, hers carefully neutral. "You can come in too." She shrugged. "If you want."

Her icy demeanor was making me angry—I wanted to take her by the shoulders and kiss her until she loved me again—but I nodded and followed them through the garage into her condo.

The place was almost completely empty.

"Your stuff is all gone!" Luna said.

"Yeah, the moving guys were here this morning and got it all loaded up." Winnie sounded a little wistful.

"But where's Piglet?" Hallie sounded worried.

"She's here." Winnie smiled. "She's been hiding out in the pantry all day because of all the commotion. You know how she is with strangers."

"But we're not strangers," Luna said adamantly. "We're friends."

"Maybe she'll come out if you ask her."

Luna went over to the pantry and got down on her knees, while Hallie continued to look around. "Is your bed still here?"

"Nope. My bed is on its way to Rhode Island." She smiled ruefully. "I have to sleep at my parents' house tonight."

"You could sleep at our house," Hallie offered. "Daddy can sleep on the couch. You might not even hear him snoring down there."

Winnie and I exchanged a glance—did I imagine the flicker of warmth?

"Thanks," Winnie said, "but I'll be good in my old room. Since it's my last night here, my family wants to be with me."

I wanted to be with her on her last night here—I wanted it so badly I had to press my tongue to the roof of my mouth or I was going to say it aloud.

Luna came out of the pantry holding Piglet. "She let me pick her up," she said softly.

"Good job." Winnie smiled at Luna. "She knows you now."

"Do you think she'll miss us?"

"Definitely. So you better be sure to email me, okay? I'll read your messages out loud to her. And send pictures too, so

I can show her." Winnie went over to the counter and picked up two little white plastic bags. "Here. I have something for each of you."

Hallie went rushing over, and Winnie handed her one of the bags. After Luna gently set Piglet on her feet, she eagerly reached for the other.

"Oooooh!" Hallie pulled bright blue nail polish from the bag along with a pair of fluffy lavender socks and a little notebook with a cat on the cover. "Thank you!"

"For when you want to show off your toes and when you want to be cozy," Winnie said with a smile. "And for writing your stories."

Luna stuck her hand in her bag and pulled out cotton candy pink polish, fluffy white socks, and a box of princess Band-Aids. "Thank you! Now I don't have to wear Daddy's boring brown ones."

"And if you run out," Winnie said, "just let me know. I'll send you another box."

Luna threw her arms around Winnie's waist and Hallie followed suit. Knocked off balance, Winnie laughed and embraced them. I stood ten feet away with my arms folded over my chest feeling sorry for myself.

"I wish you didn't have to go," Hallie said.

"Me too," added Luna. "Are you sure you have to?"

Winnie's eyes closed a moment. "I'm sure."

"But don't forget us, okay?"

"I won't." Releasing them, Winnie took a breath. "I should probably get going. I have to drop Piglet off at my mom's house, and then I'm meeting a friend for dinner."

"Come on, girls." I gestured for them to go out the door to Winnie's garage. "Go on back to our place. I want to talk to Winnie a moment."

Thankfully, they didn't argue. Chattering about their new

nail polish, they went outside, pulling the door shut behind them.

She stood across the kitchen from me, legs together, her arms wrapped around herself, hands lost inside the big sleeves of her sweater. That carefully cool expression was gone, replaced by eyes that glistened with tears and a trembling lower lip. My gut instinct was to embrace her, and I took a step forward.

She put out one hand. "Don't. Please. There's nothing you can say at this point that won't hurt, and I'm already thirty seconds away from a really embarrassing ugly cry."

"God, Winnie." Defeated, because she was right—there wasn't anything I could say that wouldn't hurt—I stood there with my chest caving in. "This sucks. I don't want to leave it this way between us."

"I don't either, but I can't help the way I feel, just like you can't help the way you *don't*."

"But what if—what if it's not just about the way we *feel*?" Desperate, I took another step closer to her. "What if it's just that the things we want are too different?"

She shook her head. "I don't understand."

"You're so young, Winnie. You're so young and so beautiful, and you have so much of your life in front of you. You want all these things, and you deserve them all, including your dream job and someone who can devote himself completely to you." Closing the gap between us, I cradled her face in my hands, my eyes burning. "And as much as I might wish I could be that guy, I can't. No matter how I feel, I can't."

"You *won't*." Tears clung to her lashes.

Swallowing hard, I shook my head.

She pushed my arms down. "Then what are you *doing* here?"

"I don't know." I closed my eyes. "I guess I was hoping we could at least say goodbye as friends."

A solitary tear slipped down her cheek, and she didn't wipe it away. "I need more time before I can be your friend."

I nodded, understanding.

"Take care of yourself, Dex."

"You too." My voice was barely a whisper. Forcing myself to walk away, I went to the door and hesitated, my back to her. I swallowed hard. "I lied to you."

"What?"

"I lied to you when you asked me how I felt. I said I didn't love you."

I heard her quick inhale, and that was it.

I pushed the door open and walked out.

Twenty-Four

Winnie

"I**T WAS AWFUL." SEATED AT THE ISLAND IN ABELARD'S** kitchen, I blew my nose in a soggy tissue. "I wish he hadn't even come over. I made it all day long without crying, and now I can't stop."

"Why'd you even let him in?" Ellie flipped our sandwiches in the pan. I'd begged her to make me one of her gourmet grilled cheeses for dinner. I needed comfort food.

"I told you, he was with the kids." I went over to the trash, threw my tissue away and grabbed another one from the box on the counter. "They'd given me a gift and I had one for them. What was I supposed to do, make him wait in the driveway?"

"Yes." Ellie turned down the gas under the pan and poured two glasses of red wine.

"Well, I couldn't. He looked all sad and hot at the same time."

Ellie sipped her wine and studied me. "Do you think he was telling you the truth about his feelings?"

"I don't know." I blew my nose one more time and tossed out the tissue. "But what reason would he have for saying he lied? Just to mess with me?"

"No." She thought for a moment. "But it seems kind of selfish of him to drop that bomb on you and run away."

"I don't think that was his original intention." I went back to my chair and dropped into it. "I think he only meant to ask me if we could be friends and it . . . escalated."

"Because being friends with someone you're in love with always works so well." Ellie checked the sandwiches and turned off the gas.

"He didn't exactly say he was in love with me."

"Based on what you told me, I think he made it clear." Ellie lifted our sandwiches from the pan with a spatula, setting them on a wooden cutting board. "He loves you, but he doesn't think he can handle being the guy who loves you. It's fucked up, but it's clear."

"Yeah." I sniffed. "This is a new one, huh? A guy breaking it off because he *does* love me, not because he *doesn't*?"

"It's not your fault," she said loyally. "Those unavailable asshole types really know how to get under your skin."

"I guess." I fidgeted in my chair. "But he was so *different* than those guys. He wasn't a selfish jerk. He sewed my dress, and he brushed my hair, and he cooked for me—badly, but he tried—and he's so protective and brave and determined to be a good father . . . he isn't an asshole deep down, Ellie. I know he isn't."

She eyeballed me over her shoulder. "Don't tempt me to like him again. I don't want to."

I bit my lip. "He rescued children from a burning house."

"Goddammit, Winnie." Ellie pulled a big knife from the block on the counter and sliced each sandwich in half. White cheese oozed out over thick slices of bacon.

Despite my broken heart, my mouth watered. "What kind is this again?"

"This is bacon and brie with peach bourbon jam." She licked her fingers. "And it's so good, it's going to make you forget all about hot single dads who rescue children from burning houses."

"And sew."

"And sew." Ellie placed each sandwich onto a plate next to a pile of salad greens tossed with vinaigrette.

"And adopt cats."

She grimaced as she set one plate in front of me. "And adopt cats."

"And have magic hands and big dicks and give you multiple orgasms every time."

Ellie shook her head. "You're killing me."

"Sorry. I had to get it out." I picked up my sandwich. "But this looks delicious and it's going to make everything all better. Dexter who?"

She laughed as she poured us more wine. "I mean, it might not give you multiple orgasms, but it is a damn good sandwich."

After dinner, Ellie walked me out to my car and hugged me goodbye. "I'll see you in two weeks," she said, "and I'll miss you like mad in between."

"Same. Thanks for dinner—and for always making me feel better."

"Of course." Releasing me, she folded her arms over her chest. "You gonna be okay?"

I nodded, happy that my throat didn't close up. "Yes. I have my family, I have you, I have my cat, I have a new job waiting for me—how much more can I ask for?"

"You can ask for anything," she said fiercely. "And you'd deserve it."

"Thanks." I smiled and glanced up at the sky, taking a deep breath of cool autumn air. "I'll try to remember that."

"Win, I'm curious. If Dex had asked you not to take this job and make this move, would you have stayed?"

"Honestly, I don't know." I thought for a moment. "But it would have been nice to know that he felt strongly enough to ask for something big and crazy like that." I laughed. "That's how I want to be loved—big and crazy. Because that's how I love."

She nodded. "I know. Drive carefully, okay? And text me all the time."

"I will. Love you."

"Love you too." She blew me a kiss, and I drove away.

The next morning, I left my parents' house bright and early, kissing them goodbye and setting out for my new life, determined to leave my broken heart behind.

Twenty-Five

Dex

THE CRUNCHING WOKE ME EVEN BEFORE THE SHIT-TALKING. Through the haze of a dream—in which I was trying to climb a tree to rescue Freddie Purrcury, who just kept jumping from branch to branch—I heard the crackle of a bag and then loud munching. Were those little shitheads eating chips for breakfast?

"Daddy's earlobes are funny. Don't you think?" Crunch, crunch, crunch.

"Funny like how?" Luna asked.

"I don't know." Hallie stuck something in her mouth and spoke around it. "They're just so big and *lobey*."

Luna giggled. "Yeah."

More crackling of the bag. More crunching. And if I wasn't mistaken, I felt some crumbs drop onto my chest.

"Hallie, look what you did. You got Cheetos in Daddy's chest hair."

I felt someone blowing on me. "Now they're gone."

"No. You missed some. Right there, it's orange. See?"

"Be careful, Luna. You're gonna drip."

That's when I felt a cold *splat* on my belly.

I opened my eyes and saw a purple blob at the top of my abs. "What the hell is that?"

"It's jelly from my toast." Luna leaned over and slurped it up like an anteater. "Sorry."

"Jesus Christ." I looked at Hallie, who held a bag of Cheetos. Her fingers were coated with bright orange. "Is that supposed to be your breakfast?"

She shrugged. "I was hungry."

"Your sister made toast. You couldn't at least pour cereal?"

"She didn't *make toast*, she dumped grape jelly on a piece of bread."

"I was scared to use the toaster," Luna confirmed with her mouth full.

I dropped my head back onto the pillow. "What time is it?"

"It's after seven. We got an email from Winnie, want to hear it?"

No, I didn't. Just hearing her name was hard enough. She'd been gone for ten days, and it seemed like she'd been on my mind for every minute of them. Every time I thought about her, my chest hurt. I'd picked up my phone to call her a thousand times, but hearing her voice wasn't going to make me miss her less. I thought about texting, but it seemed self- ish—she'd asked for time, and I wanted to give it to her.

Plus, I didn't exactly trust myself not to say something crazy.

I'm an idiot. Come back. I love you. Stay with me.

But I was desperate for news about her too. Was she okay? How was her new apartment? Her new job? Did she love it? Did she miss home? Did she miss *me*? Every time I thought of her in that soft white sweater, I pined for her a little more. Was it possible I'd never hold her in my arms again?

"Can you read it to me?" I asked.

Hallie went to get her iPad, and Luna wiped her sticky hands on her nightgown. "I got some jelly on the counter," she told me. "And on the floor."

"Great."

274

"And Freddie Purrcury stepped in it."

I frowned. "Even better."

Hallie returned, carrying her iPad instead of her Cheetos. "Dear Hallie and Luna," she read. "I was so happy to get your email and the photos you sent. You did a great job painting your nails! I miss playing salon with you too. My new job is keeping me very busy. I meet lots of new people every day. Piglet misses you too. She isn't used to our new home yet, and I think she is mad at me about the move. But it's very nice, even if my next-door neighbors are not as fun as you. You asked when I was coming home for a visit, and the answer is next weekend. I will be there from Friday to Sunday for a work event at Cloverleigh Farms. I don't know if you will be with your mom or your dad, but let me know and maybe we can work something out. After that, I am not sure when I will be home next. Write back soon and send me more pictures. Here is one for you. Love, Winnie."

"Did she send you a picture?" I asked, desperate to see her face.

"Yes." Hallie showed me the screen, and my heart lurched at the sight of Winnie's deep blue eyes, soft smile, and pink cheeks. She held Piglet, who looked about as happy to be in the photo as I felt staring at it. Something the size of a golf ball was lodged in my throat.

"Where are we next weekend, Daddy?" Luna asked. "Can we see her?"

"Uh . . ." I had to think. "That's your mom's wedding."

"But that's Saturday," Hallie said. "Couldn't we see her Friday when she gets here? Or Sunday, the day after?"

"Maybe." I tried to swallow and couldn't. "I'll—I'll text her and find out when she gets in. I also need to check with Mom about the wedding schedule."

"Okay. Can we go out for breakfast?"

"I guess." But I didn't want to go anywhere. I just wanted to stay in bed, stare at her photo, and feel sorry for myself.

"Can we go to Winnie's bakery?"

"Can't we go somewhere else?"

"No, that's our favorite place on Saturday mornings." Luna giggled. "You still have Cheeto dust in your chest hair."

Dropping my chin, I gave her my best grumpy Dad face. "Go get dressed, and put that nightgown in your laundry basket. It's got jelly all over it."

"Can you text Winnie right now and ask about the weekend?" Hallie pleaded.

"No." I needed to think about exactly what I was going to say to her. "I want to talk to Mom first. I'll do that when I drop you guys off today. Now go get dressed."

That afternoon, after hugging the girls goodbye in the driveway, I asked Naomi if she had a minute.

"Sure." She sent the girls into the house with instructions to clean their messy rooms, and turned back to me with her arms folded. "What's up?"

"Winnie is going to be in town next weekend, and the girls want to know if there's any time they can see her."

Naomi sighed. "Next weekend is going to be really busy with the wedding."

"I know. I can tell them it won't work."

"No, no, don't do that. They talk about her all the time, and they'll be sad if they miss her visit completely." A chill October wind blew her hair across her forehead, and she tucked it behind her ear. "How long will she be here?"

"Friday to Sunday."

"Is she staying with you?"

I made a face like the question was crazy. "No! I have no idea where she's staying. Why would she be staying with me?"

"Take it easy." Naomi held up her hands. "The way the girls have talked about the situation, I sort of thought you might be more than friends."

"Well, we're not. She's not in town to see me."

My ex studied me carefully. "But you care about her."

I closed my eyes. Clenched my jaw. "Naomi, don't."

"Dex, come on. Don't get mad. In the two years since we split up, the girls have never once mentioned a female friend, and after she came around, it was nothing but Winnie this and Winnie that. It's obvious she was around a lot."

"She was," I admitted.

"It's okay. It's not like I expected you to be alone forever. And you've always been very accepting of my relationship with Bryce."

"Me being alone forever is a lot more likely than a relationship with Winnie."

"Why?"

I scowled at her. "Why do you even care?"

"Because I care about *you*, Dex." She poked a finger at my chest. "Maybe you find this hard to believe, but I do actually want you to be happy. It's true that our marriage didn't work, and I don't think you tried hard enough to save it, but I don't believe it's because you weren't capable. That's what drove me crazy all the time. You *could be* a good partner to someone—if you let them in."

I rubbed a hand over my jaw. "You should know better than anyone, that isn't my thing."

"Oh, believe me, I know." She sighed. "But maybe you and I were just the wrong fit. Maybe I was never going to get over feeling shut out. Maybe your emotional baggage and mine were always going to prevent us from giving the other what they needed. And I wasn't going to settle for being unhappy, Dex. That's why I asked you to leave."

"I know."

Her voice softened. "And you didn't fight me."

I shook my head.

"At the time, I was hurt, but I came to accept that we were better off apart. And now I found someone who can give me what I need."

"I'm glad for you," I said, and I meant it.

She smiled. "Thanks. And we'll figure out something for that weekend. I need them Friday for the rehearsal and Saturday is the wedding, but I was going to have my mom take them back to her house at maybe ten or so. They'll be tired."

"Why don't I just pick them up from the reception?"

"That works. Let's say ten-thirty in the lobby of the yacht club?"

I nodded. "I have to work Monday, so I'll have them back Sunday evening."

"Okay. Thanks again for letting me have them during your weekend. If you'd like them for an overnight during your off days this week, just let me know. We can work it out."

I thought for a moment. "I have some coaching sessions Monday and Wednesday, but Tuesday would work."

She smiled. "Perfect. I'll tell them you'll pick them up from school. Oh—they have dentist appointments that day. I think at four-ten and four-forty."

I took out my phone and put the appointments in. "Got it. They'll be there."

"Good." She paused. "I wasn't going to say anything about this, but I ran into your sister the other day and she told me about your dad. That's . . . that's tough. And I'm sorry."

I adjusted the cap on my head, feeling guilty because I still hadn't talked things out with Bree. "Yeah. Thanks."

"Are you going to see him?"

"I don't think so."

She nodded. "I get it."

"Do you think I'm being too harsh?" I asked. Naomi had been around since high school and all through my mom's illness, so she knew the history.

Exhaling, she lifted her shoulders. "I think you have a powerful sense of right and wrong, and you've always known which side of the line he's on. But I also know that letting go of painful shit from the past feels better than hanging on to it."

"Yeah." I hefted my keys in my hand, impatient to leave. "I'm still thinking about it."

"Good luck. And Dex . . ." She put a hand on my arm. "I know your first instinct is to shut down when things get emotional, but don't shut Bree out. She's worried about you."

I stiffened, annoyed even though I knew she was right. "I know. I'll talk to her."

Twenty minutes later, I knocked on Bree's back door. Justin pulled it open, holding Prescott over his shoulder. "You knock now?"

"Wasn't sure if I'd be welcome." I rubbed my jaw. "Last time I was here, there was some, uh, shouting."

He shrugged. "Family shouts sometimes. Come on in."

Their house smelled delicious, and something about it reminded me of childhood. I messed around with my nephew Peter in the family room for a few minutes, then took Prescott from Justin and held him out from me. "Hey, buddy." He made a gurgling noise and smiled at me.

"Good, he likes you." Justin sank onto the couch. "How about you carry him around for a while? Every time I put him down, he screams."

"I'll take him." I actually liked holding babies. They were

so tiny yet chubby at the same time, and they fit right in the crook of my arm. And they never shit-talked.

I tucked Prescott against my side and ventured into the kitchen. Bree, stirring mushrooms on the stove, looked over at me. "I thought I heard your voice. Are you here for dinner?"

"If I'm invited."

"Of course you're invited. I'm making Mom's stroganoff."

"That's what it is." I inhaled deeply. "Mmm. I haven't had stroganoff in years."

She turned the heat off under the pan and scooped the sautéed mushrooms into a big blue pot. "I don't make it too often, but I was in the mood for it. I've been thinking about Mom lately."

Prescott started to fuss, so I put him over my shoulder and patted his back. "Did you see Dad again?"

She began filling another pot with water. "Yes. I saw him last Sunday. And I'll see him next Saturday—a week from today."

"How is he?"

Placing the pot on the stove, she shrugged. "Sick. The visits aren't long. But I brought Justin and the boys last time."

"He never mentioned it."

"I asked him not to." She turned on the gas under the water. "It upsets you."

I took a breath. "I'm sorry about that. I lost my temper the last time I was here."

"You did," she agreed, "but I shouldn't have provoked you that way. I know it's a sensitive subject."

"Which subject? Dad? Or Winnie?"

"Both." She turned to face me, one hand on her hip. "Is she gone?"

Stroking Prescott's back, I sniffed his head—he smelled like baby shampoo. "Yes."

"Are you guys . . ." She struggled for a word. "Friends?"

"Not exactly. I apologized for what I said, but she asked for time."

Bree nodded. "That's understandable. She must have been really hurt."

"She was." My stomach hollowed out all over again. "But I told her what I said wasn't the truth."

"What is the truth?"

"The truth is probably closer to what you said."

She was caught off guard. "Really?"

"Yeah."

"Which part?"

I kissed the side of Prescott's head. "All of it, I guess. That I felt more for Winnie than I wanted to admit. That I hated Mom for taking Dad back all the time. That I don't like being vulnerable to other people."

My sister looked stunned. "I never thought I'd hear you say that."

"Yeah, well . . . I'm stubborn."

"So now what?"

"Now nothing. Now she's gone." I decided not to mention her upcoming visit just yet.

"She's gone because you didn't tell her how you felt. I bet she'd have reconsidered that job if she'd known."

"She knows," I said.

Bree's eyebrows shot up. "You told her you loved her before she left?"

I hesitated. "Kind of. Yes."

"What did she say?"

"Nothing."

Her eyes bugged. "You told her you loved her and she said *nothing*?"

"I didn't exactly give her a chance to reply," I confessed. "I walked out right after."

Bree put the heels of her hands to her forehead. "Why?"

"Because there's nothing to be done about it," I said, carefully keeping my volume in check. Holding a baby definitely helped.

"But Dex, you *love* her. Don't you want to be with her?"

"If she was here, maybe. But I couldn't ask her not to go. After knowing each other for six weeks? That's insane."

Bree parked both hands on her hips. "On our second date, Justin—"

"Yes, I know. He told you he was going to marry you. That's insane too."

"But it was true. Look at us now."

"Winnie and I are different. I don't want to marry *anyone*. And I don't want more kids."

"Yes, I can see how having more children would be terrible for you." She gestured to Prescott. "You obviously hate babies."

I frowned. "Look, I faced my fear, okay? I told her how I felt. It sucks that she's so young and took a job somewhere else, but it was never going to work, she's gone now, and I'll be fine without her."

She sighed, turning her attention to the water boiling on the stove. Grabbing a bag of egg noodles, she ripped it open and dumped them in. "Okay, Dex. If you say so."

"I do."

"Because you don't look fine. You look like you haven't slept in a week."

"I said I'll *be* fine—once I stop missing her."

She nodded but said nothing.

"What?"

"Nothing. I don't want to argue."

"But . . ."

"But I still think you're throwing away something that could be great because you don't want to risk rejection, and that hurts me to think about. But I'm not going to say anything more, because I hate when there's weirdness between us, and the last two weeks have been weird." She sniffed. "You're the only brother I've got, and you're always in my corner. I hope you know I'm always in yours."

Touched, I swallowed hard. That was something our mom used to say—if you loved someone, you were in their corner. Always. "Thanks."

Later that night, I lay in bed staring at my phone in my hands. Three times I tried to start a message to Winnie and ended up deleting every word.

Finally, I forced myself to get it done for the girls' sake.

Hey. I hope you're doing well. The girls read your email to me, and it sounds like everything is going great in Newport. They would like to see you next weekend while you're in town. Unfortunately, Naomi's wedding is that weekend, so Friday and Saturday are out. Could we meet you Sunday before you head out? Maybe at your mom's bakery after church? No pressure. Let me know.

After rereading it a hundred times, I thoroughly despised every word. It said nothing about how I felt, how much I missed her, how badly I wished she was coming home to see *me* in addition to working her event. Maybe she'd have stayed with me—we could have had the entire weekend together. Slept two nights in my bed. Woken up together—I'd never gotten to wake up with her.

Angry, I hit send and put my phone on the charger. Then I switched off the lamp, rolled over and yanked the covers to my shoulder.

Miserable. Frustrated. Alone.

Twenty-Six

Winnie

I WAS SITTING ON MY COUCH IN THE NEW APARTMENT WORKING on some social media content for The Alexander when the text from Dex came in.

Holding my breath, I read it through three times.

Exhaling, I closed my eyes. Tears welled behind my lids, which surprised and annoyed me. Why should he still have the power to make me sad when things were going so well?

I loved my new job, and I liked all my co-workers, especially Sandra. She was in her fifties, recently widowed, and had moved away from Manhattan to start a second chapter in her life. Her kids were in college and she lived alone, so sometimes she and I worked late nights together and ended up having dinner while we worked. She was fast becoming a mentor, if not a friend, and I really admired her work ethic, style, and grit.

The Alexander was beautiful, and I had a small office of my very own with a view of the gardens. My new apartment was tiny—just one bedroom and one bath—but close to work, not far from the beach, and I could walk to downtown Newport within minutes.

It just didn't feel like home.

I told myself to give it time—it had only been ten days,

after all—but inwardly I worried that I'd never feel like I *belonged* here. Ellie and I were in constant touch about our wine tasting dinner, and that kept me feeling close ties to Cloverleigh Farms too.

But I was determined to push forward, be successful, and meet new friends. I'd promised myself I'd start saying yes to some of my co-workers' invites to drinks after I got back from Michigan next weekend—that is, if I survived seeing Dex, I thought, as my eyes ran over his words a fourth time.

It didn't even sound like him. There was no grumpy humor, no dirty words, no personality. It was just straightforward, polite, almost formal.

Had he gotten over me already? Maybe he wasn't afraid to see me. Maybe out of sight was out of mind for him, and I was nothing more than a girl he used to know. My throat squeezed with the need to cry, but I fought back.

After a deep breath, I picked up my phone and replied, being careful to adopt the same polite formality he'd used.

Hey Dex, thanks for the note. Things are going well here. I enjoy getting emails from the girls and miss seeing their faces. I can meet you all on Sunday morning at Plum & Honey, but it will have to be before church because my flight leaves at 11:10. Let me know if that is okay.

I hit send and stared at my phone in my hand. My pulse quickened as I imagined him reading it. Where was he? Was it a work night? Was he in bed or on the couch? Would he write back again tonight?

Suddenly three dots appeared, and I held my breath. But they only lasted a few seconds, and then stopped. No reply arrived. Disappointed, I set my phone aside and went back to what I was doing, ignoring the tear that slipped down my cheek.

I didn't hear back from Dex for two days.

Sorry for the delay. We will meet you at 8:00 at the bakery Sunday morning.

As soon as I read it, I burst into tears.

It was so impersonal! Not even a greeting this time. And his tone was even more flat. Would it have killed him to say he was looking forward to it? Or wish me safe travels? Or ask how I was? How could he go from holding me in his arms almost every night and confessing that he loved me to this *nothing*ness?

I read the text right before a meeting with Sandra. Since I was due in her office in ten minutes, I quickly ran to the bathroom down the hall and tried to clean up my face.

When the meeting was over, Sandra asked me if I was okay.

"I'm fine," I told her, reaching for a tissue. "I'm sorry if I seemed a little out of it. I promise I got all the details we discussed written down."

"I trust you." She smiled at me from across her desk. "I just noticed you seemed a little anxious today. I haven't seen you smile once."

"I think it's this wine tasting dinner back home," I lied, dropping my eyes to my notepad. "I want everything to go well, and I'm not there to oversee things."

"Of course. But knowing you, everything is under control, and the event will be a huge success."

"Thank you." I stood up. "I really appreciate the time off so I can be there, and for the offer to look in on my cat. She's just getting accustomed to her new home, and I think traveling would be really stressful for her."

"Of course." She hesitated. "How about you? Still getting accustomed?"

I hesitated. "Yes, but I really love the job."

"Good. I'm glad to hear it. Are you getting out at all? Or

do our late nights at work make up the bulk of your social life?"

Blushing, I dropped my gaze to the surface of her desk. "I don't have much of a social life here. To be honest, I haven't felt much like going out."

"Why not?"

I wasn't going to get into it, but suddenly I heard myself blurt, "There was someone at home."

Her expression was surprised. "Oh."

I blinked several times, trying to prevent tears. "I'm sorry. I'm trying to forget about him, but it's hard."

"You broke up because of the move here?"

"You could say that . . . although we weren't together very long. We just met this summer, but unfortunately I developed some pretty strong feelings for him in a fairly short amount of time."

She nodded, closing her laptop. "Do you want to talk about it?"

"Thank you, but I don't think that will help. I just need to move on." I wiped my nose with the back of my knuckles.

"I know that feeling." Her smile was sympathetic. "Easier said than done, isn't it?"

I took a shaky breath. "Yes. I don't have good control of my feelings."

Sandra laughed gently and nudged her tissue box closer to me. "Oh my goodness, honey. Does anyone?"

"Most people have more than I do. I have a history of falling hard and fast for the wrong guys."

"I was that way too. And then I finally found the one that deserved me."

"I'm working on that." I blew my nose. "But what's so great about this feeling that I keep going after it?"

She smiled again. "When you find the right person, you'll know the answer to that. Don't give up on love, Winnie."

I grabbed another tissue. "This guy is a single dad, and I got to know his girls a little bit. They asked to see me while I'm home this weekend. I said yes, but now I don't know if I should. It's going to be hard to keep it together."

"Just remember that you're stronger than you think." She paused. "And also that he'll be *really* sorry someday. Does he honestly think he'll find someone better?"

I smiled. "Thanks. But he's pretty set on remaining alone for the rest of his life."

"Ah. He's *that* guy." She nodded knowingly and leaned back in her chair. "I was married to that guy for twenty years. Trust me on this. He's probably stewing in a big pot of misery right now."

I shrugged. "Hard to say for sure. He's pretty spare with his feelings in his texts."

"Listen, if you decide to see him, make sure you wear something amazing, just to rub it in a little. He deserves it."

That made me laugh. "Okay."

"And when you get back, let's get you out and about. I know some nice young guys I'd be happy to introduce you to."

The idea had less than zero appeal, but I tried to smile and nod. "That would be nice. Thanks."

Thursday evening, I called Ellie while I was packing. After going over some details for the wine tasting, I told her I was seeing Dex and the girls on Sunday.

"You are?" She sighed. "Why doesn't that surprise me?"

"The kids asked to see me! How could I say no?"

"I guess you couldn't. I saw him the other day."

I gasped. "Where?"

"The dentist, of all places. In the waiting room. He was there with the kids."

"How did he look?"

"Grumpier than usual."

"Did he recognize you? Say hello?"

"He gave me a grunt and a nod."

I smiled sadly. "Sounds about right."

"So you're meeting for coffee?"

"Yeah." I stared at the clothing in my closet. "Sandra says to wear something amazing."

"Do it. Make him crazy."

"But it's cold there, right? I don't think I own any make-him-crazy sweaters and jeans. He used to like the skimpy stuff."

"You know what? It's not the clothes, Win. It's you. It won't matter what you wear. Show up and just be yourself—that's who he fell in love with, right?"

"I guess." I pulled a dresser drawer open and took out the white sweater I'd been wearing the last time I saw him. It was soft and cozy and oversized—I wore it when I wanted to hide from the world, not when I wanted to set it on fire.

But I folded it up and tucked it into my suitcase. It wasn't tight or revealing or the slightest bit sexy, but it was comfortable and warm, and I felt like *me* in it.

If plain old me wasn't enough for him, there was nothing I could do about it.

Twenty-Seven

Dex

FRIDAY AFTERNOON, I PULLED INTO THE COMPLEX PARKING LOT and noticed an unfamiliar car in Winnie's driveway. At first, I assumed it was the real estate agent or maybe someone looking at the place, but then I saw Winnie herself come out the front door and check the mailbox.

My breath caught, and my heart hammered in my chest. My foot slammed on the gas, my tires screeching as I swerved into my driveway. I didn't even pull into the garage, and I nearly forgot to turn off the engine as I jumped out and ran for her front porch.

Her eyes went wide as I raced up the steps, and she backed up against the door, hugging the mail to her chest. "Dex. Hi."

"Hi." Breathless, full of pent-up feelings for her, my entire body vibrated with the need to touch her. My hands twitched at my sides. "Did you just get in?"

"Yes." Her eyes glanced at the strange car in her driveway. "I borrowed my mom's car to run by and grab the mail and just, um, check on things here."

I nodded, although I barely heard a word she said. She was so fucking beautiful. It had only been two weeks since I'd seen her, but it felt like she'd been gone for a year. How had

I forgotten the midnight blue of her eyes or the gold in her hair or the way her cheeks grew pink when she looked at me?

Her thick black lashes lowered as she studied our feet. "Did you just come from the gym?"

I glanced down at my running shoes. "Yeah. I had a couple private coaching sessions."

"How's that going?"

"Good." But I didn't want to talk about that. I didn't really want to talk about anything—I just wanted to kiss her. I wanted to kiss her so fucking bad. Would she shove me right off this porch? Or would she kiss me back?

When she looked up at me, I nearly lost it and put my mouth on hers. Her lips fell open, and I swayed forward.

"I should go," she said, breaking the spell. "I'll see you Sunday." Then she zipped past me without so much as bumping my elbow.

What the hell? Were we strangers now? How could she be so cool when I was losing my mind?

"Winnie, wait." I jumped off the porch and chased after her, catching her arm halfway down the walk.

"What?" She pulled her arm from my grasp but turned to face me. "I—I'm running late. I have to meet Ellie."

I struggled for words. Shifted my weight from one foot to the other. "Can I see you later tonight?"

She shook her head. "No, Dex."

"Why not?"

"Because I'm trying to move on from you. And spending time alone with you after dark won't help."

"But I've missed you." It was torture to keep myself from embracing her. "I've missed you so fucking much."

"I've missed you too." Her eyes filled, and she blinked back tears. "But the answer is still no."

"It wasn't supposed to be this way," I said angrily. "You

were the one who told me not to fall in love with you. You said no love, no happily ever after, and no Frostys."

"I know." Her shoulders rose and her tears fell. "I wasn't supposed to love you either, Dex. I thought I could be with you and guard my heart, but suddenly I looked and it was gone. Same old story."

"No." I took her by the shoulders. "I am *not* those other guys. You don't get it. If I was younger, if I thought I could offer you any kind of future, I would."

"So what exactly are you offering me right now?" She laughed bitterly. "A night? A weekend? A quickie?"

"I don't know," I said desperately. "I just know I can't see you and not want to be with you. I told you I loved you, Winnie. Isn't that enough?"

"No." Wrenching free from my arms, she took a step back. "I want more than that. I want someone who isn't afraid to take a chance on a future with me. I want someone who doesn't hide behind excuses. And I *want* the fucking Frostys."

I couldn't argue with her. But I couldn't bring myself to take the chance she was asking for either.

When I said nothing, she rushed to her mom's car, jumped in, and took off.

Frustrated, I glared at her taillights and stood there a full two minutes after she left.

Then I stomped over to my car like an angry toddler, got in, and slammed the door. Sitting in the driver's seat, I gripped the steering wheel with both hands and breathed hard through my nose. I felt like what I wanted was right in front of me, but I couldn't reach it. It was like fucking Freddie Purrcury in my dream—just when I was close enough to reach him, he hopped to the next branch.

"Fucking women and cats," I muttered, opening the garage and pulling in. "They're impossible."

I spent another restless night staring at my ceiling, burying my head beneath my pillow, and trying not to think about the fact just a few weeks ago, she'd been right here next to me. I missed her with an ache I hadn't felt since losing my mom.

But I refused to pick up the phone and reach out to her. There was no point. I was never going to be that guy she described, and she wouldn't come near me otherwise.

I just had to get through Sunday, and try to forget about her.

The following afternoon I was still sitting around my place feeling sorry for myself when I got a text from Chip.

Hey, I'm in town unexpectedly. Time for a beer?
Definitely.
Name the time and place and I'll be there.
Let's meet up at Southpaw Brewing Co at 5:00.

Relieved to have something to do tonight, I sent back a thumbs up and went upstairs to take a shower.

Just before five, I walked into Southpaw Brewing Co., which was owned by Tyler Shaw. In a couple hours, it would be packed, but since it was still early, I was able to find a seat at the bar. After looking over the menu, I ordered a Knuckleball Ale and a basket of wings. I'd just taken my first sip when Chip showed up, clapping me on the shoulder before dropping onto the stool next to me.

"Hey man," he said. "Good to see you."

"You too. How'd you end up in town?"

"Mariah and I decided to run up here and check out some possible wedding spots." He signaled the bartender and ordered a Bandbox IPA. "We saw several today, and then April took her over to a bridal shop just for fun. Thankfully, I was excused."

"So when's the wedding?"

"We're thinking early February, although we could do later that month since I won't have to be at spring training."

I paused with my beer halfway to my mouth. "Did you retire for real?"

He nodded and thanked the bartender who set his beer down in front of him. "I haven't announced it yet, but I told my folks."

"How do you feel about it?"

He took a drink from his beer. "Fucking great, actually. I'm ready for the next chapter of my life, and so's my shoulder."

I laughed. "I'm happy for you."

"So how've you been? I heard Tyler has you doing some training at Bayside."

"Yeah. That's going well, actually."

"And the kids are good?"

"Kids are good." I rubbed the back of my neck. "They're at Naomi's wedding reception tonight. I'm picking them up later."

"No shit. Naomi got remarried?"

I nodded. "To Bryce Vogel. Remember that guy?"

Chip squinted. "Red hair? Lacrosse team? His parents gave him a sailboat for graduation?"

"That's the one."

"Huh. Interesting." He glanced at me. "You okay with it?"

"I'm fine."

"How come you don't sound fine?"

Exhaling, I took another sip of my beer. "I did something stupid."

"What?"

"After your party, I started spending a bunch of time with Winnie, and even though we both agreed it was supposed to be casual, somehow it didn't stay that way."

Chip laughed, shaking his head. "Oh man, I saw this coming."

I frowned. "Well, I didn't. Not in time to stop it, anyway. Then she got this great job offer in fucking Rhode Island."

"April told me about that today. So she left, huh?"

"Yes. And before she left, she told me she wanted to try to make things work with us, even if we had to do it long-distance, but I panicked and broke it off instead. Now she's been gone for two weeks, and I'm a fucking wreck without her."

"So tell her how you feel. Is there any chance she'd come back?"

"I don't want her to come back! Not for me, anyway," I said.

He gave me a strange look. "Why not?"

"Because I don't want her to make that kind of sacrifice and discover I'm not fucking worth it. I mean, we were only together for a month, maybe six weeks. That's not enough time." I hesitated. "Is it?"

Chip took a long swallow from his beer. "You might be asking the wrong guy here. But for what it's worth, I knew the day I met Mariah I would marry her."

I groaned. "What is *wrong* with everybody? How can you know that shit so fast?"

He laughed. "I don't know. It was just a gut instinct."

"My gut instincts told me to run the other way the day I met Winnie."

"Because she's so young?"

"Yes. She just *did* something to me, and I didn't like it. I didn't want to feel those things for someone, especially someone who's twenty-fucking-two."

"Mariah's twenty-four," he said. "That's not much older."

I took a drink and considered it. "Yeah, but we're different. I've already been married and failed at it. I've had my kids. And I don't have major league money."

"Winnie isn't the type to care about money."

"I know she isn't," I grumbled. "But I just can't wrap my head around asking her to come back here when I can't promise her what she ultimately wants. I mean, what if she wound up regretting it?"

"What do you think she ultimately wants?"

"Eventually? To get married and have kids. But let's say she's not ready for that for five more years—I'm going to start another family at fucking *forty*?"

Chip shrugged. "Why not? But let's say she was ready in one or two years. Would it change your mind?"

"No."

"Exactly. Because it's not the age that really bothers you. It's something else."

Annoyed that he could read me so well, I plunked both elbows on the bar and locked my fingers behind my neck. "What if I'm bad at being in a relationship? What if I've always been so careful not to give away too much of myself that I don't know how to do it? I mean, maybe all the shit Naomi said is true."

Chip took a deep breath. "Okay, listen. I wasn't there when you married Naomi, but I was there when you guys dated before, and it was not a good relationship. You two did nothing but piss each other off, fight, and get back together, probably because there was nothing better to do. I was shocked at the news you were getting married."

"Yeah. It wasn't a good idea." I shrugged. "But Hallie and Luna were worth it."

"How do they feel about Winnie?"

"They adore her."

"So let me ask you this. Does this thing with Winnie feel different from what you had with Naomi?"

"Night and day," I told him.

"Do you think maybe you could *try* to give away more

of yourself, at least enough to make Winnie feel like you're not going anywhere, no matter what? Because that's the only way to get her back."

I looked at him sideways. "That sounds scary as fuck."

"I know. And don't do it unless you mean it, or I'll have to kick your ass. She's still my little cousin."

"I know."

"And if it works out and we move up here, our kids can play baseball together. We can coach them. Or we can be those asshole dads on the bleachers that know everything."

Laughing, I picked up my beer again. "If I'm ever that guy, *please* kick my ass."

We hung out another hour or so, and then Chip had to leave to meet up with Mariah for dinner with his mom and stepdad. After he left, I noticed I had a text from my sister.

Hey, if you're not busy, can you come by? I have something for you. We just ordered pizza and salad and you're welcome to eat with us.

It wasn't even seven and I had no plans until I was scheduled to pick up the girls at ten-thirty, so I replied that I'd swing by in about twenty. I paid my bill and headed out.

I let myself in their back door and found Bree in the kitchen. As soon as she saw me, she handed me an envelope that said *Dexter* on it. The handwriting was unfamiliar.

"It's from Dad," she said, holding up her palms like she was innocent. "I didn't read it, I don't know what it says, I'm not pressuring you to read it. I only said I'd give it to you, and now I have."

I leaned back against the counter while Bree took out plates, forks, and napkins. Staring at the envelope in my hand, I grappled with conflicting emotions. "You saw him today?"

"Yes."

"Did you take the kids?"

She nodded. "We all went."

"How was it?"

"Okay, I guess. He can't get out of bed anymore, so we just visited for a little bit in his room."

"That sounds depressing."

She shrugged. "My kids are so small, they don't know anything. Justin said hello and went back to the living room. He mostly sat with Gloria and the kids out there while I talked to Dad."

"What does he say?"

"He actually did more talking today. He told me about the way he grew up, his abusive father, his mother's nervous breakdowns. It was sad, but it gave me a lot of insight into him." She opened the fridge. "Want a beer?"

"No, thanks."

She took one out for herself and popped the cap off. "I don't think he has too much more time."

"Months? Weeks?"

"I didn't ask." She tipped up her beer. "So tonight was the wedding, right?"

"Yeah. I have to pick up the girls from the reception in a few hours. We're meeting Winnie in the morning at eight."

Her eyebrows rose. "Winnie's in town?"

I nodded. "She had a work event at Cloverleigh Farms tonight and she's flying out tomorrow."

"Have you seen her yet?"

"Just briefly on the porch yesterday." I grimaced. "I didn't handle it too well."

She smiled. "What did you do, ask her to spend the night?"

"No," I said, although that's exactly what I'd had in mind. "I just asked if I could see her later, because she was in a hurry. But she said no."

My sister shrugged. "You can't blame her, Dex. If you want her back, you have to make it clear something has changed."

"I know," I said, tapping the letter against the palm of my hand. "I'm thinking about it."

Although I didn't have much appetite, I ate some dinner with Bree and Justin and headed home around eight.

When I got there, I stared at the envelope on the counter for a solid fifteen minutes before working up the courage to tear it open. I did it less out of curiosity for what he had to say than to prove to myself I could still do hard things.

Unfolding the typed pages, I began to read.

Dear Dexter,

I am sorry this letter isn't written by hand, but I asked Gloria to type it for me because my writing is too shaky and I want every word to be clear.

I don't blame you for not coming to see me. If I was in your shoes, I don't think I would come either. In fact, I was in your shoes, years ago when my own father was dying. He didn't ask to see me and I didn't go. I can't say for sure that I am sorry, but sometimes I wonder what he might have said if I'd seen him then.

I think a lot about what I would say to you if you were here. I know that I was not a good father to you, and I would tell you I was sorry. The words would not be good enough, but I'd mean them. I do mean them.

I would tell you how proud I am of you. You did everything you said you were going to do. A man is only as good as his word, and that means you are the best kind of man.

Bree tells me you are an incredible father and I believe her. I can see that she's a wonderful mother too, just like your mother was.

She used to amaze me with her patience and kindness and generous heart. I see so much of her in your sister, and I know she is in you too.

I regret that I didn't pass on to you much of anything good. I never knew how to be a good father and now I know I was too scared of failing to try. But if there is still time to pass on one thing I have learned, it would be this:

Never let fear get in the way of being the kind of man you want to be.

When you look back, what will matter most?

Dad

At first I was mad and wanted to ball up the letter and burn it. His regrets weren't my problem.

But once my temper was in check, I took a few deep breaths and read it through again. And again. And again. Eventually, the anger dissipated and I took a step back, looked a little deeper.

He wasn't asking forgiveness, he wasn't begging me to show up, he wasn't placing any burden on me—he just wanted me to have one thing from him that wasn't shitty, one piece of advice that might serve me.

And I had to admit, the advice was timely. I *was* letting fear get in the way of the kind of man I wanted to be.

But it was the question at the end that really stuck out to me.

I put my jacket back on and went out to the patio. It was chilly, but the cool air felt good in my lungs and on my face. I sat there until it was time to go get the girls, thinking about what he'd asked.

When I looked back, would it matter that I was strong enough to keep my heart in a vault? Would I be proud of that? Would I wear my loneliness like a badge of honor?

Or would I forever regret letting go of someone I loved

and walking away from someone who made me happy, all because I wanted to prove I could?

Looking at it that way, I saw how wrong I was. How misguided. And I didn't want to spend the rest of my life being iron-willed instead of happy.

I had no idea what the future would bring, but I loved Winnie enough to take a chance on us.

I loved her enough to believe there might *actually* be a happily ever after.

And in the morning, I'd tell her so.

Twenty-Eight

L ATE SATURDAY MORNING, I WENT TO THE SALON WITH MY mom for a manicure, which she'd scheduled as a surprise for me.

At first, I balked at taking the time out of my day for a personal indulgence—I wanted to oversee the table setting on the patio at Cloverleigh Farms, make sure the tent was up, ensure heaters were there and working, check in with the chef, and go over my notes with her on the evening's menu.

But my mother would hear none of it.

"Come on, it's one hour. And you need to relax a little before your big night," she scolded at the breakfast table. "Plus I took the morning off just to spend it with you, so you have to deal with me."

I gave in eventually, and we headed into town around eleven. As my mom checked us in at the salon, I took a seat on a pink velvet couch and pulled out my phone to send a quick text to Ellie. **Hey, my mom sprung some mother-daughter bonding time on me. Can you pick me up at 3:00 instead of 2:00?**

A moment later I heard my name.

"Winnie's here!"

I looked up in surprise and saw Hallie and Luna racing

toward me. "Oh my goodness! Hi, girls!" Sticking my phone back into my bag, I rose to my feet as they barreled into me.

I laughed as they threw their arms around my waist. They were dressed casually in jeans and zip-up hoodies, but their hair was formally styled—Hallie's usual straight locks cascaded past her shoulders in soft waves, and the front was twisted back and held in place with sprigs of baby's breath. Luna's curls were soft and shiny, and she wore a headband decorated with flowers.

"You two look beautiful," I told them, admiring their tresses. "Is this for the wedding?"

"Yes. We're flower girls," Luna said excitedly.

"But this isn't what we're wearing." Hallie gestured to their casual clothing. "Our dresses are at home."

"Oooh, what do they look like?" I asked.

"They're sparkly on top and swishy on the bottom," said Luna, twirling in a circle.

I smiled. "What color?"

"The top part is gold and the bottom part is ivory." Hallie pointed at her sister. "Hers is short and mine is longer. I wanted a long dress."

"I bet they're so pretty." I touched her dark waves. "Your hair looks gorgeous."

"What's this?" My mother came over and smiled at the girls.

"Don't they look pretty? It's their mom's wedding today."

"That's right!" Glancing around, my mom spotted a woman I assumed was Naomi in one of the chairs and waved. She smiled and waved back.

I smiled too, although my stomach felt funny knowing I was looking at Dex's former wife. She was very pretty, with blond hair and fair skin, and I saw the resemblance to Luna right away.

Hallie tugged at my hand. "What are you doing here?"

Tearing my eyes from the bride, I looked down at the little girl. "Getting my nails done with my mom."

"Where's Piglet?" Luna asked. "Did she come with you?"

"No, Piglet doesn't like to travel, so she's back in Rhode Island. I have someone to watch her for me."

"Does she like her new house now?"

I put out my hand and tilted it this way and that. "She's still getting used to it. How's Freddie Purrcury?"

"Good," Hallie said. "Daddy says he's rude but we love him."

I laughed. "What does he do that's rude?"

But just then, Naomi walked up. "Hello. You must be Winnie?"

"Yes." Nervous, I offered a hand. "It's nice to meet you. You look beautiful."

"Thank you." She shook my hand with a cool, firm grip. "I'm Naomi. Nice to meet you too. The girls talk about you all the time."

I smiled at them. "They're such great girls."

"How was your move?"

"Oh, you know. It was a move," I said, wondering what else she knew about me. "But I like my new job and I'm settling in."

"Good." Her smile seemed genuine, and I returned it.

"You look gorgeous, Naomi," my mother said. "I can't wait to see pictures."

"Thanks, Frannie." Naomi smiled warmly at my mom. "How are you?"

"I'm wonderful this weekend since I have my Winifred home." My mom put an arm around me and squeezed. "I'm not going to want to let her go again."

"It's hard being away from your kids." She looked down at her daughters. "What do you say, girls? Should we head out?"

"Bye, girls," I said, giving each of them a hug. "It was so good to see you."

"Bye, Winnie. We'll still see you tomorrow, right?" Hallie looked up at me imploringly. "Daddy said we will."

I nodded, although the thought of facing Dex made my chest feel hollow. "Yes, I'll see you in the morning."

They filed out, and I waved through the glass as they passed in front of the salon. Then I put my hand on my stomach and took a breath.

"You okay?" my mom asked, concerned.

"I'm fine," I said. "It's just a big day, and my nerves are a little jittery."

"It's going to be great." She put an arm around my shoulder as we walked back to the nail stations. "Have some faith."

Later that night, Ellie and I sat at the bar at Cloverleigh Farms, toasting our success. The event we'd planned had sold out and gone off without a hitch. The guests had raved about everything from the setting to the food to the service, we'd sold a ton of wine at the end of the night, and both Henry DeSantis and Mr. Fournier, who'd been on the premises but stayed out of sight, were thoroughly impressed. As an added bonus, Ellie and I'd had a ball together—it had hardly felt like work.

"Cheers." Ellie tapped her whiskey glass to mine. "Here's to the first of hopefully many ventures together."

"Definitely." I drank with her. "That was so much fun."

"I wish you didn't live so far away," she said with a pout.

"Me too." I stared at the whiskey in my glass. "I love my new job, but . . . I don't know. Something just doesn't feel right. *I* don't feel right in my skin."

She sat up straighter and rubbed my back. "I'm sorry. That was selfish of me to say. Give yourself some time to get used to things there, Win. It's only been a couple weeks, and you're coming off a shitty breakup. I'm not sure you'd feel right in your skin anywhere, even here."

"That's true." I took another sip. "Seeing him yesterday sucked." I'd told Ellie all about my run-in with him on the porch. "I can't imagine still living next door to him."

She tipped her head onto my shoulder. "Yeah."

I squeezed my eyes shut. "I don't want to see him tomorrow."

"I don't blame you."

"Can I cancel?"

Ellie sighed. "I don't know. That would disappoint the kids, wouldn't it?"

"Yeah. But I saw them this morning, right?" I shook my head. "And I just can't face him and pretend my heart isn't breaking."

She sighed. "See? This is why love sucks. I don't know why everyone thinks it's so great."

For once, I didn't argue with her.

Just before Ellie and I left Cloverleigh Farms, I sent Dex a text.

Sorry to cancel on you, but I can't make it tomorrow morning. I'll email the girls. Take care.

I felt awful—like a coward—but told myself there was no other way.

Someone had to protect my heart.

Twenty-Nine

Dex

O
N THE WAY HOME FROM THE RECEPTION, THE GIRLS TALKED a mile a minute about everything—getting their hair done, seeing Winnie at the salon, their fancy dresses, the music and dancing, the cake . . . I was exhausted just hearing about it, but they were hopped up on so much sugar and excitement I worried they'd never fall asleep tonight. It was already after eleven, and they showed no signs of slowing down.

We'd just gotten in the house when my phone vibrated with an incoming text. I glanced at the screen and saw it was from Winnie. At first the name made me smile.

Then I read her message and panicked. "Shit!"

The girls finally stopped talking and twirling around in their dresses and looked at me. "What's wrong?" Hallie said.

I made a split-second decision. "Come on, girls. We have to go somewhere."

"Where?" asked Luna.

"To see Winnie." I grabbed my keys. "And we have to hurry."

"Yay!" Both girls cheered as we hustled back into the garage and got in the car.

"Do either of you two know where Winnie's parents live?"
I asked.

"Hmm," said Hallie. "Somewhere by that horse barn?"

"Maybe they live at the bakery," Luna suggested.

I pulled over and made a desperate phone call to Chip.
"Hello?"

"Thank God you answered."

"Dex? You okay?"

"Yes, but I need a favor. I'm really sorry to bother you so late, but I need to know Winnie's parents' address."

"What? Why?"

"Because I have to see her tonight. I promise to explain when I can, but I really need that address."

"Okay. We're at Tyler and April's, so I can ask. Give me a minute and I'll text it to you."

"Thanks, man. I owe you."

The wait seemed endless. Every fiber of my being was radiating with nervous energy. My leg bounced. My thumbs tapped the wheel. My stomach tied itself in knots.

"What's the big emergency?" asked Hallie.

"I have to tell her I was wrong about something. But she won't want to talk to me."

"So how will you get her to listen?" Luna asked.

"Good question." I looked at them in the back seat. "What would the ogre say to Princess Minnie to get her to forgive him?"

"Well, he has to rescue her cat," Hallie pointed out. "And to do that he would have to face his fear of heights."

"Okay, but let's say he's ready to do that," I said impatiently. "Let's say he's ready to face his fear, climb the tree, and rescue the cat. What does he tell her?"

Hallie tapped a finger on her lips. "He'd fall to his knees and apologize for being a jerk. He'd explain that he was only scared before but he's going to be brave for her—like a knight.

Then he'd rescue the cat and ask for another chance to be her friend. Because that's what the ogre really wants—a friend."

"Girls," I said. "I have to tell you something serious."

"Is it that you're in love with Winnie?" Hallie asked. "Because we already know that."

I stared at them in disbelief. "You do?"

"Yes, we made it happen," said Luna triumphantly. "With our noses."

"*What?*"

"Winnie taught us how to cast magic spells," Hallie explained.

"It worked for the cat." Luna shrugged. "So we figured it might work on you guys. Although we weren't supposed to say anything about it. Even Winnie doesn't know." She turned to Hallie. "Do you think we messed it up? What if it only worked on Daddy and not Winnie?"

Hallie shook her head. "We did it the same way for both. She *has* to love him."

I was still staring at them in disbelief when my phone lit up with a text from Chip. "So you're okay with it?"

"*Duh*," Hallie said. "We love Winnie. And she makes you less grumpy." Then she turned to Luna. "But I think we might need to cast another spell to get her to move back here."

"I might be able to help with that." I glanced at the address on my screen, typed it into my GPS, and hit the gas. "I'm at least going to try."

The MacAllisters lived on a narrow side street lined with two-story brick homes and shallow front lawns. When I pulled up in their driveway, the house was dark. I took out my phone, praying she was still awake—I didn't want to ring the doorbell, but I would.

"There aren't any lights on, Daddy." Luna sounded worried. "What are you going to do?"

"I'm texting her to see if she'll come out."

Winnie, I need to talk to you. Please.

Nothing.

I have things I need to say to you,
and I don't want to do it over text.

Silence.

I'm parked outside your parents' house,
and if you don't answer, I'm going to
knock on the door and wake everyone up.

Do NOT do that.

Adrenaline surged—she was awake!

Then come out and talk to me.

I don't want to see you, Dex.

That only makes it worse.

Give me a chance, Winnie. One chance.

Hear me out.

If I give you a chance,
you could hurt me again.

Then open your window, because I have something
to say to you and

I can't hold it in any longer.

Fueled by love and the fear of losing her, I jumped out from behind the wheel and ran onto the MacAllisters' front lawn. Behind me, I heard the girls getting out of the car too. I glanced over my shoulder and saw them huddled against the passenger door, watching with rapt attention.

"Stay there," I told them. Clinging to each other, they nodded.

"This is so exciting," Luna said.

"I know," Hallie agreed. "It's even better than Mom's wedding."

Standing in the cone of light thrown by a streetlamp, I looked up at the dark second-story windows in front of me. None of them had opened, but I decided to go for it.

Forming a megaphone with my hands, I yelled at the top of my lungs. "I love you, Winnie MacAllister! I love you, and

I'm sorry I didn't say it before! I was stupid and scared. But nothing is right without you, and if I don't try to get you back, I'll regret it for the rest of my life." Remembering Hallie's advice for the ogre, I dropped to my knees on the grass. "Please give me another chance!"

Breathing hard, I waited for a light to come on, a door to open, a sign that she still loved me . . . but the house remained dark and silent.

Crickets chirped.

I glanced over at the girls, who seemed just as distraught as I was. They looked at each other, and then back at me.

That's when I heard a feminine voice come out of the darkness behind me. "Hey Winnie? Yeah, it's Audrey. There's some guy across the street yelling at the Wilsons' house, but I think he's talking to you."

Oh, *fuck*.

Horrified, I spun around on my knees. A teenage couple stood under a front porch light at a home across the street. The girl was talking into her phone.

"Dude," the guy called out. "I think you're at the wrong house."

Fuck. Me.

Behind the couple, the front door opened and a barrel-chested man came storming out the front door wearing jeans, a USMC sweatshirt, and a scowl. "What's going on out here? Who's shouting?"

"That guy over there is telling Winnie that he's sorry and he loves her, but he's at the wrong house," said the girl. "I feel *really* bad for him."

"What?" The man's chest puffed out further and he squinted in my direction.

Then Winnie's mom appeared on the porch, pulling a cardigan around her. "Is everything okay?"

No. Everything was not okay.

"Who is that guy?" her dad asked, and by his tone I could tell what he meant was, *Who is that fucking idiot?*

"Is it Dex?" Frannie leaned forward and squinted. "Is that you, Dex?"

"Yeah. It's me." I'd never wanted a sinkhole to open up and swallow me as badly as I did at that moment. If my kids hadn't been there, I might have taken off on foot.

Just then, a car pulled into their driveway, and my stomach lurched when Winnie jumped out of the passenger side. Her friend Ellie got out of the driver's side and looked back and forth between Winnie and me. "Holy shit," she said.

"Dex?" Winnie started walking down the drive and stopped at the sidewalk, gaping at me kneeling in the spotlight from the streetlamp above. "What on earth are you doing?"

"Hi, Winnie!" Hallie and Luna started jumping up and down and waving like mad. "Hi!"

And then, because apparently there wasn't a big enough audience, another car pulled up in front of the MacAllisters' house, and a second teenage girl jumped out. "Bye!" she yelled, waving as the car drove off. Then she noticed everyone outside. "Oh, crap. Did I miss curfew or something?"

"No," the first teenage girl said, hopping down from the porch. "Omigod, Emmeline, this is amazing. Kyle was just leaving when this man pulled up, jumped out of his car, and starts shouting to Winnie that he loves her and he wants another chance—but he was yelling at the Wilsons' house, not ours. Not that it mattered, because she wasn't even here."

"Audrey, be quiet!" Winnie put her hands on her head. "Dex. What is this? Why are you on your knees?"

"We told him to do that!" Hallie shouted proudly. "Because that's what the ogre would do!"

"He was begging you for another chance, Win," Audrey said eagerly. "Are you going to give it to him?"

"Audrey, enough." Frannie put a hand over Audrey's mouth from behind. But nobody else moved.

Reluctantly, I got to my feet, took both girls by the hand, and crossed the street. When we reached the sidewalk, I told them to stay put and moved closer to where Winnie stood frozen at the end of the driveway.

"I'm sorry," I said. "This was supposed to be a big romantic gesture, but it turned into a demonstration of public humiliation."

"Oh my God." She wrapped one arm around her middle, bringing the other hand to her mouth.

"But I guess I'm too far in to turn back now, and you know what?" I shook my head. "I don't want to."

"Because he loves you," Luna said from behind me. "Daddy, you have to say that part again, because she didn't hear you."

"Because I love you," I repeated, looking her right in the eye. "I know I'm too old for you, and you could have anyone you wanted—someone with a bigger bank account, someone younger and smarter, someone with way less baggage."

"Someone less hairy," said Hallie.

"That doesn't snore," added Luna.

"As I was *saying*," I went on, throwing a brief but menacing glance over my shoulder at my kids, "I know you could find someone better for you. But you won't find someone who loves you more. Or wants to be with you the way I do."

"But what about all the things you said before?" Winnie asked with tears in her eyes. "About how we should go our separate ways?"

"I said things to push you away because I was scared," I confessed. "You ignited a fire in me I couldn't put out. I couldn't control my feelings for you, and I'm someone who likes to be in control all the time. But Winnie, that fear was nothing compared to how scared I've been that I lost you forever. I never should have let you go without telling you that I love you, I want to be with you no matter where you are, and even though you were in fucking *kindergarten* when I graduated from high school, you've taught me something incredible."

"What?" she whispered, tears falling freely now.

I smiled at her. "To believe in happily ever after."

"Now you kiss her!" crowed Luna.

"And the spell will be complete!" Hallie finished.

I cradled Winnie's face in my palms and pressed my lips to hers.

"Holy shit," Ellie repeated.

"Dude," said the teenage guy.

"What do you say?" I whispered. "Can I have one more chance to make you mine?" I glanced back at the girls. "Or maybe *ours*?"

"Yes," Winnie said, laughing and crying at the same time. She melted into my arms, and held me tight. "I love you too, and *yes*."

The girls rushed forward and circled both of us in their arms, and my heart had never felt so full. After a moment, we turned to face the stunned crowd.

"I got that whole thing on video!" shouted Emmeline, holding up her phone.

"You know," said Winnie's father, scratching his head, "something about this seems very familiar."

"I thought so too," said his wife, slipping an arm around his waist. "And I think this calls for some cookies and hot chocolate. Who wants to come in for a minute and let these two have a moment alone?"

"Me!" shouted Hallie and Luna, racing toward the porch.

"Thanks, Mom," Winnie called. "We'll be there in a minute." We watched as the MacAllister family, Kyle, and the girls trooped inside the house.

"I'm going to head out," Ellie said. She gave Winnie a hug and shook my hand. "Dex, that was . . . something else."

My face was hot. "Yeah."

"I'm just glad I was here to witness it. And you." She pointed at Winnie. "Owe me the thing."

Winnie groaned. "Shit, I guess I do. When?"

"We'll talk. Night, you guys."

She got into her car and drove away, leaving Winnie and me alone—finally. When I took her hands, she shivered.

"Are you cold?" I asked. "Let's get in my car."

"No, I'm not cold." Laughing, she shivered a second time. "I'm just shocked and happy. Is this a dream?"

"For a while there, it felt like a nightmare."

"You poor thing, over there on the Wilsons' lawn." She threw her arms around me and clung tight. "But no one has ever done anything like that for me."

"What, made a total fool of himself?"

"Yes. It means everything! When I got out of that car and saw you there on your knees, my heart melted. I was mush."

I kissed her nose. "But you still made me give the speech."

"Of course I did—running through the street is only half the big romantic gesture. The guy still has to say all the things."

"Did I say them all? I feel like I left out half the stuff I wanted to tell you. The crowd was making me nervous."

"Tell me now that we're alone."

I looked down at her blissfully happy face. "I want to be with you no matter where you are. And I know asking you to leave your new job and move back here just for me is shitty and unfair."

"But you want me to do it?"

I nodded. "I'd be lying if I said I didn't want you with me all the time. You make every single day better." I kissed her lips. "You make me better."

Her eyes closed, and she tucked herself against me. "I want to be with you all the time too. We'll figure it out, Dex. I love you so much—God, it feels good to say that."

"It feels good to hear it. Better than I even imagined."

She leaned back at the waist again. "What made you change your mind?"

"Apart from feeling like you took a huge piece of me with you when you left and there was a gaping hole in my life?"

She smiled. "Yes."

"Conversations with people who matter to me. My sister. My girls. Justin. Chip. Even Naomi, believe it or not."

Her eyebrows rose. "You told Naomi about us?"

"She sort of guessed, based on things the girls have said, and I didn't deny it." I kissed her forehead. "I'm done hiding and pretending. I don't care who knows I'm in love with you."

Her smile warmed my entire body. "Me neither. I can't wait to introduce you to my dad and sisters."

I winced. "Your dad must think I'm such an asshole."

"No way. Sometime I'll tell you the story of the day my sisters and I made him go declare his love for my mom at her job in the middle of the day." She smiled at the memory. "Tonight really brings that moment full circle."

"I can't imagine thinking anyone is good enough for my daughters, let alone some guy so much older who already has two kids."

She laughed. "You just described my dad and Frannie— he's ten years older than she is, and he had *three* kids when they met. He has no room to get weird about that."

"Still doesn't mean he'll think I'm good enough for you."

"Well, you are." She tucked her head beneath my chin again, and I held her warm, soft body to mine. "You make me happy, and that's all a dad can ask for."

"I got a letter from my dad," I said quietly.

"You did?"

"Yeah." I cleared my throat. "I'll show it to you. It was also part of what made me realize how stubborn I was being.

How stupid it was to let my fucking ego call the shots. When I think about my life and how I want to live it, you're there."

She kissed my chest and held me tighter.

"I want to take care of you," I said gruffly. "I know you don't need it, but I do."

"I love that you're protective of me." Her tone was adorably ferocious. "I love that you're older than me. I love that you're a dad and a firefighter and always trying to keep the people close to you safe."

I rubbed her back. "Even though I'm a hairy ogre at heart?"

She laughed. "Even so. You're *my* hairy ogre, and I'll be your princess forever."

My forehead rested on hers. "I wish we could spend tonight together. I want to wake up next to you."

"I want that too, but we'll have lots of nights together."

"Can the girls and I still take you to breakfast in the morning?"

"You better." She leaned back again. "What was that about a magic spell?"

"That was your doing—I assume you taught them about the nose wiggling?"

"I did, but I had no idea they remembered it." She laughed as we started walking toward the house. "Are they going to claim responsibility for this?"

"Of course they are. They said it worked for the cat, and now it worked on us."

"They'll probably ask for a dog next," Winnie said as we stepped onto the porch.

"Or a baby brother."

She looked up at me and laughed. "Does that terrify you?"

"Actually, it doesn't."

Her jaw dropped.

Grinning, I pulled open the front door. "Come on. Our family is waiting for us."

Thirty

Winnie

Two Months Later

"**I** CAN'T BELIEVE I HAVE TO DO THIS."

Ellie was not sympathetic. "Hey. You took the bet, you lost the bet. Now you pay."

I looked around the crowded Mexican restaurant, which was always filled to capacity on karaoke night. Unfortunately for me, it was also the night before Christmas Eve, so in addition to all the regulars, the place was jam-packed with holiday tourists from all the nearby ski resorts.

Did I mention every single member of my family was there too? Also Dex, Hallie and Luna, Bree and Justin, Chip and Mariah, and half the Sawyer clan? Somehow they'd all heard about tonight and thought it sounded like a good time—I was going to murder Ellie if I lived through this.

Our group occupied a bunch of tables near the stage, where someone with way more talent than me was currently belting out a Whitney Houston song.

"You're supposed to be my best friend," I whined. "Can't we work something out?"

"Dex, she's trying to get out of it again," Ellie said to him across the table.

"Dex knows how bad I am." I turned to him. "You hate my singing voice."

"I don't hate anything about you." He tapped my nose. "Plus this is going to be hilarious."

"Ellie, I'm begging you." I clasped my hands under my chin and pleaded with her. "Don't make me get up there. I will die."

"You're not going to die." She plucked a corn chip from the basket on the table and crunched happily. "You're just going to know total and utter humiliation for like three minutes. But what's three minutes compared to the lifetime of happiness you two are going to share?"

"And shouldn't that count for something?" I bounced in my chair, panicking as "I Wanna Dance with Somebody" wrapped up. "I mean, this is real love! This wasn't like those times before—I didn't fall in love with a jerk, I fell in love with my soul mate! We've been together for months! I gave up my dream job for him."

It was all true. After Dex's big romantic gesture on the Wilsons' lawn, I'd flown back to Rhode Island and been honest with Sandra Elson about what had transpired on my weekend visit home. She encouraged me to take time to think about my decision, but in my heart I knew where I belonged. With sincere apologies, I thanked her for the opportunity and gave my notice a week later. She was sad to see me go, but said she understood and wished me well.

Dex came out to Newport to help me pack up and make the move, and we spent our first full night together in my bed. When we woke up the next morning, the sun streaming through my bedroom window, he'd wrapped me in his arms and told me how grateful he was for me, how much he loved me, and how he would do everything he could to be the man I deserved.

I was back at home before Thanksgiving, and since my

place had never sold, we were next door neighbors again—although we spent every night he didn't have the girls in the same bed.

"I definitely agree you guys are the real deal," Ellie said, reaching for her margarita. "It's just that I don't recall any sort of *condition* on the bet. You swore off men—all men, even soul mates—until Christmas. And I believe it was sometime in October I heard you declaring your love."

"After everything I've done for you, you're going to make me get up there?" I cried. "I saved you from dealing with brides every day! I rescued you from your mother!"

In a fabulous stroke of luck, Ellie's parents had decided to go through with their dream of spending extended time in France—which meant Abelard needed a new events manager. When she heard I might be moving back, she called me and asked if I'd be interested in taking over the job. I'd jumped at the chance, not only because it would mean working where Ellie did, but because I'd always loved Abelard Vineyards. It was half the size of Cloverleigh Farms, and much less majestic than The Alexander, but it was intimate and romantic, and my first month there had been a delight.

Ellie pretended to consider this as she sipped her drink. "You did save me from brides, that's true. And my mother is off my back since you came on board."

"See?"

"But no." Her eyes gleamed. "I still want the song."

I glared at her. "You've watched way too many episodes of *Friends*."

"True," she admitted. "But I'm not sorry."

The previous singer left the stage, and the emcee called my name. Everyone around us shouted and clapped. "Come on, Winnie!" Millie yelled.

"Winnie! Winnie! Winnie!" Hallie and Luna chanted.

"I'll pay you," I said desperately.

Ellie laughed and shook her head. "Get up there, MacAllister."

Dex patted my shoulder. "Break a leg, babe."

Reluctantly, I stood up. "If I pull the fire alarm, will you still love me?"

He shoved me toward the stage.

My eyes sought out the red EXIT sign over to one side of the room and I honestly considered making a run for it. But instead, I put my shoulders back, held my head up, and mounted the stage.

Taking the mic, I wished for the millionth time I could sing.

Over at his laptop, the emcee looked at me, and even though my knees were knocking, my hands shook, and my mouth felt drier than the Sahara, I nodded.

The music began, and I put the mic to my lips and tried to find the right notes.

"Her name was Lola."

My family and friends hooted and hollered encouragement, but I wanted to die. My pitch was even worse than usual because I was so nervous.

"She was a showgirl."

I looked at Ellie, who was laughing so hard, tears were streaming down her face. I caught Dex's eye, and he winked, stuck his fingers in his mouth, and whistled loudly. Hallie and Luna had jumped out of their chairs and were dancing between the tables. My mother looked mortified for me, but all four of my sisters and my dad were on their feet, cheering me on.

Not because I was good—I was really, *really* bad—but because they loved me and supported me no matter what. Somehow it was enough to get me through the song, and thankfully, people had started to sing along, so I didn't feel so alone.

By the end of the tune, I was laughing too, and when it was over, the place erupted with applause—I'm sure many in the room were just happy it was done. I handed the mic back to the emcee and quickly ran back to my seat. Flushed, I sat down and grabbed my margarita for a huge gulp.

"That was everything I wanted it to be," Ellie said, still wiping tears.

"It wasn't terrible?" I said in surprise.

"Oh no, it was terrible," she assured me. "But I loved it."

"You were very brave," Dex said, clinking his beer bottle to my glass. "And even though I'm so grateful you went through that for me, I'm going to have to ask you not to gamble anymore. My eardrums can't take it."

"No worries." I held up my hands. "My betting days are over."

"I still can't believe you made that wager in the first place," said Ellie.

"Hey, I had one hundred percent confidence in myself." I tipped my head onto Dex's shoulder. "It wasn't my fault I lost."

"Are you blaming this on *me*?" Dex asked.

"Entirely. If you hadn't moved in with your grumpy scowl and tight T-shirt, we all might have been spared tonight."

"Don't make me give you a lecture on how a man's clothes are not to blame for a woman's behavior," he scolded.

I laughed. "Let's call it even."

"Deal." Leaning close, he whispered in my ear. "As long as I can call you mine."

Epilogue

Winnie

One Year Later

"WORKING ON ANY NEW STORIES?" I ASKED HALLIE, dropping onto the foot of her bed. It was the night before Christmas Eve, and we'd spent the evening wrapping presents and baking Christmas cookies at Dex's place. Snow was falling outside the girls' bedroom window.

"I'm finishing an old one," she said, hugging her stuffed penguin.

"Oh yeah?" Dex tucked Luna in and sat on the edge of her bed. "Which one?"

"The one about the ogre and the princess. It's turning into a love story."

"Oooh," I said. "Tell me about it."

"Well, they've been very good friends for a while, but the ogre would like to marry the princess."

"But he's an ogre," Dex argued. "Are they even allowed to marry a princess? I thought her parents wanted her to marry the cruel prince."

"They did, but this princess doesn't care what other people say. She makes her own decisions." She thought for a moment. "She's a feminist princess."

I laughed. "Good for her."

"So do they get married?" Luna asked eagerly.

"Well, at first the ogre is afraid to propose. He thinks she's going to say no because he's not a prince. But he asks her anyway."

"Because he's learned to face his fears?" asked Dex.

"No, because her cottage is much nicer than his cave, and he really wants to live there with her."

Dex harrumphed. "This ogre gets a bad rap in your stories."

"What does she say?" I thumped Hallie's feet through the blankets. "Don't leave me in suspense!"

"She says yes, because she loves him and believes even ogres deserve a happily ever after."

Luna grinned. "That's a good ending."

"It's a perfect ending." Smiling, I rose to my feet, kissed my fingers and touched Hallie's forehead, then did the same to Luna. "Love stories are my favorite."

"What about you, Daddy?" Hallie asked. "Are they your favorite too?"

"They're growing on me." Dex kissed his daughters goodnight while I leaned in the doorway. "See you in the morning."

"You're coming early in the morning for presents, right, Winnie?" Hallie asked.

"Yes," I promised. "Just have your dad text me when you wake up." Since the girls were spending tomorrow night with their mom, we'd told them Santa would drop by early to bring some gifts to open here.

"And you'll come in your pajamas?"

"I'll come in my pajamas."

"And we can make chocolate chip pancakes for breakfast?" Luna asked.

"Yes—my mom's secret recipe."

"Goodnight, girls," said Dex. "You have to go to sleep or else Santa won't come."

"You're sure he knows to come early?" Luna sounded worried.

"Positive." As Dex walked toward me and reached for the light switch, I saw both girls look at each other and wiggle their noses before the room went dark. I laughed softly as we went down the stairs.

"What's funny?" he asked.

"The girls. I think they're trying to cast another spell."

We reached the bottom and he put his arms around me. "What could they possibly want now that they have a cat, the ogre has the princess, and I have you?"

"I don't know," I said, "but I definitely saw some nose wiggling in there."

"Hmm." He kissed the top of my head. "Maybe they were just making a Christmas wish."

"True. Santa *is* coming tonight." I lowered my voice to a whisper. "Should we give it an hour before we bring their presents over from my place?"

His hands slid down over my butt. "Can we spend that hour making out on the couch?"

I laughed, running my hands up his chest. I always wanted to be close to him. "Definitely."

The following morning, I went over to Dex's in my flannel pajamas, as promised. It had snowed about eight inches overnight, so I had to wear my boots, but I took them off at the door and tugged on the fluffy cat socks the girls had given me last year for Christmas.

While holiday music played from the speakers and snow flurries continued to drift, Dex and I drank coffee and watched the girls sit by the tree and tear open presents from Santa, their dad, me, and even from my parents. Over the last year, Hallie and Luna had become almost like grandkids to them—my mother adored when I'd bring them over to the bakery, and my dad was always excited to see us when we popped over to Cloverleigh Farms. Last week he'd gotten the old horse-drawn sleigh out of the barn and taken us all on a ride through the snow. He said it reminded him of my sisters and me growing up with their endless questions and squeals of excitement.

My parents got along well with Dex too. My mother loved how happy he made me, and my father respected his military career, his job as a first responder, and his devotion to his daughters as a single dad. We all went to Sunday dinners at their house as often as possible.

I'd grown close to his sister as well. Bree and I had bonded over our shared frustration with Dex's grumpy moods and stubborn nature, and he often had to put up with teasing coming at him from both of us at once. If Dex and Justin had a Saturday night off, we often spent the evening at their house playing cards. Bree was especially grateful to me for supporting Dex when he decided to visit their father a couple times before he died last spring. While he hadn't ever brought the girls with him, he said he'd found some peace in forgiveness and would always be grateful for the letter. I noticed him talking more about his mom and dad with the girls afterward, describing good memories from his childhood—that made me happy.

Millie sometimes jokingly asked when she should start planning our wedding, but I told her we weren't in any rush. As much as we loved each other, it wasn't just about us, and we wanted to make sure the girls were ready for us to take that step.

But as far as I was concerned, Dex would always be the only man for me.

When all the packages had been unwrapped and paper, ribbons, and bows littered the floor, Hallie and Luna sat amongst it all and exchanged a distressed look. "But Daddy," said Hallie, "there's something missing."

"There is?" Dex calmly sipped his coffee.

"Yes. The thing we got for Winnie," Luna whispered, as if I wasn't sitting right there.

I smiled at them. "But you got me plenty! The book I wanted, the new sweater, the toy for Piglet, the gift card for the salon. You spoiled me!"

"But there's something else," she insisted.

"Hmm." Dex frowned. "You know, you're right. There is one more thing."

Hallie popped to her feet. "Where is it?"

"I think it's in her stocking."

"My stocking?" I looked at the banister, where yesterday three stockings had hung, personalized with *Daddy*, *Hallie*, and *Luna*. Today there was a fourth one hanging alongside them, and it said *Winnie* across the top. "Oh my goodness!"

Luna jumped up too. "Go look in it!"

I glanced at Dex—he said nothing, but his eyes sparkled with mischief. Setting my cup on the table, I went over to the stocking and stuck my hand inside.

My fingers curled around a small box.

Gasping, I looked back at the three of them. Hallie and Luna were jumping up and down.

"Is anything in there?" Hallie asked.

"Yes." My heart raced as I pulled it out—it was gift-wrapped in shiny silver paper with a red velvet ribbon tied into a bow.

"What did you get?" Dex asked casually.

"I don't know yet."

"Who's it from?"

I looked at it again. "There's no tag. It's a mystery."

"Well, bring it over here. Let's see if we can solve it."

The entire room felt like it was tilting and spinning as I walked back over to where Dex sat on the couch and the two girls clutched each other in nervous excitement by the tree. When I reached him, I held it out. "Any ideas?"

He glanced at the box as he set his coffee cup on the table next to mine. "Hmm. I *might* know something about this."

"He does!" Luna cried.

"Shhh," Hallie admonished.

"Maybe you should open it," Dex suggested.

With my pulse pounding hard, I untied the ribbon and unwrapped a small white gift box.

"Keep going!" shouted Luna.

I lifted the top off—inside was a black velvet hexagonal box. My breath caught and I looked at Dex.

"Keep going," he said.

With trembling fingers, I removed the lid, and gasped at the diamond ring that winked at me in the tree lights. I blinked at it in disbelief, and when I looked up again, Dex had gone down on one knee at my feet.

"Oh my God," I whispered.

He took the velvet box from my hands and plucked the ring from the cushion. Taking my left hand, he said, "Winnie, the last year has been one of the happiest of my life. You've brightened every single day with your smile and your spirit and your heart. All three of us agree you belong in our family."

"Is it time for us now, Daddy?"

Dex glanced at Luna with a rueful smile. "I wasn't quite done, but okay." He looked up at me again. "The girls helped me pick out the ring, and they wanted to be part of this. I couldn't say no."

"Of course not." My eyes filled as Luna and Hallie came and stood behind their father.

"Winnie, my favorite thing about you is your hugs," said Hallie, as if she'd practiced her lines. "You always make me feel good if I have a bad day. Even if kids at school aren't nice or I'm frustrated about something, I always know that when I see you, you'll give me a hug and make me feel better."

I sniffed. "Thank you, Hals. I love your hugs too."

"My favorite thing about you is how you always have fun Band-Aids at your house," said Luna. "And good snacks. I also like when you play salon and Barbies with me."

I smiled at her through tears. "I'll always have fun Band-Aids for you. And I love our playtime too."

Dex spoke up next. "My favorite thing about you is the way you see the good in everyone, the way you treat people with generosity and kindness, and the way you love with your whole heart." He slipped the ring on my finger. "I know I'm just a big hairy ogre who doesn't deserve a princess, but it would make me the happiest ogre alive if you'd ride off into the sunset with me."

"With us!" Luna added.

"We told him to say that part," Hallie whispered.

I half-laughed, half-sobbed. "It's good."

"What do you say, Winnie MacAllister? Will you marry me?"

"Yes," I squeaked, because I could barely find my voice. "Yes!"

I only looked at the ring for a moment before leaning down to kiss him. He stood up, wrapping me in his embrace, and I looped my arms around his neck.

As my feet left the ground and his little girls cheered, I felt his heart beating against mine and knew I was safe.

I knew today was just the beginning of our life as a family.

I knew I'd never forget this moment as long as I lived, and it would be a story we told our grandchildren someday.

Overcome with emotion, I buried my face in his shoulder and shed tears of joy—I was loved, I was cherished, I was home.

THE END

Want a peek into Dex and Winnie's future? Subscribe to my mailing list and you'll get instant access to an exclusive IGNITE bonus scene! Just use the QR code below.

Already subscribed? Just check your last newsletter for the link to my bonus materials! If you can't find it, you can simply resubscribe and the scene will be yours in minutes.

Also by

Melanie Harlow

Want a reading order? Head to my website:
www.melanieharlow.com.

Acknowledgments

As always, my appreciation and gratitude go to the following people for their talent, support, wisdom, friendship, and encouragement. . .

Melissa Gaston, Brandi Zelenka, Jenn Watson, Hang Le, Kayti McGee, Laurelin Paige, Corinne Michaels, the entire Social Butterfly team, Anthony Colletti, Rebecca Friedman, Flavia Viotti & Meire Dias at Bookcase Literary, Nancy Smay at Evident Ink, Julia Griffis at The Romance Bibliophile, proofreader Michele Ficht, Stacey Blake at Champagne Book Design, Katie Robinson at Lyric Audiobooks, narrators Kirsten Leigh and Stephen Dexter, the Shop Talkers, the Sisterhood, the Harlots and the Harlot ARC Team, bloggers and event organizers, my Queens, my betas, my proofers, my readers all over the world. . .

And once again, to my husband and daughters, whose hilarious conversations inspired many scenes in this book.

About the Author

Melanie Harlow likes her heels high, her martini dry, and her history with the naughty bits left in. She's the author of the Bellamy Creek Series, the Cloverleigh Farms Series, the One & Only series, the After We Fall Series, the Happy Crazy Love Series, and the Frenched Series.

She writes from her home outside of Detroit, where she lives with her husband and two daughters. When she's not writing, she's probably got a cocktail in hand. And sometimes when she is.

Find her at www.melanieharlow.com.